The
CASCO
DECEPTION

Bob Reiss

LITTLE, BROWN AND COMPANY
BOSTON–TORONTO

FIRST EDITION

Library of Congress Cataloging in Publication Data
Reiss, Bob. —
    The Casco deception

    1. World War, 1939–1945—Fiction. I. Title.
PS3568.E51718   1983   813'.54   83-689
ISBN 0-316-73965-0

BP

Designed by Dede Cummings

*Published simultaneously in Canada
by Little, Brown & Company (Canada) Limited*

PRINTED IN THE UNITED STATES OF AMERICA

*For John Gardner, 1933–1982
prince of writers, teachers,
friends*

A very special thanks to John Crowley and the Star Foundation, Congressman Dave Emery of Maine, Steve MacAllister and Annie Compton, the McKay family, Esther Newberg, Bill Phillips, John Rabb, Ruth "Duke" Ravenel and Curt Suplee.

The
Casco
Deception

ONE

————————♦————————

February 1942

"HAPPY BIRTHDAY, SHITHEAD," Ryker said. He bowed to his reflection in a shop window and leaned heavily against a lamppost. A pigeon, shaken from its comfortable perch, squawked into the winter sky. Ryker formed his hand into a pistol and blew its head off. He burped and leaned back against the pole.

Something struck his knee. A soccer ball bounced away, pursued by boys in kneesocks. In triplicate, Adolf Hitler glared at him from a steeple wall. The medieval square, alive with blood-colored flags, smelled of washed cobblestones, laundry, bread, horses, and gasoline. Soldiers goose-stepped out of a side street. A work battalion tore up a water main. Each clang of the pickax made Ryker want to kill somebody.

He'd come into the Alps two months ago to shoot animals and sleep under the stars, but on his fortieth birthday even that had not calmed him. So he'd tried the village. Forty! He traced the number on the store window, flexed his muscles, and watched his jacket expand. VICTORY IN NORTH AFRICA, screeched a sausage-sized headline at a kiosk nearby. Beside the paper, Ryker made out the words "Pearl Harbor" on a magazine. It looked like a big naval battle had occurred while he'd been out of touch, but the letters went in and out of focus and he'd never heard of Pearl Harbor anyway. He was still drunk the morning after. He hadn't worked in six months and he hated the waiting around. Maybe he'd drive to Berlin to renew his American passport. He could break all the speed limits in the Romeo.

He wasn't a big man but he seemed that way, with powerful shoulders and the tight mouth of a hunter. His blonde beard was flecked with grey, his bottle- green eyes narrowed by the sun and long devoid of any boyishness. His pupils were deep, flinty. He had a weather-beaten look, and his mouth was sensual and violent, lending eroticism to his face but not affection. Indistinct elements of brutality, discipline, and sadness touched his wide Tartar features.

Reflected in the window, Ryker saw an incredible sight.

A Jew was walking across the square.

In 1942 Germany, hardly any Jews remained in the cities, let alone the mountain towns where they hadn't lived in the first place. Like something out of a grotesque fairy story, a tattered Jew was just strolling through town. The dirty armband was the color of pus. The Jew was small, of indeterminable age but bent like an old man. His coat was torn. Ryker, who knew more than anyone should about suicides, understood immediately that he was watching one.

All activity was stopping in the square, as if a Zulu chief or Goebbels himself were appearing before these people, but there was no antagonism in their eyes, none of the fury Ryker had seen in the cities, only simple amazement. A Jew was walking through the town, a martian, an African.

In Tanganyika as a boy, Ryker had once watched a crippled gazelle stumble into a pride of lions. The lions, not believing their eyes, had simply watched at first. They'd risen as if to pay homage. They'd followed for a distance, the gazelle unaware or steeped in its own pain, the whole scene the biblical tale, lions led by a gazelle. Then they'd ripped the animal to shreds.

Had the Jew been running for Switzerland? Had he been hiding here, in an underground station or the home of a friend? Had he been eating all his meals in an attic for the last two years? Why had he given up? Ryker pushed himself off the post.

The Jew bought a newspaper, turned, passed Ryker without looking up, and continued moving in his measured step back in the direction from which he had come. There was terror in the man's posture and a sense of control pushed to the limit. The head was down, waiting, the hands trembled slightly. The cap, the city man's cap, was tilted to block the enquiring eye.

The Jew with Ryker following passed through the square. The soldiers, lounging against a wall, watched their movements. The Jew moved into the labyrinthine passageways of the old town, past neat houses and shops. Merchants appeared in the doorways, wiped fat hands on aprons, and whispered to people inside. A shutter opened above. The February wind, forced into the narrow walkway, knifed through Ryker's thin safari jacket. He willed himself to feel no cold. A pair of small boys attached themselves to the Jew. He ignored them. He looked like a pied piper or a fagin. Some brave soul, recovering from surprise, said hello to the Jew. The Jew ignored this man also.

The inevitable black car arrived. The Jew was just leaving the maze of streets at the junction of a picturesque park. He walked toward an empty bench overlooking an ice-glazed pond. He unfolded the paper. The action had the rote quality of a ritual. He'd probably read a newspaper in the park every day before Hitler, but his hands were shaking too badly to read today. He must have heard the screech of brakes, but he did not alter his step or direction. The slam of doors followed and then a harsh shout. The Jew seated himself on the bench. Ryker's breath was a sharp frosty line. Four SS men hurried toward the Jew. They surrounded him, barking at him, hands on their belts. They pulled him off the bench. They pushed him back and forth between them. The newspaper, freed from the Jew's hands, scattered and blew against the bench and into the pond. A gust swept a dirtied page into a branch, which impaled it with a ripping sound.

One of the SS men slapped the Jew. When two others pinned his arms, Ryker found himself approaching. The blood pounded in his head. Maybe this was what he had been waiting for. "One at a time," he told them, avoiding the Jew's face, and when they turned on him, which was a big mistake, he felt the tension break within him. His boot connected with the first German's jaw. A second was doubled over in the grass, holding his stomach. The third struggled with his holster. Ryker slammed the arm around and heard the *crack*. The Jew, awakened from whatever suicide he had planned, was a pair of flapping coattails in the street, and soldiers poured into the park from another direction, rifles up. The fourth German, facing Ryker, put his hands at his sides and smiled winningly. Ryker kicked him in the balls.

The police station, complete with stone turret, looked like a miniature castle. Two soldiers stood rigid in guard boxes outside. Their heads remained immobile when the driver honked. At the side of the building a garage-sized door swung forward. The car slid into an alley.

Ryker's hands were bound. Every time the car hit a bump,

every time he tried to say something, his head struck the muzzle of the rifle behind him. He was bleeding from his mouth and ears.

In the alley, moisture ran down stone walls and trench-coated police walked German shepherds. Everyone's breath was frosting.

"Out!" Inside, it looked like a thousand other police stations he'd seen: bare walls, wooden desk, fat sergeant eating sausages. They pushed him through narrow hallways and into a cell. They strapped his arms and legs to a chair. Sunlight streamed in through the street-level barred windows. A pair of boots moved by outside. Somewhere in the town a lunch whistle was blowing. Ryker's neck ached where the soldiers had clubbed him. *Don't think about the pain.* A pair of pliers lay on a table nearby.

The man he had kicked in the face entered and sat at the table. His hands were knobbed like a farm boy's. They rested casually on his thigh. His boot, swinging back and forth slowly, was two feet away. Stained gauze covered his jaw.

"We caught the Jew. He was hiding in a bakery."

The German tossed the American passport beside the pliers. He rubbed his face and yanked his hand away. He'd forgotten he was injured.

Softly, expression partially obscured by the bandage, he said, "John Ryker."

Ryker said nothing.

"That is your name, isn't it? The name on your passport."

The sun struck the blonde hairs on the back of the man's hands. Ryker looked into the approaching pale blue eyes. The man was slim and carried himself with the belligerent movements of a brawler.

"You helped the Jew," he said. "Why?"

"There's something you'd better know," Ryker said.

The German punched him in the stomach. Ryker doubled, straightened slowly. He looked the German in the eye. He smiled. The German's expression, which had been one of gloating, faded. He rubbed his knuckles. He seemed ready to hit Ryker again but he sat down.

"You are John Ryker, yes?"

"That's me."

"An American." They spoke in German. On the table, the pliers were open slightly, like a mouth. "And a Jew."

"You know as well as I do I'm not a Jew."

The German jerked. The anesthetic was probably wearing off. "I know what happens to people who assault authorities in this country. In your country you might treat them lightly; here we know how to deal with them. What are you doing in Germany?"

"I live here."

The eyebrows went up.

"In Berlin. I want you to call a phone number at the . . ."

"What are you doing in this town?"

Ryker growled, "Listen, I'm telling you . . ."

The German stood up.

Ryker said, "I was hunting, that's what."

"Hunting what?"

"Rams."

"Where?"

Ryker lifted his head toward the mountains dwarfing the village.

"So, you were hunting rams." The German smiled triumphantly. He pulled a small-nosed automatic from his jacket pocket and pointed it at Ryker. He tossed it on the table. "With this?" he said. It was a Mauser, range fifty yards, not a ram-hunting gun.

"I use a crossbow," Ryker said contemptuously. "It's at my hotel. With the hunting license."

"Which hotel?"

"The Alpine."

"Room?"

"Three ten."

In a question, the German nodded at the gun.

Ryker tried to shrug his shoulders but couldn't. He was strapped in too tight. "I always carry that."

"What would you, an innocent hunter, need it for?"

Ryker made a disgusted face. "I've been trying to tell you. I work for the government."

The German nodded. Pride lit the damaged features. "The American government," he said.

Ryker laughed harshly. "The German government," he said. "The Reich. You'd better call that number."

The German's look faded. Ryker said, "I work for the military."

Nothing. A blink. "The military? The German military? You, an American?"

"I live *here*."

"What do you do for the military?"

"Call the number."

The German seemed less sure of himself. "A secret, eh? I can make you tell me."

"Make me tell you and you'll be sorry when you find out."

The SS man stared at Ryker. There was sweat on the American's forehead but the eyes were calm. The man was strapped, helpless, the hallway outside filled with soldiers. The pliers sat on the table. Racks and rubber hoses waited downstairs. Yet the German was the one fighting fear. Something crazy was opening and closing in Ryker's mad green eyes. The man was hurting, he had to be hurting, but it was the SS man who wanted to leave.

He batted down the feeling. He said, "I don't believe you work for the military, an American."

"That's your problem."

"And if, if you worked for the Reich, why would you help that Jew? Tell me that." He leaned closer, emboldened by logic. "If you worked for the military you wouldn't have helped the Jew."

Ryker looked at the ceiling. The pulse pounded in his temples.

"Yes, explain it to me," the German said, taking two steps back. Now he was angry at his own fear. "Why would a man like you, who works for the Reich, who lives in Germany, a foreign citizen, risk his life for a Jew? You attacked four SS. The soldiers could have shot you in the park. Why do something like that, eh? Are you going to answer me? Answer me!"

Somewhere in the building someone was clanging on steel. Ryker shook his head. "You wouldn't understand," he said.

"I think I understand very well."

The shadow of the bars stretched long across the cell. Ryker heard dripping noises and the footsteps of guards. He looked at the stained bandage encircling the German's mouth. He said quietly, "All he wanted to do was die. Bravely."

The German straightened. "I don't know what you're talking about." He picked up the pliers and moved them from hand to hand. "I think he was running for Switzerland. You were his guide."

Ryker snorted. "Yeah, his guide. I guided him into town so he could buy a newspaper."

The German flushed. "All right. Enough games." He put down the pliers. "There's a military installation near Walchen and we both know it. Mountain troops. You're a spy."

"I thought you said I was a guide."

The German unbuttoned his tunic. His voice quivered with malice. "I've wanted to get out of this town," he said. "Berlin, that's the place. And now I've caught the first American spy. The first spy of the new war."

Ryker's neck twitched. "We're not at war with the United States," he said.

The German straightened, the prideful look back on his face. "You don't give up, do you? You know quite well the United States has been in the war for two months. Airplanes of the Empire of Japan bombed your Pacific headquarters at Pearl Harbor. Your fleet was destroyed." He sounded like he'd been memorizing radio broadcasts. "The Führer has joined our allies and together we will annihilate the foe."

Stunned, Ryker could only repeat, "War?"

"With America."

"I haven't been in America in thirty years," Ryker said.

The German, throwing the pliers on the table, said, "Give me that number in Berlin."

They left him alone in the cell. After a while the light faded. The boot sounds outside became regular. Soldiers were drilling. There was a whimpering on the other side of the wall, a thud, a cry. "Jew?" Ryker called. "Are you all right?" A harsh voice answered, "Shut up!" He heard a scraping sound in the hall. He figured they were dragging the Jew away.

His wrists were numb and he'd lost all feeling in his

shoulders. To calm himself he daydreamed about hunting. He was up in the Bavarian Alps, carrying a crossbow. Framed against the dark sky, a bighorn moved along a crest. I'm not afraid, he told himself. This is an adrenaline problem, not a fear problem.

The lights came on in the hallway. Ryker heard heavy doors being slammed and steel bolts drawn. He wanted something to eat. The regular slapping noises began again next door. "Jew! Can you hear me?" The door swung open. The guard hissed, "Last warning!" A cockroach the size of a baby's fist was crawling down from the window.

Two more soldiers looked in, grinning. "So you're the one who kicked Kurt in the mouth." They laughed uproariously. "Bad for you. Soon he'll come."

He came after midnight. The dripping sounds seemed louder then, in the semidarkness. Framed in the doorway, the light at his back, the SS man seemed larger. "No reply from Berlin in seven hours," he said. "Too much time. No one we reached had ever heard of a Colonel Becker."

"You didn't call the number I gave you then."

"No one answered that number. We called others. No one's heard of you. No Ryker. No file."

He advanced into the room. His face, framed in the light for an instant, was eager, flushed. The hallway was quiet outside.

The German moved near the table. When he spoke there was a whistling noise in his mouth. "I lost two teeth," he said, "Jew lover." The pliers scraped on the table. "You lied about the army. What were you doing in the mountains? Where are you from? Why did you wear that holster?"

He pulled Ryker forward by the hair. "I didn't touch you before because of what you told me. Now it's going to be much worse. I've been waiting." Silhouetted, he rolled up his sleeves. He smelled like a hospital.

There came the sound of hurrying boots in the hallway. The door was flung open. A soldier whispered into the German's ear. The German gasped, dropped the pliers. "Light!" he cried. Ryker blinked madly. "Untie him! Untie those hands! Quickly! Now!" To Ryker, "I . . . I'm sorry. You should lie down. There's a bed upstairs. Something to eat? Get him something to eat! Untie him already!"

Ryker stood up. His ankles were throbbing. He rubbed his wrists. Soldiers ran in and out. In the harsh glare, the SS man's face seemed transformed, imploring. He swallowed. He said, "If only you would have explained completely . . . a man in my position . . . I was only trying to find out who you were."

The cell seemed smaller now that Ryker was free. Pain coursed through his shoulders. The German was saying, "After all, we have an installation near Walchen. We can't have strangers . . . and the Jew . . . you understand, don't you?"

Ryker smiled. Normally he looked so menacing that the effect of any warmth was to instantly put those around him at ease. He said, "Forgive you? For only doing your job?" The German, nodding, looked slavish. The soldiers in the hallway were whispering, "Martin Bormann . . . Bormann wants him in Berlin."

Ryker said, "I want to see the Jew."

"The Jew?" The German looked uncertain.

"For a minute," Ryker said. "Before I go."

"I . . . I don't know."

Ryker just stared at him. After a moment he said, "Of course. He's next door. Take him in, Corporal."

"Alone," Ryker said.

The German nodded. "Open the door and wait outside."

Ryker closed the door behind him. The Jew lay on a straw bunk, leg twisted. It looked broken. Only one nostril flared when he breathed. The mouth was purple, the skin white. He was rattling.

"Easy, easy," Ryker said. He touched the chest. "I'm the one who helped you in the park."

The fear cleared out of the swollen eyes.

"Why'd you come out? You were hiding. I know it."

A tear collected and dripped down the face.

"Okay, forget it." Ryker knew they were watching through the door. "You need anything?" he asked. "If I can do it I will."

Slightly, the Jew nodded.

His lips moved.

Ryker bent close, listened, closed his eyes.

"I don't know," he said, his voice suddenly loud. "Getting you out of here is something I can't do. You shouldn't have come out." While he spoke he placed his hands on the Jew's neck, feeling for the right place. The Jew was crying with gratefulness. "I helped you in the park but I can't really do *that*." Effortlessly, he snapped the neck. "You just relax here. I'll get a doctor."

He stood up. "Don't worry," he said.

Outside, he smiled at the Germans. The SS man came close. This time when Ryker's boot slammed into the jaw he knew he'd broken everything. The German went down, dripping.

Ryker looked at him before he went out. "You'll get to Berlin, all right," he said.

TWO

In early 1942 the borders of the Third Reich stretched from the English Channel to the Black Sea, and from Moscow to Tripoli. Rommel chased the British toward the Suez. The Luftwaffe ruled the skies of Europe. Martin Bormann, Hitler's private secretary, was the second most powerful man on the continent.

On the night of February 9, filled with anticipation, he awaited his Führer in the map room of the Berlin Chancellery. It was a glittering palace of a room, lit by chandelier, roasted by roaring tree trunks. The wall map showed the northeast United States, slashed by red arrows and boxes. Air Marshall Hermann Goering fidgeted in a chair. Admiral Wilhelm Canaris, chief of German Intelligence, whispered uneasily with Navy Grand Admiral Erich Raeder. If Hitler had ordered a meeting this late, the likelihood was trouble.

With courtly disdain they glanced at "the inevitable Bormann," as Bormann was referred to at Hitler's court. Bormann, who accompanied the Führer to every dinner, every gathering, on every trip, who had introduced Hitler to Eva Braun, who had the Führer's ear and the key to his office, was probably the only one present who knew the purpose of tonight's meeting. Why else would he look so gleeful at their own discomfort?

They were right. Hitler had elicited Bormann's aid in drawing up the stunning plan the Führer would reveal this evening.

They stood at attention when Hitler marched into the room. Tonight the Führer's tense aspect seemed heightened, possibly because of America's recent entry into the war or news of surprising Russian resistance in the north. His eyes were burning, his movements jerky. The beginnings of a stoop showed themselves. Anger warred with anticipation upon his features. He looked like a man battling unwanted premonitions.

Striding to the map, he said, "We have only just declared war on the United States, but the United States has been at war with us for a year and a half. We drove the English from Dunkirk. The Americans sold them half a million Enfield rifles, field guns, machine guns. We sink British ships. Roosevelt gives them old destroyers. The English have ordered ten thousand planes, trucks, tanks. This material is shipped from two cities." Hitler poked the map angrily. "Boston," he said. "And Portland.

"Without this help the British would have cooperated long ago. Depth bombs! Gun mounts! Propelling charges!" He picked up a letter opener. He ran the point along the East Coast. "The Americans build ships here! Load supplies here! Their battleships train here!" He glared at the men as if they, not the Americans, were responsible for these offenses. "You! You do nothing!"

They were suitably cowed. Raeder, the Prussian career admiral, spoke first. "My Führer," he soothed. "We have been working on the problem. We are dispatching swarms of U-boats into this area." He lifted his arms in circles, conjuring like a wizard. "*Swarms.*"

"Why didn't you send them *before?*"

Raeder had not done so because Hitler had ordered the American convoys untouched, but the admiral prudently chose to avoid that subject. Instead he said, "Their coast will be littered with wrecks."

Hitler nodded, strutting in front of the map. This was what he liked to hear.

"Their coast is uneven, filled with isolated inlets and bays. Admiral Canaris will be landing agents at key points." Raeder indicated Long Island and Maine. "There are also islands. The submarines can surface to recharge at night. However, the cities you mentioned will soon be ringed by fortifications."

Hitler's smile was fading.

"The Americans," Raeder continued, "are planting sonic buoys in the harbors. They'll be able to detect U-boats. Our intelligence is good in New England. We have some friends among the fishermen. The deep channels are protected by big guns. Dirigibles patrol the offshore areas."

Hitler snapped, "The point." He had lowered his hands to protect his genital area. He did that when he felt threatened.

"My Führer, we can seriously damage their shipping on the open sea, but please understand the reality of their port defenses."

"The reality! Ha! The Japanese understand the reality! They've crippled the Americans in the Pacific. I only hope they attack the West Coast!"

Goering piped up, "Excellent pilots, my Führer. The Luftwaffe could have done no better."

Hitler whirled. "You miss the point! If the Japanese can

successfully attack Pearl Harbor, why can't the Third Reich do the same to the Atlantic Coast?"

He set himself like the statue of a conqueror. A gleam of excitement passed between Hitler and Bormann.

Raeder said, after a pause, "An, er, thought-provoking idea, my Führer."

Goering boasted. "We are certainly as able as the Japanese!"

"But my Führer," Raeder continued bravely, "the Japanese attack, coming during peacetime, succeeded because of surprise. And Pearl Harbor is on an island. Numerous approaches presented themselves. You yourself have wisely suggested one day securing Iceland as an air base against North America, but currently our long-range bombers could never reach Boston. We haven't any aircraft carriers. The sinking of the *Bismarck* showed . . ."

"*Don't talk to me about the* Bismarck*!*"

Hitler stomped to the balcony. Cheering crescendoed below. "Come here," he ordered. He raised his arm in salute. His face was rigid. "Brave men," he said. "Dying for Germany. You think I want miracles. The Third Reich *is* a miracle; but reactionaries like you have called my dreams impossible at every step on our road to destiny." Hitler mimicked Raeder. " 'My Führer, I mean no disrespect. My Führer, it is impossible to destroy American shipping.' I don't believe it! I've heard it before! It was impossible to join with Austria, to take Czechoslovakia. Impossible! Ha! For us, nothing is impossible!"

Incredibly, Raeder took a step forward. "I still say a Japanese-style attack would fail."

Hitler screeched, "Of course it would fail! Did I say we had to copy the Japanese! Aren't there any original thinkers here? Why is it always I who has to think up ideas? Use your minds! I'm always alone! You want an original way of reaching an American port? A *German* Pearl Harbor? Better than Pearl Harbor?"

His mouth snapped shut. His forehead was laved with sweat. The mustache quivered.

Hitler told them his original idea.

When he was finished, the only sound in the room was the crack of logs. The map was raked. Hitler had been striking it. His jaw thrust forward so that he resembled Il Duce.

Awed, Goering whispered, "My Führer, brilliant." He wasn't acting this time.

Canaris looked up slowly from the carpet.

Raeder paced in excitement. "An incredible idea! It could work!"

Firelight sculpted Hitler's face. "Total surprise," he said.

"You could wipe out half the city. They'd have no one to blame but themselves."

Raeder ran his finger down the twisting American coast. He was absorbing knowledge. His face had a faraway look. He said, "But could our men ever get out? That's the problem, yes. Still, something could be done, but what? And the talent." A log snapped in the fireplace. "Where would you find the talent?"

It was the moment for which Martin Bormann had been waiting. Grinning in triumph, Hitler turned to his private secretary. He said, "For the past several days, our loyal Martin Bormann, acting under my orders, has been searching through files, *hundreds* of files. While the rest of you have been wasting yourselves, plodding, blinded to your duty, Martin Bormann found the man."

◊   ◊   ◊

The meeting broke up after midnight. Bormann moved through the marble hallways toward his office. Hitler worked late so Bormann worked late. No one talked to Hitler without Bormann's knowledge. He would have it no other way.

Guards stopped and saluted. Ahead, a figure emerged from under the bronze bust of Bismarck.

"Muller," Bormann said.

He kept walking. Hans Muller, Bormann's aide, was a former policeman who had helped Bormann cover up the murder of Hitler's niece, Geli, with whom the Führer had been having an affair. She'd been found beside Hitler's revolver. The Führer had transformed her bedroom into a shrine, which he would visit on the anniversary of her death, meditating for hours.

In contrast to Bormann, Muller was the Aryan dream, tall, handsome, lean.

"I found Ryker in the mountains," he said. "He's in your office. Herr Reichsleiter, the meeting went well, I hope."

Bormann grinned wolfishly. "You should have seen their faces."

"And your plan, Herr Reichsleiter?"

"The *Führer's* plan." Generally when Hitler proposed one of his bizarre military schemes, Bormann agreed enthusiastically, reported as the problems came up, and waited for the project to be dropped. This time it was going to be different. Hitler was jealous of the Japanese. The only problem was how to avoid responsibility if the project failed. Shrugging, all Bormann said was, "Never take responsibility, Muller." His eyes narrowed. "Unless I tell you to."

"Of course, Herr Reichsleiter. There is something you should know about Herr Ryker."

He leaned close; Bormann frowned. "He killed the Jew?"

They stood under the portrait of Hindenburg. "Why would he kill the Jew, Muller?"

"I have no idea, Herr Reichsleiter."

"Maybe the Jew knew him, knew something about him."

"Possibly, Herr Reichsleiter. I really don't know."

"Born in America," Bormann said. "That bothered me from the first."

Muller's face darkened. "He's a contract soldier."

"Yes, but some of our best fighters are hired. The Finns, for instance. Ryker is talented, no doubt about it; on paper the best I could find. Still, if I choose wrong . . ." Bormann shuddered. "Perhaps I should give him a different job first. To test him against the Americans."

"Herr Reichsleiter, forgive me for saying so, but my concerns are more immediate. You endanger yourself by meeting this man alone. His loyalties are unclear."

"What would you suggest?"

"That I remain in your office."

"No." Bormann scanned the concerned face, and his own softened. "Muller, don't worry. You installed that system in my office, didn't you? The one Becker has?"

"Yes, Herr Reichsleiter. Three machine guns: inside the desk, behind the mirror, behind the vase. Push the button on the desk and they fire simultaneously. Anything in front of the desk is hit."

"So relax, Muller."

"He's very quick, Herr Reichsleiter."

"I'll keep my hand by the button."

"Yes, Herr Reichsleiter."

"He'll sit on the other side of the desk."

"Yes, Herr Reichsleiter."

"It's a big desk. And you'll be right outside. But Muller, I'm angered by this business of the Jew. The Führer has announced I've found Ryker, so at least I should meet with him, but I'm not sure what I'll do afterwards. What do *you* think of him?"

Muller shifted uncomfortably. "I'm only a soldier, Herr Reichsleiter. He's quiet, but there's something there. It's hard to explain. A force. It radiates from him." Muller looked embarrassed. "Death."

They stopped outside the oaken door. Bormann's voice was dry. "You have a dramatic streak in you. I didn't know that." He patted Muller's arm. "I'll keep what you say in mind. If he threatens me, if he moves too quickly, maybe even if I don't like what he says, I'll just push the button."

Martin Bormann smiled warmly. "Are you a drinking man?" he asked.

"Yep."

"Scotch?"

"Rye."

"The bucket holds ice."

Ryker poured three fingers into the cut crystal. The liquor warmed his belly so he poured some more. Shielded by a tank-sized desk, Bormann watched every move, relaxing slightly when Ryker sat down, but never moving his right hand on the desk.

"Fascinating file," Bormann said.

The Reichsleiter resembled a lady wrestler. He was short and puglike, soft yet bull-like. His peasant face was flat, dark, shrewd. The backs of his stubby, fat fingers were thick with black hair. On his honorary SS tunic, he wore the Führer's Order of Blood, reward for some murder, probably.

His eyes scanned two or three files. Ryker could not make

out the contents. Automatically, he memorized the office. Above the Reichsleiter's head, the Führer had been painted astride a white horse. The Führer wore armor but didn't look like a knight. Photos of the wife and children flanked Bormann, and Bormann with Hitler, Hitler with Bormann. The plundered Flemish oils and silk curtains seemed designed to impress, not decorate.

Not looking up, Bormann said, "You lived in Maine." The word transported Ryker. He was a boy, shivering. The iced window, high above, was out of reach. Superimposed over opaque glass, shifting fingers of snow clawed, beckoned, seeped through the cracks and dropped to the floor. His mother stuffed rags around the window. The fire burnt smoky. The cabin reeked of alcohol. His father sat in the same seat, grinning crazy at the fire, oiling, wiping, cleaning the rifles, oiling the fishing reels, wiping the traps. His father said, "Your grandfather shot himself when he was forty. Killed himself. Not me."

Bormann's voice said, "Son of a guide, eh?"

Ryker heard the shotgun blast. His mother lay in the kitchen, one shoe off. The leg hairs spread in different directions. His father, beside the empty bottle, turned slowly, like a marionette, the twin bores in his mouth. A big man, he didn't see Ryker anymore, didn't see anything.

"At age eight you went to live with your uncle in German Tanganyika," Bormann said. "Why was that?"

Control your breathing. "My parents died."

Bormann closed one file and opened another. He said, with exaggerated cordiality, "Well, growing up in Africa must have been fascinating. And you speak six languages. A mountain climber, expert shot, long-distance runner. We could have used you at Munich. Two years in military school."

Bormann's voice dropped. "You struck an officer. Expelled."

Ryker said nothing. Bormann said, "Spain, nineteen thirty-eight. Engineered a prison escape at Pedro Ramez Penitentiary, freed four important Franco officers. How did you do that?"

"Trade secret."

"France. Nineteen forty. Destroyed an enemy communications center an hour before our advance. Belgium. Norway. Using your American passport. Smuggled mortars to German sympathizers. Captured but escaped, killing four. Awarded the Knights Cross and Oak Leaf Cluster." Bormann looked up. "Not usual honors for a civilian. Where are those awards?"

"At home."

"Why aren't you wearing them?"

Ryker's teeth were pearly. "I have them in a little box."

"You should *wear* these awards," Bormann said stiffly. "Ah, Poland."

"I don't talk about Poland."

"Poland. You machine-gunned Polish cavalry while our troops were repairing stalled vehicles nearby. You saved German lives."

"They were on horseback."

"Excuse me?"

"I didn't know they'd be on horseback. I wouldn't have done it . . . taken the job . . . if I had."

Bormann looked at him sideways. "There's no shame in saving Germans."

"The Poles just charged out of the woods. Swords out. Yelling. They deserved better."

"But if they hadn't been on horseback they might have killed *you.* Brave, crazy, it's all the same when you're dead.

If I were you I'd be thankful. Why do all your jobs have to be more difficult anyway?"

"That's the contest. Anyway, I'm paid well."

"The pay." Bormann flipped pages. He whistled. He looked like he was considering changing jobs.

"A lavish spender. I like that. A million for Norway. Gone by March. Drinking. Vacations. Ladies." He looked up. "A Swiss bank account? I'm amazed. Rather prudent for a man like you, isn't it?"

Ryker was silent.

"I mean, throwing away most of your money then carefully banking the rest. When you're broke you don't touch it, don't eat but don't touch it. What's the money for, Herr Ryker? I'm curious."

Ryker noted that since money had entered the conversation he was being addressed as "Herr."

"I asked you a question, Herr Ryker."

"It's my money."

"You fail to understand. People don't talk to me that way."

"I do."

A muscle jerked in Bormann's neck. "You don't get along with authority, do you, Herr Ryker?"

"You might say that."

"Up until now you have survived, even carved this comfortable niche for yourself because you're so talented, but my guards are outside. I know what you did to that lieutenant in Urfeld. What makes you think you have the right to injure an officer of the Reich, to hospitalize him, to address me in this fashion?"

Ryker watched him.

"And helping that Jew." Bormann shifted angrily in the chair. Ryker caught sight of a book title: *Society Against the*

Presumptuousness of Jewry. Bormann said, "I see nothing in your file about personal ancestry. Perhaps you've Jewish blood of your own."

"My grandparents were Presbyterian, Reichsleiter. That Jew shouldn't have been treated that way."

"He was a Jew." Bormann's lip curled. "Perhaps he knew something about *you,* Herr Ryker, so that you felt obligated to help him."

"He'd never met me before."

"You killed him."

"He asked me to."

"Who are you to decide what people deserve and don't deserve? You. You're a professional killer."

"So are you."

Bormann's face turned black. His lips went thin and bloodless. The cords on his neck stood out. His right hand, which up until now had not moved, began to tremble violently. His mouth formed words but nothing came out.

He lifted the right hand off the desk and started to run it through his hair.

Instantly Ryker vaulted the desk, grabbed the wrist, and pinned it behind Bormann. *"Muller!"* Bormann screeched. The door burst open. Two guards, flanking Muller, pointed Schmeisser machine pistols at Ryker, but he was too close to Bormann for them to fire.

Ryker's knee was on Martin Bormann's back. He'd twisted one of the Reichsleiter's arms up to the shoulder. Ryker's other hand was poised dangerously by Bormann's neck artery. Bormann's cheek was squashed against the desk.

Muller growled, "Let him up."

Ryker cocked his head. *Adrenaline problem.* He said, "Relax, Muller. I would have hurt him already if I wanted to."

Muller glanced anxiously at Bormann. "Let him go."

"No shooting now," cautioned Ryker.

Bormann was groaning. "My arm."

Muller addressed the guards. "Put down the guns."

Reluctantly, they lowered the machine pistols.

Ryker said, "Into the corner. And your Luger, Muller." The guns clattered onto the floor.

Slowly, Bormann straightened. He rubbed his wrist. His shoulders were heaving. He tensed to move but Ryker touched his elbow. He stopped.

Ryker, watching Muller but indicating Bormann with a movement of the head, said, "See? He's fine. A little pain but no damage. I didn't want to hurt him."

The room was very still. Muller folded his arms. "You'd have a hard time convincing anyone else of that."

"I don't think so." Ryker slid the desk blotter aside. He pointed to the tiny red button underneath. He smiled at Muller. "Shall I push that?" he asked.

Muller, who was just inside the door, went pale. He glanced fearfully at the mirror. Ryker said, "I thought that's where it was."

Bormann gasped. "You knew about that?"

"You never shifted your hand, Reichsleiter. Am I wrong, or is the safest place in your room your own chair?"

Muller's eyes were a deathly glow. Ryker shrugged. "Self-protection, Herr Reichsleiter. You're looking for a good man. I hope my qualities recommend themselves to you."

Bormann staggered to the door. When he was out of reach Muller retrieved his Luger, the guards their machine pistols. All three muzzles pointed at Ryker.

"Hands in the air. Don't move otherwise," Muller said.

Ryker said calmly, "Where did you think I was going to go?"

Bormann's breathing returned to normal. Muller said,

"Kill him, Herr Reichsleiter?" His face was white but his hand steady.

A strange respect lit the flat peasant features of Martin Bormann. He looked from Muller to Ryker, from Ryker to the guards.

"I have a better idea," he finally said. "I'll let him kill himself."

The Reichsleiter cradled a brandy between his third and fourth fingers. Muller and his guards had left the office so now only the bust of Hitler sneered at Ryker from the desk. Between the Italian brocade curtains and a fleshy Rubens, a map pictured an enlarged emerald mass set in the flat blue sea. Narrow at the bottom, curved in the north, the island resembled the rearing head of a serpent.

Martin Bormann said, "This is Captains Island. A twenty-minute ferry ride from Portland, Maine. Perhaps you were there when you were a boy. The cliffs offer a nice view of the sea."

Ryker was not aware of any draft, yet something cold touched his neck. He brushed it away, like an insect.

Bormann said, "The Americans have constructed a coastal artillery complex on the northeast corner of this island, to house two immense guns, sixteen-inch, sixty-foot-long guns, which comprise a major link in an artillery chain around the harbor.

"Fifty, sixty ships a day steam under those guns. Battleships in training, oil tankers. A convoy occasionally. Portland is a fueling and training center for the North Atlantic fleet. Civilians occupy the harbor side of the island. They fish or work in the Portland shipyard. The Atlantic side houses the army base. A hundred and fifty troops, watchtowers, and the guns. A direct hit from one of those cannons would blow an enemy ship out of the water."

Ryker said, "Enemy ship?" He looked disgusted. "In *Portland?*"

"That tone, Herr Ryker."

Ryker jerked his head toward Hitler's office. "Afraid he's listening?"

"Herr Ryker. Herr Ryker." Bormann, less stern since Ryker had pinned him against the desk, drummed on the wall. "We are not planning a sea attack on Portland. But if we were, let me remind you, we successfully invaded Norway from the sea."

"I didn't see *you* there."

Bormann exhaled. "Will you brag about this later?" He puffed out his chest. " 'I talked back to Martin Bormann.' You're acting a little childish, don't you think?"

Ryker threw his leg over the arm of the chair.

"Well, I revel in the knowledge of where you're going. We were farsighted in keeping up your American passport, in keeping your American cover all these years. This job is by far the most dangerous we've asked you to accomplish. I can't think of anyone else who would even consider it, but you'll go. You'll probably die. Getting interested? Getting angry? Thinking, I'll show him? Good. Think that. There's an outside chance you *will* pull it off, *if* you're smart enough, *if* you're brave enough, *if* you're lucky. I'm planting hooks. You're flushing, Herr Ryker. You'll be able to double that Swiss bank account of yours. You'll have carte blanche within the Reich. Whatever you need. Whomever you want. You'll earn a place in history, posthumously, but you'll go. You can't help yourself. So push me. I don't care. I win in the end."

The walls were Italian teak. A silver tray of Swiss chocolates was arrayed before them. Footsteps sounded in the hall. Reclining on the baroque sofa, Bormann spoke with the thick, sensual tones of a voyeur. "You have an opportunity, Herr Ryker, to change the war for the Americans. It is still early for them, they are allocating resources; how much for Europe, for the Pacific. How much for defense at home.

"If a panic were to force Roosevelt to pour his war chest into defense instead of aggression, America might be kept out of Europe for at least another year. We could finish England, hurt Russia. We could perfect weapons we have been developing."

"What kind of panic are you talking about?" Ryker asked.

Bormann said, "The Americans have yet to realize the pitiful nature of their coastal defense. Their supply convoys refuel in Portland. In the open sea the ships are guarded, attacks expected."

"You want to hit a convoy in Portland?"

Bormann bit into half a candy, looked at the remaining half, and frowned. "If some extremely crucial, strategic convoy were to be sunk *while still in Portland Bay*, with a great loss of American lives, the terror and demoralization up and down the coast would nudge Roosevelt in the proper direction, don't you think?"

Ryker laughed. "I thought you weren't planning a sea attack on Portland."

"That's right. It wouldn't work. An insane idea."

"Then I don't understand. I destroy the guns on Captains Island and you destroy the convoy, isn't that it?"

The brandy glass jerked. Head sideways, Bormann's spreading grin made him appear suddenly porcine. "I'm amazed. Herr Ryker guesses wrong. Is he fallible? *Destroy* the guns? I want you to *use* the guns. Use them for the Reich."

THREE

FOUR THOUSAND MILES AWAY, in Portland, Maine, the last ferry of the night chugged into deep, blanketing fog. The dock and waterfront shops, blacked out because of the war, disappeared. Duke Ellington's "Mood Indigo" faded across the water. A green light atop the ship went round and round. It had trouble penetrating the wall of mist.

Thomas Heiden stood at the prow of the boat, a young woman at his side. He wore a bulky military raincoat and a soft peaked cap. His shoulder was almost touching the girl's. Trying to keep from smiling, he said, "We're lost." He had a low voice and he was moving closer.

The girl wore a padded black wool hand-me-down, brushed clean but faded, which exaggerated her trim figure. "You're making up another story," she said.

"No, I'm certain we're lost," Heiden said, peering into the fog. "When the weather clears we'll be in Rio. The pilot got lost and headed out to sea. It will be summer this time of year. We'll see palm trees, hula girls."

"There aren't any hula girls in Rio."

"Did I say Rio? I meant the South Seas."

Their gloved hands rested six inches apart. Fog slicked

the white slatted deck. Paint peeled off the latticed railing, which curved, with the oval boat, back to where two other passengers, bundled, smoking, glanced between the couple and the bay.

Heiden, at twenty-seven, was tall, slim, with the developed shoulders of a swimmer. A flushed and eager youthfulness lit his angular features, slanting cheekbones, and strong jaw, but a brooding aspect clouded the high forehead. Wide brown eyes, curious, seeking, bestowed an intensity to his face. He always conveyed a hint of tension, even now, when he was smiling. Periodically he lifted the cap with one hand and ran the other through slightly unruly black hair, as if it had been longer before the army cut it, and he was not yet accustomed to its new length. He was greatly conscious of the girl beside him.

The girl said, "I was a hula girl in the second-grade play."

Heiden tipped closer. "Is this where I kiss you?"

"It's where you keep your hands on the railing."

The girl was even more alluring in the swirling fog, tilted against the rail, one slim thigh outlined against the soft ankle-length dress, black hair coiled carefully. She had a cool, slanting jaw and a small, wet mouth. Her eyes were deep violet. She had a pinched waist, a happy, confident smile, and an air of quiet strength and composure.

Behind them, through the mist, the bearded face of the pilot was a shadow behind a window glistening with condensation, shaved by wipers. The harbor echoed with horns and bells. Amber lights floated by far away. The engine's growl was deep, throbbing.

Heiden said, "At least tell me your name. After all, I've told you mine."

"*Guess* what it is."

He pursed his lips. "Bertha."

"Ugh! That's a terrible name!"

"Yes, Bertha. Or Olga."

"Well, it isn't Bertha or Olga. It's Corrice. Corrice Kelly."

"And you live on the island with your father. And you work as a typist on the base but I had to wait for a Portland dance to meet you. What else? You used to fish with your father."

"Do you always remember everything?"

She liked William Powell in *Shadow of the Thin Man* and he liked Ruth Hussey in *Married Bachelor.* He knew the names of the constellations. Her father had taught her to steer boats by the stars. He liked motorcycles. She'd lived on Captains Island for all her nineteen years. He changed the subject when his past came up.

She said, "The army won't allow civilians on the Atlantic side of the island. I used to picnic there all the time. What do you do on the base?"

He leaned very close. "Oh, nothing much." He glanced around to make sure no one was listening. "Arrest spies."

Her misting breath came quicker. "On the island?"

"We've caught—don't tell anyone—*three* spies just this week. A spy was trying to set fire to the Bath Iron Works. A spy came ashore at Bailey Island, landed by a submarine."

"You! You're making this up!"

"Shhhhh. Twenty-one spies were captured in a Waterville five-and-ten. The Germans love candy but Hermann Goering eats it all. They got so excited they were ordering in German."

"You're probably not in intelligence at all."

"I don't know why I'm telling you this. You could be a spy yourself."

Her throat, tipped back, was almost luminous. She brushed one slim finger against his chest.

She said, "You win. What gave me away?"

"Hmmmmm. Your legs."

"Lieutenant!"

"Mata Hari had legs like that."

The island appeared through the mist, rising swiftly: a jutting dock raised on thick, watermarked timbers; a narrow cobblestone street, black buglike Dodges and Packards, parked for the night; a wooden grocery; a fisherman's shack. The smells were of fog, salt, wet earth.

From below, there came the tramp of feet on the steel staircase. The night shift was coming home from Portland.

"Who was Mata Hari?" the girl asked. The ferry bumped the dock.

"A German spy, that's who. You know how she used to steal information?"

"I don't think I want to hear the rest of this." She held a Woolworth compact in one hand and patted her hair with the other. The mirror threw green light on his eyes.

"It must be wonderful growing up in a place like this," Heiden said. "Do you know all these people?"

"When you grow up in a place with thirty people, you know them, all right."

They waited on the edge of the dock for the green light to disappear again. A mournful wail came from the fog. On the strip of dark sand below, wooden boats beached for the winter lay on their keels, peeling, empty.

Everyone else had gone home. They strolled past sporadic clapboard houses. Heiden said, "Actually, I've just been assigned here, but there isn't that much to do. Important things, I mean. I hope they send me to Europe next."

"Too many people are going to Europe."

"I joined up to go." He hunched his shoulders in agitation and thrust his hands deep into his pockets. A vehement note entered his voice. "And anyway, I should go. If I don't get over there soon, the war might be over."

"Would that be so bad?"

They were on a dark, narrow dirt road devoid of lighting. Oaks loomed above them, stripped, massive. The neatly painted houses had porches, turrets, swinging chairs. Dim, up the sloping hill, another couple was entering a house, the man's arm encircling the woman. Across the street a light went off, a curtain shifted, a cat meowed.

She said, "Maybe you'll be assigned to the prisoner-of-war camp they're building near Unity."

Heiden half drew his hands from his pockets. "What prisoner-of-war camp?"

"Everybody knows about it. The government's been putting up shacks on lumber-company land. The company's complaining it has no men to cut timber. The government needs timber and our men are gone."

Heiden said, "I knew you were a spy."

"Oh, I know some things. I know about those guns on the other side of the island. Huge, tremendous guns. We couldn't believe it when they were unloaded. We thought the dock was going to collapse."

Heiden said, "But I don't want to guard prisoners. It's important to fight them, the Germans." He seemed aware that his own explanation sounded hollow. "It's just something I have to do."

"Don't you like it here?"

"Yes. It's beautiful. The people." He blushed. "But I have to go there."

Her face showed deep criticism. "Men. You're always trying to prove things."

When he looked at her sideways she added, "It was

awfully nice of you to take me home from the dance."

"Oh, the base is nearby anyway."

"This is where I live. Do you like cocoa?"

An hour later she stood illuminated in the lighted doorway, saying good night. Her makeup was still in place but her hair, lustrous and uncoiled, fell wildly and obscured the tops of her shoulders. One hand rested on a hip. From the street, where he was grinning again, he said, "Is *this* where I kiss you?"

"No, this isn't where you kiss me. This is where you march back to your barracks. Do you want a flashlight? The island will be dark."

She watched him stride off. In the hallway, she danced two steps of the shag, pulled her dress up, looked at her calves, and giggled. She cocked her head at herself in the round mirror. "Mata Hari," she said. The house was chilly and very neat. A pair of yellow slickers dangled on hooks by the banister, beside an oil of lobster fishermen battling a storm. In the living room, strewn with throw rugs, the buckshot eye of the deer head watched her take the cocoa cups off the fireplace.

She was thinking about the shy way he walked, with his hands in his pockets. He was a bold talker but at bottom, pretty shy. Otherwise he would have tried to kiss her anyway. She wondered why he didn't like to talk about himself more.

Heavy footsteps began dragging up from the basement. Her smile died.

The door opened. A red-bearded face peered out. No mustache. Just the beard.

She said, "You were quiet down there."

"Wasn't listening to you, if that's what you mean. How about some dinner? Your old Da's pretty hungry."

She was exasperated. "Did you forget to eat again!" The kitchen had pine timber floors and an immense steel stove she lit with a match. She said, "A soldier took me home from the dance."

"Hmph. Not like you to let someone do that." He sniffed the air. "Is that cocoa I smell? You made him cocoa?"

"He was cold. It was nothing special."

Her father summed up his skepticism with a single Maine "Ayuh."

She wore a cardigan over her dress. Thick steam rose from the boiling fish chowder. Her voice faltered. "He said he's an intelligence officer, Da."

"Hurry up with the food, will you? I've been working all night."

"Have you, Da?" She left the stove and pulled up a chair beside him. She stared into his face. "Then why didn't I hear any noise down there?"

He fished in his pocket, pulled out a pipe, and began packing it. When it was smoking, he said, "What do you mean?"

"You know exactly what I mean. It isn't like before. Everything has changed. We're in the war too. Da, look at me."

He pushed back the chair, the muscles in his throat working. "I promised, didn't I? Didn't we talk about this, Corrice? Come down to the basement. I'll show you, okay?"

Her black J.C. Penney pumps beat a hollow cadence on the stairs. The lone bulb, when it was turned on, swung slowly back and forth, casting pendulous shadows on the homemade workbench, the neatly hung hammers and chisels, the paint cans, the half-finished tables, the broken chairs to be repaired. Everything smelled like sawdust and concrete.

Frowning, she flipped through a series of pencil draw-ings on the workbench. She said, "When you told Captain Gottfried you wouldn't take his radio, I had the feeling you were just saying it because I was there. Why did you let me go to the base, Da? It isn't just the English fighting them now. We're in it too."

He held his stomach when he laughed. "Saints preserve me from worrying women! Do you see a radio here? Food? Do you? Fuel for them? I'm out of it. I told you!" He draped his arm around her shoulder. "You think your old Da is a madman? Come on. You like my drawings of the new boat?"

She said, "I just didn't hear any noise."

"From a pencil? Back to dinner. You going to see that intelligence officer again?"

"Oh, maybe. I don't know."

"Ayuh."

After dinner, he smoked while she cleaned the dishes, then he watched her go upstairs to bed. The light above her door went out. The springs on her bed compressed. He didn't move, though, at the bottom of the banister. He was a big man with a beer belly, hands like grappling hooks, and a broad slash of a mouth. His arms were immense.

After a while he turned back to the basement. This time he locked the door behind him.

Downstairs, he unscrewed the toolboard.

The radio lay behind.

In a light drizzle, Tom Heiden picked his way home. The thin road was a dark ribbon, barely visible in thick-ening fog. Spruces alternately crowded up against the pit-ted surface or dropped away to reveal high grassy areas, which smelled of brackish ponds he could not see. He heard a frantic rustle in the bushes, the frightened cry of a small animal, a sucking noise. The island was dripping. His shoes made rubbery sounds.

He'd been taking the long way home. After leaving the girl, he'd strolled around the tiny village, admiring the wide, decklike porches and widow's walks and white picket fences, the iron sheds filled with grey lobster traps. He'd gone to the wharves to watch the bay. He'd stood before the colored glass on the island steeple.

"Halt! Who goes there?"

He had to squint to make out the gate and the great-coated sentry who challenged him. He identified himself.

"Advance and be recognized."

The guard looked miserably sodden, shivering in the drizzle, Enfield pointed at Heiden.

Heiden touched his shoulder. "You're doing a fine job," he said. "I couldn't see *you* in the fog. How'd you see me?"

"I heard you coming, sir."

"Very observant, I'll write it up."

"Thank you, sir." The man straightened. Heiden still had two hundred yards of wooded road before he reached the barracks. Fifty yards earlier, in the middle of the island, Heiden could have sworn he was in a wilderness. But passing onto the parade ground minutes later, he found himself in a neat cropped square complete with bare flagpole, two jeeps, and an army truck. Low, long wooden prefabs lined two sides of the parade ground. The third periphery was a mass of high grass leading up a ridge, toward the forest. But the dominant border of the parade ground was the battery itself, forty feet high, hill-shaped and curling completely around the eastern edge of the base, covered with packed earth and blue spruce for camouflage. Enemy bombers, if they ever reached Portland, would see trees, not artillery.

Two tremendous concrete entranceways had been blasted into the hill. BATTERY MACALLISTER, read the lettering sandblasted into the high portals. From within came the harsh glow of unfiltered light and the sound of engines and other metallic groans. At opposite ends of the hill, the twin guns of the battery looked out over the Hussey Sound and the convoys and battleships that daily sought the protection of Casco Bay.

His own barracks was a smaller prefab. No new notices had been placed on the bulletin board but a lone envelope marked his mail slot. "Heiden" was written in the base commander's neat hand. He pocketed the letter. He was in a wooden hallway heated by a coal stove. Outside his door, he ran into another officer, wrapped in a towel and emerging from the bathroom. The other man, who was balding and wore thick glasses, leered when he saw Heiden.

"Some guys get all the luck at dances," he said. "Every guy on the base has been after that broad."

"Her name's Corrice, Mariani. And she's pretty nice."

"Nice. She was nice, all right. You score?" The officer held up pudgy palms. "Okay, okay. None of my business. Me, I got a fat one tonight. Something to hold on to, know what I mean?"

"Mariani, you know anything about a prison camp?"

"Huh?"

"A prison camp. Did you hear anything about a camp on the mainland?"

"Nah. Nobody tells me anything. Fix the guns. Clean the guns. Polish the goddamn guns."

Heiden laughed. Mariani said, "Why? Did you hear something?"

Heiden frowned. "I'm not sure."

He opened the envelope in his room.

Tom:

We've just received some interesting films of the German raids over London. The Kiwanis Club wants to arrange a little presentation . . . show the movie, give a talk on incendiary bombs (Ha, ha, as if there's anything to worry about here). Plan on doing that tomorrow night. Good community relations.

Major Savage

His fist closed over the note. He dropped it in a ball on his desk, beside a half-completed application for transfer to Europe. There was also a photograph on the desk, of a man standing proudly by a small sailboat. The man was Heiden's age and vaguely resembled him, but the photo was yellow with age, cracked, carefully taped, as if it had been carried around for years. Palms on the desk, he stared at the photograph. "Give a talk," he muttered. "I didn't join the army to give speeches."

He turned off the light and pulled the blackout curtains from the window. He seated himself by the window beside a telescope on a tripod, which he patted lovingly, a homemade affair of junk metal he'd shaped and old lenses he'd ground himself. He turned it toward the sky, which tonight was impenetrable. The drizzle had stopped. Remarkably, on the small segment of ocean visible through his rear window, the fog had lifted. He aimed the scope toward Europe. The horizon was a blacker shade of grey.

Just beyond his vision, he knew, dark ships were steaming toward harbors, and navy dirigibles were searching for German submarines. What was going on out there tonight? Had there been an attack? Sometimes the men in the watchtowers saw yellow flashes. Was someone looking back? Were sailors drowning out there, in the black cold?

He found the note he'd crumpled on the table, smoothed it, reread it, then tore it up and dropped it in the wastebasket.

Under the covers, he pictured himself advancing through bombed rubble. He saw himself crouched, ripping a grenade pin with his teeth while the earth vibrated from an approaching tank.

The telescope glinted at the window.

He thought about Corrice Kelly and the way her throat tipped back on the boat, the way her hair dropped around her shoulders.

In Maine, at times the truth was that he had trouble remembering that the war really existed. Sure, the radio reports were full of battle news and the harbor was filled with troops, but the troops were so young and clean. The Germans weren't *here*. Could a war really be raging when the air smelled so fine and the birds wheeled and he went to dances on Saturday night? Wasn't it really the huge impersonal battery, with its immense hidden guns, that was an illusion? Or the gigantic battleships that dwindled in the distance and disappeared?

Four thousand miles away, Martin Bormann, whom Heiden had seen once in a newsreel, whom he had never dreamt about, never even thought about, had decided he should die.

FOUR

"WHO ARE YOU ANYWAY?" the pilot said. He stared at Ryker but got no reply. They'd been flying east since noon, away from the sun and over the Russian Steppe. Dull yellow Plexiglas colored everything below, wavy crust, stark, endless. In antlike columns, the German army struggled through the drifts. The pilot banked the Messerschmitt to match their direction, toward black smoke twisting in the north. He said, scanning the skies, "Ivan's been bombing Klin for two days now. Why do you want to go *there?*"

Bormann had asked the same question. "You can have any men in the Reich. Why do you want to use troops who almost killed you last time?"

"Because they're good."

"But they mutinied; you had to shoot one of them."

"They learned from it."

Bormann had said in disgust, "Your own men will probably murder you in Russia before the mission begins."

Now the plane pitched in an updraft. Ryker said, "I have to see some people." Over the pilot's fur-lined collar, he memorized the movements of the black gloves on the instrument panel. The movements were sure but the voice unsteady. Since taking off, the pilot had kept up a nervous monologue: about his sons, his squadron, airmen who had been killed. He'd talked about bakeries. He'd talked about automobiles. He said, "Couldn't you meet them somewhere else?"

Ryker winked. "It's a surprise."

"A surprise. A surprise. You don't talk like an officer. You're not Gestapo either, I don't think. I've flown plenty of each. But they gave you a plane." He waited for a reply.

When Ryker said nothing he shifted his shoulders. "We'll talk about something else, then. How did you hurt your hand? It's stitched up badly."

"Watch the road."

Muttering, the pilot went back to the sky. His neck was red and crisscrossed with little folds of age. A moment later he jerked. Ryker read his lips. "Planes. Russians."

Two distant dots, framed against steel-colored nimbus, rushed toward them. The pilot gripped the throttle. The world went vertical. The Messerschmitt raced for the clouds. Then the prop began sputtering and the pilot spoke to it. "Don't stop. Climb." The approaching aircraft grew larger. The pilot fought the jerking wheel. The altimeter was going crazy. The engine coughed, smoked. "Baby, baby, baby," the pilot said. He fixed on the clouds above, protective but out of reach. Ryker, monitoring the attackers, touched the leather shoulder. "They're Focke-Wulfs. Relax."

"You're sure? Yes, Wulfs. I see them now."

The cockpit filled with a musty, acrid odor. The Messerschmitt leveled. The Focke-Wulfs wagged wingtips and their pilots waved.

Minutes later, when the sky had swallowed them, Ryker said, "I saw seven Spitfires painted on the side of this plane."

The blue goggles swung in his direction. The voice grew

measured. Once this pilot had been brash. "That's right. Seven."

"You shot them down?"

"We did. The plane and I." They flew in silence. The pilot said, "I've been fighting for four years. The thermos, please."

Steam curled over his flying cap. He said, "Do you believe in luck?"

"Maybe."

"If you believe in luck, you believe it runs out sometime."

The town below was a patchwork of dirty lumps, an interruption in the snow. A black line probed out of it like a tentacle. The pilot said, "We've destroyed the planes the Reds were supposed to have. Where do the new ones come from?" He stretched a leather-sheathed arm east, toward the Urals. "What are they building out there? They've got a few thousand miles until the ocean. Yes, I shot down seven Spitfires. But I'm afraid. I admit it. No matter how good you are, luck doesn't last forever."

Ryker said, "How long until we get to Klin?"

A muscle jerked in the pilot's ear. He began the slow crisscross of the sky again, searching. "Fifteen minutes," he said. "If the Russians haven't blown up the runway."

The runway was framed by burning machinery, a Heinkel on one side, propped on one shredded wing, a truck on the other. Balls of smoke burst in the distance. Work teams scurried to avoid the Messerschmitt, which began skidding immediately. It spun around, tipping, rushing toward a shed. With a jerk, it stopped. A fierce grin of pride was the pilot's good-bye.

Soldiers threw pailfuls of snow on a burning Stuka. The runway was cluttered with blasted steel and ice. Amid shouts and careening-ambulance bells, Ryker felt an iron grip on his shoulder. The lieutenant who confronted him had a prematurely unforgiving face and a Hartz Mountain accent. "Who are you?"

He glared at Ryker's identification. "Come with me." A voice shouted, "Incoming mail." Ryker hit the ground and the far end of the runway exploded in powder and glowing metal fragments.

The church, which lay over a drift-covered rise, was a complete surprise, alone in endless white. Ryker saw no town, no parishioners, no other evidence of Russian life. The unreal scene seemed a mirage. Binoculars flashed in the steeple. A half-track and field car warmed up outside. Inside, where the air was furnace hot, everything radiated gold, the gilt-covered cross and gently suspended incense burners. The floor was smeared with mud and melting snow. Under the oval, Byzantine eyes of the icons, booted officers clustered at the pulpit, gesturing, arguing. Their sleeves were rolled, their forearms white and veined with blue. A private circulated with a mess tray. The lieutenant jabbed Ryker playfully. "Doberman," he said, indicating the steaming meat.

The major general in charge, a more cheerful man, was a crisp, stocky Prussian with a grey block of a head and a sparkling wedding band. He said, "The Russians are finally showing themselves. I know their positions. Three weeks from now I'll be in Moscow."

He examined Ryker's paper with amusement. "Give you anything you want, eh? Paintings again?"

"I'm looking for a squad of Austrians. Light infantry. Seventeenth Army. Commander is named Meltzer."

"Sounds Jewish."

"It isn't."

"Heinrich, find out about these troops." The general gave his ear to a corpulent, blotchy-faced officer in a tightly fastened tunic. "Luck for you, Herr Ryker. They're six kilometers from here at a farmhouse, the tip of our defense of this town. You may call them on the wireless."

"I need to talk to them in person."

The general's eyebrows arched and faced the map. "These Russians have been lucky for a hundred years. Napoleon almost beat them. The Finns slaughtered them. If it weren't for winter we would have too, but we will. They're overplaying themselves. In a day or so, when the situation has eased, you may visit your squad."

"I need to go now."

The aides flashed Ryker antagonistic looks. Clearly, he had been dismissed.

He said, "General."

"Are you still here?"

"General."

The general didn't look up. "I have no way to get you to your farmhouse," he said.

"I saw a truck outside."

"To move troops, not you."

"Give me a horse, then."

"Horses, Herr Ryker, are more valuable than autos. The snow is impassable in places. The Russians are using cavalry! Cavalry, in the twentieth century! A band of damn Cossacks is breaking through my lines ten kilometers from here. Temporarily, of course. I need my horses."

The corpulent officer was unsure whether to interrupt. "Contact. Southern sector." His manicured finger stopped short of a wooded area on the map. It wasn't too far from the farmhouse. "Horses and sleds are pulling the Russians."

The general looked at Ryker as if to say, You see? He

told the officer, "We have the third Panzer near there, don't we? Can they move in the drifts? Move them."

Ryker saw that a road passed the farmhouse.

The general was saying, "Check the runway. Fly me in more coats. I don't need more ammunition. I need more coats."

Ryker said, "I'll go on a motorcycle."

The lieutenant found a BMW in a shed, sidecar attached. "Waste of good machinery," he said. "We cleared that road but it might be snowed over. The Reds may have cut it. The general's right, you know. We'll have the Russians on the run soon. The man in the field doesn't see the whole picture. You'll kill yourself if you go out now. Why don't you wait?"

Because it was so cold, it took Ryker several kicks to start the engine.

Ryker steered the BMW in the icy rut of a Panzer. Poplars and pines crowded up against the narrow track, oxcart width, as if waiting to crush anyone caught in the middle. Flying snow slashed at his face. His kidneys ached from the bumping. The engine died. In the sudden silence Ryker bent by the carburetor, then spun. A silver hawk watched from a branch twenty feet away. The hawk's eyes were hooded. Ryker wore goggles. Moments later he was underway.

The wind grew fierce. Ice particles lodged in his teeth. When the odometer told him he'd gone six kilometers, he stopped to reconnoiter and a voice from a clump of firs said, "Don't move." A figure wearing a Wehrmacht helmet and woman's fur coat stepped into the path, pointing a Schmeisser. The coat wasn't funny. A hair-trigger expression covered the pale, unshaven face. The soldier slid close, boots crunching. He looked into Ryker's face a long time. Then he said, "Shit. Ryker."

Ryker grinned. "Where's Meltzer?"

"Meltzer died."

"Who's in charge then?"

"Teacher."

Atop a short but steep hill, he leaned the bike against the farmhouse, a low expanse of half-buried timber. Inside, Ryker felt like he was in a bunker. The house was dim, low-ceilinged and octagon-shaped. People here would huddle for warmth. Throw rugs littered the floor. The radio, three feet high, was Soviet issue. Wooden ice skates dangled from the door. Behind dull red beads, a bed outlined itself in an alcove. Stalin eyed him disdainfully from the mantel. The Christ was one of the bloodiest ones Ryker had seen in Russia.

A thin, balding man crouched at a table, blowing on coals under a samovar. His grey tunic was filthy, as were the sticklike wrists protruding from the cuffs. Sensing Ryker, he straightened with a slow elegance, looked up, glanced at the automatic rifle propped against his chair. Wire-rimmed glasses magnified his pale blue eyes. His voice was quiet, disappointed, amused.

"I thought you were dead. Back outside, Axel."

The fur coat rumbled out. The room reeked with a smoky, unwashed odor. Ryker saw piles of straw or folded rugs where the men slept. He crouched by the fire. His thighs, open to the flames, began to burn. Melting show dripped down the back of his neck.

He said, "What happened to Meltzer?"

The Teacher's teeth were black or missing altogether.

He looked as if he had never been to a dentist in his life. He said, "Was that a motorized vehicle in which I heard you arrive? A troop transport, perhaps?"

"Motorcycle."

"I suppose a truck would have been too much to hope for. You want to know about Captain Meltzer? The Russians began their attack three weeks ago with a bombardment. Geysers of snow. A poetic sight. Shrapnel got him, in the head."

"I liked Meltzer."

"He didn't like you. None of us does."

"That doesn't bother me." Ryker drank from Teacher's cup, watching him over the rim.

"Of course not. Did Mephistopheles crave Faust's affection? The agreement sufficed."

"I have a plan."

"Obvious. You're here."

"It will get you out of Russia."

Teacher's uniform was dirty enough to render the rank anonymous, but the Knights Cross and Oak Leaf Cluster were visible at his neck. "You know, Ryker, I've discovered an essential truth about the army. The more you perform miracles, the more you're *ordered* to perform miracles. Since working with you in Norway we've been given every suicide assignment the generals could think of. I used to think it was the other way around. Succeed at hazardous duty and reward was yours. Mistake. Mistake. Come outside."

He coughed harshly and drained his cup, pinky extended. Wind lashed their faces when they opened the door. The barnyard rose and fell in drifts. The storm was worsening. Ryker saw a barn to one side, conical-roofed, then, backs to his face, a dozen immobile soldiers, seemingly frozen in place, rooted by a wall made of ice.

Teacher cleaned his glasses by pinching two fingers. "We can't dig protection in this ground, so we rolled snow, thawed more snow in the house, then poured the water on the wall. Layer by layer. Will packed ice deflect bullets? We'll know soon."

The snow-swept panorama was divided into segments: meadow, forest, iced pond. "The kind of Christmas view I'd have written verse about in the old days," Teacher said. "Now I'd put the flamethrower to the woods to see who's hiding there. May I introduce our new recruits?"

He turned to the soldiers by the wall. They were, Ryker realized, made of snow. Snow peeked out from under the long military greatcoats. Snow was framed under the Wehrmacht infantry helmets.

Teacher said, "This is Otto, Claus, and Albert. Otto, Claus, and Albert, this is Ryker. Otto, Claus, and Albert have extensive experience outdoors and a remarkable ability to remain in a single position for hours without complaining. There are only twenty-five soldiers here. The Russians see forty. We found clothing in the attic. The Ottos wear our uniforms. Kurt!"

Several soldiers away, one of the figures looked up. Teacher said, "Meeting in the farmhouse in ten minutes. One sentry to stay here, one at the gate. Ryker, look at the woods. We wired grenades down there. No explosions yet but the Ivans are there. I feel them. You can hear them on the radio sometimes. Nasty-sounding language. I always think they're discussing us."

"You talked afraid in Norway too until the fighting started."

Teacher grinned brightly. "Luck runs out." He sounded so much like the Messerschmitt pilot that Ryker had to suppress a shudder. He told himself, *I'm not afraid.*

On the far end of the hilltop, tilting like a dead behemoth, a Panzer Mark Four lay disabled in a drift. Broken tread spilled from the damaged frame. The long-barreled gun tapered toward the house. Teacher yelled into a jagged hole in the armor.

"Erhard!"

A youthful voice answered. "Wired it back up but the battery is dead. Barely, but dead. Anyway, the turret's probably frozen. What's this? Herr Ryker!"

Ryker nodded. "Hello Erhard. Still fixing things?"

"You saved my life. Thanks to you."

Teacher exhaled in frustration. "If it hadn't been for Ryker your life wouldn't have needed saving in the first place."

"I don't agree. You all blame Ryker for Norway, but nobody made us volunteer to go."

Teacher said, "In that case, Erhard, would you like to go with him again?"

"Are you crazy?" The head disappeared into the tank. Teacher called, "Ten minutes! The farmhouse!"

Back inside, he said, "By the way, what is this idea of yours? I haven't even asked."

Ryker poured tea from the samovar. It was cold. "I'll tell you after you volunteer."

Propped on their bellies under the pines, the Russians wore white sheepskin coats, which blended with the snow. They took turns with binoculars. The cold didn't seem to bother them.

"I count eighteen at the wall," the older one said. "Tough, if they're out in this weather. But the wall blocks the farmhouse. I wish I could see what they have in the yard. Think the colonel will attack tonight?"

"He'll take it right away if he thinks his precious tank won't be damaged. And we freeze waiting for him to make up his mind."

The older soldier rolled onto his side, stuffed snow in his mouth, and sucked thoughtfully. "One more look and we'll report back." He moved the field glasses in an arc. He stopped. Excited, he punched his companion in the shoulder. "Look at the third soldier. From the left. At his face."

"I can hardly see the people in the storm, let alone the faces."

"Take the glasses. Look at his breath. It's frosting, see?"

"So?"

"Now look at the others. Aren't they breathing too?"

The younger man frowned. "I don't understand," he said. Then he said, "Wait," and "Son of a bitch!"

They inched back into the forest and started running. Ten minutes later they were in a clearing, surrounded by more Russians in white, stomping and clapping to keep warm. The shadowy form of a T-34 tank loomed in the falling snow. A bulky man with a red star on his fur hat planted his hands on his hips. "Well?"

"They've dressed snowmen in German clothing, Comrade Colonel. They must be in bad shape in the farmhouse."

Most of the men Ryker remembered were dead. The tough soldiers arrayed on the floor were strangers, a welcome contrast to what he was accustomed to seeing in Berlin. They held none of the arrogance in their eyes, no zeal, no sense of mission, but no friendliness either, just cunning, weariness, universal skepticism. The uniforms were a collection of German summer issue and hardy Russian winter clothing. Some men smoked. A few wolfed food from cans.

They all looked at him with the same suspicious clannish-ness, as if they had a single brain, and it was telling them he was an outsider and therefore trouble. He saw Iron Crosses, Eastern Winter Campaign badges, tank destruc-tion badges, war wound badges, assault and close combat badges, Spanish Military medals of valor—enough deco-rations to fill a division, not a squad.

Teacher strolled amid the sprawled grey bodies. "The vote is," he said, "do we leave the safety of this warm, lovely country house and travel to parts unknown with Herr Ryker? Or do we remain? If we go, we've been promised honorable discharges. Herr Ryker, if he has no other positive qualities, is a man of his word. Still, let us examine the bargain. Some of us remember the two-month furlough we got for Nor-way, where half of us were killed. If *that* reward was only eight weeks, what could be the nature of Herr Ryker's new adventure? Alas, he will not tell us unless we agree to go. So let us, before we decide, imagine possibilities. Perhaps Herr Ryker has convinced the High Command that he could kidnap the entire British Parliament with thirty-five brave men. Maybe his plan is to have us fight our way to the nearest warm-water port, swim to Cairo, and surprise the British rear. Then again, knowing Herr Ryker, the job may not be that simple. In the United States, people vote out of ignorance all the time. Look who they landed up with, Roosevelt. All in favor of going with Ryker, hands up."

No one moved.

Teacher frowned. "I can't understand what's gotten into them. Generally they're so pleasant and cooperative. Could it be, do you think, that they actually want to hear the plan before they vote on it?"

Ryker couldn't stop one corner of his mouth from rising

in admiration. "You were wasted in secondary school, Teacher."

"How fortunate this war arrived to save me. Men, I'm deeply ashamed of you. What is our orderly Reich coming to when common soldiers demand explanations? So sorry, Ryker. They won't budge."

A voice in a corner growled, "I vote we shoot ourselves in the feet. That will get us out of Russia. Hold loaves of bread to the guns so the bread will take the powder burns."

After the laughter died Ryker stood up. None of the men averted his eyes. He said, "The order to keep the plan secret came from high up. I don't care about those bastards, but I care what happens to me. So if you vote no, and the news gets out, I'll find the person who told."

Someone tossed a can against the wall, where it made a loud clatter. The men muttered, stirred.

Teacher said, "Agreed. Our secret."

"Also, no more voting if you come with me."

Teacher said, "Those of us who were with you in Norway remember the sad fate of Lieutenant Buchalder. If we commit ourselves, we are putty in your hands."

Ryker heard the quick hiss of a match. A ball of smoke spread in the front row. The cigar smelled rank.

"Okay then," he said. "We're going to America."

In the silence that followed, Teacher whispered, "America. No." A muffled explosion sounded outside. A soldier by the window remarked, "Here come the Ivans."

FIVE

THOMAS HEIDEN HAD BEEN SHOWN, on his first day as a recruit, an army movie called *Hitler*. The earth, in this film, split into two spinning globes, one brightly illuminated, one black and ominous, in a thundercloud sky. The dark globe was covered with swastikas. The war was deadly and hung in the balance, but it was also clear. Simplicity was something he craved. By 1941, he'd had enough of the other kind of life.

Graduates of his prep school already occupied bank boardrooms, 4-F slips tucked in mahogany drawers. He had met senators at his parents' home, read *The Iliad* in Greek, had once appeared regularly at debutante balls.

At twenty-seven he could also build a car from parts, cook a mean chili, and play boogie-woogie piano in the key of his choice. Where he came from, these talents were referred to as "hobbies," not skills.

Until he met Corrice Kelly, he had not had more than a momentary interest in another woman in three years, not during the initial debilitating grief, nor the slower recovery. Women who didn't know the story still thought he was shy.

He'd met Liza Tate in 1938, when he was a history major

at Boston University, arguing Wells and Tolstoy on the
Common, chain-smoking Camels in the Cambridge coffee-
houses while Hitler marched into Czechoslovakia. Liza was
a perky brunette with an eye on the stage and a talent for
mime. He saw her sing in New York and instantly fell in
love. She was only a little girl, one hundred pounds, with
raven-black bangs and great brown eyes, a flower in her
hair, but her voice had seemed limitless in its possibilities,
sweeping up to reach high notes, shattering mental crystals,
dipping into the low, husky ranges, becoming breathy, se-
ductive, hurt, angry as she shifted to a blues rendition of
"God Bless the Child," becoming little-girly, an eight-year-
old trying to be coy on stage, reaching up to grasp the
microphone like a child holding a doorknob or ice cream
on a stick. He'd played Ellington for her. They'd toured
the clubs.

During that happy time, the impending war in Europe
had, for Heiden, been the perfect focus for a doctoral dis-
sertation. His title was "Is Democracy Dead?" Liza's career
took off. "I shall sing by the Pacific," she giggled one night
in her Greenwich Village cubbyhole. She clutched an in-
vitation from San Francisco. "Thousands of admirers and
aren't *you* jealous." She mimicked Marlene Dietrich, ex-
aggerating every note. "FA-lling in LUve, I theenk that I
am FAlling in LUve . . ." They rolled around the floor in
hysterics. Three weeks later he was typing the final draft
of "Is Democracy Dead?" when the phone rang. "The plane.
It was snowing in the Rockies and it hit . . ."

Friends helped him through the worst time. The moment of revelation came when he tried to finish the dis-
sertation. The title leaped out at him cruelly. He saw that
he was a pampered academic, toying with theory while
flesh-and-blood people wept and died. He would realize

later that Liza's death had simply hastened an inevitable reappraisal. But he left the university and went to New York where, with the passion he always showed at the beginning of things, he threw himself into playing jazz at the clubs. He loved the intensity, the smoky, blue-lighted rooms and late-night drunks, the backroom jam sessions. He'd found his answer, he decided, but after a year saw he'd been wrong again. The dissipatory activity seemed pointless after a while, experience for its own sake, and when the war broke out, in a kind of relief he volunteered. "I want to go to Europe," he told the recruiting sergeant at Whitehall Street. "Europe," he told the board, which gave him an officer's commission because of his undergraduate ROTC training.

Sure, they said. They'd send him to Europe, and he was sure that this time he'd escaped the long-ago trouble. But the army tricked him and sent him far from the war, to Captains Island, that jewel of an island he loved but hated, that beautiful, maddening trap.

And it was here, on the day he made the worst mistake of his life, that a voice in his doorway said, "I saw something strange last night. I better tell you about it."

As intelligence officer, with little to do, Heiden had been scanning the *Portland Press-Herald* in his prefab cubicle. BOMBS FOR BERLIN . . . TERROR IN TOKYO, read the Esso ad. Hitler and Tojo cringed while racks of bombs fell at their heads. Outside, under flak-shaped clouds, sentries glided under the camouflage spruce. Light, unreal in its starkness, spilled from the battery. It might have come from the center of the earth.

With a calmness he did not feel, he said, "Sit down." He had recognized his visitor.

Jeremiah Leeds was the only civilian permitted unlimited

access to the base. He was a salvage operator who owned miniature salvage subs docked by island caves. On mornings after sentries reported flashes on the horizon, Leeds sailed out to return pale and uncommunicative. Heiden was not privy to his reports.

Leeds fell into a chair with barely veiled contempt for everything not local. He was dressed in rubber boots and a slicker that opened to his undershirt. At fifty, he had a babyish face, lined by the weather, a grey, prickly crewcut, and the raw skin of an outdoorsman. A strong tobacco smell radiated from him, and his fingers and teeth were stained yellow. He moved like a man who was comfortable, proud, and independent.

He said, *"You're* the intelligence officer? You look kind of young to me."

Heiden grinned. "I was twelve just yesterday."

Leeds spit into the trash can. His boots were stained kelpish green. He bit off the ends of his words. "I live on the Knob, highest point on the island. Last night I'm listenin' to Gabriel Heatter on the radio. I see a light by Ruth's Cove. I'm wonderin' what it is. There aren't any houses on that part of the island. The light goes off, on. Lasted ten minutes. It was a signal."

Heiden felt ticking in his ears. Only this afternoon he'd read a report entitled "False Alarms in Maine." Most of the report concerned fishermen who had started panics by mistaking navy buoys for U-boat conning towers. The rest involved "signals." A blackout curtain blowing in and out of an open window one night had revealed a "flashing light" to a lobsterman a mile away. A couple retiring each evening at ten and turning on a bedroom lamp had galvanized a Civil Defense warden to report "mysterious lights in the woods."

"*False alarms cause panic,*" the report read.

Writing, Heiden said, "What time did you see this light?"

"Eight, eight-thirty."

"Can you be more precise, please?"

"Heatter ends at eight-thirty, so maybe it was eight. What difference does it make anyway?"

The difference was that Heiden planned to check if any base personnel were on the bluff at that time, but he didn't want Leeds to think he doubted the story. "It's just for the record."

Leeds looked disgusted. "Ayuh."

"Do people ever camp on the bluff?"

"Not when it's thirty degrees. I drove out there this morning. Didn't see no burnt ashes."

"Ashes," Heiden wrote, "No." He said, "Where would someone signal *to* from the bluff?"

"It's a deep-water channel off the island. A sub could come up and receive signals direct. *Are you going to do anything about this or aren't you?*"

"I am. I am. Last question. Why did you wait until now to report something you saw last night?"

Jeremiah Leeds pulled a corncob pipe from his slicker. He pointed it at Heiden's face, like a gun. "I thought you'd get around to that. This is a smuggling coast. I didn't think anyone I knew would be fool enough to bring in something on an army island, but I had to check." Pipe smoke obscured his eyes. He snapped, when Heiden reached for the phone. "And I ain't tellin' ya any more about smuggling."

"Don't worry. I'm calling for a jeep. I want to have a look at that bluff."

For the first time, the salvage operator appeared uneasy. "Alone?"

"You went alone, didn't you?"

"That was in the morning. You shouldn't fool around with people who flash lights at night."

"Ninety percent of all alarms received have been proven false," the report said.

Heiden made the first mistake of the day. "I'll call the base if we find something," he said. "Show me the place."

The jeep shot past the guard booth and down the coastal road. Across the marsh, the immense spires of the battery rose in the shape of a giant samurai helmet. The cannons angled toward the strait. With an evil hum, one of the guns was swiveling and, by some trick of coordination, tracking the jeep. Heiden imagined a troll deep in the earth, pulling levers.

Jeremiah couldn't take his eyes off the gun. His tone remained harsh but since mentioning smuggling he had excluded Heiden as a target. He snapped, "Why don't you put barbed wire around this base? If someone wanted to sneak in here he wouldn't just la-di-da up the road."

"We'll get barbed wire. Now we use patrols."

"Why don't they get dogs, then? Dogs would sniff someone out, all right."

Impressed, Heiden said, "I'll mention it."

Jeremiah told him to stop on a deserted stretch of forest. Brush clogged the drainage ditch. The ground was matted with leaves and vegetation. The sun was huge, red. Jeremiah said, "We shouldn't have come alone."

Wind hissed in the trees. Heiden heard the whisper of the sea but only thick forest was visible. With the salvage operator leading, they plunged through brush so dense that within moments it was impossible to imagine a road nearby. One reason he had not told anyone where he was going was that he did not want to admit how badly he wanted Jeremiah to be right about the signal. The odds were crushingly against that possibility and Heiden didn't want to set himself up for disappointment. But here, in the silent forest, anything seemed possible. He remembered what he had learned about night signaling in intelligence school. A signaler could use a slide projector to send a beam of light so concentrated that a viewer had to be in its direct path to see it.

He had a vision of himself, as he slapped the brambles from his face, emerging onto a high cliff to surprise a stranger with a signal lamp. Captains Island contained the biggest, most lethal coastal guns in the United States, a prize for any saboteur. His throat was throbbing. He felt for his Colt.

With a great crackling of brush, they broke from the forest. The wind screeched into their faces. Gulls wheeled beyond the cliff. The bluff was treeless, oval, touched by dead grass and pierced by granite outcroppings.

Below, the green ocean swelled against the rocks.

No one might have been here for a thousand years.

He was surprised by the acuteness of his disappointment. The sky was going grey to black. At his shoulder, Jeremiah insisted, "I saw the light." When Heiden said nothing, he stretched a knobby finger toward the horizon. "The army isn't telling you what's going on out there. I'm in salvage. The Germans are closer than anyone thinks."

Jeremiah's eyes were deeply veined. Heiden said, "How close?"

The moon face locked. "Can't say."

Heiden turned to the dark encircling forest. The wind went "Aaaaaaah."

Behind him, pushing back toward the jeep, Jeremiah

said, "Now what?" Heiden, certain there had never been any light, there never would be any light, there never would be anything interesting on this island, said, "Back to your house. To double-check. To watch the bluff."

The jeep wouldn't start. Pumping the accelerator, Heiden said, "Only thirty people live on this island. If someone was sending signals, maybe you have an idea who it is." No answer was forthcoming. Heiden said, "Do you?"

He could have sworn he saw sorrow fill Jeremiah's ruddy face.

"You're Corrice Kelly's boyfriend," accused Jeremiah Leeds.

Heiden shot the jeep around a bend, nearly impaling them on an oak. He'd been seeing Corrice almost every night for two weeks. He shouted over the wind, "If you're telling me that girl is sending *signals,* you can get out right now! You're nuts! *You're crazy!*"

The high edge of his rage was directed not only at Jeremiah, but at his job, the island, at complication itself. He felt tricked. He wished he were in Europe. He hated the notion that people could be different from what they seemed.

He protested, "I was with her yesterday!" as if that alone were enough to dispel Jeremiah's words. "We went for a walk! She's practically in charge of the war drives on the island! Paper, iron . . ."

"If you'll keep quiet, you'll find out I'm not talking about Corrice. I'm talking about her father!"

Heiden sucked in his breath. The father? He pictured the formidable-looking fisherman he'd met at the house.

"It's no secret Mike Kelly hates the English," Jeremiah said. "The Limeys crippled his grandfather and drove his father from Ireland. Before the Japs attacked, he used to say we should join the Germans and wipe the Brits off the map."

"We didn't join the Germans."

"This is my house."

Isolated, it was a salvage man's heaven, a battered Cape Cod surrounded by junk: tires, rusted engines, porthole covers. A shadowy form that might have been a cat or might have been something uglier darted under the stairs. The porch was heavy with salvage. Jeremiah lit a kerosene lamp in the kitchen. Face hellish from the pulsating smoke, he said, "No more light. I want you to be able to see outside."

Heiden felt as if he had stumbled into a Civil Defense warehouse. He glimpsed, in the pantry, a package marked "Bomb Scoop" and another "Official Blackout Bulbs." Jeremiah displayed a plastic bag proudly. "GI Powder," he boasted. "For incendiaries." The wall calendar was marked "Chemical Warfare Course," "Gas Warfare Course," "Air Raid Warden's Class." The only thing missing was a map with little flags.

Half-empty cans of lima beans lay on a counter, beside blue food stamps.

Heiden almost laughed at a circled newspaper headline. DALE CARNEGIE SAYS, 'TURN YOUR DEFICITS INTO ASSETS.'

The musty living room was cramped with lumpy shadows. Heiden seated himself on one.

In the blackness Jeremiah shoved a cold bottle into his hands. Could Michael Kelly be sending messages to the Germans? Visions of the ruddy Irish face and the word "spy" canceled each other out. A "spy" was a trench-coated German caught by Basil Rathbone in Sherlock Holmes movies. So what if Corrice's father had been raised to hate the English? Lots of people hated the English; were they all spies? Besides, anyone Heiden *knew* could never be a "spy."

Yet here he was, listening to Jeremiah babble and the house creak, staring at the darkened window. Jeremiah had an overactive imagination. That much was obvious. Who else but a war nut would stockpile supplies in the pantry? Heiden hadn't found any evidence of signaling on the bluff, had he? He saw now that what he had mistaken for simple directness in Jeremiah was eccentricity, except that suddenly the salvage man roared to his feet, pointing, shouting like a madman, "See? *See?*"

The light was intense, golden, blinking.

Heiden was up, ears throbbing, reaching for the kitchen phone. He yanked a grid map of the island from a back pocket. He pinned it down with a can of Liberty Beans. The phone rang once at the base, twice . . .

"Hello?"

The soldier on the other end had the high whine of a Tennessee cracker. Heiden envisioned the pimply bean pole condemned to spend nights in the radio shack. He identified himself. He said, "Call Sergeant Pulski, on the double."

He heard the phone drop. He called, "Jeremiah?" No answer.

"Jeremiah?"

A creak disturbed the living room.

On the phone, Heiden heard a door slam. This time the voice on the other end was older, Midwestern. "Pulski here."

"This is Lieutenant Heiden. I need men, thirty-five men. Do you have a map of the island?"

"Thirty-five men, sir?"

"Do you have a grid map!"

The light blinked on, off.

"There's a map on the wall here, sir."

"Good. Find coordinates, uh, G-nine. See the road? Follow it south six, seven hundred yards. It loops close to the sea. I want you on the upper tip of that loop in ten minutes, with thirty-five men. Armed men. You hear me?"

"Which men should I bring, sir?"

"Take 'em off the guns, for all I care!"

"But . . . but Major Savage said to leave the gun crews—"

"On the double!"

He slammed down the phone, cursed, dialed again. Pulski had left already, the bean pole said, so Heiden barked, "Tell the sergeant not to bring vehicles. I don't want noise. No jeeps, get it? No trucks."

He watched his reflection hang up. *Aren't you going to take men with you?* Jeremiah had asked at the base. He raged inwardly for ignoring the advice. The light might go out for good momentarily.

"Jeremiah!" When he yanked open the front door a cat bolted. He dived into the jeep, roared twenty feet, and screeched to a halt. *No noise,* he told himself.

He started running.

He was in fine shape so he moved quickly, hitting the ground hard, drawing air, feeling good because he was doing something. The sound of his breathing was loud in his ears. The cold air cleared his thinking but revealed holes in it. He'd forgotten to alert the camp commander that he was taking more than a quarter of the men off base. He'd forgotten to order Sergeant Pulski to bring walkie-talkies. He wanted to move the men into the woods in three groups but would have no way of talking to them once they separated.

A stitch squeezed his side. The growl of a truck reached

him from behind. Few people traveled this road at night. Dimmed headlights, lowered like half-closed lids of an animal, lurched around a bend. He reached for his Colt and squeezed into the brambles.

From the cab, Jeremiah's voice called, "This ain't the place, Lieutenant! It's further ahead!"

Five or six dark forms crowded in the pickup, cigarette smoke silhouetting their shotgun barrels. Jeremiah's face was a pale oval in the dark. "I brought the rifle club," he announced. "You need more men."

"I called the base. Thanks, but I don't need you. Okay? You can go back. Jeremiah?"

The men stirred angrily. Jeremiah said, "I don't know, Lieutenant. We know the woods better than you do."

He didn't seem like he cared who knew the woods better. He seemed like he wanted to be involved in whatever happened, but he had a point, and Heiden hadn't time to argue.

"Put out those cigars, and leave the truck here," he said.

He left five big-bellied islanders struggling out of the cab, rounded a bend, and saw the helmets. Many troops on Captains Island were "limited service" men, men whose physical problems weren't serious enough to keep them out of the army, but forced the army to station them in non-combat zones. Looking over the glasses, the fat boys, at one tall, thin private with a sickle back, Heiden felt as if he were at a math club meeting, not a gathering of troops.

Sergeant Pulski's permanent confused expression was more pronounced than usual. "Thirty-five men, sir," he said. He whipped and pointed. "Look!" The rifle club was gasping toward them. Some of the soldiers dropped, aimed.

Heiden hissed, "Attention!"

The moon hung overhead, a great laughing face.

In a whisper, Heiden addressed the sergeant. "Someone was on a cliff out there tonight, is probably still there, flashing signals. We're going to box in the bluff. Divide the men into three groups. Two will include guides from the, er, local rifle club."

The club was doubled in a little circle, heaving. Two men wore American Legion caps.

"The first two teams will separate and move thirty yards in either direction on the road, enter the forest, and head straight for the sea. They'll leave a sentry every nine yards.

"Five minutes after you leave, I'll lead the rest of the men into the box. As we pass the sentries they'll join my group. We'll all reach the bluff together."

For the first time, Pulski's face was flushed with excitement. "Yes, sir!"

"And keep them quiet."

Pulski hissed instructions on tiptoe, craning his neck as if he were screaming, as if that were the only way he knew how to talk to people.

The men ran down the road carefully to keep their equipment from flopping.

They disappeared into the trees.

A minute ticked by.

Someone called "Ouch" from the dark.

Two minutes.

After three minutes a white sedan barreled into view, scattering troops. Out poured women, children, a barking dog. The whole damn island had been alerted by Jeremiah.

Heiden waved his hands frantically. "Be quiet! Go back!"

He caught a glimpse of Corrice in the black coat, hanging back, and Jeremiah's words slammed into his mind. *It's no secret how much Mike Kelly hates the English.*

Was her father here? He didn't see him. Then why was *she* here? Curiosity? Could Mike Kelly really be on the bluff?

Suppose somebody shot him?

Heiden realized he'd issued no instructions about shooting.

He was sweating despite the cold.

He ordered a baby-faced corporal, "Keep those people here. None of them better follow us into the forest."

The boy looked scared. Heiden turned from the islanders, some of whom wore nightgowns under their coats. His troops were poised along a sixty-yard front. Although he'd been with Corrice the day before, it seemed much longer since he'd seen her. The rotating hand of his watch beat a cadence of images.

Twenty seconds. He envisioned the light on the bluff.

Ten. He imagined a sub surfacing beyond the shore.

Heiden looked up. "Let's go."

He plunged into the brambles and immediately lost sight of everything more than three feet away. Thorns tore his face. He slid on an ice patch but stayed up. He was making enough noise for an elephant.

And now he realized, groping through the blackness and feeling like an abysmal fool, that he had failed to anticipate an escape by sea. If whoever was on the bluff had arrived by boat, all Heiden's preparations would be useless. A simple call could have brought the harbor patrol.

He barely avoided hitting a tree, freed himself from a root, crashed through tangled bushes, and suddenly found himself in a clearing, with soldiers emerging on all sides. Not only had he actually coordinated the action, but in the bright moonlight the troops had, as a group, assumed a menacing air. The rifle club, intimidated on their own island by armed men in uniform, hung back in a Druidish circle, draped in tattered hunting jackets. It was a triumphant panorama, with the thunder of the surf below, but the spell was broken by the Brooklynish whine of a soldier with glasses. "Shit. Nobody's here."

Heiden wanted to scream, "No wonder, with the racket you made!"

Everyone was looking at him.

There was more crashing in the underbrush. Another uniformed figure burst into view, Major Arthur Savage, lantern-jawed commander and career man, who called himself "the most unforgiving man in the army."

Savage roared, *"What the hell is going on here?"*

Behind him, the women and children appeared.

So did the barking dog.

Heiden felt like jumping off the cliff.

But before anyone could say anything, a muffled grunt sounded from behind one of the granite outcroppings.

The circle of troopers quivered. The Enfields swung toward the rock. The rifle club drew into an armed knot. Major Arthur Savage stomped forward so that he stood beside Heiden. He seemed uncertain what to glare at, Heiden or the rock.

Loud, the hammer of Heiden's Colt clicked back.

He approached the outcropping, immensely conscious of the troops behind him, the major, Corrice. "If you don't come out of there," he said, surprised at the power in his own voice, "I am personally going to blow you all over the ocean."

Nothing happened at first. Then a little boy started crying behind the rock. Another young voice called, "Don't shoot, mister. We were playing with a flashlight!"

◊   ◊   ◊

Heiden made the worst mistake of his life then. He decided to ignore everything Jeremiah had told him, which included the warning about Michael Kelly.

Forty miles north of Captains Island, in a deserted cove, Michael Kelly stood in his fishing boat and watched a rubber dinghy filled with Germans approach. The Germans came from a U-boat fifty yards away. Shadowy sailors on deck trained the big gun on Kelly.

A pile of fish eyes glittered at his feet. Dead chubs and blood scallops lay there, frozen.

He had not met the U-boat since the United States entered the war, and had been surprised to be summoned. Meetings were dangerous and so no longer part of the arrangement. For the past few months he had regularly visited a cave on this island to leave lists of allied warships in Portland. He didn't know who picked up the messages and he didn't want to know. He knew only that he helped the Germans for a reason he had once refused to admit to himself, a reason that both obsessed and repelled him, a simple reason. Money.

He was awed by his capacity for greed, yet had been unaware of that part of himself in the beginning. When he'd first met the sub, by accident, before the United States entered the war, he'd conceived of himself as a simple fisherman with modest tastes. He'd been raised to work hard and expect little. When the U-boat ghosted out of the fog, he'd been afraid it was going to ram him.

Instead, a sailor had called, "Want to trade fish for whiskey?"

So he had started a side business, running vegetables, poultry, even diesel fuel to the sub. In 1939 the United States was neutral and Maine still reeled from the depression. Kelly needed cash. Any qualms he felt at profiting from a war were allayed by the fact that the war was against the British. Michael Kelly had been brought up on stories of the English beating his grandfather, of Uncle Sean's prison hunger strike, of the war of independence.

He'd even sent money to Ireland at first, but gradually stopped. Then he'd started charging higher prices. Then he'd offered to sell information on British merchant ships in Portland Harbor. By the time the United States entered the war, the natural rhythm of his cooperation and his growing lust for money controlled him as completely as heroin does an addict.

Now, eyeing the dinghy, he felt the familiar gut-wrenching excitement, only tonight it was dampened by a pain between his eyes. He could not rid himself of a nagging Corrice voice in his mind. She had known about the Germans at first. Later, he'd told her he'd stopped trafficking, but she suspected the truth. Her voice said, *They hang collaborators.*

He uncorked a bottle of Wild Turkey. "Fuck England," he said.

The dinghy bumped the boat. Lugers in hand, sailors slid over the gunwale, tense, suspicious. In the past they'd smiled at him. Tonight they scanned the sky. The captain, who followed, was iron-faced, distant, more formal than before. He shook hands crisply and asked about Corrice, but seemed less interested. He spoke in Oxford-accented English. "Sorry we have to rush. You have a pass enabling you to sail inside Portland Harbor. May I see it please?"

"My pass?" Kelly experienced a stab in his groin. "Why do you want my pass?"

The captain was frail-bodied. His dark skin seemed more Italian than German. "For your cousin," he said. "To print one for him."

The air was very still. "What are you talking about?" Kelly uncorked the bottle, changed his mind, and stuffed it in his jacket. "I don't have any cousin."

"Sure you do. You remember your cousin. Your cousin who's coming to visit. Your cousin whom you will show the harbor. We need to find out about a ship. You don't know what to look for. He'll be gone within a week."

Corrice's voice was louder now. *You've got to stop.*

Kelly said, "Too risky. I won't do it."

"A thousand dollars."

"No."

"Five thousand."

"I said no. I don't want anyone at my house."

The captain's eyes filmed over. "Do you realize what would happen to you and your daughter if the Allies discovered you've been selling information?"

"You need what I sell too badly to threaten me."

"We need it, yes, but we can get it somewhere else."

Kelly looked into the captain's face. "I don't believe you."

"Why do we have to argue? The man will stay only a short while. He'll have plenty of identification. Your cousin, from far away. From Wisconsin. From California. Canada."

"No."

"Ten thousand dollars."

Kelly said nothing. The captain said, "An old friend, then. A boarder! You never even met him until he knocked on your door. Twelve thousand. You can buy a new boat."

"Twelve thousand dollars?" The captain flicked a hand and a sailor with a Luger extracted Kelly's wallet. The captain held the plastic pass to his face. "You're useless if you say no," he said. "Worse, you're dangerous. We can't have operatives refusing orders. That kind of thing is bad for morale. Your service has been good, but we haven't paid you all this time for information alone. Poor Corrice. What will she do when you've been arrested?"

The fish eyes glittered. Uncertain, Kelly said, "What if the army checks his background?"

The captain waved a hand. "We've taken care of everything. He was born in the United States. He has genuine records here. He'll use his real name. No one will ever tie you to something we do months from now, thousands of miles from here. Besides, you've told me yourself, once the authorities see someone's pass they leave him alone. They don't check out summer visitors on the island, do they? A million civilians move around in Portland Harbor and no one has time to check them all. Besides, the army doesn't consider your island vital. It wouldn't allow civilians there at all if it did. So tell your neighbors he's a cousin. Or tell them you met him in Portland. Tell them he's helping you fish. Think of something. Tell them anything. But put him up. Fifteen thousand."

Kelly uncorked the bottle. "What do I tell the harbor master? I'll have to replace my pass."

"Tell him you lost your wallet."

"But I didn't lose my wallet."

The captain opened his fingers. The wallet hit the water with a smack, spread open like a pair of water wings, and drifted out of sight. The captain turned away.

"Yes you did," he said.

And when they were back in the dinghy, pulling away, Kelly called out to them. He was surprised to find that his voice sounded the same, sounded normal. "And the man who will be coming? How will I know him? Tell me his name!"

The answer was a hiss over the dark water.

"John Ryker!"

SIX

IN THE STILLNESS THAT PRECEDES BATTLE, the clanking of the Soviet tank was unusually clear. Far down the sloping meadow it churned toward Ryker through the drifts, throwing off snow, long, raised cannon outlined against the indifferent sky.

At the ice wall, the Austrians watched in silence, jamming on their helmets or cocking Schmeissers. They spaced themselves and readied light machine guns at the ice slits. Cradling a knapsack-sized mortar, two soldiers struggled across the barnyard, their pockets bulging with potato-shaped missiles. They embedded the whole contraption in the snow. Sighting between the wall and the tip of the forest, they adjusted the mortar.

Although no Russians were visible yet, a plume of black smoke over the forest indicated that one of Erhard's grenade traps had exploded.

Teacher's mouth formed a cynical curve flickering behind a haze of cigarette smoke. He never took his eyes from the approaching tank. His voice was quiet so that only Ryker could hear. "I've heard about that monster. The

T-34's the best they've got. I can't imagine people associated
with that thing except as fodder."

Low to the ground with sloping plates of steel, the tank
looked as if it were sniffing them out. It moved steadily
along the forest wall.

Teacher knelt by a field telephone. "Come in," he said.
He cranked the phone. The red star grew clear on the
tank's turret. "Someone's answering." He identified himself, explained the situation crisply, and asked for aid. Startled, he held the receiver from his ear. In a thin, triumphant
voice, a stream of haughty Russian issued from the German
phone.

Recovering quickly, Teacher winked at the men. "With
that accent, I would have thought Berlin."

One man laughed. The earth was starting to vibrate.
Ryker glanced at their own disabled Panzer, tilting like a
ship broken on rocks.

Below, the tank stopped.

Ryker said, "Down."

Before he had even finished speaking, a yellow cloud
balled out from the turret, followed by the boom and screech
of a shell. The ground rocked. A fountain of snow pelted
them from the other side of the wall. Ryker felt the force
of the blast sweep over his head.

The clanking started up again. A minute later the tank
stopped in front of the forest.

The second shot screamed over their heads to tear a
corner off the farmhouse.

The third disintegrated the ice wall, shattering it into a
thousand cutting fragments.

A deep cry went up from the woods.

Russians poured out of the trees.

They came on across a hundred-yard front, alternately

running or dropping to earth, firing all the while. The tank boomed. Ice splinters flew off the wall to the steady thwack and ricochet of machine-gun bullets.

Ryker readied his Walther, but the attackers were still out of range. Teacher, fully exposed to the fire, was roaring directions. There was no hesitation, no fear, no sign of the theorist in the orderly way he issued instructions. "Cover fire on the left! On! On!" A trooper beside Ryker grunted, hunched, and sank to his knees. He pitched into the snow. Ryker untangled the Schmeisser from the body, rose, and sprayed the lead Russian. The man threw out his arms and danced sideways like a fighter as the bullets smashed into him. A great spurt of blood leapt from his neck. He collapsed in a heap.

But the attacking wave was gaining ground. A hundred men were creeping forward. Ryker stood to shoot but was forced down again by fire. Teacher, miraculously untouched, was still up, ordering the mortar crew. "Move it right. Another inch. Now."

A mushroom of snow burst ten feet from the tank.

The flat Slavic faces of the attackers were growing features, they were so close.

Another mushroom burst, almost on the tank.

Ryker stood to fire.

The tank was backing up.

The machine gunner beside Ryker clutched at his eyes and rolled away in the snow. His partner grabbed the trigger and kept firing. Ryker's Schmeisser jammed. He threw it away, pulled out the Walther, and squeezed off a clip.

The advancing Russians seemed to sense that the tank was gone. The line faltered. Men stopped to look back. Ryker screamed, "Rapid fire! Everything!" and all the Austrians jumped up, cheering, firing furiously.

The Russians stood up to it for a moment, shooting back. Then some of them turned and ran.

"Close range!" Ryker roared at the mortar crew. The bursting shells catapulted fleeing soldiers into the air. The attack had completely broken off.

A minute later, the last moving Russian disappeared into the trees.

The hill was littered with bodies. Amid the carnage, a lone hand clutched at the sky and fell. Blue smoke swirled above the snow. An Austrian fired one last volley into the trees. The air smelled of cordite. Someone coughed. Someone began moaning.

Slowly, the Austrians lowered their weapons, looked at themselves, looked at each other. A few brushed off their uniforms. The machine gunner who had been shot lay against the wall beside Ryker, who looked into the grey, open face. The helmet tipped toward the sky. The strap clenched a rigid jaw.

Troops clustered about the dead or wounded while Teacher moved from group to group, speaking softly. A medic directed the carrying of the wounded into the house. The snowmen had been truncated during the battle. Grotesque round faces leered from the ground, stone smiles amid spent shell casings. Other snowmen, cut in two, hung inside the clothing in which they had been wrapped. Teacher patrolled the wall with a heavy-jawed corporal with a bullet hole in his helmet. "Fill in the spaces," he ordered. "Then five minutes of rest. Then I want barricades in the farmyard . . . there . . . there." He stomped through the drifts like a mathematician calculating angles.

Ryker helped with the barricades, dragging furniture from the house, then found Teacher inside, vainly trying to relight his samovar. The coals had disintegrated to dust. He poured a cold cup of water anyway.

"Suggestions?" he asked pleasantly. His face was exhausted.

"You seem to be handling everything."

"Oh, definitely. Five dead. Five wounded. Do you think that Siegfried, our national warrior hero, became concerned at times like this?"

"You don't fool me," Ryker said, dropping into a chair. "You know as well as I do we'll get out of here."

"Voilà! A medium! Didn't I see you on the Hamburg stage before the war? You guessed what people had in their pockets."

Ryker said, "I don't have to guess what's in your head."

"Then perhaps I can join the act. Audiences will know me as Mr. Transparency. You amaze me, Ryker. Ivan will be back momentarily. If that human-wave attack failed last time, it will nevertheless have convinced them that the hill isn't mined. That means the tank will lead their attack next time. The tank, Ryker. That steel behemoth we saw. As for us, we can't go anywhere until dark, especially carrying wounded. So why are you so sure we'll leave at all?"

"Because we're good. We've gotten out before. People like us can do what we want."

With pinched thumb and forefinger, Teacher dropped tiny green leaves on the surface of the water. Color seeped pathetically from the edges. Teacher said, "Tea at four. Civilized, don't you think? You said 'people like *us*.' Is it your opinion, Herr Ryker, that you and I are the same?"

Ryker grinned. Teacher cradled the cup in both hands, watching the water wash back and forth. He said, "So the philosophy emerges. Everyone's the killer, right?"

"That's right. Everybody. You. Me. The milkman. The

cabdriver. At bottom we're all the same. I admit it, that's all. It gives me a jump on most people. If you admit it you have to be better at it."

"I feel like I'm back in class, arguing with students. And love, Ryker? Tell me about that. How can you love anyone when you might have to kill them at any time?"

"You're twisting what I said."

"Not if you follow it through." The facade of indifference seemed for a moment to have lifted from Teacher's face, and in its place the hollow academic features took on a haunted aspect. Teacher, almost as if he had forgotten that Ryker was there, looked up and down at the filth caking his wrists. He put down the cup. He rotated his hands.

"I love people," he said.

Ryker said, "You can heat up the samovar with wood."

"Wood. Yes. Wood. Of course." For an instant Teacher lost his animation, blinking under the spectacles. Then the mouth reformed itself into its cynical curve. His back grew straight. He picked up the cup again. "The luxury of philosophy. Now to more immediate problems. It's occurred to me that you could go for help on your motorbike."

Ryker snorted. "I'm not going anywhere, not without you."

"Afraid we'll run off while you're gone?"

"My men are here."

"We're not your men."

"You will be."

The open doorway framed a figure in light. Teacher said, "Technically, I could order you to go."

Ryker unfolded the same paper he'd shown the major general. Teacher exhaled angrily after reading it. He said, "What was the point of asking us to vote before? You can make us go with you."

"I won't though. That part is your decision."

Teacher appeared mollified. Ryker felt the subtle power shift in the room. He said, "But the motorcycle idea is good. Why not send someone else?"

"You can't send anyone!" cried a third voice. They turned to Erhard, who had moved up beside them. "I *need* the bike. I think I can get the Panzer going with it."

Ryker and Teacher voiced the same thought, "You *think?*"

"If this doesn't work, we won't have time to get help," Teacher said. The cycle was raised off the earth on a block. Bare wires ran from the battery to a small black box on a log. Erhard explained what he was doing as he hooked more wires from the box to the back of the Panzer.

"The bike runs on six volts, the tank on twenty-four. Impossible to use one battery to charge the other? Ta da! That little machine on the log is the transformer I took out of the radio in the farmhouse. A transformer is a voltage booster. It's just possible, if the charge is sufficiently heightened and the tank barely dead to start with, to get this monster running again. There's one shell left in the breech. The manual gun controls are frozen but if we can swing the cannon around electrically, we'll have one chance to fire when the Ivans reach the barnyard. We start the Panzer. Someone waits inside while we lure the Russians here. Then, kapooey!"

Teacher said, "Let us hope it is we who 'kapooey' them."

"The trick," Ryker said, checking the wires, "is to convince them the Panzer's dead. We'll move the bike to the front of the yard after we start the Panzer. Ivan will have heard the engines. We'll hook the bike to the radio, and they'll think we were using it for that."

Erhard started the bike. Clouds of gasoline fumes enveloped them. Teacher said, "And whom shall we choose for our human sacrifice?"

Ryker looked over the mass of grey steel. "I'll do it," he said.

Ryker patrolled the grounds like a commander. The soldiers at least nodded to him now, although they still preferred their sullen clannishness to conversation. Gaps in the wall were filled with debris: the sidecar, the bed. Elsewhere, under the supervision of the corporal, troops piled logs to form more barricades, none near the Panzer.

The cold made Ryker's temples throb and teeth ache. He did not normally believe Nazi propaganda, but he was reminded at this moment of the party line on the inhuman Slav. How the Russians could thrive, unprotected, in the woods down there was beyond him, although he imagined them fashioning snow caves and lining them with birch or fir, burrowing like animals.

The men at the mortar displayed two missiles. "Last ones," a soldier said. At the wall, soldiers used field knives to widen the firing angles in the gun slits by shaving the ice. In the barn, on packed straw, the wounded men looked grateful when he arranged their blankets and gave them water. He conferred with the medic. Could the men fight? And if they couldn't fight, could they be moved? Preferring the cold to the illusion of safety in the house, Ryker trudged down to the road. He could see Axel's fur coat gliding amid the pines. There were no other preparations to be made, and the only task remaining was the one of calming himself. He located a thick tree trunk that would shield him from the wind and wedged himself into a niche. He closed his eyes. The lines of his face softened. No one could have guessed how far away he was;

no one would have guessed what he was thinking . . . .
In his mind the snow was gone. The wind disappeared.
Ryker, in his fantasy, reclined in a high-backed wicker chair
on the bank of a misty jungle river, lush, meandering, calm.
He watched a boat race. Twin wooden prows, heavy with
boisterous paddlers, shot around a bend to laughter and
applause. On shore, half-naked, coffee-colored women beat
time on their thighs with wooden ladles, and naked sway-
backed children watched from the shallows, beside thatched
huts raised on stilts. He couldn't see faces. Parrots squawked
in the tall palms. Mangoes and pineapples lay at his feet.

He was not a man celebrated for a peaceful imagination,
yet what idle musings he had, had, for thirty years, been
concentrated on this vision. His uncle had told him about
Colonel Suplee, the French mercenary who, in 1890, carved
a kingdom for himself in Siam. His uncle had said the rest
of the world was becoming too crowded for strong men.
Ryker had been ten when he'd first heard the story. He'd
been banking a special fund to afford his expedition. In
Asia, people would love him. In Asia, simple Asia, Ryker
could relax, become benevolent. A childlike smile lit his
face. Laughing children snatched bananas from his feet.
The rowers, somehow hazy, never in focus, howling with
glee, were neck and neck at the finish line.

The spatter of gunfire opened his eyes.

"The sun's in our eyes," Ryker said. "Now I understand
why they waited."

Amid eerie silence, shielding his brow with his palm, he
watched the Russians trotting out of the forest. Instead of
charging, they were staying away this time, separating into
two groups, flanking the yard.

Teacher said, "No firing yet. Save bullets."

Ryker eyed the forest. "The tank will come up the middle. We'd better break into three groups."

The soldiers looked to Teacher, who nodded agreement and pointed out each man's place with his index finger.

Then everything broke loose at the same time.

The Russians began advancing and firing. The tank burst into the open, machine guns blazing, churning up the hill. More Russians followed in its wake, the whole assault unrolling speedily in a trident shape. Bullets swept the wall. The cannon roared and the piled furniture shattered into a thousand pieces, the clatter of falling debris sounding amid the whine of shell fragments. The tank lumbering into the sun began glowing. Ryker ran for the Panzer.

A hail of bullets filled the barnyard. Wincing at the frigid touch of the hatch, Ryker lowered himself. Abruptly he was entombed with the underwater sound of his breathing and the scrape of his boots. The firing outside became a metallic echo. Blood-colored light shafted in through the narrow slits and shell hole, and dripped across the white-washed walls and cramped, slanting deck. The gunner's chair, raised in the turret, was darkened by shadow. A rope dangled nearby. This was the firing mechanism.

The chair was freezing, too, the cold biting Ryker's back. His gloved finger poised by the electric starter. Too soon to push it. A pounding was starting in his head. *Calm down.*

He pushed his face up against the gun slit, but the Panzer's plating restricted his view. Across the yard, between Ryker and the farmhouse, the Austrians had taken up positions behind the second line of barricades. Teacher poked his head up and fired. One of the troopers splayed backwards into the wall and slumped like a rag doll. A crimson spot welled on his forehead.

Ryker craned to see. The first white-clad Russians hurled

themselves through the breach in the wall, then the clanking of the tank grew loud and the front end smashed into the barnyard. Russians fanned out from behind. Others, firing from the turret, moved in circles.

Abruptly, bullets raked the Panzer. Ryker ducked, hoping the attack was only a kind of reconnaissance, that the Russian gunners were making sure no one would return fire. The smack of bullets stopped, but Ryker heard a scrambling noise on the outside of the Panzer. Ryker readied the Walther. The hatch began to open, then Ryker fired, there was a cry of pain, and whoever it was thudded off. Ryker looked out of the gun slit. Across the barnyard, by the blasted barricade, Teacher touched his finger to his helmet. The Russian tank boomed. Part of the house disappeared.

When the tank filled the view through his gun slit, Ryker punched the starter. The engine coughed, caught. He activated the turret control. He could see the troops on the Russian turret, alerted by the growl of the Panzer, turning in horror, pounding on their own tank.

Both cannons were swiveling.

Ryker yanked the firing rope.

The breech recoiled past Ryker's face as the Panzer rocked. The compartment filled with the choking, semisweet stench of spent ammunition and much smoke. When it cleared, Ryker was astounded to see the turret of the Russian tank upside down. A man half hung down the side, crushed. Black smoke etched upward. Abruptly, the tank exploded with roaring volleys as its ammunition caught fire.

It was almost night. The Austrians began retaking the barnyard.

Under cover of darkness, with Ryker leading them back to German lines, they voted to go to Captains Island.

SEVEN

TWO DAYS after Thomas Heiden disrupted Captains Island because of the boys with the flashlight, Major Kenneth Levy, head of harbor security, arrived on the army mail launch, met with Major Savage, and ordered Heiden to show him the cliff where the incident had taken place.

Heiden thought he was going to be chewed out again, but he was wrong. Looking out from the bluff, Levy shielded his palm with his hand. The water was flat and sparkling. Gulls wheeled overhead. A battleship steamed toward the harbor. He remarked, disturbed, "We've been picking up U-boat signals." He was tall and dark-haired, with wire-rimmed glasses and a softspoken, serious way.

"Always the same U-boat," Levy said. "He signs off the same."

At the words "U-boat," Heiden felt the pulse thicken in his ears. *Germans. Germans off the island.*

Levy said, "We haven't been able to decode the messages, but we figure they're instructions, because no one ever answers. We could find them if they did."

The battleship seemed huge, even half a mile away.

Levy said, "Don't misunderstand me. There's no reason

to suspect anyone on Captains Island. I'm visiting all the islands, Falmouth and South Portland too."

Heiden kept the excitement out of his voice. "Whatever you need, I'll do it."

"Good. First, don't get overexcited. Curb your natural enthusiasm. Keep your eyes open, that's all. Make sure all the radios here are registered. I wish we could confiscate them but fishermen need radios. And the Civil Liberties Union would be all over us if we tried to take them. Anyway, chances are the person we're looking for isn't here. A half-million people live around this harbor. And Lieutenant?"

"Sir?'

"I read your report on the flashlight episode. You were right to call troops that night. You got a little carried away, but you learned from it. I just wanted you to know, your efforts are appreciated."

The mail launch tipped high when Levy left the lagoon. Heiden was already figuring quiet ways to check out the radios on the island. For the first time, he felt like he had something important to do. Some days, his job didn't seem so bad after all.

EIGHT

⸻

LATE IN JUNE OF 1942, an obscure railway clerk in Portland, Maine, fell from a warehouse window and, in so doing, changed the war in the North Atlantic.

For Henry Meeks, life had been an unending stream of bad luck. Born in Germany before the First World War, he was ten when Bismarck marched into Belgium. The French took revenge upon his parents while he hid in a hayloft. He left the gutted farm for the safety of Berlin, only to suffer four cracked ribs the day he arrived. Heinrich Meeks was caught, that day, in a street battle between German Bolsheviks and Royalists.

His marriage to a towheaded waitress named Helga produced triplets just as the German mark reached its all-time low. He found work in Lisbon. Helga wired that she'd met someone else. After a period of drunkenness, he secured passage on a States-bound tub, but his uncle in Maine died two weeks after he moved in. Finally, he got a job in the Kaufman warehouses, for serf's wages.

He was forty the day he died, and had changed from a man who dreamt of success to one who hoped for it, to a man satisfied with a dark corner in which to nurse his wounds. He was slight, with pasted-down hair and eyes of intense black. He still limped because of the Berlin injury. This morning fate had even robbed him of his primary daily pleasure, a peaceful breakfast. Micah's Egg 'n Muffin had been invaded by a stranger who wore a suit like a lawyer but had ears like a farmboy, who'd unfolded the *Portland Press-Herald* all over Meeks's scrambled-egg special and ranted about how the Allies would push Rommel back in Africa and crush the Wehrmacht in Russia. Roosevelt was the greatest leader since Julius Ceasar. U-boats were being sunk by the dozen.

Meeks had been tempted to scream into his face, to reveal his secret.

Instead he'd hurried out, eggs uneaten.

Commercial Street brought him along the busy wharves, which were bustling with soldiers, dockworkers, short-order cooks dumping grease in empty oil drums. Unshaven sailors lounged against a hissing locomotive, right on the cobble street. Trucks rattled through the fog to clanging from the shipyard. He smelled fish, gasoline. Beyond Portland Head, the foghorns were deep and dangerous.

His stomach rumbled. The warehouse sprawled where the railyard met the sea. In the cavernous, half-lit interior, rock-jawed men strained with bales of navy whites. The stairway shook all the way up to the office. Someone would probably fall before Kaufman replaced the railing. Meeks looked down. A rat tail slithered into shadow.

His desk was sixteenth in line, beside an immense streaked pane of glass and its view of a crane rearing like a dinosaur, and a line of immobile boxcars in an overgrown field. The pile of paperwork seemed to have grown overnight. He dropped his cheese sandwich in his drawer, folded wire rims over his face, and, like a million other clerks who ran a war, bent to the first business of the day.

He leaned closer, reading.

The paper began to tremble.

The War Department was ordering all three Kaufman warehouses empty by August 16 to accommodate unspecified rail cargo from Washington. "Clerks and stevedores stay home. Army personnel will unload and transfer shipment to convoy, on August 19."

Meeks folded the paper but his hands were shaking and he had trouble getting it into his pocket. He'd never realized simple breathing could make so much noise. When he dared glance up, the clerks were sickle-backed, scribbling.

From outside came the low, powerful moan of a steam locomotive releasing pressure.

At his window, Meeks pretended to watch the Liberty ships loading beyond the freight yard.

The exit seemed farther than normal. The shopkeeper's bell above the door went off like a bomb when he pulled the knob.

When he got outside, he had to keep from running.

Thomas Heiden picked his way along the long cobble beach, over granite balls and immense clawed boulders. He carried a wicker basket on his arm and stared at the tide line. He was looking for something. Another soldier patrolled two hundred yards ahead, basket in hand. And behind, far down the beach, a sergeant walked, eyes peeled.

"Lieutenant Flashlight!" called a boy's voice a few feet away.

Heiden threw up his arms and spun at his nickname. "Ya got me, Copper," he said. A boy and girl stood, wide-eyed nine-year-olds.

"Ya lookin' for *bodies*, aren't you?" the boy cried.

The girl said primly, "Oh, Johnny!" They wore sweaters even in July. On slabs of granite, back by the road, white-faced matrons offered chins to the sun. Their knees were puffy above rolled trousers.

The boy said, "Find any yet? Bodies?" The girl looked disgusted and the boy said, "Why do you think all the soldiers are out here! Whaddya think that noise was last night! The whole sky was orange! The navy blew up a U-boat, didn't it? Didn't it, Lieutenant?"

Heiden joked, "You'll never get it outta me, Copper," but the truth was that he didn't know. He'd been at Corrice's when the explosions started, mighty blasts that shook the porcelain cats on her windowsill. Quiet had descended by the time he walked back to the base.

"Get out there with the baskets again," Savage had ordered this morning. Heiden had tried hard to learn what had happened, but the major only said, "It's classified. Take the civilian side." The fog had burned off and Heiden scanned the frothy wavelets. In clear tidal pools, kelp swirled like the long hair of a drowned swimmer and spilled from cracks in the rocks. The shoreline was an angular destruction, sharp cliffs where the rocks had crashed into the sea. He saw a clamshell, broken; a sidestepping crab, trapped until high tide; a squirming raft of tiny blue worms; a piece of washed-up Coke bottle; a shredded fisherman's twine. And out on the calm morning sea, bobbing, a chain of hollow unspiked mines holding the submarine nets. Past that, a high-prowed lobster boat, painted Michael Kelly's yellow and green. Kelly heaved a lobster trap over the side.

The boy said, excitedly, "I was asleep. Boom! We open the window! Hap Hardy's runnin' around with his helmet and whistle. 'Close those curtains! Kill those lights! You want a U-boat to see a ship?' Come on! You blew up a sub!"

He stopped. Something sickly white bobbed in a sea hollow, hidden from the kids by a rock. Something about a foot long.

The boy said, "No one tells us anything."

A blue vein trailed in the water, like a tapeworm or gigantic leech.

The boy said, "What are you looking at?"

Heiden whirled and went German. "YOU VILL BE QVIET VEN I SPEAK VISS YOU!" He wanted to get the kids away. He saluted madly, like Hitler. "I em looking for a tiny U-boat vich slipped inside der nets, full of tiny Germans your size. You must be zese Germans. Sergeant Pulski! I haff found der tiny Germans!"

Way up the cobble beach, a figure started running.

"On der double, Pulski. Und now you two I catch!"

He roared and the children fled, laughing uproariously. They scrambled up a footpath and stopped by the blueberry bushes. "Nah!" the boy cried. "Lieutenant Flashlight!"

His heart was snapping like Mariani's snare drum. When he reached down he thought he might be sick. The arm thudded in the basket. Dripping, it hardly weighed anything.

Was this what a German arm looked like? Like any arm? The wrist was puffy. A blue dullness streaked the fingers. Skin trailed from the thumb, where some creature had nibbled. He tried to picture a U-boat, tail up, black smoke rising, sliding into the ocean for the last time. Then he saw the ring.

Pulski ran up and looked in the basket. "Shit, Lieutenant. I never thought we'd really find something."

"It's a class ring," Heiden said, pulling it off. The gold sparkled with droplets from the sea. He read, "Evanston Township High School. Class of 1941."

They found nothing more. In the jeep, five of them shot through town, toward the base. The basket with the arm, separated from the others, stood on one side of the back. The soldiers perched on the rear of the jeep, as far as possible from Heiden's find, glancing at it as if they expected the top to start screwing off. One said, "So it was a merchantman blown up, not a U-boat." And another: "I just graduated high school." The third kept twisting his own class ring while Heiden explained that the arm must remain secret, the islanders must not find out about it. Now they were all quiet.

Outwardly he had composed himself for his men, but he was remembering the puffy feel of the skin, the wriggling vein, the glint of gold. He saw a lumbering merchantman in the night sea. He saw the phosphorous trail of the torpedo. He remembered the rumbled explosion last night and envisioned one of his own nineteen-year-old privates, thrashing, one-armed, in burning oil.

He was enraged and frustrated. He burned with fierce protectiveness for the island.

"Cah-dee-lac," said Pulski, hitting the brake.

The dirt harbor road, spotted with porched houses, was completely blocked by a jet-black automobile with Massachusetts plates. MINE. It was empty. Heiden had never seen it before. The doors were flung open. On the bay, between the pincer-shaped headlands, the weekly car ferry was tiny toward the inner islands.

A tall blonde woman glided in their direction, down a garden footpath from a high gothic porch. The turreted mansion had been empty for as long as Heiden had lived here. It was the largest house on the island.

"Assholes," said Private Shannon, who was from Trenton.

Drawled Schroeder, "Ain't no cars here, hardly. Prob'ly nevuh had to worry about traffic before."

They glanced at the basket, embarrassed that petty difficulty impeded its progress. And ashamed, unimportant beside death.

The skirt was white cotton, tight, the blouse the color of roses. She swayed like an eighteen-year-old, but close up Heiden realized she was at least forty, and only then from the lines around her eyes. She had a small, tanned face, a delicate nose, and a mouth that glistened. Her eyes were deep violet. Her wrists were slender, fluid, and jeweled. She had long fingers, like a model.

Heiden, out of the jeep but still in that dark night sea, was aware of black pupils fixing him with frank appraisal.

She said, "If you're here to check our passes, go away. I resent the way every shallow nobody in uniform uses this war to harass innocent people. We showed the IDs on the Portland side."

Thin strap marks ridged her shoulders. Her voice was low and ice-cold. "Do you know how hard it was for the judge and me to get here this year?" The judge had come from the house now, too. Silver hair ran under the straw hat. A watch chain looped from seersucker trousers. She said, "Gas rationing! Rubber rationing! The Hudson family has lived on this island since seventeen fifty-five!"

People started to collect, appearing, as usual, out of nowhere. Heiden remembered what Major Savage had said about new people on the island. A window opened. The blonde called, "May Belle! You know me!" Framed, a fish face nodded.

Major Savage had ordered no confrontations with civilians. Heiden said, "Hold it," and held up his hand. "I know the coast guard checks passes. I'm not here for that. Sorry you had a rough time."

"Why *are* you here then?"

"You're, uh, blocking the road."

A boy laughed. The red started at the woman's forehead, just below the roots, and touched the eyes, slid down the high cheeks, stopped, reversed itself.

"Oh," she said, tapping his chest with one red fingernail. She cocked her head, charming like a five-year-old, but Heiden wasn't fooled twice. She was coming back at him. "I know who you are," she said. "You're the one they call Lieutenant Flashlight, aren't you? The one who made a fool of himself that night."

He felt the urge to throw the arm in her face. The husband laughed coarsely, like a drunk. "Don't shoot, mister! We were playing with a flashlight!" His voice was filled with despair. So they hated each other. So they'd trapped Heiden. She addressed the old ladies and children. "*My* son is in Africa. Fighting." To Heiden she said, "Of course we'll move the car. We've never had to worry about traffic here. Oh my." She smiled into his eyes, mocking. "I forgot where I put my keys. Judge? Honey? Can you find your keys? You can never find anything, can you?"

"Not me, uh uh. No keys."

"Then I'll just have to *look* and *look*," she said. "You soldiers can sit here while I do. Or find another way back. You don't seem too busy anyway. What pretty baskets. Been having a picnic?"

Heiden just repeated it. "A picnic." In the jeep, Pulski watched his face. They understood each other. Heiden said, "Another way back, Sergeant. You heard the lady."

"Yes, sir." Pulski was already aiming the tires at her tulip bed.

Screeching, she faded, a lone figure in the middle of the road.

"What is it about you, Heiden? I'm tired of apologizing for you."

Twenty minutes later, Heiden stood before Major Savage and his gigantic steel desk. A ceiling fan pushed hot air into his face. On the curving spruce wall of the Quonset hut, beside the diploma from South Carolina's Citadel Institute, the major's wife and daughter glared through glass, Savages in tandem.

The basket stood on the edge of the desk, unopened. Heiden pointed to it. "There's something I found, sir."

"Quiet."

Savage's face was branded with a permanent expression of lock-jawed belligerence, which, combined with his shiny pate, had earned his own nickname among the troops, "Il Duce." A short man, he moved with the angry, exaggerated jerks of someone afraid his insecurities are showing. "Did you get a kick driving over her flowers? Stop looking cheerful!"

"No, sir! Not me, sir! I'm not cheerful!"

Savage looked at him sideways, suspicious. "The Hudsons own half this island," he said. "She moved away but she's still a Hudson. I don't care if that woman is a screaming banshee from hell, you keep her happy!"

"Yes, sir! A screaming banshee from hell, sir!"

Three inches away, Savage's face was shiny, shaved. "I'll

bust you down to the kitchen," he said. "That village was here before we were. We sponsor dances. We let the islanders on base for movies. Everyone seems satisfied except you. I've even heard that damn flashlight story at Fort Williams." He squeezed his eyes, exorcising. "You're a focus. Everything they don't like. Next they'll call you Lieutenant Tulip. Doesn't it bother you to be a laughingstock? It bothers me!"

"Sir, what bothers me isn't the issue, sir. I overreacted on that cliff because I was new, but I was still right to call the men. The light was blinking, and checking it alone would have been foolish. If I live here twenty more years and win the Medal of Honor, I'll still be Lieutenant Flashlight to these people. So they gave me a name. So names stick. I'm supposed to do a job."

Savage said, "Aaaaaah," and started pacing. He'd been a college fullback and still had the shoulders. Outside, in the cropped-grass square, a flag snapped. A sergeant drilled troops. A truck arrived with the week's rations.

Savage halted before a green-and-white topographical map of Casco Bay. "The guns," he announced, "are obsolete. Face it." He stubbed his finger into Captains Island, which lay beyond the mass of brown inner islands. "The guns were outdated the day they were installed. In nineteen thirty coastal guns were important. But in nineteen forty-two, what are we going to do with cannons that shoot twenty-five miles? What German ship is going to steam within range? Even if the Krauts had a navy, which they don't, our planes would hit them hundreds of miles out." He breathed hard. He didn't like the truth either. "If the government didn't move so damn slowly, they probably would have canceled these guns before they were put in.

"So why are we here? To fight? No, to make people feel

secure. The navy goes after the U-boats. We're just a pre-caution. Our job is to run the base smoothly. But if the islanders disrespect you, they disrespect me. They disrespect the base. They disrespect the army. I smell something funny," he said, sniffing. He glanced at the basket. He said, "Apologize to Mrs. Hudson."

A hammering began outside. Heiden felt it in his fore-head. "*That's* the way to lose respect," he said. Savage's head came around slowly. Heiden's control broke and he dropped both hands on the desk. "Transfer me. I'm not a caretaker. If the names bother you so much, why won't you let me go?"

Savage jerked once, as if surprised by the outburst. More gently, he said, "I can't let you go. No one can let you go." He opened a drawer and tossed a file on the desk. Heiden saw his own name, in block letters. "Open it. Go ahead. I can't figure out the damn thing.

"Highest score I've ever seen on the officer's exam," Savage said. "But trouble all the time." Heiden read about the high-school motorcycle theft, the time he hit the policeman. There was a comment from someone called Captain Je-rome, M.D.: "*Lieutenant Heiden is a hard worker but has trouble, over the long run, committing himself to a job. If he ever buckles down he'll be a remarkable soldier.*"

Yeah, Heiden thought. Send me to Europe and I'll show you a remarkable soldier.

The order to which Savage referred was neatly typed on a page all its own. "Lt. Heiden is not to be transferred off Captains Island for the duration of the war."

Signed: General Omar Bradley.

My God, Heiden thought. *I can't even escape it here.*

Savage was returning to his normal agitated state. "Who the hell are you anyway? I've never seen anything like this."

The throbbing in Heiden's brow was very bad now. He had to muster all his strength to keep a straight face. "You could lose the order. Things get lost," he suggested off-handedly.

"Forget it. I want out myself." Savage returned to his chair. "What's the story here, Lieutenant?" he demanded. He glared a moment. "Won't say? All right, then. Dismissed. Apologize to Mrs. Hudson and report back to me. You forgot your basket."

"I didn't forget it," Heiden said at the door. "There's something in there you might want to see."

Outside, the sun seemed far away. The red-flower sumac trembled across the compound, where the dark forest met the base. Two corporals passed, chatting as if nothing had ever been wrong in their lives.

A private rushed out of Savage's Quonset hut holding the basket at arm's length. He acted like it contained a cobra, not an arm.

Heiden counted the change in his pocket. He strode past the two-story barracks to the officers' club, which, since it served only three people, consisted only of a partitioned room with a coffee table, magazines, and a pay phone.

He dialed a special number in Washington, D.C.

"Burchette," said the voice that answered, crisp and impatient. Heiden envisioned a severe-faced young man in a pressed grey suit. He said, "It's Tom Heiden. I'd like to speak to the senator."

There was a brief silence, then the voice said, slightly wary, "Tom, can you tell me what this is in reference to?"

"The senator knows." Heiden talked low, glancing around to make sure no one had come in.

"The senator's in a meeting right now. Perhaps you can leave a number so that he can call you right back."

"Interrupt him. He'll come when he hears who it is."

The man sighed. "This is a particularly important meeting. I'm sure if you tell me what this is about someone else might—"

"I said get him! Didn't you hear me?"

"I . . . well . . ." There was a muffled sound of a hand over the receiver and a clatter as if the phone had been placed on a desk. He heard a slamming door, footsteps, the sound of the receiver lifted again.

"Tom," boomed the voice, honey dripping. "How the hell are you? It's been months!"

"Get me off the island, you son of a bitch." Heiden's voice was flat and low.

"Excuse me?"

"I saw my file. What was written. You people get out of my life. I want off. Now, now, you bastard."

There was the sound of inhaling breath, then the voice became wheedling, low. "Tom, listen. We've been over this a million times. Ask anything else . . ."

Heiden hung up.

Enraged, he strode across the compound, away from the spruce-camouflaged battery and the sea. He plunged up the weedy rise and into a thicket of birch and poplar. The forest floor cleared. Soon he was in cool shadow, oak canopy overhead. A mockingbird screeched. The scrape of shovels came from directly ahead. Three soldiers dug under a chicken-wire fence.

A Chinese private with a Boston accent addressed him. "I don't understand why you want us to *widen* this hole."

Heiden plucked an apple from one of the low-lying trees by the fence. "Kids come over the fence for the apples.

They're not going to stop because the army says so. I don't want them to get hurt."

He followed the fence away. Those bastards can't keep me here, he thought. I'll go to Europe myself. But even as he thought it he knew it was childish and impractical, and once he got to Europe what the hell would he do anyway? The army wasn't like school, he couldn't go away if he felt like it.

The islanders never traveled through the forest here. He felt like a tourist in New York City, where natives never visit the Statue of Liberty. At length he reached the berry bushes, the base gate, and the road.

He walked a mile into town, the brisk pace calming him a little. He knocked at a neat shingled bungalow with a bright red roof and rose garden.

"Late today," called a spry, elderly voice from inside. Clara Chadborne was white-haired, petite on rubber-heeled shoes. She moved with a cane but had the bright, untroubled eyes of a sixteen-year-old. "Sit there!" she commanded, indicating the redwood stool by the piano. It was a one-hundred-year-old Behr upright grand, its body carved with baroque design. Heiden brushed the B-flat and forgot Savage, at least for the moment, in the bright, sweet tone.

She said, "Show me that 'A Train' song again, then I'll teach you the nocturne. Fudge? I made it this morning. There's a bottle of honey too, from my bees. Share it with the other boys. I heard you had a run in with Mrs. Hudson, that bitch. Ha ha!" She balanced by an oversized reading chair, aimed the cane critically at one of eight or nine oils on the wall, island scenes. "I don't think I painted that lead duck right, do you? But a soldier offered to buy it. And what was that explosion last night? It's all everyone is talking about."

He didn't tell her about the U-boat, but he laughed with her over Mrs. Hudson. These weekly piano meetings with Mrs. Chadborne were one of his public-relations duties Heiden enjoyed.

But when he left an hour later he remembered his file. The sun was turning orange and the air had cooled. His own tasks were complete. Corrice had to work until eight. In his room, he did one hundred push-ups and three hundred sit-ups. In shorts and sneakers, he ran around the island. Then he went to the pistol range. Alone, on a bluff and bundled against the dusk chill, he pumped round after round into a cardboard man a hundred yards away. The heart was round and red. It grew pulpy. Sometimes he thought of the U-boat while he fired, sometimes Major Savage. Sometimes he thought about an office in Washington, D.C.

The sea was coming in. He fired to the pounding in his temples and the blood in his ears.

He was becoming very good with the gun.

In Portland, Henry Meeks, the railroad clerk, found a phone booth off Commercial Street. The glass doors closed him into the coffin-shaped box. He turned his back on the traffic.

"Hello?" the man who answered said. The voice sounded normal, even disinterested. Maybe Meeks had dialed wrong. "Hello?" He unfolded the warehouse schedule he'd stolen and spread it on top of the Yellow Pages. The voice said, "Who is this? Come on!"

The line went dead.

Meeks dropped more money in the slot and tried again. He got the same voice, annoyed this time. "Hel-lo!"

Meeks said, "My name is . . ." but then stopped because he remembered what he was supposed to say, which sounded stupid now that he actually had to say it for the first time, but he did so anyway. "So many freight trains in the yard today," and instead of answering, "Who is this?" or hanging up again, the voice actually responded, businesslike and very interested, "Which are you shipping on?" and the call had now developed a momentum of its own, so despite certain misgivings, Meeks told the voice exactly what was written on the paper. When he was finished the voice said, "Okay," and hung up. That was that.

Meeks left the booth, taking ten steps before he realized he'd left the list by the phone. He went back. The door was open but a sailor was inside, hat tipped rakishly, a smile emboldening his face as he whispered into the receiver. The paper wasn't on the Yellow Pages. Meeks experienced a bolt of horror and had to keep from fleeing. Then he saw the paper under the sailor's shoe. The sailor hung up triumphantly, hitched his belt, and winked at Meeks as he stepped past. "Ooh la la," he said.

Meeks crumpled the paper in his shirt. It was smudged now, impossible to put back in the pile. Should he rip it, throw it out? Pausing by a corner oil-drum trashcan, he shredded the paper, watched the pieces fall away, soaking up blue oil on the bottom.

Only twenty minutes had elapsed since he left the warehouse. The length of a coffee break. On wobbly legs, he pointed himself toward Kaufman's.

He had not meant to join the Bund, not at first. From his holed-up existence at the boardinghouse, he had followed the rise of Adolf Hitler with approving interest. After personally experiencing the chaos of post–World War One Germany, Meeks knew the value of a strong leader. But he had a deep belief in his own bad luck and fear of political action.

He had been persuaded, partly out of curiosity, partly from boredom and boardinghouse camaraderie, to accompany a fellow resident to a German-American Bund meeting one night.

The people had been so warm, so friendly, asking question after question about Germany, expressing sympathy over his story, soliciting opinions.

But the biggest surprise had been the speaker, a middle-aged uncle who resembled England's sober Prime Minister Chamberlain, not the ranting Nazi robot portrayed in the American press.

Hitler, the speaker told them, had achieved an economic miracle in Germany, putting idle youth back to work and building great highways.

Meeks found himself nodding, sliding to the edge of his folding chair, caught up in the air of brotherhood. And when the speaker discussed the United States, Meeks felt as if he alone were being addressed. Of course, his boss, Mr. Kaufman, was not mentioned personally, but Meeks understood who "certain elements" were. And Roosevelt. Lend-Lease. The Civilian Conservation Corps. Weren't those the types of programs a Red would sponsor? Didn't Meeks realize his bad luck was not luck at all, but a carefully plotted campaign to oppress hardworking men and women? Germany and America should be friends, not enemies.

When he signed up after the meeting, the registration form included a box marked "Employment." Two days later the speaker surprised Meeks by showing up at the boardinghouse. They took a long walk by the wharves.

Meeks found himself opening up to the man. They played checkers, discussed politics. Meeks knew what was happening, that the conversations were being steered and that he was being tested, but strangely, he didn't care. Some weeks later the speaker slyly hinted about the bottom-line purpose of his visits. Would Meeks be willing to pass along occasional information about the movements of war supplies in Portland?

Meeks's name, the speaker said, had never been entered in the Bund roles. He would not be permitted to attend meetings or fraternize with members. But high-ups in Germany knew who he was and valued his friendship.

Now he stopped in the middle of the street.

What are you worried about? he asked himself. *You did it!*

He picked up his step. In the tracks, by the high grass, men in overalls and peaked caps laughed, leaning against the Maine Central Railroad cars. A gramophone blared Fats Waller tunes. The fog that had oppressed the wharves had cleared. The locomotive cowbells sounded like joyous pealing from a church.

After forty years of bad luck! People made their own luck! The speaker was right! He suppressed a whoop of triumph. He was seized with a love of Germany, of Portland, of everything around him. He took the steps two at a time. The dangling rows of fluorescent lights seemed comical, not oppressive. He wanted to embrace the other clerks, like brothers.

Then he saw the man with the suit, standing in front of his desk.

Meeks blinked. The obnoxious, college-faced man from the breakfast shop, the man who had spread his newspaper and ranted about the great Roosevelt. Why was that man here? And Kaufman beside him, pale face furrowed. Two accusing sets of eyes. The suited man leaned forward, hand outstretched, offering something. Senses clogged, Meeks reached out, watched his hand pluck a small black-and-white square from the extended fingers.

The square became a photograph.

Outside, the cowbell noises grew loud. Steam rose in fitful bursts past the streaked window.

His senses were clearing.

He was looking into a group picture and he saw his own face.

It was a photograph of that first meeting of the Bund.

Now he saw the silver badge pinned to the man's wallet, and was vaguely aware of the other clerks swiveling, like white slugs or dead people in a horror movie, and Mr. Kaufman was saying something through the roar. "I didn't know you were attending Bund meetings, Meeks," and the suit wasn't grinning anymore, only looking earnest, like a district attorney on his first job. "We know you never came back after this first meeting, Mr. Meeks, but I was wondering why . . ." and the word snowballed in Meeks's mind. "Whyyyyyy," with the bells and screams outside. This was the worst trick of all, to show up so soon after the call.

Meeks had to get away, to escape. He turned, running already, and of course the cord was there, the long black cord from the desk light, snaking across the wooden floor. And he was floating and the window came to meet him. He felt the hardness smack against his face, he heard the shattering glass. The crane waited below, steel teeth rushing. The air felt so cold.

CLERK FALLS TO ACCIDENTAL DEATH, read the headline in the *Portland Press-Herald.* The censors reviewed everything before it went in the paper.

◊   ◊   ◊

They never found out about the message, which had already been relayed to an Argentinean freighter in Portland Harbor. The first mate handed it to a diplomat in the Argentinean Consul General's office in New York. The news traveled by diplomatic pouch to Lisbon, and by coded radio to Berlin.

Martin Bormann said, "*This* is the convoy we want. *This.*"

Muller stood respectfully by the sofa and reclining Reichsleiter. "A cruiser has already been dispatched. Ryker will rendezvous with the U-501, at sea."

"You told Ryker?"

"You first, Herr Reichsleiter. As always."

Martin Bormann smoothed the message over the sofa and ran his fingers along the lines. "Call Ryker now," he said.

NINE

RYKER CROUCHED BEHIND A ROW of pine hedges and peered into the village beyond. The predawn sky was purple and orange. A few stars glowed white. Teacher and the other Austrians waited behind other bushes, cradling Schmeissers, all down a line.

The only sound was a glasslike tinkling that came with the cool sea smell. At their backs, a country cart track and dark pine forest. The houses across from the hedges were small, neat, and dark.

Of all the towns and cities spread through the Third Reich, the Norwegian village of Sticklunden most resembled Captains Island, Hitler's intelligence arm, the Abwehr, had decided.

Like Captains Island, the village lay on the North Atlantic. Like the island, it consisted of roughly twenty homes, which emanated, along with a church, from the long, waterlogged dock.

Like Captains Island, Sticklunden was isolated, cut off by sea and forest, yet in actual miles the port of Trondheim was close. No German troops were stationed in Sticklunden, but the army manned sixteen-inch coast artillery several kilometers away.

The major difference between the two towns, the difference that would matter most this morning, was one of which the Abwehr was unaware. Sticklunden's pastor liked to wake early, climb the church tower, and watch birds.

Five hundred yards from Ryker and the Austrians, seventy-year-old Oyven Swenseid puffed into the bell tower and caught his breath.

The roofs below were close and steep, in perpetual readiness for winter. The fjord was calm. Black circles spread where fish rose and cormorants shot past, inches above the surface. The buoys tinkled like crystal.

To Swenseid, who spent much time dealing with villagers' petty concerns, the predawn peace filled him with daily, cleansing appreciation for his town.

Thanks to his prized Weisz field glasses, which he now removed from their case, he had actually seen a brown eagle yesterday, first one in three years.

A puff of smoke etched into the brightening sky. His wife was up, preparing Sunday breakfast.

A dog barked in the village.

Through the glasses, the forest seemed inches away. Needles trembled in the breeze. Swenseid saw the brown flakes of the pinecones.

He scanned the treetops. The eagle wasn't there, not yet. Lowered, the round binocular sights revealed cool shadow grottoes in the green forest. The hedges at the edge of town blurred, they were so close.

He adjusted the focus.

A sleeve sharpened into view. An olive-drab uniform. A slanting German helmet over a set jaw.

Other German troops, behind the bushes, started into

the village. A powerfully built man in a safari jacket issued instructions by hand signal.

Swenseid thought, *They can't be here.* The invasion was over. The town minded its business. Norway had surrendered and people didn't like it, but that was that.

The man in the safari jacket stood and jerked one arm into the air.

Immediately the soldiers burst through the hedges, spreading through the village, as if they'd known its passageways for years. A dove cooed in the bell tower, yet no voices sounded below. No equipment jangled. Swenseid couldn't even hear footfalls. The soldiers moved amid silence that suppressed the very cry in his throat. He'd had a nightmare as a child. Danger barreled toward him and he could not get out of the way.

Buoys tinkled, bumping boats. Buoys tinkled, like crystal.

The soldiers reached the smaller homes, at the outskirts of the village.

Three Germans paused outside Olaf Michael's door, then disappeared inside.

Three entered Narvik the drunk's cottage.

Move, Swenseid thought, but the unbelievable shock held him in thrall.

They're looking for someone, he thought. *That's it!* A prisoner had escaped. A British flier had landed and the Germans thought he was here. That was why they'd come at dawn. It was all a mistake. They'd leave without finding whom they were looking for.

The soldiers reappeared, running toward adjacent homes.

Swenseid kept his eyes on the doorways they'd left. The roused villagers would crowd into the street, gawking. They'd tell the story for years, and laugh.

A second ticked. The doorways gaped, empty.

Swenseid's jaw hurt it was clenched so tightly. *Where are they?* He knew the story of the Czechoslovakian village. A German was murdered nearby and the inhabitants were shot, the town bulldozed.

Directly below, the soldiers burst into his own cottage.

Oyven Swenseid moved.

The Germans froze as his binoculars shattered a foot from the nearest trooper.

Swenseid grabbed the bell rope. The pealing shattered the silence. He dropped down the ladder like a boy of twenty, his cassock ripping on a nail. *Got to fix that.* He'd seen soldiers streaming toward the church. He burst down the main aisle as the front doors came inward. Light shafted through the bay windows of his study. He was not a cowardly man, nor an indecisive one. He had simply not wanted to believe the Germans were here.

The shotgun in the closet was more of a blunderbuss, unused against the Danes forty years earlier. The first German through that door would leave in pellet-sized pieces.

Dust billowed when he broke open the breech. Steady handed, he loaded. He seated himself behind his desk. The gun was heavy, but it did not waver.

He had lived his whole life in Sticklunden. In less than five minutes, the Germans had wiped the village out. *I'm ready. Come on in.* His wife would have been at the stove when the soldiers came in, her hair in long braids, thick slippers on the oak floor. She would have heard the commotion at the door and thought, *Oyven's back early.* She would have been stirring porridge.

He heard the sound of running men on the ceiling.

Maybe, if he'd rung the bell earlier, she might have gotten away.

The doorknob turned. A bit of green came into the room.

The explosion almost knocked Swenseid out of his chair. An enormous pain ripped his right shoulder, from the recoiling gun. The uniformed being before him seemed to dissolve. The machine pistol, flung outward, clattered once. The face was shredded and strips of flesh hung downward. A hand had been lifted to ward off the attack. Light spilled through the palm, then blood filled the holes. The uniform, half torn, hung from the riddled torso.

The soldier slid down the edge of the door, leaving a trail. His boots splayed inward. His chin struck his chest.

Swenseid half rose. *I killed him.* But the chest moved once. He was torn with the desire to aid the man, then he realized the silence was back. Smoke drifted in the light. He had not reasoned beyond the first shot and he thought, *They're afraid.*

Then shouts came from the vestry. He didn't hear gunfire, but the glass behind his head was falling and splinters flew off the desk and he understood their guns were silenced.

He dropped behind the desk. *Thwap* was the noise the bullets made. A thin strand of smoke rose from the shotgun. The shell box lay across the open doorway. He had not thought to keep it close. In pieces, the office was coming apart around him, and the soldier's body, propped against the door, would keep it from closing.

He thought, preparing to try for the shells, Lord, here I . . .

There was a tremendous shattering at his back and a voice said, in Norwegian, "Drop it."

The shotgun thudded against the floor. The voice said, "Slowly. Look at me."

He saw, perched amid the wreckage, sphinxlike, a pair of slanting green eyes in a red earthy face. The pupils flickered between the pastor and the body. The voice was toneless. "Not a Christian act, that. Was it, Father?"

The Pastor's shoulder was on fire. He squeezed it, wincing despite himself. "I suppose you're proud of yourself," he said. He regretted the limitations of his own voice, which made him sound, he felt, as if he were chastising a Bible class. Bitter, he said, "Murdering people in their beds."

The man squatted on the windowsill, like an Oriental, smoking a cigarette. He holstered a fat-bored automatic. He said, as much to himself as to the pastor, "We didn't murder anyone. The problem was, could we take the village without alerting anyone." He glanced about, at the wreckage. "We took it."

"You mean, you mean you didn't hurt . . ." The man nodded. The pastor said, "My wife? Narvik? None of them?" The man raised his palm like a Boy Scout. "Word of honor." But with Swenseid's flooding relief came a new realization, that he had killed one of them, that he had changed the situation. He remembered the Czechoslovakian village. "I didn't know," he said. His voice sounded weak.

The man stepped down from the windowsill, drew a long breath through his cigarette, and tossed the butt outside. The glass hung in knife-edged patterns. Already, villager voices came from the street outside. They were worried about Swenseid. The pastor said, "I was in the tower. I saw you coming. It was all my fault."

The man wasn't listening. "I sent them into the houses," he told Swenseid, brandishing an imaginary gun. "Stay in your beds! It's just an exercise! Stay out of the doorways! Reverend, relax. I'm not going to hurt them." But at the same moment, a harsh voice in the hallway said, "Kurt?" and soldiers entered the room.

They spread, a half dozen of them, into a semicircle

around the dead body on the floor. One of them kneeled, looked long into the single open eye.

The trooper fingered the shredded uniform. "Kurt?" He placed his hands on the shoulders. The head rolled sideways. He said, "Damn."

A thin, filthy soldier wearing wire-rimmed glasses addressed the man who had come through the window. "Ryker, *der Brud* . . ."

"Speak English," Ryker said. "All the time now."

"Those two are brothers," the trooper said. Swenseid, who understood English, was amazed at the lack of German accent.

The soldier on the floor stood away from his brother. He drew the bolt on his machine pistol as the other muzzles came up too. The expression on the man's face was unreadable but the gun trembled.

Ryker stepped toward the soldiers. His weapon remained holstered and his hands were on his hips. "Next time," he said, "take the highest building first." Ryker stepped in front of the dead trooper's brother. He did not look at the Schmeisser, which almost touched his belly. He said, "Your brother knew better than to just walk in here." The soldier didn't say anything, but one of the larger men spat sideways on the floor. They all looked much harder than other soldiers Swenseid had seen. Ryker said, "The Father didn't know it was a practice. He saw the whole thing."

The dead trooper's blood soaked into the wooden floor. Swenseid, filled with sickening expectation, felt Ryker battling them. In a way, this was almost more frightening than the actual danger, that a single human possessed that much strength of will.

He wanted to sit, to explain, but sensed Ryker might interpret that as weakness, and lose interest.

Ryker said, "The street. Now."

The gun bore wavered. The men became ordinary troopers again. The wire-rimmed soldier said, "Advice, Father. Stay inside while we're here." He didn't seem to be threatening, just explaining. And when they left, Ryker said, "After three months of training, they're bored." He bent by the dead soldier, closed the staring eye with one finger. He retrieved the shotgun. "You look tired. Sit down." He turned the weapon over in his hands. "Beautiful. Quality work." In a single, shattering motion, he slammed the butt against the desk. It split like a cantaloupe.

As Swenseid watched in weary horror, Ryker hammered the rusty barrel until it bent.

Ryker said, "The army doesn't let Norwegians own firearms, but you don't own a firearm anymore, do you?" He looked at the body. "One mistake. Just one."

He stretched over the desk suddenly. Swenseid smelled dirt, wood shavings, rust, but no sweat or even breath, as if Ryker weren't human and had come directly from the earth.

He remembered a magazine photograph he'd seen. A scientist and an orangutan were looking into each other's face. The orangutan's expression was innocently human, yet at the same time the camera angle emphasized the animal's dangerous unpredictability and killing power.

The caption read, "Is he thinking?"

Ryker said, "You can tell me now. You were afraid, weren't you?"

The pastor replied, "The Lord decides." He longed to get out of there. He wanted to see his wife, to take a hot bath. He wanted to sleep.

Ryker said, "You were afraid." He seemed disappointed. "How old are you, seventy?"

Swenseid nodded and Ryker muttered, "Almost twice as old as me. And the Lord." He straightened. "The *Lord.*" You would have thought it was the first time he'd heard of the idea. He shook his head, vastly amused. "*The Lord!*" The grin disappeared. "You killed Kurt and got away with it. The villagers might interpret that the wrong way. If I ever hear of another German death in this town, I'll come back. Do you hear me? Do you know what I'm talking about?"

After he left, the townspeople crowded in. Swenseid's wife was in the lead.

Two hours later, while Muller's call was being routed north, Ryker pressed his eye into a telescopic sight and squinted through the crosshairs. He saw, over a blurred dandelion field and twenty-foot clif, the grey North Atlantic. An early-summer storm brewed the swells into unreal slowness.

He was in a coastal battery a few kilometers from the fishing village.

Magnified, the rust-caked prow of a merchantman entered the view. Any national markings had been scraped off the side.

Ryker wore thick earmuffs but still heard the angry voice beside him. "You aren't using the gun properly! You don't wait until you *see* a ship. When they said to teach you artillery, I thought you wanted to do it right."

Unlike American batteries, which were protected by twenty feet of earth and concrete, German coastal artillery was often a battleship turret completely encased in steel onshore, surrounded by camouflage trees. American and German guns operated almost identically though. One dial in this battery even read "Made In USA."

Ryker leaned away from the scope. Axel grasped a fist-thick firing rope next to the barrel, which was wider at the base than both men together. In immense welded sections, parallel to the ground, it telescoped out sixty feet. The entire structure was an encased, rotating platform of grey steel. The Austrians watched from steel-grid catwalks. Railings protected them from the twenty-five-foot drop into the gun pit.

On the ceiling monorail track, six-foot-long bullet-shaped missiles hung, chained in a row. The track led to a loading pan.

The criticism of Ryker's artillery skills had emanated from a stocky bearded gunnery lieutenant with ROSENBERG on his nameplate. His eyes shone pale blue behind thick glasses. He snapped, "Gunnery is an art. You make it like a carnival shooting match!"

The merchantman wallowed where it had been abandoned by retreating tugs. A quarter mile farther, hundreds of yards behind, another tug towed a series of twenty-foot-high wooden targets, plywood pyramids.

Ryker said, "Seven shots in four minutes. Accuracy and speed. First the ship. Then the targets. Thirty seconds to load. Fifteen seconds to find the target. Maximum use of the gun, eh, Herr Rosenberg?"

"My ass! What type of crew is this anyway? How did you get coast command to let you sink a ship? Let me tell you! Even your dummy shell will tear out her insides. Like blowing up a rabbit with a tank gun!"

Axel swished the rope back and forth. Teacher and two troopers spun hydraulic wheels. Ryker swiveled, with the gun.

Erhard broke ranks from the watching troops. "Phone!" he called.

Rosenberg said, "You know how you're *supposed* to do it? Spotters in towers see the ships, far away. They use the targets, the gun, and their own position to form a triangle. On a plotting board, they figure speed and distance."

Ryker snapped, "Left. To the left."

"They figure wind. At thirty kilometers, wind is important!"

Erhard waved his arms. "Berlin is calling!"

"They phone the information to the gun crew. The gun crew can't even see the target, that's what makes it an art! A child could fire the gun your way!"

Erhard came right up to Ryker. "A Major Muller is calling."

Ryker said, "Stop!" The gun ceased moving. A slow smile spread on Ryker's face. "Graduation. This is it," he said. "Look!"

Out beyond the targets, a German cruiser steamed, full speed, toward Trondheim.

"I feel it. That ship's for us." Ryker said, "Next time we shoot for real. This time, perfect. Weight of the powder charge?"

"Three hundred pounds!" the Austrians said. This was their drill.

"That's half the standard charge. Why?"

"So the shell will drop to the waterline."

"And hit?"

"The powder magazine."

Ryker snapped, "Speed of the shell?"

"Two thousand meters a second."

They were changing by the minute, becoming animated, radiating force. Ryker said, "We fire the American guns. But where are their troops?"

New question. They were silent. One of them said, "Dead."

Another man repeated it. Their voices were low, like monks at vespers. "Dead. They're dead."

Rosenberg muttered, "Shit. Jesus." Dawning understanding lit his face.

Erhard called out, "What about the phone, Herr Ryker?"

On the pitching sea, the cruiser issued a deep whistle. The men were flushed, the platform rotating. The merchantman wallowed, helpless. Ryker leaned into the scope. Rosenberg, now that he had an idea why he had trained these men, boasted. "There's nothing in the world this gun can't destroy. At a mile, it's unstoppable." Ryker said, "Fire," and Axel pulled the rope.

TEN

◆————————————————————◆

IN THE CRAMPED U-BOAT CABIN, Ryker had the nightmare again. He couldn't stop the dream. Tiny fans spun like spiders above his bunk.

He was eight, snowed in the cabin. Wood popped in the fireplace. His father oiled the Winchester, his mother scraped a frying pan in a trough. They didn't look at each other, they didn't speak. Only their hands moved, slow, mechanical. Endless motion fought off madness.

On the floor, Ryker played with the dancing man, a wooden doll impaled with a handle/skewer. Holding the skewer, he bounced the jointed legs on the floor. The doll danced.

His father growled, "Stop that laughing."

The dancing man clattered by the icebox. Ryker, perched on a crate, barely reaching the window, knew what was coming next. Wind rattled the sill and the trees seemed tiny through the storm haze.

The snow turned red.

First the falling flakes, then the drifts. Balled newspaper stuffed in the cracks absorbed color. Red oozed from the roof and stained the rafters. Oblivious, Ryker's father slugged whiskey from a pint bottle and wiped his mouth with the back of his hand. He said to Ryker's mother, "Stop that scraping." He kept slipping shells into the breech, so many shells Ryker thought the gun would burst if he didn't stop. The dancing man turned red. So did the plastic Jesus on the shelf. His mother kept working. "Did you hear me?" his father asked. Red crept up his flannel shirt, crossed his face like a shadow.

Ryker's mother blew, chest forward, into the washbasin. She said, "Gaaaa."

The shotgun pointed at the boy. Ryker tried to reach out, to grab his father's trousers, but he could not move his arms. Hot metal smoked an inch from his face. Ryker screamed, "Daddy!"

Outside the snow was white again. His father rocked by the fire. The back of his head was missing and blood ran along his face. His expression was mild, his voice strong and reasonable. "Your grandfather killed himself when he was forty. We all do. Don't let the fire go out. Cover your mother. She's cold." He winked and lay on the floor. Light spilled through the open doorway. An immense stranger's face bent over Ryker, smelling of tobacco, wearing a stocking cap. "Christ, kid, you must have been with these bodies a week!"

Ryker opened his eyes. A tall, skinny sailor stared from beside the green curtain partition. "Bad dream, sir?" Ryker swung his legs over the bunk. Sweat ran down his belly to tickle his thighs. The walls dripped with condensation. Sopping towels littered the floor. "I don't dream."

The disbelieving eyes did not leave Ryker's face. The U-boat felt like the nightmare, people who have been together too long. "Captain says you go ashore in an hour. We surface in ten minutes." The sailor was nervous and, under the polite, military explanation, the voice filled with accusation. "It's dangerous this close to Maine, but oxygen's a problem." *Your fault*, the face seemed to say. "Extra men." He put a harmonicalike shape to his mouth and drew deeply. "Carbon capsule. Helps purify the air."

The low ceiling forced Ryker to slouch and he had to keep his arms close to avoid knocking against the cramped bunk, confining walls, or tiny sink. When the sailor drew the curtain, his father's words were a dream echo. "Your grandfather killed himself when he was forty."

The last few months of his life, Ryker's father had been obsessed with Ryker's grandfather's suicide, and his own lessening physical prowess brought on by middle age He devised unpassable tests for himself. Could he still do two hundred pushups or was he down to one hundred? Could he carry heavier packs for longer distances?

Ryker thought, Don't think about it. You have work to do.

But in the confined space the memories uncharacteristically lingered. *You want to end up like your father, blowing your head off?* That was his uncle's voice, in Tanganyika, where eight-year-old Ryker had been sent to live. *Then go ahead, keep thinking about him, keep asking questions.* Or there was the other response to Ryker's inquiries: *Shut up or I'll send you out of camp again, out in the bush again, alone.*

He'd spent ten years with his uncle and their porters and wealthy German clients. Real men, his uncle told him, never asked idle questions. Real men could control their emotions, and if Ryker learned to control himself, just maybe he wouldn't end up like his father. Real men went off alone if something bothered them, to find a challenge so acute it kept them from turning weak.

In ten years, Ryker learned to shoot better than his uncle,

to trap, to track and smell like an animal, skills his uncle and the Africans respected and admired. He learned to live by himself in the wild. *Don't depend on other people, boy. They're weaker than you.*

No friends. Ryker's adolescence. At eighteen he became a military cadet in Berlin.

He tossed the capsule on the bunk. He shaved without water, concentrating on each stroke. Showers were not permitted but he didn't mind. From the locker, he extracted a faded red flannel shirt, old work boots and oil-smeared trousers. The Abwehr had tried to issue him a grey vested suit. Where did they think they were dropping him, Times Square?

The long hallways felt like a jail, a steel world reverberating to diesel engines and the clanging of pipes. Sailors wedged like prisoners into a cell-sized mess. The air boiled. Ryker smelled frying potatoes and unwashed bodies. Men sucked on unlit cigarettes. The ship's office was half the size of a small closet, with its crouching yeoman in a tiny chair, a typewriter, steel cabinets.

He swung through portals, under hammocks filled with hard sailor's bread, and by locked cases of carbines. ALL AMMUNITION DANGEROUS. KEEP CARTRIDGES OUT OF SUNLIGHT. Sunlight? Ryker hadn't seen sunlight in days.

Ahead, he heard Erhard's voice, pleasant as usual. "I'll go back to my garage. You, Axel? What will you do at home?"

"Women."

Ryker swung into the forward torpedo room as Teacher's voice said, "Sweet self-delusion. To actually believe you might come back."

One by one, they noticed Ryker. They peered, like

animals, out of the low, oblong cave. Normally thirty men bunked here, in two shifts, wedged between chain-suspended racks of brass-colored torpedoes. But the sub had been stripped for room. Only two torpedoes lay in place. Otherwise the racks were covered with air mattresses, the air mattresses with men in black underwear. White, rash-blistered arms dangled. A card game progressed. Masses of coiled pipe and wire descended to obscure the ceiling, and Ryker saw wheels everywhere. Wheels to open hatches and wheels to close them. Wheels for valves.

Teacher's breathing was a labored whistle, but his wry expression remained in place. He looked Ryker up and down. He pursed his lips. "Monsieur Ryker's fall collection," he said. "Le Paul Bunyan."

Ryker grinned. Teacher said, "The mighty invading army steams toward the mainland. Each soldier lies in his bunk. Will he be alive tomorrow? He awaits the naval bombardment which will precede his landing. What? *No* naval bombardment?"

Ryker said, "You voted to come."

"Free elections. How could I have forgotten? With Russians outside the polling places." Unflinching, he looked into Ryker's face. "Temper, temper. Am I damaging morale?" Raised on one elbow, he addressed the troops. "Men, it's true that there are only forty of us, that we are about to attack a fortified American city, that several thousand troops defend Portland, but do not be discouraged by numbers. Our hearts are pure. To the brave go the spoils. Surprise is on our side. How am I doing, Ryker?"

"Very sincere."

"Humor? Is there hope then?"

"We're not attacking a city," Ryker said. "Only an island."

"Manhattan is an island. The heart of New York."

"That's enough." Ryker's voice was a whip and Teacher quieted immediately. Ryker said, "Changing your vote?" He moved next to Teacher's bunk. He added, softly, "I didn't hear your answer."

Teacher sighed. "You know I'm not."

"Good! Then! The island is not in New York. We'll all return to Germany. I know how. The problem is getting *on* the island, not off. Maps!"

Life and *Colliers* magazines lay scattered through the room. The crackling of paper filled the air. The Abwehr had drawn these maps back in 1936, just in case. Portland and South Portland lay in the pit of a great brown mainland indentation, with points marked SHIPYARD, RAILROAD, DOCKS in German. Little cross streets ran by the sea. Extending outward, a huge lagoon was titled OIL TRANSFER FOR FLEET. Then came the circular fleet of islands that shielded the harbor. There was a Great Diamond Island and a Peaks Island and a Long Island. A Great Chebeague and a Littlejohn Island. A Cushing Island. A Cliff Island. In the green map sea, rearing like a serpent's head, Captains Island was the furthermost piece of land, a mile in diameter, carved into black numbers in Ryker's heavy hand.

Ryker said, "A few civilians. A few troops." The men were getting excited. He could feel it. "Oh, there are soldiers on the other islands, but by the time they realize who we are, we'll be gone."

The sailors watched with a kind of disbelief. Ryker said, "I'll go to the island alone and scout it. When I send for you, I'll radio a number. Land only on the corresponding part of the island. I'll be waiting. Problems? No? I leave in ten minutes."

Teacher's tone was light again. "Send a postcard. Something with a lighthouse on it."

Ryker said, "Watch for shore patrols. And if the weather is clear, dirigibles will be out, looking for U-boats."

"U-boats?" Erhard piped up. "Are there U-boats here?" They laughed together. *Good omen*, Ryker thought.

The house was crowded, the layers of smoke thick. Faces leered in the firelight. "Happy birthday," sang the islanders. It was the worst night of Corrice Kelly's life, but if she showed it, if they guessed it, Da would be the one to suffer. "Happy birthday to youuuuuuu." She was nineteen.

At the piano, Heiden finished with a flourish and a roll of Lieutenant Mariani's drum. She couldn't catch Da's attention. Under the buck's head, a heavy wooden table bent under turkey, ham, blueberry pies. Teenagers, newly arrived summer visitors, clustered by the radio. The house vibrated with soldiers' laughter, voices. Heiden launched into "Take the A Train." Her path to Da was blocked by Mrs. Hudson.

"Lovely present," said the older woman. As always, her tone was a sneer. She said, "Your father must love you to give you something so expensive." Corrice suppressed the urge to laugh in her face. Didn't people see anything the way it really was?

She said, "Excuse me." Da was in a corner, fingers wrapping a whiskey tumbler, head bent with Major Savage. He said, "Once a year the coast guard finds a lobster boat, going in circles. No one aboard. Get your foot caught in the buoy rope and the trap drags you down."

She struggled to keep her face composed. "Da?"

Da said to Savage, "You're all alone. One mistake and you're gone."

She smiled at the major. "Da, can we talk?"

When he drank, his face swelled, his laugh was thick. "Must be important to take me away from your boss here. Afraid I'm going to tell embarrassing stories?" He winked at Savage, who said, "Hyeh, heh." They were having a wet night at the fireplace. "I'll find you," Da said.

From the wide porch, the sky was turbulent. Mist collected, diagonally across the dark road, in the high grass. It felt like autumn, not midsummer. The music sounded desperate, the faces inside seemed vulnerable. The birthday present burnt her clenched fist. Mrs. Hudson had said, *Lucky you.*

The muffled party sounds grew loud. Her father's eyes were hidden in shadow, his mouth slack from drink. "What could be bothering the birthday girl? Leaving your own party."

As if pained by the moonlight, the necklace twisted in her open hand. Golden links chained a heart. Drawn to it, he said, throaty, "I want to see you wear this." But she held it up to his face instead. "How did you afford this?"

At his laugh, revelers grinned out from the hallway. Father and daughter, they figured, having the time of their lives. She closed the door.

Da said, "You wouldn't be wantin' me to tell the price of a gift now. Besides, nothing's too good for my daughter."

The heart spun back and forth. He said, "The way you worry about money."

"It isn't money I'm worried about."

"Don't you like the necklace? I picked it out."

"Da, it's beautiful."

"Then put it on! Put it around your neck! That's right! Tom Heiden'll come pantin' now. You been seeing him for five months! A man likes a little decoration on his sweetheart."

"You listen to me!" Her fingers were tiny on his massive wrists. The door opened and Jeremiah Leeds lurched out, hiccuped, and leaned against the railing. "Back to work," Jeremiah said. "In the morning."

He stumbled into the night. Corrice felt her face blazing. "This!" she said, shoving the necklace toward him. "This! You hardly talk anymore! You stay in the basement! You're having a boarder, you say. When Mom was alive you hated boarders!"

At the word "boarder" he peered into the dark, as if the man were standing there. But his voice was annoyed. "You'd better explain what you're talking about, because what I think you're saying is that I been lying to you. Calling your father a liar."

A searchlight stabbed into the sky, from Portland. High above, impaled in the yellow beam, a plane droned in from the sea. It seemed trapped, exposed.

Michael Kelly said, "I draw my new boat in the basement. You know that. And I'm quiet." He shook his head. "I'm quiet and that's terrible. You're throwing a fit because I'm quiet."

"I don't want anything to happen to you!"

Her mother had told her, *When you have a feeling, it's based on a thousand little facts. You might not remember the facts, but you'd better trust the feeling.* Islanders had said her mother had a sixth sense. *No such thing. There's only common sense.*

He became soothing. She was his little frightened girl. "Honey, what could happen in the basement? The basement is the safest place in the world. Oh hell." He put his hands on her shoulders. "We shouldn't make each other mad. The boarder sent a letter. I told you a month ago.

His friend stayed here when Ma kept the extra room. I saved for the necklace. Aaah, you take the fun out of life. What am I doing, making excuses to a nineteen-year-old? I'm going back to the party."

His eyes, when he turned away, stayed on her face an instant too long.

"Da."

"What now?"

Arm's length, she held out the necklace. "I'm not going to wear it. I'll put it away. I'm not part of what you're doing and I won't be your excuse. You're selling food to them. People are hanged for that. And there's something funny about the boarder. It isn't like you to want a stranger in the house. When I know . . . when you've stopped, I'll put this on, then."

He looked old, heavy shoulders drooping. "You're dreaming, Corrice." But his heart wasn't in it. Music burst from the party. He squeezed his forehead, an actor 'til the end. "Your old Da's pretty drunk. I wonder if I'll remember anything tomorrow."

The pathetic offering, she thought. A comedy to live with. Still, she lacked the willpower for cruelty. Lowering the jewelry from sight, she said, "Yeah, you. You never remember a thing."

On the bay, the foghorn sounded its first note, a guttural rolling. Mist inched into the road. The noise grew loud again and this time Heiden stood beside her. "Are you okay? What's the problem?"

You, she thought. Men and their stupid secrets. People who have to prove things. She said, "We're going to have a boarder." It sounded like a confession. He waited for more. "Yes?" In her vision she was twelve. Her father hauled heavy wooden traps on the boat. He said, "A hundred pounds and we'll celebrate. You, me, your ma." The image changed. Da had told her about Uncle Ambrose, hanged by the British in Ulster, with his face black and his eyes squeezed out of his head. *Oh Da, Da. What are you doing?*

She became conscious of Heiden's watching eyes. What was she supposed to say, "Da sells supplies to the U-boats"? Three months ago Heiden had aroused the whole island over a report of a "spy." She heard herself snap, "Why are you always asking questions!" She knew she shouldn't turn on him but she couldn't help it. "I tell *you* things. All you do is make jokes. Tell *me* something!"

He grinned. "Something."

"Get away from me. All of you." Whirling, she was startled to see Da peering at her from the window. He turned away. Oh, Heiden had faults. He was as secretive as Da in his own way, and that had intrigued her at first, then frustrated her. The difference was that she sensed goodness in Heiden, strength. She trusted him. She'd been waiting for him.

Now that was changing too. She told herself that maybe if she and Heiden had been closer, if he'd opened to her, she might be sharing instead of hiding things now. Her father was cutting her off from Heiden as well as everyone else.

Heiden said, "Don't be mad. Corrice? I'm sorry I hurt your feelings."

"You did not hurt my feelings."

"You act like I did."

"*You* could never hurt my feelings. My feelings are just fine, thank you."

From behind, he put his arms around her. Their bodies were close, but not pressing. At the warm contact, she wanted to melt, to tell the story. Her feelings were all mashed up. She wanted him to sweep her up. She wanted him to kiss her and reassure her, to divine her needs. For the thousandth time, she wondered how she would feel sleeping with him, sleeping with a man, that hair and muscle. She wanted him to take her from this horrible party, to obliterate the necklace and turn back the time. She was angry at him for failing and with herself for making impossible demands.

It was all too much. She raged, "I don't know anything about you! Where you come from! Your family!" They weren't looking at each other but she felt him shift uncomfortably.

He said, "My family is . . . is in Virginia. I haven't seen them for years."

This was safe and more distracting than the oppressive silence. Not really caring, just talking, she said, "What do they do?"

"My father works in Washington." She didn't say anything. He said, "In the government."

"Your mother?" she asked.

"At home."

The silence was returning. Corrice said, "Is that everybody?"

"Yes," he said, clearly lying.

At any other time she would have been fascinated. It wasn't worth the effort now. From inside came the rapping of Lieutenant Mariani's snare drum. Whoever was playing it didn't know how.

Heiden said, "You talked about a boarder. Is that what upset you?"

"No, no." She was talking much too quickly. "I just mentioned it." She thought, Now we're both making up stories. "I just came out for a minute."

His hands were in his pockets now, instead of on her shoulders. He was giving up also. "Oh. I wanted to see if you were okay."

She squeezed his hand. "I'll be inside in a minute."

The wind rattled the birches. She longed to be on the coast road, but her dissatisfaction, if hinted at too openly, would become island property.

The party noises hit her almost physically when she opened the door. In the red, leaping flames, a pagan joy lit the island faces. The crowd was hornpiping to the gramophone. The turkey was a carcass. Blueberry residue smeared the pie pans. "Birthday girls don't do work," said Mrs. Chadborne when Corrice piled dirty plates. Major Savage gripped her wrist. "One dance." The men howled at jokes, by the punch bowl.

In her room, a couple stood up when she turned on the light. "Sorry, Corrice," they giggled, smoothing down their clothing. The bed was small even for two teenagers. PARIS, CITY OF ROMANCE, read the magazine advertisement over the pink bedspread. A wooden doll watched from the windowsill, head tilted against blackout curtains, one-hundred-year-old doll eyes wide. A knitting pattern lay crushed on her pillow. Dresses, draped neatly over a chair, awaited alterations. She was shortening hems, narrowing waists. A handout on the rolltop read, "Corrice Kelly, chairman of the church scrap drive." War work or guilt work. Girl or woman.

Framed between her mother's jewelbox and her mother's Irish clock, her mirrored face seemed remarkably composed. Her mother at nineteen had been married. Heiden's photograph lay pinned by glass on top of a dresser, beside her mother on a beach, her father in the army, baby Corrice, cheerleader Corrice, Corrice in the cute uniform she wore on base.

The necklace radiated light. Her finger traced lines on her neck. A single strand of gold, seducing.

It occurred to her that the boarder would sleep across the hall, in the dark room ten feet away.

"Quite a gift for a teenager," said a slightly mocking voice from the doorway. Mrs. Hudson surveyed her, a hand on her hip. "Expensive too." The older woman advanced into the room. "For a lobsterman."

Corrice said, "He saved up." Mrs. Hudson's perfume cast a choking radius of at least six feet. Her hair was long, lustrous. She said, "What did your boyfriend get you? That lieutenant?" On the bed, she lifted one leg, straight out, stretching. "Cute boy," she said. She met Corrice's eyes coolly, like a rival. *Stop me*, her face seemed to dare.

The older woman changed the room. No longer in transition, it seemed in conflict with itself.

Corrice said, "Wish you were young again?" She was surprised at the sweetness in her voice and her triumph at the twisting response, but her stab of jealousy was already buried by other emotions. Mrs. Hudson was interested in distraction, not resolution. The two of them would forever be talking about different things. "I was going," Corrice said.

The stairs were packed with well-wishers. The padlocked basement opened to her key. She drew the bolt behind her. At the bottom of the shadow steps, her father's presence was everywhere, in the pipe tobacco aroma, in the wood shavings on the floor, the tools, the homemade workbench, the scattered drawings of his new ship.

A lot of money for a lobsterman, Mrs. Hudson had said. It

was one thing for Corrice to mistrust Da, quite another for someone else to do so. She was shamed by Mrs. Hudson's voicing of her own suspicions. All Da had done was to buy her a beautiful present. Was she, a mere nineteen-year-old, infallible? Couldn't she make a mistake?

If he were still selling food, she would find evidence here. He spent all his free time in the basement. Whatever he was doing was centered in this room.

The drawers were filled with tools. Hammers and mallets hung over the table. Concrete wall lay behind the shelves of paint and turpentine. She argued with herself. Boarders *had* stayed at the house when Ma was alive. The lobster boat did need repair or replacement. Da was capable of saving for a present.

The old cardboard boxes were filled with *Portland Press-Herald*s. At the table, she scanned the shadows, relieved. Maybe she'd needed privacy. Maybe, on her birthday, she'd wanted more than just friendly attention from Heiden. Maybe her period was coming on, although she was not prone to emotionalism at such times.

Upstairs, a voice cried, "Where's Corrice?" She became aware of the music and watched her fingers tapping to the beat. She would grow her nails long, like Mrs. Hudson. She rapped on the table. She'd been too hard on Heiden tonight. She'd make him a cake. She rapped on the glass jar full of brushes. She rapped on the toolboard.

It made a hollow thud.

Corrice stared at the hammers and mallets. Her stomach was starting to burn. She tapped the board again, located a screwdriver, began unfastening the six screws.

The board was heavy.

A radio lay inside.

She reached like a blind woman, ran her hands along metal and wire. Steadying herself, she donned the earphones. They muffled the party. She flicked a switch.

Tap. . . tap, tap, tap-ta—

He was still selling supplies to the Germans.

She stuffed the earphones behind the radio and fell into the chair. Music blared upstairs. The ceiling went up and down, with the dancers. A voice cried, "Where's Corrice?"

Her arms formed a circle on the table, her head on her wrists. The radio's green light penetrated the dark pocket she had formed. It was a sickly little light. Suddenly, the basement was very cold.

Corrice Kelly started to weep.

On the bridge of the U-boat, Ryker watched sailors drag a rubber raft across the deck. The sailors moved quickly, glancing at the sky. Clouds rolled across the moon. The sea was glass, the breeze almost tropical. "Dangerous, that moon," the captain said, "If it comes out before you get ashore, you'll make a pretty shadow from the air."

The raft splashed softly. A sailor held it by a rope.

Ryker examined his wallet, driver's license, Social Security card, library card. The brown cardboard pass was supposed to get him on the island ferry, but the Abwehr had made mistakes already. The money consisted of soiled fives instead of the crisp new bills they had tried to give him.

"I admire you," the captain said. Straight-backed, silver-haired, he wore the camouflage jacket of a Wehrmacht private. Silver hammerheads adorned his shoulders. Likewise, a painted shark leapt, on the conning tower, at victims' flags: British, American, French.

The captain said, "I don't know what you're planning on that island, but I have a good feeling about you. When you're finished I'll be there. Depend on me." Ryker placed his hands on the ladder. The captain said, "I should reach the island by tomorrow. I'll stay under and wait for your signal. The Americans have installed a line of sonic buoys around Casco Bay, but the enclosed area is two hundred square kilometers, large enough so they won't find us if we aren't moving. With luck, they'll decide waves set off the buoys. Herr Ryker?"

"What?"

"I opened the curtain and saw you dreaming. I have a nightmare too. I don't tell anyone about it. We've sailed into a convoy, at night, on the surface. We blend with the shadows. We torpedo six or seven vessels, then submerge. The destroyers look for us. We hear the asdic as the ships pass overhead. Then I hear a new sound, a terrifying sound. Tearing, rending. The ships we torpedoed are breaking up around us. Their bulkheads are crumbling. They're sinking a few meters away. What a way to die, crushed by your victims."

Ryker said, "I'd better go now."

The raft rocked. A small spade and canteen lay in the bottom. He waved to the captain and heard the hatch slam. The night was filled with the roar of flooding sea tanks.

The U-boat left a phosphorous wake.

Ryker began the steady shoreward pull. Maine was a black line. Behind the clouds the droning of an airplane grew loud, then passed to the north. He would never be more vulnerable than he was right now.

His arms felt good. He was exhilarated to be out of the U-boat. A hissing burst from the sea and the back of a whale surfaced only thirty feet away. With unreal slowness, the animal submerged again. Teeming life under Ryker's feet. The raft lifted in the resulting swells.

Twenty minutes later the shore shaped itself into a reaching promontory. The moon came out, flooding the ocean with light. Thin silver birches rose from black granite. Portland lay slightly over one hundred miles to the south.

In three days, the convoy would pass Captains Island. *Maine*, he thought triumphantly. The first moment was always the best. His boots touched rock and tiny sandpipers fled. He pulled the raft onshore and dragged it toward the bush. Ahead, the forest was a jagged line against the moonlit sky.

ELEVEN

————————◆————————

RYKER HAD LANDED NEAR the town of Milbridge, Maine.
Forty minutes later, in the same spot, Civil Defense Captain
John Crowley picked his way along the granite ledges by
the sea. The moon was bright. He shut off his flashlight.
Normally he carried a revolver as well, but it had jammed
during practice and awaited repair at home.

The strap of his old First World War helmet clenched
his jaw. He looked like a pudgy, fifty-year-old doughboy,
but he was a milkman near Milbridge, father of three, a
coast-watch volunteer.

The sea glistened. "Coolidge!" he called. A lean, sloping
shape shot from a spruce copse, raced around his feet, and
danced ahead.

Nose to the ledge, the Labrador sniffed excitedly between a dark promontory and patch of brush. Probably
found an animal, Crowley thought, or picnic leftovers. "What
do you see?"

He switched on the light. The dog's head protruded
from the brambles, its eyes red orbs in the beam.

The moon disappeared behind clouds.

Crowley followed the animal into the bushes. An owl

hooted nearby . If he ever did find anything, he mused, he would have to run half an hour to reach the nearest phone. Civil defense authorities kept promising him a walkie-talkie. Crowley figured the war would be over by the time he got it.

The ground was wet from recent rain. Ahead, the dog was digging. Dirt flew between its hind legs. Crowley moved up to watch and that was when he saw the footprints.

They were all over the forest floor, some still filling with water. Air bubbles frothed on the surface.

From behind came an odd scraping, as if something were rubbing against a tree. Like other coast residents, Crowley had heard rumbles out to sea some nights. The navy never explained them, but a swordfisherman named Grady told a story about a U-boat surfacing near his trawler, on the foggy outer banks.

"Hello?" Crowley said.

No answer.

"Is somebody there?"

The ground smelled like mulch. He bent to scoop wet earth. Moments later, he pulled a black rubber strip from the ground, and another. He dug some more.

He breathed, "It's a goddamn rubber raft."

He found a canteen and a spade.

Now he really wished he had the walkie-talkie.

"Coolidge?" The dog was gone.

"Coolidge!"

He didn't think smugglers would slash up their own raft.

Something rustled in the bushes. Leaves glistened in his circling flashlight beam. Crowley backed up a step. The shadows shifted.

Something touched his neck. A low-hanging leaf.

Twenty minutes later he pounded on a cabin door in

the woods. Lights went on overhead. His face swelled where a branch had hit him.

"I have to use the phone!"

"Ride, friend?"

Ryker peered into a jowly, middle-aged face. The driver patted the passenger seat. American cars were gigantic. "Middle of nowhere," the man said. He had slicked-back hair and a rumpled suit. "Car break down?" Ryker had traveled in the woods all night, keeping off the road until midmorning, when a hitchhiker would not arouse suspicion. He hadn't even stuck out his thumb and the car had stopped. *Good omen.* The countryside began flowing by.

"Where you headed?" the driver asked.

"Brunswick." Thirty miles from Portland.

"Toot! Toot! The Brunswick Express." The man had the ingratiating grin of a salesman.

Half turning, Ryker saw the carotid artery throbbing on the man's neck. He said, "That old Ford's trouble." He didn't think he had an accent but it was easy to fool yourself. "Broken axle." Lots of little turnoffs offered themselves, and thick, protective woods.

Sandwich wrappers and newspapers cluttered the floor. The driver glanced at cardboard boxes piled in back.

"Baby shoes," he said. " 'Want to comfort baby-woo? Buy a Protech baby shoe,' ha, ha. Dumbest little slogan y' ever heard, but it works. Last week a ship got torpedoed off Halifax. Military secret, but I know because of the cargo. Ten thousand baby shoes, floating in the ocean. My name's Halloran. You?"

"Marshall. Steve." Ryker didn't want to use his real name until he reached the island.

The driver said, "You live around here?" He jerked his head to sum up the area. "Maine people. All they do is get drunk, beat their wives, and invent things. But they buy shoes, yessiree. I'm from Boston. Fart City." He looked at Ryker strangely. "Get it? Fart? Boston? Beans? Ain't you got no sense of humor?"

"Oh sure. Boston."

"Hell! You'd think you never heard of Boston baked beans! Marshall, that an English name?"

"English," Ryker said.

"Don't mind my questions. I'm a bored salesman and I like to hear myself talk. Two more stops today, then home. Peace and quiet, ha. Seven kids and fertile Myrtle's expecting. Hey! Listen! I pull into the Esso in Milbridge. It's the middle of the night. I see *soldiers* all over the place." Ryker turned slowly. "Maybe a hundred troops, all roaring toward the ocean."

The gears made a heavy, dragging sound. Below the cliff road, bleaching tree trunks lay broken on boulders.

The salesman said, "I asked the soldiers, 'What are you doing?' Some captain answers, 'An exercise!' Hell, at three AM, soldiers on exercise look bored. These guys were excited, know what I mean?"

Ryker said, "Excited." He shifted his body imperceptibly. The steering wheel wasn't blocking his left hand anymore.

"Coast guard spotted a U-boat, I bet. Maybe a German came ashore. It happened last winter, no kidding. A kid saw two men walking on Route One. Dressed right out of a fashion magazine, in the middle of the night. Everyone up here knows this story. The FBI got 'em."

Ryker said, "A hundred soldiers, you saw."

"That's right."

"Dogs?"

"Didn't see none of them!"

"The army better set up roadblocks if they want to catch the fellah," Ryker said, watching close.

"No roadblocks either. Hell, maybe nobody landed."

Ryker asked, "How come it took you so long to get down here from Milbridge? It's only thirty miles."

"Shucks, friend. Paid a lady a visit."

Ryker thought, *Roadblocks could be everywhere by now.*

The salesman seemed disappointed about the lack of dogs and roadblocks. "Hell, I thought I had a war story." Ryker smiled sympathetically and brought his hand onto his lap. The car left the coast area and plunged into the forest. Up ahead, a dirt track led into the trees.

The salesman said, "What do *you* think happened in Milbridge?" He pressed the brake to slow for a curve. No cars approached in either direction.

Ryker struck once, with the wedge of his hand. "I think you might have figured it out later," he said, taking the wheel.

In Portland, the soldiers spaced themselves every thirty yards, carbines in hand, to form an olive-drab cordon for the incoming train. Rain lashed in from the sea. The locomotive stopped with the high squealing of brakes.

More troops peered from the opening boxcars. Massive brick warehouses lined one side of the tracks. On the other side, Portland rose steeply in a house-covered hill.

Two men stood a small distance away from the soldiers and watched canvas-topped trucks back up to receive cargo. The first, who wore an expensive camel-hair coat, controlled gambling, prostitution, and waterfront unions in Portland.

Joseph Cardi frowned. "I'll be glad when this shipment is gone," he said.

His companion said, "Not as glad as me. I had to ride all the way with it." He was taller, square-jawed, and wore a grey fedora and the shiny black shoes of a law-enforcement official. Charles Evans was special liaison between the office of Naval Intelligence and the OSS.

Smoke burst fitfully from the locomotive stack, as if to color the sky. Rain drummed on their umbrellas. One of the stranger alliances of the Second World War linked Naval Intelligence and organized crime. Recognizing the mob's hold over waterfront unions, the navy asked Charles "Lucky" Luciano for help in protecting dock areas from sabotage. In return, Luciano received early release from Great Meadow Prison in New York.

Cardi eyed the wooden crates in the boxcars. "Gas bombs," he said. "I saw what they did when I was a boy. In Italy. The Austrians left and we went over the battlefield to look for clothing." He grimaced. "The soldiers' eyes looked burnt. Froth dripped from their mouths. Their faces were swollen, like blowfish from the sea. And blue."

Evans said, "Sounds like phosgene gas. It's a quarter of this shipment. The rest is mustard. Invisible fire, they call it. It burns out the lungs."

The first round of trucks pulled away from the boxcars.

Cardi said, "Two hundred thousand bombs."

"To stockpile in England."

"That gas would wipe out my docks, my shipyard, my railyard, and half my city."

"Only if the wind is right."

"The wind is right every time the tide comes in. First Kaufman's clerk kills himself. Now the civil defense finds the raft. You should have sealed Milbridge off right away."

Evans said, "We hadn't any soldiers up there. We don't know how long the raft's been buried. Besides, there's no certainty the Nazi's coming to Portland."

"Is that why you woke me at six AM? The Germans know about this shipment, all right."

"Okay, okay. We're setting up roadblocks." Evans paused. "It's funny, though. You and me. Working together. We'll probably try to kill each other after the war."

Cardi blew his nose on an embroidered handkerchief. "Yeah, philosophy. Just get the gas away from here. I don't even like being in the same city with those bombs."

"We load the convoy," Evans said, "then I can go home."

High above, on the overlook, Ryker watched the last truck pull away. A second train awaited unloading. He wished the pay-telescope stand beside him had not been stripped of its viewer, but obviously the authorities had removed it for fear it might be trained on the railyard.

He'd left the salesman's car in the woods. Even if someone found it, and the body in the trunk, the police would need days to trace Ryker to the bus that took him to Portland.

He'd bought a rain slicker and had been wandering the city, familiarizing himself for later.

Tugs churned through the rain below. In the crescent-shaped harbor, large fleet units clustered around a monstrous service ship, the crane lifting a cruiser from the bay, for repair. Three battleships steamed toward the open sea. They would probably pass close to Captains Island, but in the fog, the islands seemed little more than scattered, lumpy masses. Anyway, Ryker hoped Captains Island couldn't be seen from the hill even on a clear day. The farther it was from the mainland, the better.

He checked his ID, which included his real name, a

"Summer Visitor" stamp, and a black-and-white photograph. But the ferry would be guarded and a mistake on the pass fatal. A V-shaped squadron of B-19s blanketed the sky, flying low, toward Iceland. Below, tankers and merchantmen fueled.

He'd never visited Portland as a boy but had spent his first eight years in the north, mostly in the woods. Twice this morning, his father had come into his mind. Both times he had batted away the memory.

A car pulled into the overlook. Doors slammed and children in blue slickers ran to look at the ships.

Ryker wrapped his own slicker close and left the parking lot.

It took a few minutes to realize that gold stars in windows signified sons killed in service, and not Jewish ownership, as they would in Germany. Vegetable gardens were everywhere. The waterfront was filled with ironworks, warehouses, soldiers. Women drove the trucks. OFFICIAL MAPS OF CASCO BAY, read a sign in a nautical supply store. Ryker was astonished. Was it this easy to obtain information? He browsed among the ropes and compasses, waiting for someone else to buy a map first. He would check the new map against the Abwehr's.

Steel double-decked ferries left hourly, for various islands, from a long public pier. Forty soldiers could easily seize and defend the ferry, he decided. An open-air roof protected him from the fitful downpour. Dead mackerel floated in the greasy water after falling from incoming fishing boats. A hundred yards across an inlet, on a private commercial pier, stocking-capped swordfishermen stacked immense orange floats on a rusty deck.

The waterfront impressed Ryker with a sense of rawness and vitality. The troops seemed young and well fed. Even the middle-aged ferry passengers exuded strength, those pipe-smoking shipyard workers with composed faces and grey cropped heads. Summer residents wore more colorful clothing. A beagle bayed, tied to a camper's canoe. Coast-guardmen with holsters walked the pier.

Ryker thought about Nazi propaganda, which pictured weak, spoiled Americans. The Wehrmacht is in for a nasty surprise, he thought.

A ferry whistle blasted. "Peaks Island," yelled a voice. The guards blocked the ramp to check passes.

Ryker thought, Make sure your pass looks right. Take the last ferry. The guards will be tired.

The ticket seller shoved a schedule out of a wire-mesh booth. Back on Commercial Street, Ryker bought an old suitcase. After all, he was supposed to be a tourist. Then he looked for a bar. Problems, even big problems, made the whole job worthwhile.

Heiden and Corrice turned left under the marquee and walked toward the waterfront. She'd been given the day off at the base, for her birthday. The rain was easing. Heiden rumbaed with an imaginary partner. "Rio . . . Rio Meeeo. Come on, Corrice. You love Abbott and Costello." She didn't answer.

Heiden said, "What was your favorite part of the movie?" Slowly Corrice let out her breath. He said, "Mine was Costello dancing." Corrice looked at the sidewalk. Heiden imitated her voice, "My favorite part was the chase." In his own voice he said, "I didn't like the chase." In hers he said, "*You* never like the good parts."

She burst out crying.

High Street was a corridor of shoppers and plate-glass windows. Flanked by bobbing black umbrellas, Dodges and

Packards cruised. Under lace mesh hats, passing matrons scowled at Heiden, and eyed Corrice sympathetically. One hissed, "Soldiers!"

"Corrice, you're giving me a bad name."

"Sorry." She fixed her face in a Rexall window. OFFICIAL BLACKOUT BULBS ON SALE, said the sign. Heiden said, "We'll go eat, okay?"

"Okay. I'm . . . I'm not really hungry."

"Museum?"

"Not today."

"Another movie then. The mail launch can take us back."

"You can't be having a good time."

He went Bogart. "No shweat, kid. I got duh day off for your birthday." Her smile flickered, but then she said, "We can wait for the ferry at Craun's."

"But you hate Craun's. It's impossible to talk there."

"Who wants to talk?"

I do, thought Heiden. He wanted to knock down the terrible barrier that had sprung up between them. After parting uncomfortably from the party last night, he'd returned to the base, sat by the telescope, gazed out to sea as usual. But for the first time, he had not wanted to think about Europe, had not even wanted to go to Europe. The whole idea of daydreaming in the dark seemed childish. His little argument with Corrice had bothered him more than he'd first cared to admit.

In his room, he'd experienced a sudden flash of precognition. It was a powerful moment. Something was about to fundamentally change his world.

Now his problem was more than how to tell Corrice that he had fallen in love with her. It was whether she cared.

He was as miserable as the lowest adolescent. *You never talk about yourself,* she'd snapped last night. He'd decided to tell her everything about his family, why he'd been kept on the island.

But from the moment he'd picked her up today, she'd seemed a pale apparition of herself, gripped by solitude and alienation.

"Is it me?" he said. They turned at the doric-columned courthouse, toward the docks. The narrow street closed in upon them. Thick fog lay ten feet overhead. "Did I say something wrong?"

"No, no." She squeezed his hand, but when he put his arm around her she moved away.

She said, "I really need to get to work on the rubber drive. The army wants two hundred pounds by Friday."

"That's a lot of pounds." Even mundane conversation was better than silence.

"I'll send the kids to crash around in the bushes. People threw away tires before the war."

"A one-woman war effort."

"Plus I'm baking chocolate-molasses brownies for overseas."

Heiden licked his lips. "The home front loves brownies."

"The home front gets first choice."

He didn't believe her. He was as powerfully attracted to her as he had been the first night they met. Her hair fell in ringlets tonight. He looked into her violet eyes and sensed her smooth limbs working under her padded black coat. He ached to make love to her, that moist fragrance and milk-white skin. He'd never tried.

On her birthday, he now realized, she had wanted more than a piano-playing buddy. She'd needed affection last night. Selfishly, he'd left the porch.

He took her hand. CRAUN's, blinked the neon sign above

their heads. He said, "You sure you want to go in there?"

Night was falling.

The door opened, like a mouth.

Craun's was every waterfront bar Ryker had ever visited. He might have been in Oslo, Marseilles, even Hamburg. Only the uniforms looked different. Under rotating ceiling fans, the smoky room was packed, noisy, full of round tables and booths. A pay phone rang. A dancing couple crashed into other customers. The long bar doubled as a dinner table.

"I saw her first. The perfect fuck," said a sailor beside Ryker. His friend caught his arm. "Flip you for her." Backs and elbows touching the bar, they ogled an entering couple. The girl was pretty in a slim, un-made-up way. Her escort, a lieutenant, was due for trouble. Ryker had seen enough bar fights develop to recognize the sailors' tone. They were ugly drunk and had been rejected by a sarcastic bar girl five minutes earlier. The first man ribbed his buddy. He had a coarse Southwestern drawl. "Yours is the masculine type." Their laughter was harsh. "We'll take him outside."

Ryker had learned, just sitting here, that they served on the battleship *Alabama*. He'd learned that longshoremen had the day off while soldiers unloaded the rail shipment he'd seen.

By asking a drunk clerk about his new baby, he'd gotten the man to open his wallet and had caught a glimpse of a ferry pass. It matched his own.

Lots of ferries would chug into the fog tonight, but the only one to stop at Captains Island would leave in forty minutes.

The first sailor growled, "Desk drivers get all the snatch."

He was a towheaded Texan sucking on his tenth beer. "We go to sea. They get laid. Not fair. It's not fair, is it, Arnie?"

They seemed bored, angry, happy. They couldn't decide.

"That fucker."

"That shithead."

"The girl don't even like him. They're fighting."

"Let's rescue her."

"We'll plaster him."

The Texan ground his fist against the bar, drained his bottle, and weighed the empty. Ryker thought, *Keep out of it.* He sipped watered whiskey. He'd never approved of two against one, unless he was the one.

Full of purpose, the sailors pushed into the crowd.

"You're not wearing your father's necklace," Heiden said, placing a beer and Coke on the table. "How come?" Normally, he loved Craun's. It reminded him of the crowded clubs he'd played. Tonight the boisterousness seemed designed to keep him from talking with Corrice. He said, "It sure is a beautiful necklace." In the din, he had to lean across the table. She reached to touch her neck, looking guilty, as if she had lost the necklace.

She stood up. "Back in a minute." She pointed to the ladies' room.

The room throbbed with the high, free sound of wartime pleasure. The jukebox blasted the Earl Hines Orchestra playing "Boogie Woogie St. Louis Blues." Finger in one ear, a sergeant shouted into a pay phone. The dancers bumped Heiden's chair. Beer slopped onto the table.

He was getting mad now. Even if Corrice were legitimately angry, she was handling it the wrong way. He traced her mood. She'd been fine before the party yesterday, had screeched with delight at the "Surprise!" and had kissed him madly when she realized he'd helped arrange it.

Next thing he knew, she was on the porch, moping.

People didn't change so fast. Scowling, he realized a half hour had passed between the time she gleefully opened her presents and the time he found her on the porch.

Had someone upset her during those thirty minutes?

A scissor-legged brunette at the next table watched him. He noticed her wedding ring. Smiling into his face, she slid off the ring, then shrugged when Corrice returned. A soldier immediately took the chair beside her.

Corrice spoke more quickly than usual. "Jeremiah Leeds must have tons of rubber in his junkyard. Maybe he'll give some to the kids."

Heiden, still trying to reconstruct the party, said, "Yeah." He was trying to remember whom she'd talked to while he played the piano.

"Of course, Jeremiah has rats in the yard. The kids would have to wear gloves and long pants."

Heiden mused, "Strange reversal. *You* want to talk about the war. *I* want to talk about anything else."

With forced gaiety she said, "The island talent show, we'll talk about that. What are you going to play?"

"Damn it, Corrice, what's the matter with you? What the hell is going on?"

"Nothing is the matter with me."

"Couldn't be better, huh? Happy-go-lucky Corrice. I'm glad I'm not around when you're depressed."

"You don't want to be around, you don't have to be around. Do you hear me laughing at your funny joke?"

"I don't hear you saying a damn thing."

"Then the shoe is on the other foot for a change, Lieutenant."

A third voice drawled, "This gent bothering you, miss?"

Through the red rage haze, Heiden looked up at two of them, looming ensigns swaying with alcohol or anticipation. Red cracker faces, tattoos and long arms. They looked like a couple of prizefighters in white. Corrice said. "He isn't bothering me."

"Oh now, honey. You can tell us." The sailor spun a chair backwards and sat, draping his arms. His friend placed his hands beside Heiden's beer glass. "Get rid of this desk driver. We'll show you a good time."

Heiden felt the blood rushing in his temples. He had never been in a bar fight before.

The first Texan said to Corrice, "We're shipping out tomorrow."

"Leaving."

"This is our last night in the continental U.S. of A."

Corrice said, "Tom, let's go."

Heiden heard himself say, "I like this table."

"That's the spirit," the Texan said. "What are you drinking, hon?"

Corrice stared at him coldly.

Heiden dropped his voice. "I'm asking nicely."

"Rum and Coke? Is that it?"

His friend said, "I think it's plain Coke, Arnie."

"We'll buy her a rum and Coke *and* a Coke, then."

Heiden stood up. "You'd better go."

Both sailors rose, but they didn't look like they planned on leaving.

The first sailor addressed his friend. "Sounded like an order to me."

"Army giving orders to the navy."

Heiden said, "Corrice, move back, okay?"

"I think we should go."

"Corrice!"

Her chair scraped. Glenn Miller's "In the Mood" blasted from the jukebox. The sailors edged around the table in both directions. A burst of laughter came from the bar. Heiden stepped inside the bigger man's arms, lowered his shoulders, and drove his right fist up as hard as he could. The man's toes lifted, the eyes opened in surprise. He tipped back and away. Heiden spun as the Coke glass whizzed by his ear and shattered on the table. He twisted and rammed up his right knee. The second sailor's mouth dropped open but the scream came from behind them. The first man had crashed to his knees in front of the bar. His hands clutched his back. He looked like he had crashed into the bar.

The sailor Heiden had kneed was doubled over, gasping. Less than seven seconds had elapsed since the fight started. Already, customers were turning back to their drinks.

Heiden stared at his fists. He said, "Hey, I did it!"

Corrice said, "You! You! We could have left." She hit his chest repeatedly with one fist. He loved it.

But one image bothered him. He saw his fist strike the broad white shirt, saw the sailor throw his arms wide. He remembered a single blurred movement from a customer on a stool, an instant before the backpedaling sailor would have struck the bar. *Then* came the howl of pain.

Heiden thought, So, I had help. But the circumstances had been confused, and the customer's movement so quick, that he doubted himself. Besides, the man seemed completely disinterested, sipping his drink at the bar.

The horn blast of the arriving Captains Island ferry cut through the din.

The moaning sailor lay on the floor. Shipmates helped him to his feet.

The customer slapped money on the bar. Heiden and Corrice joined the crowd funneling toward the door.

Heiden reached to catch the customer's attention. Beneath the bulky rain slicker, the shoulders were surprisingly muscled. The eyes, when they turned, were utterly emotionless, yet at first glance the stranger radiated a startling and extraordinary violence, in the huge, rough-hewn face, the brutal, sensual mouth, the corded neck. Up close the man did not seem as large as he had earlier, but there was absolute command in even the slightest movement. Heiden had never felt such strength in a person, especially on sight. Under normal circumstances he might have been intimidated, but he believed the stranger had aided him. The violence did not seem malevolent. Heiden was drawn, not repelled. He was fascinated, grateful.

They stood in line for the ferry. Ahead, the guard checked passes. The storm had stopped. Half a mile away, the clanging shipyard blazed like a city on fire. A single switch could douse every light.

Heiden said, "I don't know what you did to that sailor. I couldn't have handled them both."

The stranger's eyes were flinty and unreadable. "You moved fast." The rough, knowledgeable tone filled Heiden with pride.

"Good thing they were drunk," Heiden said. "I'm surprised I'm still standing." He extended his hand. "Tom Heiden."

"Ryker. John."

"Summer visitor? I haven't seen you before."

The guard said, "Passes." He was a pimply teenager in oversized khaki. His girlfriend gazed at him ten feet away.

She loved to watch him check the IDs. The boy reached for Ryker's wallet. "Captains Island," he read solemnly.

Heiden laughed, delighted. "Where you staying? It's a small place."

"With a lobsterman. Kelly's his name." Ryker seemed friendlier now that he realized they were going to the same place.

"Corrice! You hear that? John Ryker, may I introduce your hostess? Corrice Kelly."

Ryker said, "Charmed." Heiden, seeing her face, thought, *She's in that mood again.*

Ryker said, "I'm visiting for two weeks. First vacation in years." He looked into the girl's face and kept talking. "I was born in Maine but I never saw the islands. Been working in Detroit. The plant burnt down. My big chance to visit East."

Heiden said, "I'm glad you got here today, all right."

"Are you in Portland on leave?" Ryker asked. The ferry pulled away. Heiden laughed. "Leave? I'm stationed on the island."

"There's a *base* on the island?"

Corrice said, "Excuse me," and crossed to the other side of the prow.

Ryker watched her back. "I saw you two in the bar. Nothing serious, I hope."

"She's just moody today."

Ryker said, "Well, I don't mind riding by myself." The effect of his smile, as usual a welcome surprise, was to create warmth. "But tell me. I didn't pick the wrong island for my vacation, did I? The soldiers won't be drilling under my window?"

"We keep to our side of the island. Don't worry. There are only a hundred and fifty of us."

Ryker looked like any relieved tourist, discovering that his vacation was not, after all, ruined. "You'd better talk to your girl," he said. "I want to see the harbor anyway. I don't want to miss a thing."

Ryker looked over at the looming battleships. White froth billowed below, phosphorous. Buoys tipped like shadow drunks, green eyes blinking. He scanned dark islands, which rose from the jet-black bay. *Which one is it?*

The ferry stopped at inner islands. The shipyard glow diminished and soon only a dozen passengers remained. A girl smiled up at him. "Raffle?" She held some kind of booklet and looked fifteen. "They're only a dollar. For mats for the wrestling team." Ryker unfolded a bill. An old woman was saying, "I've practiced that damn harmonica for two months. Sure, I'll play in the show."

So this was Casco Bay, two hundred square miles, eighteen miles at the mouth. The great natural division of Maine. The moon came out. The islands lay like a great fleet at anchor, presenting stone facades to the sea. "Forts," the old woman told a summer visitor. "Built that big one during the Revolutionary War, *that* one during the Great War. See the eight-sided fort? See the cannon holes? Jefferson Davis built that before he became President of the Confederacy."

Ryker memorized channels, berths, ships, fuel tanks. You never knew when you'd need information. Portland Harbor had girded for attack for two hundred years, arming itself against battleships and bombers, building steel nets to repel U-boats. Troops drilled on a dozen islands. Spotter planes flew overhead. Now the attack began with the price of a ten-cent ferry ride. Ryker had to keep from laughing.

He recognized Captains Island when he saw it. In the vivid moonlight, the serpent's head reared. A few homes clustered, pale boxes by the luminous sea. Farther back, above a black forest canopy as thick as any South American rain forest, protruded a high, rectangular artillery watchtower. But it faced the same direction as all the island's defenses, away from the bay and toward the open sea.

Ryker measured the wide expanse of water isolating Captains Island. When he turned back, the Asia dream came to him as it often did when he faced action. The same misty images never changed, the wicker-backed throne, the racing paddlers without faces and the coffee-colored women, the vague blue sky and jungle haziness. Soldiers prayed to God when they went into battle, but Ryker had never been in a church in his life.

In Asia I won't have to fight anymore.

After this job.

He blinked to clear his head. The peaceful feeling evaporated and his wariness returned. The ferry chugged through a narrow headland into a lagoon, where he saw lobster boats anchored in still water. On deck, a toddler supported himself against Ryker, with the unquestioning touch of a child. A teenage ferry attendant threw a loop of rope to secure the boat to the pier. Engines throbbing, the ferry bumped the dock.

Ryker breathed, "My island."

Behind him, a voice hissed, "Spy!"

TWELVE

NONE OF THEM slept that night.

The dying chimes announced one AM. Fully clothed, Ryker slipped off his bed. Moonlight impaled the cheap sturdy furniture and snapshot of the Kellys. He pulled the suitcase from under the bed and removed a black sweater and bowie knife. He hooked the bowie knife in his belt. He dropped a pen flashlight in his pocket. Slowly, he reached for the knob.

Corrice's door was open across the hall. Her back rose and fell in the dark.

He did not see her eyes open.

His luck had started going bad on the ferry. When the voice hissed "spy," he had needed all his training to keep from attacking. A ten-year-old boy had been teasing him. On the walk home with Corrice and Heiden all his senses had screamed danger. This girl did not want him here, that much was obvious with the first killing glance. And the father was a frightened blowhard who had kept glancing at Heiden all through dinner, as if expecting imminent arrest.

Fortunately, the lieutenant, preoccupied with Corrice,

had missed the looks and fake, booming laughs. But Heiden had acted with prompt intelligence in the bar. He would figure it out.

Ryker reminded himself that within twenty-four hours the Austrians would land and Heiden would be dead and unable to realize anything.

Softly, he shut the front door. Dark windows looked down upon him along the street. He walked casually, feeling naked. When he couldn't see the houses anymore he smeared dirt on his face and hands.

He'd allotted himself only a few hours to prepare for the Austrians. He would have no second chance. The moon glowed, pale and vaporous. He waded through glistening masses of neck-high weeds. Night moths rose to brush his face. He pushed through berry bushes and jungle-thick grass. Sumac trunks reared like reaching hands. He counted steps, listened for patrols. Birch forest closed in around him.

He had a perfect sense of direction and had memorized both maps. At length he broke onto a high, treeless bluff, spotted with boulders. He retreated into the shadows and waited, but when no guard passed after thirty minutes, he decided to risk discovery. He crawled to the edge of the bluff. The ocean swelled against the rocks below. Ryker knew that U-boats needed at least sixty feet of water to submerge safely. He had ruled out the deep-water army side of the island as the Austrians' landing place. It was too well guarded. But according to the map he'd bought, two locations on the civilian side provided adequate depth too. The bottom dropped ninety feet four hundred yards off this cliff.

Belly flat, head over the cliff, Ryker scanned the seemingly bare rock face, searching for a path, a handhold, anything the Austrians could use in ascent. A hairline crack fifty feet below looked like a ledge. It would have to do.

He was back in the trees two minutes later when the guard passed. The footsteps faded. He hurried north, toward the base. Ryker wondered how many soldiers guarded the fence.

When Corrice heard the soft click of the front door, she slid from under her covers and crept to the window. Below, the boarder moved up the road toward the forest.

Her nightdress brushed the tops of her toes. She tiptoed to her father's room and opened the door. Michael Kelly's snores rattled the windows.

When she'd sensed Ryker standing in her doorway, she'd wanted to scream, feeling those eyes on her back. He'd moved so fast in the bar.

His door was unlocked. Yellow moonlight bathed his quilt.

The dresser was empty. Unused hangers dangled in the closet. The room emitted a musty, un-lived-in smell and a trace of masculine musk. His eyes had frightened her the most. No matter what expression touched his face, it never reached the flinty green eyes.

She caught a movement in the mirror and jumped at her own reflection. He was not a regular boarder, that was for sure. His suitcase lay under the bed. She muffled the springing locks with her fingers. Inside, she found an old flannel shirt, dungarees, new toothbrush, new hairbrush, new underwear. She ran her hands inside the elastic compartments and found nothing. It didn't change her feeling. He had bothered her all along.

The house creaked downstairs. She sat on Ryker's bed,

thinking furiously. Da had practically had apoplexy when Ryker showed up. They were probably selling supplies together. Da was expanding his business. Well, she would wake Da and order him to send Ryker away. Selling supplies alone was dangerous enough.

Who was she fooling? He'd never agree.

She would *talk to Ryker*. She would confront Ryker, tell him to go, threaten him with exposure. She'd be bluffing, because she would never do anything to jeapordize Da, but Ryker wouldn't know that.

Where had he gone anyway?

She would find him, tonight, just the two of them in the woods.

She dressed quickly. Outside, the banshee wail of a screech owl floated from the trees.

Ryker had taken the forest road. Since the road offered no turnoffs, he would have to come back the way he had gone.

Hurrying to catch up, Corrice went the same way.

Thomas Heiden scowled at Michael Kelly's name, on his chart. A bare bulb hung on a wire over his Quonset-hut desk. The wire looped in a noose. On the day Major Levy had told him about intercepting U-boat signals, Levy had ordered, "Make sure islanders register their radios." Heiden had done much more.

His chart listed fifteen residents who owned shortwaves, as well as the date and time army intercept units picked up the broadcasts. Kelly was included in the chart because he had a radio on his boat. Whenever Levy called Heiden about a signal, Heiden quietly checked the whereabouts of the islanders.

Levy had phoned yesterday. Now Heiden wrote, beside

Michael Kelly's name, "Home, Basement. Working on boat." Six identical entries marked Kelly's column.

Heiden had never completely forgotten Jeremiah Leeds's claim, made four months earlier, that the most likely German sympathizer on the island was Corrice's father. But the memory, an uncomfortable reminder of a bad night, seemed disloyal to Corrice and Mr. Kelly. On this small island, most fifty-year-olds stayed home at night, worked on hobbies, or just went to sleep. Heiden's chart was a precaution. He suspected no one of receiving messages. Still, with a twinge of guilt, and noting the consistency of the entries in Kelly's column, he decided next time he visited the house he would ask to see the drawings in the basement.

Heiden had also written, on a separate piece of paper, the name John Ryker and the Maine hometown Ryker had mentioned on the ferry. He planned to call the appropriate county clerk on Monday, when records offices opened, to check the story.

It was all part of Heiden's new system of checking summer visitors. He might call a vacationer's office, pretend to be a friend, and find out the man was vacationing in Maine. The perfunctory check would be over. He did not like violating people's privacy, but Major Savage opened the base for Saturday night movies, so Heiden felt the calls necessary. He kept them secret from Savage, who was over-zealous about public relations and might order him to stop.

After hearing more from Major Levy about U-boat signals, Heiden had also ordered the hole filled in under the base fence. The apple trees were off limits to the kids now. The action had started a new round of Lieutenant Flashlight jokes on the island.

He threw down his pencil. Work wasn't taking his mind off Corrice. Outside, the surf hissed beyond the spruce-covered battery. Heiden strolled through a massive concrete portal. Entranceways at opposite ends of the bunker led straight to the huge guns, because sixteen-inch artillery could only be fired two hundred times, then the steel would weaken and the gun would have to be taken back out of the installation and replaced.

The Captains Island guns had only been fired once, during a test that broke all the windows on the civilian side of the island. Major Savage ordered no more practice after that.

Heiden saluted the guard. White light bathed the concrete walls, which dripped with condensation. The swivel base of the cannon loomed ahead. From the circular-railed platform, surrounded on three sides by the battery but open to the sea, he had an unobstructed view of the ocean side of the battery; a cattail marsh, scrub-brush thickets, moonlit boulder beach and cove. He smelled concrete, spruce, sea, oil. The ceiling went on through fifteen feet of concrete and ten more of earth. The gun pointed at the black horizon.

Overhead, monorail tracks could carry one-ton, chain-suspended shells to the gun. Heiden had watched the shells lowered onto a tremendous loading pan. A steel trough ran from the pan to the breech. A mechanical ramrod shoved shells along the trough and into the open gun. The ramrod resembled a monstrous bicycle chain pushing a steel fist. As the shell moved into place, denim-clad soldiers wheeled dollies to the trough, and hefted two-hundred-pound gunpowder bales, four for each shot, onto loading position. Everyone wore earplugs. Even with sound-absorbing cork ceilings, the firing had been shattering.

Heiden stood, dwarfed by the gun. He had never been alone with it before. He was thinking that the gun and its mate were the reasons for his assignment, for his life on the island. Perhaps, as Major Savage claimed, Battery MacAllister's monstrous weapons were obsolete, but the gun seemed powerful and ever watchful, vigilant, neck up, mouth to the sea. Heiden felt an affinity with it. He understood why soldiers named guns. He patted the gigantic breech as one would an old pet. He marveled at the engineering that could propel a two-thousand-pound explosive shell, accurately, over the horizon for twenty-five miles, and was saddened that the engineering had been deemed necessary in the first place. How could such a gigantic death-dealing machine already be obsolete? He chuckled. Corrice was the one who generally thought up things like that.

The cattail swamp was lush, the sea lulling. The main tunnel served as the only connecting passage between entrances. Steel doors in the hallway led to powder rooms, unused. Bunched pipes ran along the ceiling. Bare bulbs glowed above. Heiden smelled acrid gunpowder and damp earth. The tunnel was cool. In the vast impersonal emptiness, a little loneliness returned and he wished Lieutenant Mariani were here, cursing over the guns, as usual.

Oddly, an image of John Ryker came into his head. He had spoken to no one about Corrice and was surprised to realize he wanted to confide in a stranger. He rarely discussed personal problems even with friends.

He told himself that sometimes strangers were easier to talk to.

Maybe he should visit the Kelly house, see Ryker, talk to Corrice, check the basement drawings at the same time. He'd sensed friction between father and daughter at the dinner table tonight. At the party too, come to think of it. He tried to imagine what could be wrong between Corrice and her father. Heiden emerged from the battery and crossed the parade grounds. Under the bright moon, he had no trouble identifying the footpath that led into the forest.

Could Corrice's father have something to do with her strange behavior?

The ground sloped upward. The crowding trees twisted. In the silvery dark, they seemed to change shape.

Dropping from the fence, Ryker made a soft thud. The single insolent caw of a raven protested his incursion. He had been astounded to find the base protected by nothing more formidable than chicken wire. The fence must have been designed to keep out locals. If that was the worst trouble expected here, Ryker's job would be easier than he'd thought.

He needed to scout the watchtower he'd seen from the boat, as well as the base barracks and gun emplacement. But he'd lost time on the bluff and was already behind schedule. It was vital to be back in his room before the islanders got up.

He squatted, listening. He smelled no humans, only honeysuckle and hemlock.

Conjuring his maps, he began a stop-and-go run, threading the trunks with high quiet steps. *Move like an animal.* Five steps and pause. Six steps and pause.

His uncle had taught him in Tanganyika. The best forest for silent travel is a climax forest, an old forest, where a dense canopy blocks the sun and kills off ground vegetation. Ryker hurried over a soft pine-needle floor.

At length the tower loomed. Four stories high, it crowned

the highest point on Captains Island and served not only as an observation post but a triangulation point for gunners as well. The area around the huge square base had been cleared and a large boulder lay in the clearing.

From the trees, Ryker made sure the tower was unguarded. He approached to consider the sheer concrete walls and single dark, open slit near the top, where soldiers probably even now scanned the sea. A telephone wire ran into the trees. He crept to the steel-grill door. In the black interior, a ghost staircase wound upwards. How many men worked inside?

Footsteps echoed on the stairs: more than one person was coming. Ryker retreated and the door scraped. He dropped behind the boulder. A thin, complaining voice said, twenty feet away, "We shouldn't be down here, Clancy. Leaving the top alone."

"Ah, cramped up in the dark. Who's gonna spot anything at night anyway?"

Heels snapped on concrete. Leaves cracked louder as one of the men approached.

"Sure we can see. The moon's full."

"Who are you, the werewolf?"

Pressing against the rock, Ryker slid the bowie knife from his belt. He kept the reflecting surface from the moon. He heard the quick scratch of a match and smelled tobacco. A shadow fell across his face. Back to Ryker, a soldier leaned against the boulder.

The complaining voice had not moved. "Come on, Clancy. We're on alert."

"Shit. 'Alert' doesn't mean there's a U-boat out there. It means one of those damn cables picked up movement." The smoker sighed. "The navy lays cables on the sea bottom. The cables register disturbances in the current. A big cruiser steams past and the cables pick up movement. The lights come on, on the board at Fort Williams. The army checks with the ship and everyone goes back to sleep. A U-boat sneaks by and the lights come on again. This time the army can't find a ship, so the harbor goes on alert."

"That's what I said."

"Yeah, except every time a big wave passes, the lights go on too. Ninety-nine percent of the alerts are goddamn waves."

The back shifted. The hand holding the cigarette moved down so the tip glowed six inches from Ryker's face. CAMEL, said the lettering. His eyes watered. Around the soldier's black-haired head, wreathing smoke formed a blue halo.

The first voice said, "I'm going back." Footsteps receded, climbing stairs. But the man leaning on the boulder remained in place. He looked off into the trees, blowing smoke. Ryker could see the curving corona of his blinking eye, profiled. When the man shifted, Ryker readied the thrust.

The man stood up. "Okay, okay. I'm coming."

The gate shut behind him.

Silently, Ryker thanked the men for showing him how to take the tower.

But he'd lost more time. In the forest, he picked up his pace, passing fallen trunks, great cracked timber. He still moved with high, careful steps, but he paused after longer stretches. Head up, nostrils wide, all his senses were roaring. He fully registered the twisting run, a stream to avoid, a huge oak, a humpbacked possum slithering into the trees. He noted boulders, smells, conjured the maps and superimposed them over the ground cover. Even at this rapid pace he would have heard anything moving; except when he rounded the oak, the soldier in front of him wasn't moving at all, just sitting on a fallen trunk, knee up, almost casual, head snapping with shock.

The soldier barked, "Who the hell are you?"

Half hidden in darkness, the man fumbled with his holster.

The guard said, "No one else came by, Corrice. Why do you ask?"

"I wondered who was awake, that's all." Wincing at her obvious lie, she passed into the base. The road was lined with pines. Shadows seemed to shift ahead, beyond the moonlight. Ryker was there somewhere. Corrice had changed her appraisal of the boarder in the last hour. Now she searched for him out of some kind of compulsion. She had to know where he was.

Ryker could never have gotten a coast guard pass unless her father had vouched for him, and since that act tied them together in the eyes of the law, Da must have had a good reason. Was the reason supplies? Were his supplies hidden on Captains Island? Did Da need someone to help move them?

Before Pearl Harbor, he'd generally kept extra food and oil in the basement. Afterwards, he'd transferred supplies elsewhere, north, she figured, where he "fished" near isolated islands.

But if the supplies were north, why would Ryker stay here? And if the supplies were here, why wouldn't Da take Ryker to see them personally? Why allow the stranger to go into the woods alone, at night?

Trees crowded the road. *What if there were no supplies at all?* She stopped. Her legs went weak. What if Ryker's reason for coming here *had nothing to do with supplies?*

Her stomach burned. No, that was impossible. Da was greedy but he would never sell information. Or board someone who would. *You're imagining the whole thing.* She thought she must have overlooked a logical explanation.

She saw herself coming upon Ryker in the woods. His hand shot toward her, like in the bar. He clamped her mouth shut. The trees offered thick protection. Why would the Germans want information if not to use it?

The parade ground lay peaceful, deserted. *Wake Tom!* He could stop Ryker in a minute, call out the soldiers, search the base. Her skull felt like it was going to explode. Heiden slept peacefully, fifty yards away. If, *if* Ryker were going to gather information, what would he want on the base? The answer came immediately, as a picture of the two huge guns being unloaded at the dock.

Trust your feelings, her mother had said. But suppose she were wrong? She saw soldiers dragging Da from the house, saw her Irish uncle, black-faced on the gibbet. The base was guarded, wasn't it? Ryker was just lost in the woods, an overeager tourist. He'd never even reached the base. Or he *was* helping Da sell supplies. Even in wartime, it was hard to believe the boarder in your house was a spy. Spies happened to other people, whom she read about but did not know. They happened in books and movies. There was a radio show on after Gabriel Heatter, called "Watch That Spy."

She was in a black place, paralyzed, unable to breathe. Her chest pounded in the thickening dark. She was a speck, a cinder, tiny, lost. She was powerless. She struggled to find an answer. In her mind she saw a pinpoint of light, and it grew and Da's face was in that light. She never should have let him continue to sell supplies. Her mother would have stopped him. She would press him now, make him tell about Ryker. No more excuses. No more games. Something horrible, which had come to the island with Ryker, waited just beyond the blackness. If she didn't force him to leave, it was going to come out.

Her watch read three AM. The first ferry would leave in four hours.

She headed home at a trot.

The intruder burst around the side of the tree and Lieutenant John Mariani barked, "Who the hell are you?" In the dark, he did not see the man's face and assumed him to be another soldier. But this spot was Mariani's private place. He'd been interrupted and he was embarrassed.

Everyone assumed he was nothing more than a pudgy Brooklyn wise ass, with a ready leer for the ladies. Well, he was sensitive too, even he didn't show it. He'd never told them, afraid of their laughter, that he wrote poetry.

He'd never told them that to a tough slum kid, this island was paradise. The only birds he'd ever seen, until age eighteen, were pigeons. He'd never seen a cow until the troop train brought him north. "Ocean" had meant 200,000 pasty bodies blocking his view of Coney Island Beach. "Harbor" was a greasy brine filled with floating condoms.

Mariani had worked on his poem for three months now. He called it "Oh, Beauteous Island."

He'd been out here since dusk, composing in his head, trying to think of a stanza lauding the island woodcock. Then the intruder had burst out of the dark. Mariani realized the man wore a black sweater, not a uniform.

He went for his holster, rising and fumbling with the snap; felt a punch and a tearing sensation in his neck, a slithering—odd because the intruder stood ten feet away, hand outstretched, fingers splayed. And now, at the bottom periphery of Mariani's vision, he saw the protruding bone handle and felt the weight of the knife. A red mist was spraying. The gurgling sound was his own. The heat pain started and his hands danced in front of his face. He thought, But I was only writing poetry, as if that were an argument against what was happening, and the pain grew very bad then, but in a way, it seemed as unreal as the rushing earth.

Ryker, running forward, caught the body before it fell. He pushed it onto the fallen tree. The dying soldier pounded him on the shoulders. Ryker slammed his head back, over the curve of the tree. The weight of Ryker's chest muffled the snap of the neck.

Ryker withdrew the knife and pressed his forearm against the pumping wound. Even dead, the man sprayed the ground. Ryker pulled off his sweater and wrapped the neck, squeezed the knot. The blood was hot on his face.

The moon touched the highest tree in descent toward dawn. If the soldier's body were found, the base would go on alert. If Ryker somehow managed to get the dead man outside of the base, he would never finish his job tonight. Digging was noisy and out of the question. Besides, guards might appear momentarily.

Ryker forced his breathing back to normal. He was cold without his sweater, but at least the forest seemed quiet. He knew nothing of this island's secret hiding places. A seemingly isolated spot might be overrun in the morning.

He lifted the limp body over his shoulders, making sure no blood dripped. Bent under the weight, he swayed out of the clearing. The soldier had soiled himself in death, and Ryker frowned at the smell. He waded in the stream, careful not to splash. The water felt icy. Even if the soldier's blood were discovered in the clearing, and the troops brought in dogs, Ryker would be able to fool them now.

His own tiredness disgusted him. *Forty years old*, he thought. *The body fails.* He stepped from the water. Like an altar, an immense V-shaped oak blocked his path. Ryker took one deep breath and lifted the body, with his shaking arms, onto the V. Dead men were incredibly heavy. Ryker climbed up after the man. The sweater still blocked the blood flow. A spasm immobilized Ryker's knee, but it passed.

Sweating, working quickly, he removed his own belt and the Sam Browne belt belonging to the soldier. He tied the belts together to form a harness. He propped the body against one slanting trunk and looped the harness under the arms.

It was a good thing he'd remembered this tree. It rose away from him in a series of thick, leafy boughs. With immense effort, Ryker climbed from bough to bough, hauling the body with the harness. When he was finished, he was thirty feet above the ground. He wedged the still-warm lieutenant between two branches, onto a small natural platform. Rigor mortis would lock the body in place.

Ryker sniffed the bark as he descended. He was relieved to smell no blood.

Base headquarters lay to the north. Ryker broke into a trot. At length he saw a light ahead. Spread below a wooded rise, bathed in moonlight, the parade ground lay in a vulnerable bowl, deserted, bounded by the wooden prefabs and radio shack, the barracks and tree-covered battery. The thirty-foot-high steel doors looked permanently open. A guard shadow moved across the spilling light.

He'd hated having to use the knife. Hands would have been cleaner, but the soldier had been too far away for a quiet kill with hands. Only the knife in the throat had stopped the lieutenant's cry.

Ryker saw, in the moonlight, that his hands were covered with blood, and he felt the dry flaking on his face too. The clearing in the woods would be soaked. *Rain*, he prayed. The sky was clear but the weather changeable. He knew how to take the base now, but the problem was reaching the Kelly house without being seen. The sky was lightening. The town would wake up. If a single islander saw Ryker this early, before he reached home, he was finished.

THIRTEEN

"HE'S NOT ON THE ROAD and he's not in his room. Where is Ryker?"

They faced off on opposite ends of the sofa, Corrice and Michael Kelly. A single, glass-domed lamp cast greenish shadows on the buck's head over the fireplace and the hulking black piano in the middle of the room. It was left from the party.

Da wore red flannel pajamas and a faded brown robe.

Corrice had not removed the heavy sweater she'd worn while following Ryker.

Their voices were soft against the ticking of the grandfather clock. The hands read 4:40. On the white porcelain face, the cherubic sun was rising.

Da said, "The last boarder used to walk at night, too. Too excited to sleep."

"A 'walk' isn't the same thing as disappearing into the woods, Da."

He winked. "Who knows what evil lurks in the hearts of men, eh? My daughter knows."

In the glass clock case, the swinging pendulum sliced her

reflected head, passed over her shoulders. "You're not funny," she said. She was absolutely rigid.

"The only night I get to sleep. Saturday." With an exaggerated flourish Michael Kelly raised his hands high. "Lord, has this poor widower done something to offend you?" He cocked his ear toward the ceiling. "I *gave* to the seaman's fund, I promise." He nodded, glancing slyly at Corrice. "She's turnin' red, Lord. I think she's holding her breath."

"Stop playing around!"

"A man's vital juices drain when he's asleep. Ah," he said, opening a red wooden box by the fireplace. He already had a glass in his hand. "Man's best friend."

She said, "*You* brought him here."

"Darling. Darling. He's a tourist."

"You're responsible for getting his pass."

"Do you want me to show you his letter? Where did I put that letter? Your Ma boarded his pal. Powers. From Chicago. Remember?"

She fixed on the little glass sea captain on the window, yellow slickered, the glass milkmaid, the glass cat. Everything in this room seemed breakable. Had the party been only last night?

"Where," she said, "is Ryker?"

"Talking to a wall, that's what I'm doing." He yawned mightily and she retorted, "You'll never make Broadway if you don't do it right. You have to let out more air."

"Insults," he said, rising. "I'm going back to sleep."

"I found the radio."

For an instant, his confident expression broke into a jumble of disconnected pieces. She said, "In the basement. Last night." Hollow, he replied, "The radio."

"At the party." Her jaw throbbed. He was trying to rally. She hoped he would. She was about to hurt him and she wanted him strong.

"The radio isn't what it seems," he soothed.

"Ryker. Tell me what he's doing here."

He put the glass down a little too hard. A note of pleading entered his voice. "Trust me, okay?"

"Trust what? That you're working on the boat in the basement? Or that you aren't selling supplies? Tell the truth."

"The radio . . . I'm not . . ." The normally jovial lines around his mouth had gone flat, the worry close to the surface, pushing out. "Listen to me. I can't tell you what's going on. If I tell you, you're involved."

Strong men, she thought. Is there really such a thing? "I'm already involved," she said. He picked up his whiskey, rotated it, put it down without drinking. He said, "Corrice," but didn't add anything else. She said, "I don't trust you. I love you, but there isn't any trust."

Orange dawn touched Da's face. She had never, in nineteen years, seen him at a loss for words. He was showing vagueness, disconnection, as if he were drunk, yet he had consumed only one glass of whiskey. He spread his fingers over his knees and stared down at the webbing.

"The whole thing," Corrice demanded. "Where is he?"

When Da looked up this time the fight was gone from his face. Suddenly, she felt frightened.

"I don't know," he said.

A spasm ripped her stomach. She stiffened at the sound of a car outside, but the noise passed. The truth must be pretty bad if Da didn't even know Ryker's location. She said, "They contacted you about him, right?" He didn't answer. She'd been frustrated by his evasiveness for months.

She repeated, "Right?" Slowly, he nodded. She said, "They told you he was coming." A nod. "Didn't they tell you *why* he was coming?"

"They told me—" he started to say, then the porch creaked. They stopped talking and watched the front hallway. They listened for the opening door. When nothing happened he spread his hands helplessly. "They said he was coming to find out some . . . some things."

"What things?"

His hands trembled. He hid them in his lap. "About ships. In the harbor. They said I wouldn't know what to look for." His voice became rushed. "Jail! I didn't want to go! They'd tell about me!" He was gasping. "It was nothing important, what he was going to do. He would only stay a few days."

He added, miserably, "And what would have happened to you?"

"Did they pay?"

He didn't say anything. She said, low, "Did they pay you?" She began to feel cruel. "How much money did you take?" The morning light was growing stronger and she shut off the lamp, yanked it on again, laughed angrily. "We don't have to worry about electric bills now! Turn on all the lights! We can eat in Portland! Buy a car! Isn't that wonderful? Isn't that the best thing you ever heard in your life?"

"Stop. Please. I'm sorry."

"Aren't you proud? Where did you hide the money? The boat? The basement, maybe, with your goddamn radio?"

He was cringing, as if warding off blows.

He started to sob.

"Da, Da." She was paralyzed at first. Then she went to

him, cradled the wet, streaked face. He smelled of sleep and pumice soap. He'd rubbed his coarse beard against her cheeks when she was little, making her screech with delight. She wrapped her hand around his finger, like a baby.

"I didn't mean it. I was angry." Her mother would have known how to handle him. He'd blustered and pretended these last few months, but at bottom he'd been afraid. She loathed herself for hurting him. And Ryker, she hated Ryker. She saw herself pulling the heavy steel trigger of Da's shotgun.

Da muttered, "Cousins. In Ireland. But they're family."

"What are you talking about?"

"There's fishing in Canada." Firmly, "I'll go there."

"Da?"

"No one will blame you if I go. The money's in the basement." He ran his hands through his hair. "Like waking from a drunk," he said.

She shook him. "They'd follow you. Think about Ryker. Ryker's on the base!"

"I'll tell Thomas the truth. He'll know you weren't involved."

"You're not talking to Tom." Her voice sounded firmer than she felt. "You're not leaving and you're not going to jail. We'll think. Together. Think something out." But her high, keening rage was already in decline. He wasn't moving. He was just sitting, watching. The lines in his face had rearranged themselves to suit his old age.

The clock chimed six AM. The little sun face was fully visible now, inside the glass.

Ryker couldn't stay away all day.

What am I going to do?

In the kitchen, she made tea to steady herself. The water

steamed and bubbled. She could see, through the open doorway, Da's arm, on the chair. And one slipper. Framed.

Under her breath, so that he could not hear her, she said, "I'll take care of you."

Parents become our children, she thought.

Ryker turned boldly onto the Kellys' front walk. He'd washed his hands and face hours ago, in the stream. He'd waited until nine AM to return. At nine AM, his appearance in the village would not arouse suspicion. The porch groaned under his weight. He heard voices inside.

Corrice, who had been burning something in the fireplace, straightened quickly and smoothed down her dress. Her face looked scared and defiant. The father seemed curiously indifferent or lackadaisical, sitting in an overstuffed chair, wearing a frayed cardigan and flannel shirt. A mug of tea steamed at his side.

The loud ticking of the clock mingled with the hiss of flames.

Ryker advanced to rub his hands at the fire. "Next time I go for a walk, I'll wear a sweater." He still had goose pimples from the wait.

"You did wear a sweater," Corrice said. "I saw you when you left."

Ryker laughed. "That was the late-night walk. I got up early and went out again. I can't get enough of this island."

"You better stop lying," Corrice said. Her voice was so menacing, Ryker quieted. She looked into the fire, seemingly satisfied that whatever she was burning was obliterated. "Sit down," she said. Ryker picked the chair closest to the door and the kitchen. The phone was in the kitchen.

Corrice said, "Everyone has been lying to me. I'm not

listening to more lies." At her sides, her fists were white. "My father told me about you." Her head was low, like a fighter. Ryker didn't trust the father's lack of emotion. He couldn't tell if something was building in Kelly, or if something had died. If he worked it right, he could reach them both. The closed window would muffle sound.

Forcing himself to lean back, he said, "The truth, then. But how about some coffee? It's cold out there."

"Where did you go last night?"

"We'll talk. But I need something warm, okay? Want me to get it myself? I don't know where anything is."

She glared. Her path to the kitchen brought her a foot from his splayed boots. His head rolled, following her. Casually, he rose, making sure the father stayed put. They would be in separate rooms now. When she lit the stove she said, blowing out the match, "I know what you're thinking. That you're going to do something to us."

"You should write for the pictures," Ryker said. The clock began to chime.

"You're not going to do anything," she said. "This is a small island. In forty minutes I'm supposed to be at the church, for the scrap drive. At eleven, the Lions come for the piano. For the talent show. Da has to help. If we're gone, everyone looks to you. When people say they are going to do something here, they do it. Our boat is moored. The kids who play on the dock couldn't have seen us board the morning ferry. So where are we, if we aren't where we're supposed to be?"

Ryker said, dryly, "You have quite an imagination."

A low breeze came through the kitchen screen. The day was warming. Corrice said, "Sugar?"

"Milk, please."

"Da, you want some tea?"

There was dreariness in the voice that answered, "No tea."

"Go back into the living room and sit down, won't you, Mr. Ryker? I'm not going to use the phone. Yet."

Ryker eased himself down in the plush recliner. When she came back he said, "I don't see any police." She stepped away quickly after putting down the cup. She was almost pulling off her tough act. But her eyes were wide and Ryker sensed fear. That was the only encouraging part of the situation. She said, "I want to give you time to leave. The evening ferry."

The coffee was real, it would cost a fortune in Berlin. Ryker addressed the father. "Children. No respect, eh? How old is she, eighteen?"

Animation livened the pale blue eyes. "Fuck you."

Ryker said, "You took the money."

"And I burnt it," Corrice said. "We don't want any part of you anymore." Flames wove in the fireplace. "You were blackmailing him. Anyway, what happened before isn't important."

Ryker reclined in the chair, watching the smoke rise. Little bits of glowing green. "Pretty generous," he said, looking Corrice full in the face. "The terrible enemy. All yours. Then you let me go."

Her mouth formed a tight line. He tossed one foot over the arm of the chair. "You don't tell your boyfriend about me. You don't phone the police. Very unselfish of you. But you might as well have kept the money, because I'm not leaving."

She caught her breath. It was a little sound but he heard it, a gasp. When she started to edge toward the kitchen he said, "I stay until tomorrow. Go ahead. Call them. But you won't call them. Because if they come for me" —he nodded at her father— "he goes too." Ryker smiled, relieved he'd found a hook and was not going to have to kill them. Islanders or no islanders, he would have killed them both He said, his voice filled with respect, "It was a very, very good bluff."

She was looking at her shoes. He said, "So! I need to stay an extra day. No one will be hurt. I promise. I'm collecting information, information, that's all. To be used far from here. But I haven't even been able to find it and I'm starting to think it isn't here. You want me on the evening ferry. I want to give myself one more day. Twenty-four hours, that's all." He made his voice gentle. "You tried your best."

He said, "More coffee?" Her shoulders drooped and she went into the kitchen. Ryker heard the rattle of dishes. He'd lied because he didn't want her following him tonight. He heard water gurgling and the tinkle of spoons. He heard a door open, a hollow scraping. When the shotgun barrels came through the door he started to get up. Corrice said, "Uh uh." He sat down again. Her face was all shiny and desperate.

"What are you doing with that?" Ryker asked.

"Isn't it obvious?"

"Not to me."

"You tried to rob us," she said. "You tried to rape me."

Ryker looked her up and down. "Sure. All that blood. Your dress torn."

Corrice said, "Not the ferry tomorrow. The ferry tonight. I don't know what you're doing here but I don't want you to finish it." Ryker grunted and laced his fingers behind his head. He sighed. He said, "Sorry. I don't believe you'll fire that. If I did, I would have been behind your father when you came out of the kitchen. Put it away. I can't have you thinking I can be threatened."

Corrice shook her head. "You had no idea I had a gun."

Ryker shrugged and picked up the newspaper.

There was a knocking at the door. Heiden's voice cried, from outside, "Get up! It's a beautiful morning!"

"The wonderful thing about democracy," Ryker said, looking at the door, "is that it gives you so many options." The shotgun started to tremble. The twin hammers were drawn back. "Choices. Choices. Think about your dad."

FOURTEEN

$\longmapsto\bullet\longmapsto$

THE WAVERING BORES of the shotgun did not leave Ryker's face. Slowly, they lowered. Corrice's mouth was working but all she said was, "You!" She sounded tired. Ryker suggested, in a gentle, coaxing voice, "Why don't you put that away?" She shuffled back to the kitchen.

From outside, Heiden called, "Casco Bay tours! Leaving in five minutes for bee-utiful Captains Island!" When Corrice led him into the living room Ryker thrust out his jaw, in a friendly parody of a fighter. "Well, well," he said. "Jack Dempsey."

Heiden blushed. "Are you talking about me or you? Corrice, how about a drive around the island? I don't have to meet Mariani for another hour."

To Ryker, he explained, "Last rehearsal. The Battery MacAllister piano-drum band."

To Corrice's father he said, "You sick or something?"

"No. Yes." Kelly squeezed his eyes. "Headache."

"You should sleep more, Da," Corrice said. Then, to Heiden, "He worked on the boat all night."

Heiden said, "Work, work. I'd like to see those blueprints sometime. Maybe you could show them to me."

"Why?" Kelly asked.

Ryker interrupted. "What will you play in the show, Tom?"

"Ellington. Waller." He grinned. "Heiden."

"I can't wait for tonight."

Corrice said, "Tom, I can't go with you. There's a scrap pickup this morning. But Mr. Ryker would love a drive, I'm sure. Wouldn't you, Mr. Ryker? After all," she said, looking Ryker full in the face, "he hasn't seen any of our island yet."

Ryker gave a thin little laugh. "I think Tom had a different kind of drive in mind. Young love. Sun and beach."

"He'll live," Corrice observed wryly.

Heiden said, "I don't know. The doctor prescribed female companionship."

"After the show." Corrice seemed to have brightened since suggesting the Heiden/Ryker excursion. She raised herself on her toes to kiss Heiden's cheek. "I know I've acted strange the last couple of days. I'm better now."

His eyes shone with pleasure. "Go ahead, Mr. Ryker," Corrice said. Ryker said, "Oh, call me John." Heiden said, "Let's go," and Ryker went upstairs for his jacket. He was exhausted but the ride would cut his scouting time today.

She had gone through his suitcase. He could tell because the hair was missing. He racked his brains. She'd passed up the opportunity to call the police, so why did she want him out of the house?

Outside, Heiden slammed the jeep into gear. "Our impregnable fortress in Maine," he said. "Just tell me where you want to go."

In the village, Ryker noted the number of homes and the distance between them. He counted boats in the cove. He guessed which carried radios. The church steeple, the highest point in town, reminded him of the gutsy pastor in Norway. Heiden said, "One or two homes are empty. Some of the summer people are away."

Ryker scattered questions through the conversation. "Do the fishermen work every day?" "Is this the only road in the village?"

"A couple of dirt roads cut in from the middle of the island."

"Oh," Ryker said. "*Three* roads."

"Jeremiah's probably down by the caves. Working on his submarine."

From the junk ocean surrounding Jeremiah's house, Ryker and Heiden made their way to the forest and cliff. A rocky footpath descended toward a green inlet. Pines sprouted from the cracked granite. Rose-hip bushes clawed for a perch. Below, by a wooden shed and jutting dock, an undershirted man leaned into the open hatch of a green, steel, slug-shaped machine.

Dark, low caves rose from the inlet and echoed with slapping water. Beyond the narrow headlands, the sea shimmered deep blue. Close up, the submarine, raised on blocks, resembled an oil tank car that had been guillotined in half. The top front of the turret, now the front of the whole mechanism, had been cut out and replaced with thick glass. Eight-foot, jointed mechanical arms protruded from the bottom, and rested like crab pincers upon the ground.

"For salvage," Heiden boasted. "Jeremiah made it himself."

The figure straightened at their voices. Close up, he had a skeptical middle-aged baby face. He wore rubber boots and carried a blowtorch. "You Kelly's boarder?"

The interior of the sub resembled a bathtub. Its white

curving floor had room for two men if one stood in the
turret and the other lay down. Ryker's mind churned with
possibilities. "Gasoline engine?" he asked.

Leeds's eyes widened with pleasure. "Designed it myself," he said, unfastening rivets.

The only written directions inside the chamber consisted
of scrawled words, in black paint—OPEN. OPEN. CLOSE—
beside valves that Ryker guessed had come from the ap-
pliance graveyard surrounding the house. The gauges were
unlabeled. He figured they indicated depth and pressure.

Jeremiah was saying, "Here's an idea for another invention!"

Ryker looked past the calm inlet, at the cobalt-blue sea.
"How far can you go in this thing?" he asked.

They left the jeep by the road and walked to the edge
of the island. To the north, ocean and sky merged into the
same inhospitable grey. "Rain this afternoon," Heiden pre-
dicted. Half a mile away, in the Hussey Strait, a convoy
steamed toward Portland, merchantmen and cruisers moving with unreal slowness, wallowing dinosaurs under the
guns.

Ryker envisioned Axel in the American bunker, pulling
the firing rope. He saw the belch of flame and felt the
earth's vibration. The shell whistle receded. Beneath a flaming corona, the lead ship slid into the sea. Axel pulled the
rope again. With a single thunderous crack, the second
ship split in two. The gun swiveled. Black smoke billowed.
Bobbing sailors shrieked in burning oil. By the time the
Americans understood their own battery was attacking them,
the convoy would be wreckage, dying ripples on Casco Bay.

"I said, do you play anything?" Heiden was looking long

into Ryker's face. "Guitar? Harmonica? It's a pretty informal show."

Ryker shrugged. "I don't have much talent."

"Oh, everybody has a special talent. Sports, painting. What is it with you?" Heiden's voice seemed amiable enough. He added with a flash of inspiration, "Hunting."

Ryker grinned. "I'm hopeless."

A few moments later Heiden said, "Are you going to stay in Detroit now that the factory burnt down?"

The bastard's quizzing me. "Maybe, maybe. I'm thinking of moving back East."

"You have family in Detroit?"

"Nobody."

"Steering wheels. You made steering wheels, right?"

"Windshields."

"Oh yeah," Heiden said, "Windshields."

"I think I'll watch the ships awhile," Ryker said. "It sure is beautiful here."

Heiden looked at his watch. "I'm late. Mariani will be mad. You sure I can't take you back to the house?" He walked to the jeep and waved. "Tonight!" He drove off. In the woods, Ryker found a glassy cattail pond. He lay on a sun-heated boulder. A dragonfly hovered overhead, against the vine-covered willows and dark green oaks.

The muscle spasm returned to his arm. He told himself he would quit working after Captains Island. With the money from this job plus his funds in the bank, he could hire men, maybe even the Austrians, for Asia. It was funny that the Austrians were the closest people he could think to bring.

There had been a girl a few years ago. He'd lived with her for months. A plump blonde, a filmmaker for the government. She'd had a nice figure, expensive tastes, and an acrobatic and inventive nature. Bormann's plundered Rubens reminded him of her. She'd never asked about his work. He couldn't remember why he'd left her.

He wondered where she was, then decided it was stupid to think about someone he'd known so long ago.

He yawned. He entertained himself with an image of unzipping Corrice's skirt. A little American peasant, that's what she was: fiery, fiery. He saw himself running his hands along her thighs, onto the pit of her belly, grasping the small, rounded breasts. Her legs wrapped around him. She bucked and raked his back.

The scene changed. He saw Corrice standing over the smashed radio in her basement, a hammer in her hand.

"Shit," he said. He sat up. So that was why she'd wanted him out of the house.

How was he going to contact the Austrians now?

You'll find another radio. You haven't slept in two days.

It was so peaceful here. He unbuttoned his shirt and peeled the flaps from his skin. The air had warmed considerably since dawn. He opened his mouth to the nourishing sun.

The cattail pond became a river, the oaks high palms. Ryker was surprised because he hadn't called up the dream and it had never come by itself before. Hazy faced, the jungle rowers beat time. They never finished the race in his vision. He watched, unarmed, the Walther not necessary, not with his villagers, his islanders.

Peaceful sleep reached to envelop him. He frowned lightly. He had not meant to call the Asians *islanders*.

"Where the hell is Mariani?" In the narrow church, the Lions unfolded tables and stacked programs by the door. Bunting looped over rows of pews. An oil painting over the piano showed Jesus's arms outstretched over sailors in a storm. The sailors rowed a dinghy against ten-foot waves. Heiden rapped impatiently on Mariani's snare drum. "He's never late."

He called the base from the rectory. The sergeant who answered said, "He's not in his room and he's not in the mess. He didn't show up at the guns this morning."

"But he never misses rehearsal."

"He ain't here, Lieutenant."

"Ask around. Anybody see him last night or this morning?"

The sergeant called back. "Schroeder saw him."

"Put Schroeder on the phone."

"I just *think* I saw him," Schroeder corrected. "Last night. On the base."

Heiden called the main gate. The guard had not seen Mariani this morning. The night sentry was in Portland, on leave, and would not return until evening.

Heiden drove to the dock. The kids told him no one had boarded the morning ferry.

Savage stomped around his office. "He's AWOL." He pounded his fist into his palm. "The whole island will know about it tonight."

Heiden said, "I'm afraid something may have happened to him."

"You think so?" Savage looked hopeful. Accidents were preferable to embarrassment.

"He never misses a rehearsal. Nobody saw him leave the island or even the base. Why don't I take some men and look for him?"

Savage asked in horror, "On the whole island?"

"The base, to start. The woods and the cliffs."

Savage considered a moment. "Okay, just the base. But Pulski will do it." He jabbed his finger at Heiden's chest.

Suddenly he looked angry. "You have something else to do."

"Sir?"

"You don't have any idea what it is, do you? Do you, Lieutenant? Two months ago. Think back. I gave you an order you decided to ignore."

"Uh oh."

"That's right. Mrs. Hudson called. Furious. She wants to see you today. You still haven't apologized."

"I'm sorry, sir. I'll do it. But Mariani is more important. I know the woods, Pulski doesn't. Suppose Mariani's hurt. There's a better chance of finding him if I'm there."

"You know what's important? My fucking orders are important. Not only will you apologize to Mrs. Hudson for the flower bed, you will apologize for taking so long to apologize. Do you hear me? Tell me that you hear me. Say, 'I hear you, Major. I'm running as fast as I can to the Hudson house.'"

Savage threw himself into his chair. "See?" he said. "You get to have a rehearsal."

The storm broke in midafternoon. Soldiers in olive-drab slickers moved through the woods. The bark grew dark and slippery around Mariani's body. Leaves stuck to the sodden uniform. Pools formed under the haunches and droplets streaked the pasty face. When a gust tossed the heavy branches, the corpse slid slightly in the boughs. The open eyes stared straight down at the ground.

Voices called, from the forest, "Lieutenant! Lieutenant Mariani!"

Heiden's voice was not among them.

The rain kept up, steady, indifferent.

After a while, the body shifted again.

◊   ◊   ◊

"Come in, Lieutenant."

Standing in the doorway of the Hudson mansion, she wore a tightly wrapped lavender silk bathrobe that accentuated her slim body. Her perfume was a sweet, subtle presence. "I was asleep," she said. Heiden had caught a glimpse of her at the upstairs window as he came up the walk. He'd spent the last two hours looking for Mariani on the civilian side of the island, asking questions and walking in the woods. He said, "I came to apologize." She reached to touch his shoulder. "You can do that inside."

The front door muffled the drumming rain. "The judge is in Boston," she remarked. In the oak and redwood hallway, severe-faced bankers sneered down from the walls. The living room was sunken. A plush carpet lapped the edge of the marble fireplace. She leaned against the cool stone, her expression open, amused.

Heiden, stiff in the archway, said, "I'm sorry I—"

She had a light, mocking tone. "I'm not the major. You can sit when you talk to me."

Her legs, outlined against the pressing fabric, seemed longer than he'd remembered. The sofa enveloped him. "I'm sorry about your flower bed," he said. "And that I took so long to come."

"Oh, don't even think about that. I was in a bad mood that day." He thought, So why'd you call Savage this morning? When she stretched, her whole body seemed naked. "You want a drink," she said. She swayed across the rug. He wasn't sure if the tinkle he heard was ice or the silvery ripple of laughter. Her nails, painted red, lingered on the whiskey glass. The perfume seemed stronger up close. She said, "Relax."

She leaned back beside him. "Maybe I should be the one apologizing," she said. "I forget sometimes. It isn't easy, the war. When I grew up there weren't any soldiers here. But you soldiers would rather be home, too."

Heiden said, "Maybe we were both wrong. I didn't have to lose my temper either."

"I like making up after fights, don't you? The judge and I used to fight and make up all the time when we got married. Then we stopped making up." She laughed harshly. "Then we stopped fighting."

Uncomfortable, Heiden said, "I just wanted you to know how sorry I was about the flowers."

A ripple of impatience marred the smooth features. "I heard you had a fight with Corrice at her party."

Heiden jerked. "It wasn't exactly a fight."

Her green eyes fastened on his, over the edge of the tumbler.

"We'll make up," he announced firmly. "Tonight."

She stood and said gaily. "Of course you will." She extended her hand. "I'll show you the house."

"Ma'am, there's something important I have to do on the base."

Her voice took on an edge. "To appease the wounded party, you must suffer her tedious chatter. The tour. Dry, dry men," she said, indicating the portraits. "These stairs were redone. The carpet, why don't you take off your shoes an I feel the carpet?"

"Beautiful house, Mrs. Hudson."

"Built in seventeen sixty-seven." She showed him the guest room, the judge's bedroom, the library. Her own bedroom was wide, cheerful and yellow, filled with pillows. She sat on the brass-railed bed and patted the mattress.

"Let's stop pretending," she said. Pretending seemed to be an effort for her. "Sit down."

He didn't move. She said, "Don't tell me you don't want it. That little twit doesn't have to know."

The bathrobe was loose and he glimpsed her body inside, taut and beautiful. She leaned back. She crossed her legs.

"You're hard as a rock," she said.

"I'm not hard." The rain drummed on the window. He added before walking out, "You're looking at my keys."

Ryker pushed the skiff off from shore. At dusk, the rain had stopped but the cove was blanketed with purple-white mist. At ten feet out, he could scarcely see the edge of the circular cobble beach. The lobster and pleasure boats, the dock, the headlands: all were obscured. He inserted the oars in their greased locks. Upside down, the dinghy had been lying on the rocks.

Coded foghorns bellowed in Portland Harbor. Voices floated out of the mist. On the shore road, the islanders headed for the talent show.

He'd been right about Corrice smashing the radio, but there would be other shortwaves on the boats.

Ghostly, the first vessel took shape, a sloping lobsterman. The gunwale slid past, faded, disappeared. A white-sheen wall loomed, coated slick with fog. Ryker tied the skiff and climbed onto the deck of the power yacht. Fog swirled after him into the cabin. The pinprick beam of the pen flashlight illuminated teak walls, a gleaming wall barometer, an ice bucket. The radio was clamped to the ceiling, above the wheel. He adjusted the wavelength. He put on a Maine twang.

"Charlie, where are ya? It's James, Charlie. For the fifteenth time."

He tried again. "The fifteenth time, Charlie. I've been at this for four hours."

He was telling the Austrians to come ashore in four hours, at eleven o'clock, on the part of the island corresponding to section fifteen of the map.

The receiver emitted heavy static. Then Teacher's wry voice gave the prearranged answer. "You're a pain in the ass, James. Over."

Ryker laughed under his breath.

Heiden had asked him, *Do you have any talent?*

And Corrice, brushing her hair in her mirror, raised her eyes to her own reflection. Think about your Da, Ryker had said. She'd given him his extra day and smashed the radio. He didn't know about the third part of her plan.

She and Da would take the Nova tomorrow afternoon. Tonight was out of the question because their absence would be noted at the talent show. They would chug off to Peaks Island. At eight PM, after the ferry left, she would call Ernie at the wharf and find out if Ryker had left. If he had told the truth, if he was gone, they'd return. If not, she'd turn Ryker in by phone. Then the Nova could get them to Canada.

It's just a precaution. He'll leave, he said so. Her mood had vacillated wildly since this morning. She'd saved her father. No, Ryker had beaten her. He would try to kill them just before he left, or they would have to flee. Tonight was her last night on the island.

No again. She'd made the right decision. Tomorrow a little after this time, she and her father would be free.

Her whole body throbbed with building intensity. She felt light, giddy. The night was beautiful, more lovely than she had ever seen it. She chose her best blue dress. She hummed one of Heiden's jazz tunes, fastening the ribbons at her shoulders. She was astonished by her mood switches and she could not wait to see Heiden. She'd been really unfair to him the last few days. He was the best thing in her life.

FIFTEEN

"THERE'S A SPY IN THIS ROOM," announced Jeremiah Leeds. "A HOLLYWOOD TALENT SPY!"

"Ooooooooh," said the audience.

Surprisingly professional lighting colored him red and amber, at the altar. Japanese lanterns swayed over his head. He wore a flower-print button-down and his raised voice carried. The rest of the church was dark.

"We got talent tonight. We got Bing Crosby and we got Kate Smith. We got Glenn Miller and his big band." Laughter erupted from the rows of soldiers cross-legged in the center aisle, pressed, standing, against the walls, and scattered among the islanders in the pews and folding chairs. Leeds cupped his ears toward the "wings," dangling sheets on a clothesline, painted with Tahitian dancing girls. He said, "Crosby can't make it? Huh? We got someone better? Better'n Crosby? No kiddin'! Owen McKlintock playin' 'Chopsticks'? Let's hear it for Owen!"

A voice cried, "Come on, Owen. Play something else for a change!"

In the second row, Heiden laughed and applauded and glanced anxiously at his watch. Beside him, Corrice whispered, "Don't worry. Mariani will be here." She was uncommonly affectionate tonight, and she looked radiant.

He'd spent the afternoon, after leaving Mrs. Hudson, talking to islanders, dropping Mariani's name without indicating he was missing. No one had seen the pudgy artillery lieutenant.

Ryker squeezed down the row to seat himself at Heiden's left. "I miss anything?"

Owen McKlintock had a fleshy, impassive face, baggy clothes, and the blue-veined nose of a drinker. His "Chopsticks" was s-l-o-w.

Leeds announced the "Captains Island Dolls," three seven-year-olds who clustered in a far corner of the stage and murmured "America the Beautiful." In the middle of the song, one girl cried out, pointing at the front row, "Ma, you're *looking!*"

At eight-thirty, the seventy-year-old Turners put a tango record on the Victrola and performed a vaudeville chase scene. Mrs. Turner wielded a broom and Mr. Turner's pants kept falling down.

Bobby Lee Rye played "Swanee River" on his clarinet.

Amid rising boisterousness, the Rosenberg brothers, two privates from Omaha, sang "Hava Nagila" and kicked around the stage like Russians.

Corrice walked through the church three times, to return and whisper, "I can't find him."

Heiden said that Savage could go to hell. He was going to announce Mariani was missing and ask for help. But Savage anticipated him and came down the aisle. He leaned into Heiden's face and reminded him, in a voice filled with bureaucratic menace, that he had better not mention Mariani at all. Savage promised to schedule "military exercises" on the civilian side of the island tomorrow, in reality searches for Mariani.

"He's AWOL," Savage said. "Stop worrying." He winked. "Play your heart out. What's the expression? Break your neck?"

"Break a leg."

"A leg!"

But Heiden was not in the mood to play, particularly not the earthy boogie-woogie he'd rehearsed with his friend. Ryker nudged him. "They're announcing you." To wild applause, he made his way toward the piano. Beyond Corrice, the audience merged into a dark, amorphous mass, wreathed in smoke and blue angular shadow. The piano keys looked amber. He tried a joke. "Sure is dark up here. Anybody got a *flashlight?*"

The laughter rolled in waves. He didn't feel any better and he was going to have to play something. He announced, "A surprise." From the opening brush of the C, he relaxed and began to lose awareness of the audience. The waltz began slowly. The high, narrow church seemed to capture the Chopin and suspend it. The music was light, subdued, the slow section breaking into a quicker run, then dropping back, sad, longing spaced with lonely contemplation. It was a strange kind of waltz, a waltz for one dancer. The foghorns outside punctuated the music with their plaintive, ephemeral wail. Heiden envisioned a last dance for lovers, a faded snapshot, a lone ballerina in a dark auditorium, whirling.

The final note faded into nothingness. Absolute quiet reigned in the dark, smoky church. Half turned at the keyboard, Heiden saw tears streaming down Corrice's face. He'd never seen her looking so beautiful. Her hair spilled in undulating waves. Even the children sat motionless. As if emerging from a daze, Jeremiah, in the first row, leaned back. The crowd broke into individual faces. Mrs. Hudson stood, clapping. Then the church filled with a tumult of applause.

Outside, receiving congratulations, he watched Corrice talking with her father. He'd been right about sensing trouble between them. But they seemed to have resolved themselves, at least for the moment. Bull shoulders lowered, Michael Kelly shuffled away, toward the house. Savage was saying, "We should arrange a concert at Fort McHenry. For the brass!" Corrice came up and he put his arm around her. She returned the gesture. At least one thing was going right tonight.

He whispered to her, "I thought of a place where we might find Mariani." He led her away, towards the woods. It was eleven PM.

The packed torpedo room reverberated with metallic clicks and the drawing of bolts. The Austrians, dressed in black sweaters, folded stocks on their Sten guns and tested the fit of their silencers. They lay the guns in waterproof floatable sealskin bags, along with stock grenades, walkie-talkies, grappling hooks, extra sweaters.

Sten guns were English, but Ryker had demanded them for this mission. Teacher had told the men the story. Otto Skorzeny, who would one day rescue Mussolini from prison in Sicily, had arranged a Sten demonstration for the high command. He concealed his men in a shrub garden and walked the generals through. He told the generals the demonstration would be held on the far side of the garden. But Skorzeny's men rose behind the passing generals and shot off the top six inches of hedge. The generals never heard a thing.

Silence spread when Teacher stood. The black sweater exaggerated his pale lankiness. He planted his feet by the hatch. As always, even in the U-boat, his hands and face were caked with dirt. He wiped wire-rimmed lenses with two fingers.

"Hypothermia," he said in his dry lecture voice, "results when a normally healthy Austrian soldier immerses his body in freezing-cold water. The Austrian's temperature drops to an alarming degree. Valhalla is lovely this time of year. You may wonder why an intelligent Austrian would subject himself to this sort of torture, and yet, in a few minutes, we will find ourselves in a shockingly cold sea."

Teacher replaced the glasses, blinked, removed them again and resumed rubbing the lenses with his fingers. He said, "Herr Ryker, who has vast familiarity with tortures and Austrians, strenuously insisted that the Abwehr supply us with wetsuits for our swim. The Abwehr delivered twenty suits for forty men. Herr Ryker raged, but there was no way to acquire the extra suits and reach the island in time. This U-boat is close enough to the island so that normally the swim would be cold but not dangerous. Characteristically, a problem has arisen.

"The captain reports fog so thick it obscures even the sea from the deck. So how are we to see the island? The answer is, we aren't. The captain has had the goodness to point the front of this vessel in the proper direction, but if we miss the island, twenty of us, the twenty without wetsuits, will freeze. I am an informal man and do not like to wear suits. The rest of you, draw lots.

"Those of you who lose can take hope in two tidbits of

encouragement. We are three hundred kilometers from shore, roughly a fifteen-minute swim. Axel, our secondary-school swimming champion, will lead us with his uncanny sense of direction. And Erhard has designed an invention to help us too."

Erhard's teeth flashed against the grease he'd smeared on his face, to shield him from the cold water. "A simple rope, Teacher, a fisherman's twine, marked for distance." He unraveled some rope. "Twenty meters, sixty. . . We tie the rope to the bow of the U-boat. Axel unwinds it while he swims. If we have not hit land after three hundred meters, Axel uses the taut rope as a fulcrum and swims in an arc until we strike land." The men murmured approval. Erhard said, "From the three-hundred-meter mark, we turn left, on shore, for another hundred meters. We should have then reached the approximate point Herr Ryker specified."

"Thank you, Erhard. Finally, this telegram, allegedly from our adored Führer, is to be read to you. 'Soldiers! Heroes! The eyes of the Third Reich are upon you! Do not falter in this hour of challenge and triumph! You, the first German troops to set foot on the North American continent, will pave the way for glorious victory against the enemies of National Socialism! I salute you! Adolf Hitler.'"

Teacher said, crumpling the paper, "I asked him to come along. He said he had a headache."

When the laughter died, Teacher said, "The three-hundred-meter freestyle competition will begin in ten minutes. All swimmers to the main deck, please." It was midnight.

Ryker froze at a scraping noise behind him. He was in the woods and his eyes swept the fog, his mouth open slightly so as to improve hearing. He moved his head, slowly, right to left. He heard the dripping forest and the foghorns in the bay. He returned his bowie knife to his belt, shoved a thorn branch from his path, and continued into the dark, humid woods.

Inland, the fog still lay thick, but it was thinner than the clotted mass suffocating the coast. He relied on his incredible memory for direction, but still felt as if he had been transported to a primeval version of Captains Island, or another island altogether. Tendrils of mist floated above the willows. Bathed in fog, the larger trees seemed smothered by creepers and vines. Soft, fern-covered earth sucked at his feet.

When he envisioned the Austrians paddling blindly in the sea, he cursed the Abwehr, for the thousandth time, for sending only twenty wetsuits.

He carried a rucksack containing flannel shirts and a hot-water thermos. He'd stolen a few shirts from the Kelly laundry basket. They smelled sweaty but the Austrians might need warmth. He'd found the thermos on a kitchen shelf, beside the flashlight he carried in his hand. It was off at the moment. He wished he had more shirts and thermoses.

He heard the scraping again and halted. The sound stopped too.

Roughly, noisily, he launched himself forward. Sure enough, the crunching and snapping started up, directly behind but slightly farther back. Ryker stopped, retrieved a thick twig, and snapped it. The wet stick made a muffled sound, but it must have carried, because whoever was behind kept coming. A professional would have known from the location of the sound that Ryker had not moved.

Ryker had seen Corrice leave the church with Heiden. They'd walked toward the woods but she could have broken away.

He moved casually, searching for a place to wait. The old oak stood across a clearing. It felt coarse against his face, sodden. The footsteps halted, sounded again but seemed no closer. Ryker envisioned Corrice turning in circles, listening.

He slid off the rucksack, aimed, and let fly. It descended with a crash.

The footsteps hurried forward.

Outlined in the fog, a figure stopped, eight feet away.

It wasn't Corrice, that was for sure. The man was wide-shouldered, bigger even than Ryker. The head inclined forward, listening. The man advanced into the clearing. Ryker saw the shotgun barrel, cradled over the arm.

Pressed against the oak, he slowed his breathing. The footsteps veered in the wrong direction but came close again. The problem was going to be keeping the gun from firing even if the blast missed Ryker.

When the steps were almost upon him, Ryker smelled pumice soap. The shotgun barrel slid into the lower periphery of his vision, close enough to touch.

Simultaneously, three things happened.

Ryker pushed the barrel away and brought the knife up for a belly thrust. No explosion sounded. He'd dislodged the trigger finger.

The man, moving quickly himself, shoved the barrel forward, to strike the incoming knife and knock it from Ryker's grip.

Ryker looked into the face of Michael Kelly.

The shock of recognition slowed him. He was going, with the flat of his hand, for the death spot, when Kelly hit him like an express train, smashing into his neck with both hands, driving him into the tree. Ryker tried to knee him, but the angle was bad and Kelly grunted and squeezed harder. Ryker felt cartilage crunching in his neck. He brought his hands inside the gorilla-sized arms. Kelly's eyes were glazed with rage. Ryker poked them.

With a roar, Kelly dropped back, fumbling at his face, but he stood directly over the shotgun, so Ryker launched himself before Kelly could open his eyes. Kelly went down like a tree. Ryker scrambled up the body but the hands shot out again, with uncanny direction, grabbing and flinging him to one side. Then Kelly was on top of him, squeezing. The man only knew one way to fight. He had the power of a madman.

Ryker had never fought such strength. He brought his fingers up again but Kelly twisted away, squeezing all the while. Ryker tried to slap the ears. He couldn't reach them. He faked a roll to the right and went left. He did not fool Kelly. The world was tilting. Kelly's face loomed, grotesque.

Ryker's groping hands found the flashlight. He brought the light up and switched on the beam in Kelly's face. The hands loosened. Ryker ground the glass into Kelly's face. Debris rained down on him. The air was sweet and cold. The hands came back at him but he rolled viciously, and Kelly threw up his arms.

Ryker lifted the flashlight and brought it down with all his might. Kelly grunted once. Like a child awakened from sleep, he raised his hand vaguely to the back of his skull. Blood oozed from his ears. He fell over.

Ryker finished him with the bowie knife.

Lungs burning, Ryker backed against the tree. He drew great gasps of air. The woods stopped swimming. Kelly lay sprawled, arms across his chest, feet tangled. A leaf fell across his face.

The flashlight lay in bits, shattered beyond repair.

Ryker pulled out the knife and lurched to find the knapsack.

Jeremiah Leeds had been preparing for bed when the light went on in the woods. In his darkened bedroom, the blackout curtain hung open. He wore a long wool nightgown and white sweat socks. He wore a sleeping cap with a red woolen ball on it. He was thinking about how much he enjoyed the talent show, turning back the covers on his hundred-year-old trundle bed, when he thought he saw a glow outside, from the forest near the bluff.

The glow was already gone. He sat in the rocking chair by the window. His thoughts returned to the show. Up on stage, he'd felt like Major Bowes in New York, far away from his junkyard and salvage work. He liked his job, but he had fun pretending one night a year.

The woods remained dark. In reality, he knew the only way he might ever achieve fame would be through his inventions. Someday his inventions would make him known around the world. Hadn't Maine people invented Morse code? Hadn't they given Edison the key to the vacuum tube? There was a fellah over in Portland, a doctor he'd met at Craun's who talked about joining the bones of two people the way you grafted plants. Who could tell? Leeds thought. It might work.

The idea exciting him at the moment was an electrically powered automobile. The car would start using gasoline, but then a generator hooked to the turning wheels would save gas and provide power. People could get more mileage out of their gas coupons.

Rich, Leeds thought. I'll be rich.

The light went on in the woods.

He ran downstairs, instinctively avoiding piled magazines and auto parts littering the darkened stairway. The kitchen smelled of cheddar he had not cleared away. He lifted the mouthpiece and reached to dial.

Then he chuckled and hung up.

"Kids again," he said. "Fool me twice and shame on me."

"Why would Mariani come here?" Corrice asked.

The cottage was a two-story clapboard, freshly painted red and yellow, with a white picket fence. Heiden had showed the house to Ryker this morning and explained it was unoccupied. It stood near the middle of the island, alone on a private drive.

Heiden repeated, in a frustrated, singsong voice, "Why would he come here? Why would he go AWOL? Why would he disappear at all?" The bare porch was swept clean and felt solid underfoot. He pushed open the front door. "Good a place to look as any," he said. He groped for a light switch. It didn't work.

Corrice said, "Wha'd you expect? No one's lived here for ten years."

"But the house is in pretty good condition."

"Owen McKlintock's fixing it up. The owners pay him. I guess they want to sell it."

Heiden called, "Mariani?" He advanced into the center of the boxlike room, which was empty and smelled of wood shavings. "Mariani?" Their eyes adjusted to the darkness. A hammer, pliers, and box of nails had been laid out by the sill. A pile of scrap wood occupied a corner. Heiden shouted, "Where the hell are you!"

"Maybe he did go AWOL," Corrice said.

"Sure, sure. Family emergency."

The kitchen was filled with dust and spider webs. The

pump on the sink creaked, dry. The banister wobbled. Upstairs, Heiden saw a pile of fresh blankets by a bare window. He saw a large bedroom fireplace in the same room, and a pile of logs. A newspaper lay near the fireplace, a comic book, a couple of empty rye bottles. Unlike the rest of the house, this room smelled fresh.

"He must sleep here when he's working."

"Maybe he'll come back tonight," said Corrice.

"No. It's past eleven. The whole island is asleep." Bitterly, Heiden called, "Mariani, you under these blankets? You wedged in the chimney?" They sat on the blankets. Corrice rubbed his neck.

Heiden said, "You have any matches?" He found some on the mantel. In the orange light, her blue-black hair fell in ringlets. He watched the whiteness of her neck against the fabric. At the shoulders, ribbons held up the dress.

"What you played tonight," she said, "was so beautiful."

"First time in public." He moved his hands, as if playing the waltz. He said, "Do you ever have a premonition?" He chuckled. "I forgot who I was talking to. Well, *I* had one tonight. I don't know how to explain it. Sitting there, waiting to go on, everything felt so fragile. Us, the island. But that's stupid, isn't it? I mean, aside from Mariani, everything is fine."

The firelight played in her violet slanting eyes. He felt a thickness rise up in him. Corrice insisted, "He *could* have gone AWOL. Everybody has secrets."

Dryly, "Right." Heiden tossed a log on the fire. It hissed and began to smoke. "The funny thing about secrets," he said, "is that when you finally get around to telling them, they seem so unimportant that you wonder why you kept them secret in the first place. I thought about what you said. At your party."

At the window, he leaned his forehead against the cool pane. He watched the fire's reflection slide back and forth, in its blackness.

"You asked about my family. I never see them."

She had crossed her legs and arranged herself comfortably. "I told you they live in Washington," he said. "I didn't tell you my father is a senator. I don't like people to know, especially in the army. They'd make a fuss. He's fixed it so I can't leave this island. I'm telling it badly. I'd better tell you about my brother."

He joined her on the blanket, extracted his wallet, and showed a picture of the man by the sailboat, a smaller version of the photo on his desk. "I was a kid when Scott sailed to England. Alone. In my family, that's the kind of thing you were supposed to do. They were all adventurers: climbers, divers. The house was filled with trophies and newspaper articles. My uncles, my father, all of them. But my brother, my brother never came back.

"I was ten. That day I was playing in the living room. We had a huge house near the Senate. Tremendous picture window. A townhouse. I could see the trolley go by in the street. I had this wooden boat and I pretended that I was Scott." Heiden smiled. "My hero. I was sailing the ocean too." Heiden made a whistling noise. "Wind in the sails.

"My parents came into the living room. They were always a little stiff but that day their faces were hard. My mother said, 'Scott went away.' I smiled. 'I'm going to England too!' My father picked up the boat and wrapped it under his arm. All of us started to cry then. It's funny. I don't remember them telling me more, just that we were crying." Heiden grew quiet. "They changed after that."

Corrice stroked his hand, her skin warm. "Changed?"

"His funeral was a year later. My mother wanted it even

though he'd never been found. The family has a plot, in Virginia. Two hundred years of Heidens. It was raining. Other senators came, reporters, my uncles. My father had aged. He really looked like a senator now, trim and white, but he was sad inside, dead. My mother's eyes were blazing. I didn't understand why she seemed so angry.

"Afterwards, in the limousine, my uncles tried to make her feel better. They were big men, like Ryker. They told her Scott might be alive. People disappeared for long periods and then showed up. Suddenly she exploded. She'd always been quiet, Southern. When she got mad she didn't show it. But now she was screaming. Didn't they understand why she wanted the funeral? The funeral was for *me*, for Tom! Scott was dead! She wanted me to know it! She was shaking me, yelling into my face. *'He's under the water. The fish are eating him. He doesn't even look like Scott anymore!'*

"She told me I was never going to have a boat. I wasn't going to climb, like my uncles. I wasn't going to hunt. She blamed my father for my brother's death. He didn't have the spirit to fight her. The trophies disappeared from Scott's room. She was crazy then. She didn't stop with the hunting. I couldn't go on camping trips. I couldn't join the Boy Scouts, the goddamn Boy Scouts. The Boy Scouts, for Chrissakes. I felt like a prisoner."

Heiden scowled. "Who can live like that? When I was sixteen I got wild. Stole a car. Ran away. I even hit a cop. My father took care of it. When they got stricter I became wilder. What did it accomplish, though? The truth is, they'd won."

"I don't understand," Corrice said. She rubbed his neck again.

"Well, I ran away, but did I climb the mountain? No, I went joyriding in a neighbor's lousy car. Fear. It's an interesting word. Writers write about big fears: war, famine. But I'd been infected with little fears, of difference, passion. Of risk. Smothering fears. Sleep, that's the safe thing. Christ, am I rambling."

Corrice said, "You weren't rambling. You were talking about my favorite subject: you. Except it bothers me to hear you be so hard on yourself."

The fire warmed his face. He was quiet awhile. Then he said, "I went into academics, detached myself completely. Oh, I liked it. I learned things. I had fun. And I would have been a good professor. I even fell in love. But when Liza died, I decided I'd been hiding in the library. Unfinished business, that's what I had. I decided to do something important, something big. I decided to go to Europe, and fight."

Heiden laughed. "The funny thing is, in a crazy way, maybe I owe them a favor, my parents. For keeping me on this island. I like this place. I feel comfortable, like I've come home. Savage says the guns are obsolete. Even if it's true, I don't care. I'd go to Europe, sure, but I don't need to prove anything anymore. I like being Lieutenant Flashlight, doing my job well."

He sat up. "I thought you had to be someone extraordinary to find contentment. You're so beautiful. You're important to me, that's what I'm trying to say. I'm still not telling it right. I love you. You don't have to say anything. You're right about the secrets, though. No more secrets. They only make trouble."

Her face, while he spoke, had revealed wide ranges of emotion. Fascination, at first, when he discussed his family; surprise, and compassion. Eagerness at hearing him talk. Gladness at his love for the island, but fear too, and he had the fleeting impression he had reminded her of whatever had bothered her the day before. She muttered, "Secrets. They're no good, are they?" She brushed a hair from her forehead with a helpless, childlike gesture. He ached looking at her. Her face had gone pale and unreadable. She was trembling. She had drawn herself up, on the blanket, her back curved like a bow.

The room seemed to close in on him, to shut out the rest of the world. The warmth from the fire crawled up his legs. He saw her face, close and fragrant, molten. She wet her lips with her tongue. Averted, her violet eyes seemed vulnerable, provocative. Her breath came short, audible. She repeated, in a whisper almost blocked by the pounding blood in his head, "No good at all." Every effect in this room seemed designed to heighten her allure: the simpleness, the dark shadows and guttering flames.

When he touched her shoulders her whole body shuddered. "I've never done this before," she said. He started to pull back. Firmly, she brought him forward. "I want to," she said. "I'm just afraid."

He cupped her face and lifted her mouth. She covered his face with kisses, little kisses all over his neck and jaw. She ran her fingers over his face, tremulously, like a blind person.

When he pulled one of the ribbons holding up her dress, the fabric fell away to reveal her bronze shoulder. It tasted like ginger. She fumbled at his buttons, her boldness delighting him.

The fire compacted but burnt strongly. Her breasts were small, as he had imagined, rounded and firm. She shielded the dark pubic mound with one hand. When he entered her she sucked in her breath and lay quiet a moment. Her eyes seemed gigantic. She moved slowly at first. Then she pulled his head down and her legs came up. She clutched him violently. He saw the moving flesh in broken images, his whiter fingers on her rounded sunken belly, her brown knee raised past his straining hips, her taut thigh muscles, the curved feminine arch of her foot, the sun freckles on her neck, under a lone sliding bead of moisture, glistening.

She said his name over and over.

Afterwards, the guttering light adorned their entwined fingers. They stroked each other. They did not speak. He felt so full, so happy. He had not thought a woman could make him feel this good again. The fire was starting to die. In another minute he would have to feed it. He had not made love in a long time. He was not going to lose Corrice. He was not going to leave her, or let her go.

He chuckled to himself. What was there to worry about? He felt so incredibly, incredibly lucky.

Belly flat on the soaking grass, Ryker stretched over the top of the cliff, inclined his head toward the sea, and listened. The surf lapped below but he could not see it. He heard dripping trees and coded foghorns. He heard rustling in the brush but instinctively knew a small animal made the noise. He did not hear footsteps, or voices, or the splashing of swimmers. In the freezing ocean, the Austrians were late.

Maine seacoast fog is a special kind of fog. It's no light, city fog, but the collective dank spirits of ship collisions, drowned sailors, of kelp-entangled bodies. It's the ghost of every bloated corpse that ever sank beneath the waves.

His scalp was slick from the crawling fog. Even if he had not shattered the flashlight, he had the feeling the swirling grey mass would have diffused the beam and sent it back to him.

He pictured the Austrians, bobbing aimlessly in the flat

night sea, past the invisible island. Maybe they'd gone numb by now. Maybe they could no longer move, the water was so cold. If they were close enough, his cry might bring them.

Should he risk one shout?

He jerked his head. Rubber-soled shoes, that's what he heard. Rubber-soled shoes on the glassy rocks below, splashing in the brackish tidal pools, squishing closer.

Too many people to be guards, he decided.

The footsteps stopped almost directly below. He heard someone mutter, but was unable to make out the voice, or even the language.

He whispered, ready to run if he was wrong, "Teacher!"

Through the fog, the voice hissed, "Get back."

He scrambled away from the edge. Three claw-shaped grappling hooks came hurtling through the fog. One fell back over the side, but returned moments later. Ryker ran forward to wedge the hooks behind rocks. He tugged on each rope and the lines grew taut. Climbing forms materialized, out of the mist. Teacher came over the top first, shivering. His face was filthy, as always. Condensation coated his glasses.

"Is that a thermos?" he said. "We missed the island at first. Ahhh, hot water. You should have been a Saint Bernard." His teeth chattered. The men came over the top in threes. Teacher passed out the shirts and poured hot water. "Immigration control," he said. "Passports please." Six raiders undid their haversacks, pulled out Sten guns, and formed a protective semicircle around the group. Ryker gave the men five minutes to arm and change clothes. "Let's get going," he said.

He led them in single file, through the woods. The fog obscured landmarks. Twice he thought he had lost his way.

When the fence appeared, he signaled them to wait in the bushes.

He scaled the fence alone. He had chosen the oak tree as his ambush spot the night before. His only question now was which direction the sentry would come from, and the sentry solved the problem by whistling as he approached.

Ryker reached out as the man passed, in a single violent motion clamping his hand over the mouth and plunging the knife in deep, into the back. The guard died instantly. Shadows swarmed toward the fence, out of the dark. Ryker had already removed the dead man's coat. Teacher put it on, frowning at the blood. "Goodness gracious, I'll never get this stain out."

Ryker snapped, "You know what to do."

As the main attack body cut diagonally away, through the woods, Teacher took five men and followed the fence toward the road and guardhouse. Two hundred yards later he waved the men into the bushes. Shouldering the dead American's Enfield, he continued forward with the measured pace of a sentry.

The real guard materialized, walking toward him. "What are you doing here?" the man called. Head down, Teacher kept coming. The guard said, "You hear me?" With a single lightning thrust, Teacher drove the palm of his hand into the base of the guard's nose, driving bone into brain, killing the man instantly. Sergeant Neuman put on the uniform.

When they spotted the glow from the guardhouse, ten minutes later, the three raiders not wearing American uniforms melted into the trees, angling away from the booth but toward the base road. Teacher waited until the rustling noises stopped, meaning that his men were in place. He leaned against the fence like a bored guard. Neuman crept to the booth and crouched under the window. Inside, smoke curled around the sentry's boyish blonde head.

Singing cut the night, from the civilian side of the road. An American soldier weaved out of the fog, drunk, jerking his shoulders, doing some kind of comic dance. "Where is mah ba-bee, where can she beeee." *A musical people*, Teacher thought. The guard hastily donned his helmet and stepped into the road. Teacher could not see him now, because of the booth, but he heard the "Halt! Advance and be recognized!" The sentry allowed the drunk to pass. Thirty seconds later a muffled cry came from up the road. The guard ran back outside. "What happened?" he called. Neuman lunged from the bushes. Teacher, judging the dead man's size, said, "This should fit Weissman." He folded his arms and regarded Neuman critically. "I'm waiting," he said.

In English, Neuman said, "Halt! Advance and be recognized!" The "halt" had sounded too Bavarian, like "hahlt" and not "hawlt."

Neuman tried it again.

Teacher nodded. "Much better. Let them through, all of them. I'll be here if they notice the difference."

Axel squinted up at the high wall of the base watchtower. He was concealed, with three raiders, at the edge of the clearing in the forest. "Cut the phone line first," Ryker had said. It was a single, looping wire, not a thick trunk line, which would spark if cut.

Axel shimmied up the appropriate oak and used a pair of small wire cutters. He watched the severed line fall away into the fog. Back on the ground, the four attackers circled the tower until they faced the dark open slit at the top. A red-faced private named Protzer pulled a flashlight from his rucksack. Axel shouldered his Sten gun. The two men climbed another tree. Fifteen feet up, as they broke out of the fog, they heard voices from the tower. *"Some kind of animal out there, Clancy. Are there bears on this island?"*

"There's bears in your head!"

"Gimme the light!"

Axel shoved down Protzer's head. A beam shot out of the slit, traveled the tree, twice, three times, and clicked shut. The critical voice said, "Bears. You're whacky."

Protzer aimed his own flashlight at the slit. Axel was remembering spotlighting deer in the Harz Mountains. He'd tie the flashlight to the rifle barrel. He'd shine the light in the animal's eyes and it would freeze.

Protzer switched on the light. Sure enough, two white faces appeared, blinking. "What the he . . . ," but Axel's shoulder jerked as he fired and the bullets swept into the light, across the opening. Two pairs of hands fluttered like moths. Then they disappeared. At first no sound came from the tower. Then Axel heard a groan. Then nothing.

The door wasn't even locked.

The Austrians went upstairs and saw they had done their job.

Ryker savored a deep peacefulness, looking down at the fog-shrouded base. He lay, with the rest of the troops, at the top of the wooded bowl. If Axel or Teacher had failed, an alarm would have sounded by now. Ryker's mind ranged over the rest of his strategy, seeking flaws, finding none. The battery glowed faintly. He touched Erhard's elbow and, half rising, the two of them descended toward the deserted parade ground.

He slowed his magnified senses, heard the soft crunching

of vegetation underfoot, smelled the humidity and the juniper trees. Hugging a prefab barrack, they angled toward a small wooden shack that lay midway between the barracks and the battery. A high antenna protruded from the shack. A telephone wire looped from the roof.

The grass smelled freshly cut. A tulip bed adorned the front of the shack. Erhard reached for the knob while Ryker readied the Sten gun. In the spilling light, a white, shocked face fell back, the toppling-chair sound mixing with the closing of the door. The soldier's face was shattered. Erhard glanced over the radio, placed the headphone to one ear, fiddled with the dial. He said, grinning, "No problem." Ryker opened the door again, twice, in a signal.

Moments later the Austrians silently erupted from the shadows at the edge of the parade ground, splitting up, at a run.

Raiders entered the three enlisted men's barracks from the front and rear. They walked the center aisles, pumping silenced bullets into rows of sleeping men. A few Americans woke. One even reached his pistol, but never fired it.

In the officers' quarters, Lieutenant Mariani and Lieutenant Heiden were not in their rooms. The three attackers were unconcerned. Ryker had told them one lieutenant was already dead. Teacher would kill the other one at the front gate.

Major Savage lay in bed, reading a book entitled *How to Win Support from Your Employees.* The bifocal reading glasses seemed out of place on the Mussolini face. His oversized feet stuck out of the covers. He said, scowling at the shadows in his door, "You're in big trouble, soldier." Corporal Frederick Weiss shot the headboard to pieces. "Don't move. Don't talk. Someone is coming to ask you questions," he said.

Two sentries guarded the battery, one on each gun. Three Austrians hit each entrance at a crouching run. Neither guard had time to unsheath his Enfield.

By 3:10 AM, August 20, 1942, three miles from the shore of the continental United States, German attackers had wiped out a United States military base, captured two of the biggest land guns in North America, and taken control of a one-square-mile area within the city limits of Portland, Maine.

Austrians pored over the guns, studying controls, raising the barrels and swiveling them. In the shell room, they lowered steel pincers to begin transporting ammunition to the guns. Austrians wheeled powder charges on dollies. Smaller crews would have to fire the guns, so supplies had to be readied now.

From the battery and radio shack, raiders carried American corpses to the enlisted men's barracks. When they reappeared, they wore the dead men's uniforms.

Teacher reported to Ryker outside the battery, by the artificial hill that housed the guns. Ryker had opened a heavy manhole cover in the ground, and shined a flashlight into the hole. The beam showed a steel ladder descending down a narrow tunnel. The edge of a tremendous steel tank outlined itself below in the dark.

"Oil tank," Ryker said. "Fuel for the base. Only one entrance," he mused, planning.

He slammed the manhole cover. "Follow me." They checked the supply room, the air-conditioning room, the sleeping room. At the gun, they looked out toward the sea. The thinning fog revealed white rollers. "The convoy," Teacher said. "When will it come?"

"This afternoon. I know which ships to look for so we

get the right convoy." Ryker walked the gun's platform, running his hands over the machinery. "This gun's the same as ours, almost. It'll be no problem operating it."

Teacher rapped on the railing. "I've wondered about this convoy. Why do we wait for this particular one? Why not attack another one? What does it carry?"

Ryker called to the soldiers in the corridor. "Don't pile the powder so close! Put it near the wall, in the main corridor!"

"Yes, Herr Ryker." The men looked peculiar in American uniforms.

Teacher repeated doggedly, "What does it carry, this convoy of ours?"

"Blow it up and see what floats in the water afterwards."

Teacher clicked his heels. "Herr General."

A soldier, running up, said, "One hundred and thirty-seven bodies, Ryker."

"Good that they stayed on the island for the show tonight. But that leaves twelve unaccounted for. You got six, Teacher?"

"When I left the gate we'd gotten that many."

"Was that other lieutenant among them?"

"No."

Climbing down from the gun, Ryker asked the soldier, "Did you count the two Axel got at the tower and the guards by the fence and the one I got yesterday?"

"I forgot about the tower. Sorry."

Ryker said, "Then there are four left. Four out of a hundred and fifty. They're either shacking up in the village or they're in Portland. If they're in Portland they'll come back on the morning ferry. If they're in town you'll kill them now. Take the trucks. Bring the villagers. Well?" Ryker asked. "What are you waiting for?"

"A question, that's what." Teacher's voice was low, the wryness gone. "The convoy won't come for ten, twelve hours. Five thousand Americans occupy a fort two miles away. There are five, maybe six battleships in the harbor, not to mention cruisers, troop transports, patrol boats. There's an air base in Brunswick, forty kilometers up the coast, and another at Weymouth to the south. Planes can reach us within half an hour. Even if we sink this convoy, this special mysterious convoy, how do you plan to get us off the island, Ryker?"

Ryker grinned, enjoying Teacher's discomfort. "Is that all?"

"I congratulate you if you consider forty to five-thousand odds, 'That's all.' "

Ryker snorted. "You act fancy but underneath you're more scared than anyone here."

"I never denied it."

Ryker made a face and Teacher said, "What you smell is Eau de Fear, a very expensive fragrance. Millions of Reichsmarks go into the manufacture of a single ounce. Start with a secondary-school teacher, an ordinary instructor of literature. A man who teaches and lives alone and is satisfied. Spend thousands to train him to shoot, to handle explosives, to use a knife. Send him far from home. Surround him with enemies who want to kill him. Voila! An ounce of Eau de Fear!"

"I changed my mind," Ryker said. "I'll take the men into the village. You supervise the guns. And interrogate Savage. Can you manage that much? Find the base logs. I want to know what to expect on a Sunday."

When Ryker turned away, Teacher said, "And my question? How are we going to get out of here alive?"

Ryker looked between the closed manhole cover and

Teacher's face. "Stop worrying," he said. "I told you I was going to get you back. You'll get your medals and go back to your town. The answer's right in front of your face. But I won't tell you now. Wait until I get back with the villagers."

Ryker started to walk away. He was looking back and smiling.

"When I get back with the villagers," he said, "I'll show you."

SIXTEEN

◆———————————◆

SHE WATCHED HEIDEN, prepared to wake him if he slept too long. His nostrils flared slightly when he breathed and a peaceful smile touched his face. The blanket felt smooth and luxurious against her bare skin. A few embers glowed in the hearth. He had rested one hand on her thigh, and his arm connected them like a bridge. She smelled his faint musk smell. His shirt lay beside her. She rubbed the starched, crumpled khaki between her fingers, irrationally jealous of an inanimate shirt. What would it feel like to be that close to him all the time?

"Stop, thief. I need that shirt," said his voice from the blankets. He smiled and reached for her. She had never kissed a man in the morning before. She felt excited, proprietary, shy. Outside, the moon floated, huge in the dark window. The fog had lifted an hour ago. She could tell the morning would be clear and warm.

She said, "Me Tarzan, you Jane," and pointed to the edge of the blanket. She had picked the raspberries by moonlight, right outside the house, while he slept. She put one in his mouth. He said, "No, no. *Me* Tarzan. *You* Jane."

"That's what I said."

"You're blushing."

"You can't tell in the dark."

"Berry good," Heiden grunted, sitting up, the moonlight on his pale shoulders. He pressed his palm to his heart. "Tarzan like Jane more than Tantor, the elephant. Tarzan like Jane more than Horta, the boar."

"Thanks a lot."

"More than Sheeta, more than Numa. Jane Tarzan's favorite Tangomanyani."

"I have to get back before Da wakes up," she said. Pretty funny, she thought. *My life is falling apart and I'm worried about staying out all night.* But only good things seemed possible this morning. She banished the worry from her mind.

"I'll walk you back," he said, dressing.

"No, they'll see us." She meant the villagers. Fixing the blankets together, they looked up, struck by the domestic scene, and burst into laughter. When they pulled apart, Heiden said, "How big is this place anyway?"

"Seven, eight rooms. I used to play with the girl who spent summers here."

"You think the owners will want a lot of money?"

In the silence that followed, her breathing seemed unusually loud. "I don't know."

"Maybe if Owen McKlintock didn't fix the place up, the price would be lower."

"Probably." Her face was burning. *Say something more than one word!* Outside, the sky had gone from black to deep purple.

Heiden suggested, "I could fix it up."

"I know a little carpentry," she heard herself say. "Da showed me on the boat."

She could not see his expression clearly in the dark but

she felt his grin. "Sure! A little paint downstairs, a new banister . . ."

She grew a little frightened then and dizzy. She knew what he meant and she liked it a great deal. "I have to go back," Corrice said, but they stayed a few minutes more, not saying anything important, relishing the unspoken agreement, reluctant to part. When she closed the door, Heiden's muffled whoop of joy sounded from inside. He made her feel graceful, beautiful, loved.

She hurried to reach home, change out of her evening clothes, and start Da's breakfast before he woke. The island smelled fresh and fragrant with wild roadside roses. Under bright stars and a full, fading moon, the road unwound in a pale grey strip, lined with pines, lined with honeysuckle and rich clover. She remembered the firmness of Heiden's touch and his eyes close to her face in the dark. *I could fix up the house*, he had said. She felt flushed and weak thinking about it. Happily, she picked up her pace.

Then she remembered Da again. And Ryker, who had said he needed one last day on the island. She would never see Ryker again after he left tonight. She tried not to wonder what kind of information he was gathering. *It will be used far away from here,* he had said. *I'm starting to think it isn't even here.* But she pictured the thousands of soldiers crowding the passing transports each day, the island boys who had left for Africa, and the ads and cartoons filling the papers. DON'T BE A RUMOR MONGER! DON'T BE AN AXIS PARTNER! Or the poster in the church: LOOSE LIPS SINK SHIPS! She felt dirty then, and soiled, for not turning in Ryker. She felt old. *No more secrets,* Heiden had said. She would make the lie up to him. She would love him and be good to him, would be the best wife in the world. But she would never, never tell about Ryker.

She hated Da at that moment. A bird warbled in the hidden branches. Loyalty, Corrice thought, is a horrible thing.

The church steeple crowned the treetops. The only visible life on her street was a Labrador retriever in the middle of the road. It tucked its tail between its legs and bolted. She wondered what had frightened the Hudsons' generally friendly pet.

She showered and changed into her church dress, some of her tension having drained with an undetected arrival home. Downstairs, she took two eggs from the icebox and reached for the sink cabinet, for a bowl. That was when she saw the telephone.

The receiver was missing, cut from its wire. Black masking tape looped around the bottom of the box and up to the cradle, depressing it.

She took a moment to understand. The phone could ring, but no one could answer.

Her head began to throb. "Da?" She advanced up the stairs. The house creaked. His doorknob felt cold. "Da!" She didn't know what to expect inside, but his room was empty, as was Ryker's.

In the living room, the smashed radio lay overturned, surrounded by glass and splintered wood.

The shotgun had been taken from its basement rack.

Da was nowhere in the house.

The deserted street seemed ominous now. She was afraid if she ran she would trigger the malevolence practically pulsating through the air. She turned toward the harbor with measured steps, but inside she was screaming. *Oh please, please be on the boat.* There was nowhere else he would go on a Sunday morning.

She looked back. The dog stood in the middle of the road, shivering.

The first house she reached, the Turner house, was a stone Cape Cod fronted by high sunflowers. Mary Turner tended her garden most Sundays, but not today. The front door tilted open behind the screened porch. Had the Turners seen Da?

Nobody answered Corrice's knock. She peered into the house.

The wall phone was taped up in the hallway. She stepped inside. The radio lay shattered in the den.

The Turners were gone.

Corrice bolted outside, the screen door slamming behind her. How could she have ever thought Ryker would just go away? She should have told about him, she saw that now. At a run, she rounded the corner onto the harbor road. Thin plumes of smoke rose, far out in the bay. The first convoy of the day was passing Captains Island. *I should have let Da leave.* In the somnambulant heat, the deserted street flew past, the parked Hudson Cadillac, Cora's store. The dock lay ahead.

Where were the people?

Then she saw two soldiers lounging against the Esso pump on the wharf, sunning themselves, just sunning themselves as if nothing were wrong. Da's Nova, anchored beyond them, looked empty, but she saw soldiers on several other boats.

Her sneakers thudded on the dock. "The telephone," she gasped. "The radios." Their faces lowered. The men elbowed themselves off the pump. Soldiers did not generally carry weapons on the civilian side of the island, but Corrice recognized machine guns when she saw them.

The barrels came up, pointing at her. The soldiers seemed amused.

She stopped five feet away. She knew every man on the base, but these two were strangers.

"Trouble, miss?" one of the soldiers said.

Ryker finished taping the phone in the church rectory. He sliced the receiver from its wire and carried it outside. In the sunlight, the Austrians guarded two jeeps and a canvas-topped transport set off from the other vehicles. Five Sten-wielding troopers ringed the back of the truck. The islanders were silent silhouettes inside.

HOLINESS UNTO THE LORD, read the sign on the white cedar shingling. FURNACE DRIVE. Ryker tossed his receiver on top of a pile in one of the jeeps, beside islander rifles and revolvers.

Axel, planted next to the jeep, looked over its contents and sneered. "You do everything so fancy. Why not just cut the wires to the phones? Why take the receivers?"

"Sure," Ryker said. He stood on the top step. "Then callers get busy signals. All the callers. All the time." He swaggered down to Axel and patted him on the cheek, relishing the resulting look of fury. "So they call the authorities in Portland to complain. I want those phones to ring. And I took the receivers in case you missed an islander. You don't want an islander calling out, do you?"

Axel flushed deep red. "A fucking germ couldn't have hidden from us."

A woman's strident complaint sounded from the side of the church. "When Major Savage finds out about this, you're going to regret ever coming to this island!" In silk robes and pajamas, the Hudsons rounded the building, prodded by private Neuman and his Sten gun. Mrs. Hudson looked doughy without her makeup, but her posture was regal, her bracelets in place. Ryker guessed she slept in jewelry. She snapped, "Who's in charge here?"

Ryker stepped close. "You?" she said. "But you're Kelly's boarder." She looked over the others and shook her head in disgust. "A new bunch." She indicated Private Neuman with an imperious wave of her hand. "This man broke into our home, woke us, without any explanation, and when I tell Major Savage . . ."

"Major Savage is unavailable," Ryker said.

Her head jerked. Jeremiah's voice called from the truck. "They're Germans, Isadora."

For the first time, she became aware of the other islanders. "That's ridiculous," she said. "You're not funny." No one said anything. "They can't be Germans." Judge Hudson began to tremble. "How can they be Germans? They're wearing American uniforms. In Portland! *Our soldiers are all over the island!*"

Axel leaned toward her conspiratorially. "We're not Germans." He winked. "We're Austrians."

"But the whole base!" Ryker just shook his head. She blinked uncertainly, then dawning horror stretched her features. "A hundred and fifty men? But you're . . . you're Kelly's boarder."

"Into the truck," Ryker said.

He closed the gate behind them. Civilians would generally beg and wail, but Ryker faced an eerie, implacable wall of flinty stares, the men a collection of rural weather-worn faces, wire-rimmed glasses, bristling crew cuts, and white socks; the women, in print dresses, closing around Mrs. Hudson. Only Judge Hudson and the children showed fear. Ryker decided he'd be glad when he got them all back to the base.

Then he looked into the truck again. "Corrice," he said. He whirled on Axel. "Where's Corrice?"

"Corrice?"

"'A fucking germ couldn't have hidden from us,' eh?"

Axel snapped, "We went through the houses."

"Did you find the lieutenant?"

Axel shrugged. "I figured he took the ferry. Or Teacher got him at the gate."

Ryker switched to German, breaking his own rule. "He couldn't have taken the ferry. I saw him last night after the ferry left." Livid, he hit the truck. Was this it? The one thing that always went wrong?

"You checked the boats," he said.

"We're finishing now."

"There were no empty moorings? You smashed all the radios?"

"Come on, Ryker. He's only one man"

"I'm only one man," Ryker said. He thought, *If they swam far enough, a boat could have picked them up.*

He turned to the islanders. "Where's Corrice?"

Jeremiah leaned back, in the truck. "Having problems, are you?"

Ryker paced off several steps. He closed his eyes, concentrating. He pictured Heiden and Corrice, walking into the forest last night. But the forest had been wet last night. They wouldn't have slept in the wet forest.

His eyes opened. "The houses," he said. "The empty houses." He was already running for the jeep. "Recheck the village," he called. "Teacher will know what to do with the islanders."

He ordered two privates to come with him. The houses were ten minutes away.

◊   ◊   ◊

Heiden wandered through the cottage, whistling happily and planning renovations. The building seemed sound structurally. He's have to insulate the walls for winter. The kitchen pump was dry; was the well dry too?

He would need a job after the war. Maybe Michael Kelly would teach him to lobster. They could lay a lot more traps together. Or he could commute on the ferry, teach in Portland, even finish his degree. He loved the idea of spending his life on this island.

His only problem at the moment involved Owen McKlintock, who was fixing up the house. Islanders looked after each other and Heiden didn't want to take work from Owen without coming up with an alternative job, maybe on the base.

At length he decided to return to the barracks but avoid the main gate. The men could get pretty raunchy if they knew he'd spent the night out. He didn't want any incidents when Corrice went to work tomorrow, and he didn't want the news getting back to Michael Kelly.

So instead of taking the main road, he chose a familiar woodsy path toward the fence. Morning sunlight dappled the forest. He stopped to pick some raspberries. He could still feel the copper smoothness of her legs and the circular way she moved her hips. Her waist was so small he could practically encircle it with his fingers.

He hoped Mariani had returned to the base, but doubted it. First thing this morning he would remind Savage to order the search on the civilian side of the island. Then he'd phone Brooklyn to see if Mariani had gone home. But he'd be careful not to alarm the family.

The fence appeared abruptly. He pulled himself over a wooden post, cutting a finger on a splinter. He brushed himself off, glad to be on the base but uneasy over the bad security. Still Savage refused to assign him more guards. At least the army had promised to deliver barbed wire, but the island kids couldn't resist the off-limits apple trees, and Heiden wanted to keep them from hurting themselves. He walked along, sucking the bleeding finger. Maybe he'd ask Savage to reroute the fence. A few less feet wouldn't make a difference to the base, and Heiden didn't want to cut down the apple trees.

Savage will never do it, he thought.

Then he whispered, "Oh God."

Schroeder, the Alabama private, sprawled in his underclothes, half in the bushes, blonde hair streaked with dirt. Ants crawled on a hideously contorted face.

The morning heat seemed to suck the air from Heiden's lungs. He became aware of the sun on the back of his head. Schroeder's nose seemed to have been driven into his skull. Blood spread from his mouth and ears. The woods were filled with a sweet, pervasive reek.

Jesus, Jesus Christ, who would do this? Fighting off nausea, Heiden knelt. The bulging blue eyes seemed to follow him. Shuddering at the touch, he felt no pulse. He heard a million insects all around him, hyperventilating. Close up, the body broke into blocks of disconnected color: the red smears, white flesh, the khaki undershirt.

He closed the eyes. Schroeder's uniform was nowhere in sight. The Enfield was gone too.

Footprints overlaid footprints around the corpse. Heiden guessed there'd been a fight.

Get help, he thought. He began to run.

Schroeder had been with him the morning he found the arm. Other than that they'd never talked much, but the boy had seemed quiet and good-natured, his limited-service rating due to a weak kidney and bad feet. Why would someone murder Schroeder? The solid jungle thickness alternated with birch forest. Heiden nearly fell over a humpbacked root, but he stayed up. He realized he could have run to the main gate and phoned Savage, but he had not thought of it. Now the barracks were closer, but Heiden's rhythm was off, his balance bad. He had trouble breathing and he was ducking branches like a fighter. Why would someone take the uniform? *To wear it.* A saboteur? *Seal the base. Call Major Levy at the OSS.* He'd order a reveille and check over the troops, then organize a search of the grounds. *Double guards on the guns.*

The world was spinning. The grounds seemed endless. What did the army need so much land for, a city? He had to catch his breath, just for a second. He steadied himself against an oak.

Lungs burning, he looked up.

Something white caught his attention, in a nearby tree.

He squinted. He walked a few steps.

"Mariani," he breathed.

"They were here, all right," Ryker said. He stirred the ashes in the fireplace with his foot. "Still warm." Sunlight streamed through the window, creating an aura around the Austrians by the sill. Ryker remembered a story he'd heard in military school. A French general wanted Napoleon to promote him to field marshal. The general visited Napoleon to list his skills and victories. "I know you're talented," Napoleon said. "But are you lucky?"

Now this insignificant lieutenant had eluded Ryker three

times in one morning, at the base, at the village, and, by less than half an hour, in this room.

"Does he know we're here, that's the question," Ryker muttered.

The house offered no more clues. Outside, he spotted two sets of footprints immediately. He bent and followed them. When he straightened he seemed relieved. "They wouldn't have separated if they knew."

The girl had headed for the village. The Austrians had probably captured her by now, but Ryker had no way of checking. He needed the privates here. The house had no phone. The jeep contained one of their walkie-talkies, but he remembered an incident in Poland. He had been in a Warsaw apartment, listening to regular Polish radio, when the Germans entered the city. Because of a broadcasting fluke, German field messages had drowned out the regular program. All he needed now was a passing pleasure boat picking up his inquiry about Corrice.

Heiden's footprints meandered into the woods, not down to the road, like Corrice's. The lieutenant had paused by a berry bush, probably picked breakfast, then strolled ahead. All Ryker's senses screamed for him to go after the man personally. Heiden was worse than smart, he was lucky. But the sun was up and Ryker needed to return to the base. Teacher would have found the schedules and logs by now. Mail launches might be arriving this morning, or supplies or visitors. There would be regular radio communications with the fort in the harbor. Ryker couldn't waste time chasing one soldier in the woods.

He felt a little better when he looked over the privates. "Kill the lieutenant," he ordered. They loped off, as natural in the forest as wolves. His men were mountain troops, trackers, the best in the world. He told himself that Heiden, unarmed and unaware, would be dead within the hour.

Heiden lurched along the forest floor, dazed with horror. His throat burnt, his head was on fire. He kept seeing Mariani, *tilting out of a tree,* arm dangling and face puffy.

Had he kissed Corrice good-bye only an hour ago? He jerked at a rustle in the bushes. A cardinal squawked toward the single lavender cloud in the sky. Sweat soaked Heiden's armpits. He eyed the dense bowers and thick, concealing trunks. He'd been having a good time when someone murdered Schroeder. But Mariani had been missing *two* nights. Had the killer come back twice?

His legs seemed to work by themselves. Who had done it, he kept asking himself. A saboteur? Spy? Had the killer been an islander? Impossible. Someone new on the island?

Ryker was new on the island.

He stopped but started again. The truth was, anyone could have rowed to shore during the night, concealed a dinghy in a hundred odd places, and scrambled into the woods. The civilian patrol was a joke, like the fence.

He broke out of the rise above the parade ground.

The scene below was all wrong.

A canvas-topped transport and a jeep had been driven onto the parade ground, right on Savage's precious grass. Ringed by armed soldiers, civilians climbed from the back of the truck; women and children included. The sense of menace was unmistakable. The islanders huddled by the truck.

He felt as if he had woken on another planet. The base looked the same, but none of the human activity below made any sense. The soldiers didn't even move right. He knew his own troops, the bespectacled math geniuses and fat boys, the farmers with flat feet. The troops he watched seemed crisp and confident, even athletic. He was too far away to see faces, but their manner was all wrong. And where was Savage?

As he watched, a soldier who had been bending into the jeep straightened with a load of rifles, but the rifles fell. The man's cry of pain echoed across the square.

"Scheisse! Verdammt Gewehr!"

"Speak English!" cried a voice from the other side of the parade ground. "All the time!"

Heiden's knees went weak.

He crouched in the bushes.

They couldn't have spoken German, he told himself.

I heard no shooting! How could they have taken the base!

He crept closer, the vegetation smell thick and humid. The bulk of the troops kept their backs to Heiden. The islanders were still coming out of the truck. The whole village was there.

Corrice climbed from the truck. The pain between his eyes grew very bad.

It was unreal, a nightmare. *Where are my soldiers?*

At least twenty-five men below wore American uniforms. And now he was close enough to notice the weapons, stubby machine guns held at the hip. But the base had been equipped with Enfields, not machine guns.

The sky was clear of planes. That didn't mean they weren't coming. Or had the Germans overrun the other islands last night? Were they already on Peaks Island and Bailey Island? Had they occupied Fort Williams? He sweated freely. Suppose they were attacking Portland!

He could find out in the radio shack, only fifty yards away, in the open. He wondered if anyone was inside.

He paused at the edge of the high grass, three feet from the parade ground. The soldiers' faces, visible now, showed they were strangers, but Heiden was not surprised.

A thin, balding man exited Savage's quarters. Heiden guessed he commanded here from the way the guards parted at his approach. Once inside the human circle, the man faced the islanders and bowed slightly.

"Good people," he said, surprising Heiden with loud, unaccented English, "undoubtedly our presence here shocks you. I sympathize, I really do. I envision my own small village in Austria and imagine my neighbors' reaction were the situation to be reversed."

The reasonable, academic tone contrasted sharply with the man's filthy appearance and the hard demeanor of his troops. The soldier who had dropped the rifles disappeared into the enlisted men's barracks with another load. The speaker said, "You must keep one thought in mind during the next several hours. You're safe. Really. It's true we killed the soldiers. We do not treat civilians the same way."

His words tore into Heiden's brain. *It's true we killed the soldiers.* His head swarmed with terror. *Get calm, get your mind working.* He pictured Schroeder, broken and stripped. The rifle carrier left the wooden prefab, his job apparently finished, because he walked back toward the battery. Heiden began crawling through the grass, circling the parade ground to get close to the rifles. He hoped the Germans hadn't stationed a guard in the hut.

The speaker said, "My name is Teacher. Ask for me if you have a problem. I'm afraid you're going to have to occupy some rather cramped quarters for a while, not because we want to inconvenience you or frighten you. We need to free our own men from guard duty. If you'll just go—" but Mrs. Hudson drowned him out. "Don't listen!"

The soldiers shifted uneasily. She cried, "He's lying! It's not just this island!"

The islanders grew more agitated. Teacher raised his hands, whether in menace or supplication, Heiden could not tell. "Listen!" But Corrice cut him off. "Where's my father?" She sounded frantic. Heiden didn't see Kelly anywhere. "And Tom!" she cried. "Both of them!"

He couldn't stand it, couldn't bear it, just sitting there watching. He wanted to help, to get her out of there. He wanted to let her know he was all right. His head pounded. His fingers dug into the earth. At first he was only dimly aware of the jeep roaring into the parade ground.

Then he saw that Ryker drove the jeep.

At that instant, it all made sense. *It was you.* The jeep skidded to a stop. On top of the other shocks, Ryker's appearance pushed Heiden out of confusion and into sudden brutal clarity. He remembered Ryker's late arrival at the talent show, his speed in the bar. He saw the parade ground as a whole now, the prisoners, the scurrying troops by the battery, the way Teacher ran to meet Ryker. The conversation was too low to hear, but suddenly Ryker turned and saw Corrice. He advanced to her, dwarfing her, gesturing angrily toward the village. Their noses were inches apart.

Heiden understood that Ryker was looking for *him.*

The realization filled him with pride. Luck or not, he'd eluded them.

Before Ryker's anger, Corrice seemed to stand straighter. *At least she knows I'm alive.*

But suddenly she leapt at Ryker, who parried her blow, seizing her wrists and holding her, utterly without effort, until Teacher dragged her back. She thrashed wildly, trying to reach either of them. "I should have killed you," she cried, "when I had the chance!" And Heiden caught the second movement among the islanders then, as Dick Turner launched himself toward Teacher, with all the speed of a seventy-year-old, to try to help.

Heiden didn't know whether the "Stop" came from a German or an islander. A soldier swung toward Turner. Then Turner was dancing, jerking like a puppet, crying out as he fell.

All activity stopped. Turner raised himself, painfully, onto all fours, palms inward and elbows bent, head tucked into his shoulders, like a lizard. A single spurt of blood gushed from his mouth, followed by a high, inhuman whine. He sank to the grass.

Corrice, released now, took two steps forward. She covered her face with her hands.

Nobody stopped Rose Turner from running to her husband.

Ryker planted himself before the trooper who had fired. Heiden thought he was going to strike the man, but he said something instead and the soldier turned quickly and left.

Heiden trembled with rage, with the violence of it. *Silencers. That's why I didn't hear anything.* On her knees, beside the corpse, Mary Turner held her hand, soaked with Dick's blood, up to her face. She was absolutely stiff, in shock. At Ryker's gesture a soldier gently lifted her to her feet. She was curiously compliant, like a child. The troops began moving the islanders across the parade ground. Turner's body remained, a twisted disturbance on the neat, mowed lawn.

At first Heiden thought the Germans were bringing their prisoners to the battery, but then Ryker lifted the manhole cover to the fuel room. The islanders began climbing down, one by one.

Heiden's mind screamed, *Fight them.*

So many of them? You'll die like Turner.

Then go for help.

He could try for the rifles in the wooden prefab. Maybe he'd find machine guns too. But how much good could he do with one machine gun? If he reached the village he could use the phones. Or boats. Fort Williams was so close you could see it from the spotting tower.

Were Germans in the village? Heiden remembered Teacher's words, "We have to free up men from guard duty." If Fort Williams was safe, American troops could land here within ninety minutes. And now that the first flush of panic had passed, he knew that the Germans could never have taken Fort Williams last night, not without an aerial bombardment he would have heard. Plus, any large invasion force would have been spotted at sea.

He enjoyed a savage vision of the navy roaring ashore, the troops storming the base, himself among them, the bullets ripping into Ryker, tearing him, like Turner.

He hated leaving Corrice, but at least she knew he was alive.

She disappeared into the fuel room. The soldiers were still occupied at the manhole entrance. Heiden turned to make his way back up the hill and simultaneously saw the glint, ahead, where the mass of thick vegetation met the high forest. He shielded his eyes with his palm. A barb swept into his belly.

Two soldiers picked their way through the brush, coming down the hill.

He was trapped, sandwiched. *I'm dead,* he thought bitterly. He wished he had an Enfield, or anything to use against them. At least he could die fighting.

Then he realized the soldiers were not moving directly

toward him. They were angling toward him, following his earlier line of descent and tracking him. *They had not seen him yet.*

He had, at most, a minute before they spotted him. Even if he crawled into the brush he would leave tracks. He imagined their cry of recognition, saw the soldiers turning in the square, felt the bullets smashing into him. In his mind he was Turner and Schroeder and Mariani. He saw Ryker standing over his body, satisfaction on that brutal face. *Run for the barracks.* What other choice did he have? He started to rise, readying for the mad dash, and he saw the parade ground ahead, the body lying, the troops and the islanders, and in a flash he understood his single, thin chance of getting out alive.

SEVENTEEN

CORRICE STEPPED OFF THE LADDER to make room for the next prisoner. She saw, framed by the manhole above, Ryker's legs in an inverted V. The concrete floor felt hard under her sneakers. Streaming light bathed her in its brilliant shaft, but a solid surrounding wall of black began two feet away.

She heard islanders moving around in the dark. Jeremiah's voice said, soft, beside her, "Make room." She was reluctant to leave the light but allowed him to steer her. The air grew cold.

The room issued an oily, metallic odor and smelled of pressed bodies, still rank from sleep. Vague human shapes took form, sitting on the floor, dwarfed by the elephantine swell of the fuel tank, which started by one wall and filled more than half the room. Jeremiah's touch was light. "I'm sorry about your father." She sat, wedged between bodies. She fixed on the golden shaft of light and dancing dust particles within.

The last islander stepped off the ladder and Teacher's face appeared at the opening. "Remember, you're safe."

The steel manhole cover reverberated. The room went pitch-black and a child began to whimper.

"I knew your father since we were kids. Those bastards." Corrice recognized the clipped Yankee tones of Pat Rye, one of the fishermen's wives. "At least Tom Heiden's alive." Corrice envisioned the small athletic woman. A slim arm came around her shoulders. Corrice hadn't smelled sachet since her mother was alive.

She hoped Tom had fled, swum into the channel, gotten lucky, flagged a boat. Da was dead, Ryker had told her. And Turner had died crawling at her feet.

I'm glad they didn't kill me. She hated herself for the thought. She imagined Da lying in the woods, lying on the grass, like Turner. *I'm responsible.*

In the absolute blackness, the bodies pushed in on her; she couldn't move, couldn't breathe. She felt formless. Her brain was burning. An insect crawled on her hands. She brushed it off. It returned, then she felt more of them—ants, spiders, marching up her wrists, her legs.

Jeremiah's voice pierced the darkness. "I found the light! Everybody! Close your eyes!" She opened them slowly. A lone bulb blazed on the ceiling. Her fright dissipated now that she could see. So did the crawling sensations, but her breathing wasn't back to normal yet. The forty islanders and summer people had arranged themselves in family groups, in a kind of doughnut on the floor. The fuel tank was even larger than she'd imagined, boiler-shaped and fifteen feet high, practically brushing the ceiling. Pipes ran like thin arms from the tank to the grey concrete walls, which dripped with condensation.

Jeremiah stood beside the tank, the only person on his feet. He pointed at the bulb and addressed the children.

"See that bulb?" He sounded gruff, like he was chairing a town meeting. "A Maine fellah invented that bulb." He raised a hand to ward off protest. "You're thinkin' Edison got the credit, but it was a Mainiac give him the idea for the vacuum tube. Bobby Lee Rye, what's a vacuum tube?"

"No air in it, Jeremiah."

"That's right boy, so stop sniffling."

Ten feet away, across a gap and by the tank, a circle of islanders comforted Rose Turner. Corrice looked away.

"Maine fellah invented the Maxim machine gun," said Doug Donnelly, president of the rifle club.

"Maine people invented earmuffs," said Clara Chadborne.

"And tungsten for steel. And a car battery that goes inside the car, not out," said Jeremiah. "You'd think a Maine fellah could invent a way out of here."

The heads swiveled simultaneously. People got up and put their hands on their hips.

"Don't see no vents," said Doug Donnelly.

Lobsterman Hugh McKaye said, "Lots of gasoline in that tank. Too bad we don't have any containers. Wonder what kind of wiring they used for that light."

"You ain't touching that light," Jeremiah said. "It's the only light we have."

A chorus of voices sounded. "Yeah, leave it alone." "Teacher said we were safe!" "Gasoline? You want to burn us all up?"

Abruptly, across from Corrice, Mrs. Hudson shoved herself to her feet. She'd been uncharacteristically quiet. Now her face glazed, distorted, contracted. Corrice looked into the glaring accusation in the eyes, and her bowels started churning. Their glances were locked. Mrs. Hudson stepped past bodies, the conversation faltering in her wake. There was nowhere to hide. *She knows!* She stopped a foot away, planted her feet like Ryker, arms akimbo, and leaned forward. Her mouth twisted. Everyone else had stopped talking. Corrice heard a steady dripping from behind the fuel tank. In the otherwise silent room, Isadora Hudson's voice was a harsh echo.

"What do you mean," she demanded, "you should have killed Ryker when you had the chance?"

Heiden watched the Germans coming down the hill. He did not think they had seen him yet because their heads were bent to the ground. He guessed they followed his footsteps. None of the troops on the parade ground looked in his direction. Heart roaring, he stood up.

He strode onto the parade ground, hands at his sides. Ahead, although the last islander had disappeared, raiders still clustered by the manhole. Heiden walked directly toward them. Uniformed men here were supposed to be Germans. It was the only way to reach Ryker's jeep.

His back felt twelve feet wide. The parade ground, which he had never considered strategically before, was bounded by the battery on the sea side and the low hill opposite that. Barracks and the officers' quarters composed the third boundary, and the mess and radio shack the fourth. He would have to swing the jeep in a circle and drive between the Germans and the radio shack. The road lay thirty feet beyond the raiders. There was no other way out of the base.

The jeep was fifteen feet off, just beyond Turner's crumpled body. A raider glanced back toward Heiden and turned around again. Teacher disappeared into the officers' quarters. Ryker seemed to be issuing orders. Heiden already felt the wheel in his hands. He had driven that jeep a thousand times, taken Corrice for rides in it, even shown Ryker the island in it. Every angle, every inch of the vehicle was etched into his brain. *Don't run.*

Six feet. The raiders on the hill must have seen him by now. Were they squinting, aiming? He wouldn't hear them if they fired. The tulips by the radio shack seemed uncommonly beautiful. So did the grass and the blue spruce on the battery. He passed inches from Turner, resisting the urge to feel the pulse and make sure he was beyond help.

The veiny wear marks were visible now on the jeep's leather seat. He swung himself up, reaching for the red ignition button. The engine started smoothly. The jeep jerked to a start.

The gears made a horrible grinding noise. The steering wheel felt slippery. *Shift into second.* He'd almost completed the circling maneuver. The Germans had not looked up but the two on the rise must have identified him by now. The gap loomed between the raiders and radio shack. He slammed down the accelerator. The engine roared. The jeep slid sideways, throwing up dirt, straightened, and shot for the opening.

The attackers were whirling. Heiden caught a glimpse of Ryker's face, the shocked recognition, the mouth forming a word, *"You!"* and then he was past. The jeep crashed off the parade ground onto the road. The air was alive with the slap and whine of bullets. Heiden lowered his head. Firing attackers were visible in the side-view mirror. Ryker ran toward the other jeep.

He swept around a bend. The mirror showed no pursuers. Two hundred yards ahead, on the forest straightaway, three soldiers stood in the road beside the sentry hut. They held machine guns loosely in their hands. They seemed more curious than alarmed. Heiden maintained speed. When he reached within thirty yards of them, he downshifted, slowed, until he could make out their features. Then he slammed the accelerator again, and swerved at the men. They leapt out of the way, into the bushes. He roared around another bend.

Free! The rushing air was cool, delicious. He'd beaten them! Passed them! He waved and howled with laughter and slapped the dashboard with delight. Oh, the expression on their faces when they'd jumped out of the way! The bucking jeep threw him from side to side. He raced along the coast road. *A mile to town.*

The blood pounded in his head. He felt alive, exultant, until the thinking part of his mind clamped down and he realized the Germans weren't just on the base but in town too. If Ryker had phoned ahead, they might even be waiting.

He caught sight of the church steeple, half a mile away. The inevitable pursuing jeep was still not visible, but the curving road limited his visibility. They could be close. A turnoff approached. Cursing, he jerked the wheel violently to the right. The jeep plunged up a narrow dirt track, through a poplar forest, and under overhanging branches. The poplars thinned into a field. He cut across the grass. Two minutes later, in the trees, he braked and shut off the engine.

The silence was complete. Then the insects started buzzing. He heard, from the direction of the coast road, frantic engine sounds, growing strong and then fading. Ryker was bringing reinforcements into town.

He slumped against the wheel, the surge of energy gone. His hands shook. If the Germans hadn't been in town before, they would be now.

Move it, move it, get into town. He used his officer's voice on himself.

But maybe he shouldn't head for town. Maybe he should try swimming off the island. All he had to do was walk back to the road, over the sharp granite outcrops, and into the sea. The problem was threefold. He was on the Atlantic side of the island, not the Portland side. Portland was three miles off anyway. He'd tried swimming in these waters once, when he was new here. Two minutes in the cold and his body had begun hurting. Lobstermen said it was possible to survive thirty minutes in this water, but he did not want to test the theory, even in August. A wetsuit would make the swim survivable, but the wetsuits, like the phones, like the soldiers, like Ryker, were in town.

Decide. Teacher had said, "We have to free up the men from guard duty." That sounded like the raiders might be shorthanded. Plus, if they arrived in a U-boat, which was likely, their numbers would be limited. Perhaps most of the attackers had been on the base.

Get to a phone. In the dappled sunlight, squirrels played. He fixed the jeep's location in his mind. He hoped he wouldn't have to come back later.

Avoiding a nearby footpath, he plunged directly into the brush.

The woods threw thorn bushes in his face.

He kept telling himself there wouldn't be too many Germans in town.

"What do you mean," Mrs. Hudson repeated, *"you should have killed Ryker when you had the chance?"* She towered

over Corrice, red fingernail pointing like a talon. "Tell us! We all heard you say it! You knew who he was all along!"

The nightmare had taken different forms over the last few weeks, sometimes consisting of a knock on the door, the soldiers waiting outside the screen, sometimes Heiden just walking off, getting smaller until he disappeared. At least he wasn't here to witness her humiliation.

Mrs. Hudson said, "Who helped Ryker get his pass to the island? You? Your father?"

Corrice had read about criminal trials in the papers. Guilty defendants were often described as "emotionless." But the word was wrong. They weren't emotionless. They'd gone crazy for months, worrying about the verdict. When it was finally announced it seemed quick and unreal. What the spectators saw was really narcotized shock.

Mrs. Hudson's voice dripped with contempt. "Chairman of the scrap drive. Chairman of the paper drive. Oh, you fooled us, so sweet and innocent."

Hugh McKaye said, "Give her a chance, Isadora. Michael's been killed, he's dead. Anyway, why would they stick her with us if she worked with them?"

"To tell them what we're saying, that's why. And what did she mean, she had a chance to kill him?"

Other voices rose. "When did she have a chance?" "Leave her alone, will you?" "No, I want to know."

Jeremiah's patched denims appeared at eye level. She couldn't look up at him. The knees bent. She saw the pores on his face. "You had a bad time," he said, "but don't you want to say anything? Don't you want to explain?"

The silence deepened. His gentle tones broke through and her emotions surged in. *Yes,* she thought. *I knew who he was. Explain? I want to explain.* But how do you explain?

Do you say, "When I was six Da took me fishing?" or "We used to sit in the living room at night. He told me funny stories?" Or do you try it another way? Do you say, "On that particular day, when I made part of my decision, Da felt bad, the sun was shining, all these factors affected me." What parts of a decision were the key parts? Explain? She wanted to explain how she could have let her father flee the island, and how she'd felt watching Turner crawl in the grass and die. She wanted the islanders to punish her. That was what she wanted to explain. All the possible answers crowded in, the excuses and evasions, the confessions, the rationalizations, merging into one cacophonous mass.

But as quickly as the storm had brewed, it subsided. What was an explanation but an appeal? You believed or you didn't. She had never had any other choice and had made the only possible decision. Despite her sleeplessness, her arguments, her threats, fathers had been around a lot longer than countries.

She straightened and looked Jeremiah in the face. She appreciated his kindness but didn't need it anymore. Absolutely calm, she said, "He was my father. I loved him. I did what I had to, to protect him."

They could wait for more but they wouldn't get it. She guessed she hadn't changed expression in ten minutes, but what she felt was no longer numbness but peace, resolution. A low murmur rose around her. They could do with her what they wished. Jeremiah moved off. Mrs. Hudson replaced him. "I told you," she announced to all. "She fooled us."

Surprisingly, Mrs. Turner was the first to answer. "You wouldn't have helped *your* father, would you, Isadora?"

Corrice looked up, blinking.

Judge Hudson sat almost directly against the fuel tank. "She wouldn't have done anything for me, that's for sure."

Palms out, Mrs. Hudson turned in a circle. "Why's everybody looking at me?"

The judge said, after a moment, "Sit down."

The room became quiet again. Corrice realized Pat Rye's arm had never left her shoulder. Mary Turner seemed to remember her husband. Her face crumpled. The islanders nearby went back to their own concerns.

After a while, Jack Rye said, "Jeremiah, even if we had bottles, how would we get the gasoline out of the tank?"

She knew it was going to be all right then. But over one hundred and fifty people had died because she'd tried to save her father.

The islanders left her alone when she started to cry.

The house lay twenty feet away, but twenty feet in the open. Heiden looked out from the forest. He didn't even hear birds. The neat, cropped lawn was splashed with roses. The yellow Victorian stood two stories high, featured a widow's walk below an upper bedroom window.

Where was Ryker? In the woods? In town, circling, in the jeep? There were guns in the house. Jack Rye belonged to the rifle club. *But had that curtain moved?* It wasn't moving now. He shifted his gaze to the telephone wire looping from the house and toward the harbor, Fort Williams, and help.

Heiden had racked his brain over Ryker's purpose in coming here. The raiders could have blown up the battery by now if they wanted. There was no invasion fleet, that was almost certain. The ring of sonic detectors two miles out would give Portland ample warning of its arrival, and even if the guns on Captains Island had been disabled, batteries on Peaks and Great Chebeague islands would force enemy ships down a corridor so narrow American battleships in the harbor would pick them off, one by one. Plus, the bottom of the Hussey Strait was lined with sonic mines that could be triggered from Fort Williams. He'd seen the hundred-foot-high funnels of water when the mines were tested. Germany had no aircraft carriers Heiden knew of, or air bases in the North Atlantic. Hitler's Stukas could never reach Maine.

It all meant Ryker couldn't stay long on Captains Island. *So why did he come here?* The massive fueling areas in the harbor contained enough oil to supply over a hundred ships a day. Wasn't that the reason for the whole military cordon around the city, the oil? *Do they want the oil?*

A shadow moved across the lawn. An anti-U-boat dirigible glided out to sea. Heiden broke out of the forest, running at a crouch. He leapt to the porch, wincing at the thud of his shoes. Noiselessly, he pushed open the back door. A cone of light illuminated the kitchen's wood-plank floor. The hall closets lay open. They'd been searched. Frilly blue curtains bathed the living room in shadow: the lumpy couch, wooden hutch, the china and decorative fishing floats. An iron-bellied stove occupied a corner. The shelf clock ticked eleven AM.

Had he kissed Corrice good-bye only hours ago?

The phone was on the rolltop desk, in the study. Black tape depressed the hook and the receiver was gone. On the floor the radio lay smashed. Shattered tubes had rolled against the baseboard.

He stared at the phone, trying to understand. Something brushed his ankle. He wasn't sure who jumped higher, Heiden or the cat. "Damn!" He steadied himself against the desk, where ads in the open newspaper looked obscenely frivolous. MARIA MONTEZ STARS IN SOUTH OF TAHITI!

The Siamese returned to Heiden's legs, rubbing and meowing piteously. The house must be empty, he figured, or the Germans would have appeared at his cry. "You nearly scared me to death," he said. "I guess you didn't have a good morning either. Sure. You're hungry." The phone rang. Heiden saw why Ryker had taped up the box. The rings sounded five times. He ripped the tape from the phone and threw it against the wall. He stomped away but the cat's meowing was horrible and feeding it would only take a second. "Okay, shut up!" He found a bowl in the kitchen. "Fresh cream, Ephraim. You probably don't eat this well when the Ryes are here."

The gun cabinet was open upstairs but the rifles were gone. The only thing left inside was a pair of binoculars he took off a peg. He saw the master bedroom from the hallway: the open closet, the rumpled sheets. He imagined the Ryes waking to see Germans with machine guns at the foot of the bed.

He started back downstairs but stopped when he heard footsteps on the porch. He backed into the upstairs hall, peering through the banister.

Downstairs, the front door opened.

One of the raiders who entered was the man who had shot Turner.

Heiden pressed against the wall, unable to see the men now, afraid if he moved the floor might creak. The footsteps paused in the hallway. He envisioned the men listening, pivoting, machine guns at their hips. The steps grew muffled. He pictured them on the throw rugs in the living room. The steps grew sharper. They were in the hallway again.

What if he managed to get through the bedroom to the widow's walk only to expose himself to more soldiers outside? But the raiders would surely come upstairs. Hide under the bed? Draw the bathtub curtain? The steps had stopped again. He pictured the raiders in the kitchen. They had not paused this long since entering the house. Heiden's forehead started to throb. They'd seen something. The cat!

He imagined them kneeling beside the cat, looking at the freshly poured cream, touching the surface and nodding at the icy feel. This cat had just been fed.

Moving toward the bedroom, praying the floor wouldn't creak, he was careful to stay on the thin strip of rug in the hallway.

The window opened easily. He squeezed across the sill and stepped down to the fenced-in widow's walk, glimpsing the ocean over the tops of the trees. In the distance, twin columns of smoke rose but Heiden saw no ships. The lawn seemed deserted. He shut the window behind him. Maybe that would give him more time. Binoculars around his neck, he slid over the balustrade and onto the sloping roof. He inched forward on his haunches. He'd have to jump two stories. The raiders must have finished downstairs by now. At least the drawn living-room curtains would obscure his landing. He dropped off the roof, heart roaring, and rolled when he hit the ground, like he'd been taught in the obstacle course during basic training. He felt a sharp pain in his ankle. He scrambled into the forest.

The sun reflected off the bedroom window. He could not tell if someone watched. Heiden moved gingerly back into the woods, keeping weight off the ankle until he decided the damage was not lasting. It would be pointless to try another house. Ryker was too thorough. *I should have taken a knife.* The ground was wet in places, it sucked at his shoes. He plunged into a narrow stream, wincing at the cold water. At least he wouldn't leave footprints.

He moved at a stop-and-go pace, five steps and pause, six and pause. When he heard a crunching noise nearby he crouched and listened. The sound faded. He was circling the town, working his way toward the cove and the islander boats. He needed to avoid the beach, though, so he angled toward the thin pincer of land encircling the north curve of the harbor. Surrounded on three sides by water, it would provide no protection if the raiders tracked him there.

The birches thinned as he reached the headland, but they were still numerous enough to offer concealment. He worked his way along the natural-forested jetty. Peering from a leafy copse, he saw, across a hundred-yard expanse of water, islander boats anchored peacefully. Just another summer Sunday afternoon in Maine, complete with soaring gulls and the drone of pleasure craft from the ocean side of the headland. He made his way through the birches and saw the boat, a long power launch already too far away to hail. Through the binoculars he saw the beer can in the driver's fist and the streaming blonde hair of the passenger. He watched the receding foam of the wake.

He crept back to the cove. In the binoculars, the small bobbing vessels looked invitingly empty, close enough to touch, especially the sleek Hudson power yacht. He didn't know how to start it, but he knew where Michael Kelly hid the key to the Nova.

He scanned the wharf, the gas pumps, the lobster-trap shed, the bleaching hull on the beach. The dock's continuous cluster of high-water-marked timber resembled herons' legs. The cove smelled fresh and washed from rain. A smacking sound interrupted the soft slurping of water on the rocks. He removed the glasses. Widening ripples told him a fish had jumped, mackerel probably. He'd seen the kids pull them in from the wharf.

Where were the Germans? No matter how few soldiers Ryker commanded, he would be crazy not to have stationed men by the dock, if for no other reason than to guard against the arrival of a pleasure boat. Heiden focused on the lobster shack again, waiting for movement. He tried the glass rear of Cora's grocery. Encouraged, suspicious, he turned back to the boats. They were still empty but the second check revealed the Germans had been there. A buoy hook leaned sloppily against the side of Jack Rye's Nova. A lobster trap had been left atop the side of the Kelly boat. Kelly never would have left the trap there. It could fall over the side. Items seemed out of place on most of the boats. The Germans had been searching and probably smashing radios.

He could reach the Nova in five minutes with a good crawl stroke, but the crawl was noisy and noticeable. *Try underwater.* The absence of Germans still bothered him but he told himself he wouldn't feel much better if they were in view. He realized he might have fooled them by leaving his jeep in the woods. Maybe they'd driven into town and left when they didn't find the jeep. If that was the case, he might have forced Ryker to divide up the search party. With the island encompassing over two square miles, the Germans would be scattered all over the place.

He suppressed the urge to laugh, whether from joy or anxiety he did not know. He envisioned the Germans examining the discarded jeep in the forest, tracking him to the stream, and stopping, stymied. The two in the house might have missed him altogether or assumed he'd gone back into the woods. He left the binoculars under a bush. The sun warmed him when he removed his clothes. Kelly kept extra clothes and sneakers on the boat. He hyperventilated, building up air in his body. *Remember, the water is warmer in August.* But the shocking cold wiped away the thought. He submerged himself quickly and kicked hard. The rocks looked murky and jagged below. The bottom dropped away. Filtered sunlight turned the depths green. Shadow fish scattered at his approach. *Don't think about the cold.* But he felt it in his ears first. He avoided a huge submerged timber, angling up from a vague skeleton hulk below. *So that's why no one anchors in this part of the cove.* His legs throbbed. Surfacing for air, he glanced around quickly. The boats lay slightly to the right but still ahead. He adjusted his direction.

Christ, the fish are huge. He was a good swimmer and he exhaled in small bursts so as not to leave a trail of bubbles. When he came up again the boats were farther than he'd imagined. The cold was getting worse. He went down, concentrating on the sun.

He surfaced beside the Hudson yacht and peered around the side. A dinghy rocked below the deserted wharf. A lone duck quacked hysterically near shore. Gulls swooped above the water-marked timbers. He swam to the Kelly Nova, hauled himself over the side, and lay on the bottom.

He drew great draughts of air, soaking up luxurious heat from the sun and wooden deck. A dead stone crab lay bleaching beside him. The Nova was a thirty-two-footer with a high, V-shaped prow and a flat, low stern. It did eight knots in a calm sea. He'd fished with Kelly a couple of times. The wooden bulwarks, six inches across the top, were designed to provide a perch for the traps. Kelly put them there when he removed lobsters and baited them. But the Germans had left a trap there now. Heiden imagined them searching the boat and hoped they had not found the hidden key. He was careful to avoid touching the trap's rope, coiled on deck. The rope was attached to an empty Coca-Cola bottle that would mark the trap. But wooden traps were weighted with bricks and Kelly warned him about them both times they fished. Get tangled up in the rope and you'd be dragged over when the trap went over the side.

He wished he could move the trap but that would involve standing up. It would be risky enough to expose himself and steer the boat.

A dry work shirt and pants lay crumpled on the deck. He put them on. They stank of fish, like the whole boat, although the smell came primarily from two sink-sized troughs in the front, near the cockpit. The troughs would be filled with bloody fish heads in oil, lobster bait. The cockpit was roofed and windowed on three sides. The shortwave had been removed from brackets on the ceiling. A closed door beside the wheel led to the engine room.

The key should be behind one of the square granite blocks lining the gunwale for ballast.

Avoiding the rope, crawling so as to avoid being seen from shore, he slid one of the blocks aside. Something small glinted in a crack in the wood. His heart raced when he touched the key. The headlands looked very close now. His hands still shook but not from cold. He fitted the key in the ignition switch but didn't turn it. The worst part came first.

He peeked above the bulwark. Two soldiers patrolled the beach road. He ducked. When he looked out again they were almost out of sight.

Heiden scrambled over the far side of the boat but hung on so that his hips dangled in the water. The boat couldn't go anywhere until it was untied from its buoy. He inched forward, hand over hand, keeping the side of the Nova between himself and the wharf. The only other way of reaching the rope involved climbing directly onto the prow, which would be like raising a flag to announce his presence. Straining, propping himself on the prow on one elbow, he reached to untie the rope. It dropped to the water.

By the time he returned to the cockpit the boat was drifting. He turned the key and pumped the accelerator. Nothing happened. He tried again, using the choke. Nothing happened. "Come on, dammit." The Hudson yacht grew closer. He wanted to howl with frustration. *Check the engine.* It wasn't even turning over. He reached for the door but it opened before he touched the knob. He saw the emerging gun and the fist that held it. He stared into the face of the person confronting him. It was Ryker.

EIGHTEEN

HEIDEN STEPPED BACK INTO THE SUNLIGHT. The heat seemed to grow, he had trouble breathing. He almost lost his balance when the Nova bumped the yacht. Ryker's finger, close enough to touch, curved around dull blued steel. He held a U.S. Army Colt at waist level.

With his other hand, he dangled a metal cap with wires. "Distributor," he said. His voice seemed to come from far away. "We have them all." It splashed when he threw it over the side. Heiden felt as if he had been kicked in the stomach. He'd actually believed he was going to escape on the boat.

The world condensed itself into a black muzzle. He waited for the stillness to shatter. "Hiding in the engine room," he said bitterly. "That must have been fun."

Ryker's face showed faint surprise. "No games," he said. With a vague gesture and a trace of disgust, he indicated the automatic. "Jammed safety. Your major didn't take care of his gun."

The hulls scraped, high-pitched. Ryker wore the same dungarees and flannel shirt he'd had on when Heiden drove him around the island, except now a holster and bowie knife hung from his hip. He glanced toward the wharf. Whatever he looked for, he didn't see it. "Major Savage could have lived," he said. "Now you can."

The tone, not the words, penetrated first. Heiden looked up from the gun as Ryker said, "You're coming to the base." All Heiden knew was that Ryker wasn't going to kill him, at least not immediately. Relief flooded him. "Technical questions," Ryker said with a knowing look. "When we go, we'll leave you with the islanders."

The sick feeling returned with the word "questions." Heiden's skepticism must have shown about the rest. Ryker said, "I have nothing against you personally."

The tone was too genial. Heiden knew he was lying. Ryker was going to kill him later.

"Is that why everybody was shooting at me?"

"Major Savage was alive then. Then he didn't want to talk to us."

Over Ryker's shoulder and beyond the headland, Heiden saw a gliding white sail. A second followed close behind. *A race.*

Ryker's gaze flicked back. He remained expressionless but pulled the bowie knife from its sheath. To Heiden's astonishment, he put away the .45. "No noise," he said. "One's as good as the other."

More boats appeared. Heiden's mind was functioning now. He saw weapons all around him. The bait iron, six inches away by the trough, was a foot-and-a-half-long needle for stringing fish heads. Granite ballast bricks lined the gunwale. But stoop for a brick, reach for the bait iron, and Ryker would kill him instantly. Heiden had never forgotten the man's speed in the bar.

Something quickened inside him. He'd noticed the lobster trap rope on the deck.

"Your men," Heiden said. "Where are they?" The trap perched on the bulwark, behind Heiden and to his left. He was closer to it than Ryker. The rope coiled between them. *"Get your feet tangled up in that rope,"* Michael Kelly had said, *"and you'll be over the side before anyone can help you."*

Ryker said, "In town, the woods, there's one at Jeremiah's. You were smart, ditching the jeep."

The blue sea past the headland was a patchwork of sails. One veered from the main group, toward the mouth of the cove.

Ryker said, "We'll talk at the base. We catch you lying, you end up like the major."

The sail turned back and went the other way.

Heiden needed to cross four feet to knock the trap over the side, but instinct told him Ryker would cut him down if he moved now. The man's antenna was marvelous. Green eyes swept Heiden like radar.

Ryker gestured with the knife. "The engine room," he said. "Don't worry. Just calling for the dinghy." Desperate to keep the rope between them, Heiden dimly registered that Ryker must have a shortwave on the boat. He said, "Tell me why you're here."

Ryker just inclined his head. Heiden could have sworn the flecks started moving in his eyes.

"You're asking me to help you," Heiden persisted. "I want to know who I'm helping."

Ryker took one step forward, his leg an inch from the rope now. "You, that's who."

"You killed them!"

For an instant, he thought he had gone too far. But Ryker's lowered brows rose again. "You're wasted here," he said. The same lauding tone had swelled Heiden with pride after the bar fight. Remembering his envy and admiration for the man, Heiden was filled with shame.

"I'm not like you," he said, but Ryker ignored him and stepped forward. One foot was inside the rope now. "Okay," Ryker said, "you deserve to know. We're here to use the guns, your own guns." His eyes were shining and he could not keep the pride from his voice. Heiden realized he was bragging. "There's a special convoy."

The last sail had passed the headland. Heiden said, "The guns?" His head pounded. This was worse than anything he'd imagined. "That's crazy," he said, but his words sounded crazy, not Ryker's plan. Not after this morning.

Ryker's features seemed to stretch, the cheekbones grew prominent, the lips thick, the eye sockets deep and gargoylelike. "This afternoon," Ryker said. Coarse sensuality marked his voice; some violent well was being tapped. He had been frightening before; now his low tones made him terrifying.

Heiden's laugh was high-pitched. *Say something or he'll move you.* "You think you're going to get away after that? The planes will come as soon as you start."

"Worried you won't get out?" Ryker said. "Maybe you'll get out. Our U-boat is just offshore, a few hundred feet away. Just before we use the guns we drive a couple of your islander boats to the base. We attack the convoy. It'll take only ten minutes. We run to the beach and take the boats to the U-boat. It's easy. Risky but easy. Planes will never get here in time and the convoy escorts will be afraid to attack, to sail under the guns."

Heiden hurled himself at the trap, striking it at the same time Ryker smashed into him. The box went over the side. Heiden felt a punch and tearing in his shoulder. Then he was falling. His back crashed into the deck. Ryker loomed through the shooting spray, blade flashing. Heiden screamed.

Ryker stopped and glanced down. He must have felt the slithering rope. Heiden's foot caught him in the thigh, driving him back.

Ryker's leg jerked sideways and flew out from under him. His arms flailed. He crashed against the deck and bulwark. The rope, wrapped around his calf and ankle, dragged him, chest down. He grabbed the bait trough, toppling it. Fish heads spilled in blood-red oil. Ryker dug the bowie knife into the wooden planking. The end broke. His free hand closed over Heiden's ankle. Heiden struggled but Ryker held him in a vise. He stamped on the hand. Ryker wouldn't let go. They were both sliding in fish oil, which loosened Ryker's grip. Heiden kicked again and broke free.

Ryker grunted once. His face smashed into the bulwark. Feet first, he flew over the side.

Heiden stood up. He had one last view of Ryker's powerful thrusting struggles underwater. Then Ryker was gone.

Less than ten seconds had elapsed since Heiden struck the trap. Red stained the water around the boat from oil running out of the scuppers. Heiden froze when a shadow appeared near the surface. It was only a big blackfish drifting by.

I killed him.

The pain started in his shoulder then. He realized he'd been stabbed.

He remembered the punch he'd felt when Ryker crashed into him. When he brought his hand from his shoulder, it was coated with blood. He opened his shirt. Jagged flesh oozed under his armpit. He stared at his fingers. *Get out of here.*

Fish heads lay scattered, rotting. He slid the bait iron from the fallen trough, wrapped it in an oily rag, and stuck it in the back of his pants. He had to duck in the cramped, dark engine room. Ryker hadn't hidden a radio there, only a walkie-talkie. Heiden could talk to the Germans, nobody else. Enraged, he hurled it over the side.

He tied Kelly's extra pair of sneakers together and hung them around his neck, careful to keep them from bumping the wound. Wincing, he lowered himself over the bulwark. When the salt water hit the shoulder he had to keep from screaming. The wharf looked deserted, fifty yards away; oars rested invitingly in the dinghy. But the raiders would return momentarily. Using side-paddle stroke, which was easier than swimming underwater, he turned back toward the jetty.

The initial pain wore off. The cold numbed his wound. Imagining Ryker drowning gave him some strength, but when he reached shore he staggered into the trees. He planned to cross the jetty and get back into the ocean on the other side. He hated the idea of more swimming, but if the raiders had seen him they'd be coming up the jetty.

The sun broke through the poplars. He gave himself a minute of warmth, reached the rocks, and got into the water. The beach, a hundred diagonal yards off, was a rounded mass of cobble grey where he had found the arm a month and a half ago. The sea was rougher outside the cove. Cold spray clogged his mouth and stitched his nostrils. He stumbled through the tidal pools. The rocks sloped up to a solid line of rose-hip bushes where he sank down.

He looked back to see drying footsteps mark his trail. At least the bleeding had stopped. The rumble of an approaching vehicle came from the coast road on the other side of the bushes. Jeep, he figured, but it was the Hudson

Cadillac that cruised by, a raider framed in the passenger window.

When the car passed, he lurched across the road. He was sopping and his strength was gone. He had no idea where he was going, he only wanted to get away from the beach. He splashed along a forest stream, each step firing bolts of pain through his shoulder. The chattering sound was his teeth. The trees merged, going in and out of focus. When his foot hooked something, he was powerless to regain his balance. A low branch smashed his shoulder. The treetops whirled with his scream.

The ground rushed toward him, especially one tiny purple flower. He heard the hollow thud when he hit.

The black and yellow blur focused into a tiger swallowtail butterfly. The distant sea whispered and the leaves crackled when he drew his hands from under his chest. Heiden sat up.

He grabbed his head. His shirt had opened, the wound was coated with dirt and blood. Heiden crawled to the stream and splashed water on his face. He rinsed his mouth and drank. Wincing, he washed the shoulder.

The forest smelled lush and summery.

He remembered Ryker's hand clawing his ankle, leaving a red trail. Standing brought on a round of dizziness. *They're tracking you. Move.* How long had he been asleep? An hour? Through the treetops, the sun hung overhead.

Ryker had said, "We'll use the guns this afternoon."

He pulled the bait iron from his pocket, unwrapped it, and fingered the long shaft as he walked. He'd seen a newsreel when Mussolini invaded Ethiopia, of tribesmen attacking an Italian column with spears.

The enormity, the daring of Ryker's plan staggered him.

Two months ago a German U-boat had breached the British naval cordon at the Scapa Flow, sunk a destroyer, and escaped. The attack had caused a sensation. Heiden imagined the island cannons tracking, humming. When they fired, the very earth seemed to take to the air. Dust billowed and swamp birds screeched out of the reeds.

His gait grew stronger. Ryker had said, "We'll get out of here." But the laugh was on Ryker. Ryker was dead and Heiden felt dangerous. For the first time he felt like a menace instead of a victim. The anger pumped through him. Should he swim? Hide? The Germans weren't going to flee because Ryker was gone. Heiden's rage was suddenly so intense he thought he would explode from it. Swimming was not an option, not anymore. The sailboats never passed the island twice. And he wasn't going to hide while the Germans slaughtered a few thousand troops.

They weren't going to drive him from this island. The time for running was ended. Corrice was trapped; he hadn't seen Michael Kelly and feared the man was dead. A hundred and fifty men had been butchered while they slept.

The guns could open up any second.

You'll die, warned a voice in his mind.

No I won't. They haven't found me yet.

But even if he died, there were worse things than dying. Once you realized that, death lost influence. Pain could frighten, but how much more scared could he get? Besides, what of the troops on the ships, the sailors, the islanders who would be trapped with two tons of explosive fuel when the air force blanketed the base with four-hundred-pounders, because that was what they were going to do, they weren't going to make deals with Germans.

He had wanted to do many things with his life, have babies, grow old. They passed through his mind not as individual thoughts but as an urge, a sad longing. It didn't last. It wasn't strong enough. And then it was gone like it had never existed. *I'll take plenty of them with me.*

His mind had reached another plane. He saw the island as if from the air: the base, the nestling village and pockets of searching raiders in the forest, the Hudson Cadillac, the attackers in the battery, sleeves rolled to white forearms, pushing powder charges. He saw the islanders in the fuel room, the sliced phone lines and smashed radios, even the goddamn hungry cat in the Rye house. He envisioned the Kelly living-room map of Casco Bay, his world now, with egg-shaped Fort Williams an inch away. There was one working radio on this island and that radio was on the base. It was the radio Ryker had planned to use to offer the army his deal. Nothing was going to stop Heiden from reaching it.

He checked the sun and angled right. He knew exactly where he was going now. *You'll die,* the voice cautioned again. It had no power, not anymore. He needed one of the Sten guns and Ryker had told him where to get it.

The instant Ryker had felt the rope rushing at his feet, he knew Heiden had tricked him. He'd seen Heiden tense but had expected an escape attempt, not a leap at the trap. Amateurs did the unexpected, that was the dangerous thing about them. Then Heiden had kicked him farther into the rope.

His feet flew out from under him. Whatever happened next, he must not lose hold of the knife. He tried to protect his head but the blow to the deck was savage. The rest was instinct, his grabbing the trough and Heiden's ankle.

He glimpsed Heiden's terrified face as he flew over the side. The freezing water closed over his head.

Now he dropped fast, the rope taut below, the trap a plunging outline. *Hold the knife.* Two inches of broken blade remained. He was strong enough to double over and grip the line, even as he sank. Then the trap struck bottom and the impact sent the knife spinning.

The suffocation had begun with slight tugging in his throat. Pressure mounted in his chest. The blade glittered, disappearing into the cloud thrown up by the trap. The rope made maneuvering difficult. Groping the bottom, he stirred up more sand. Then his hand struck something.

It was the distributor cap he had tossed over the side.

Don't panic. He tried again. A sharp pain sliced through his palm and he yanked it back. The knife! He reached again, fingers closing around the bone handle. Vigorously, he parted the rope.

He kicked hard. He'd been underwater three minutes, he estimated. His chest felt as if it were exploding. He had to let out the rest of the air. The whole cove was alive with the hammering of his heart. His skull rang. He was wild to breathe. He should have reached the top by now. Blackness crept at the periphery of his vision.

He broke surface.

The air was sweet, sweet. There was a taut rope beside him and he hooked his arm around it. He wouldn't sink now if he fainted. He gasped, semiconscious. When his vision cleared he saw he'd come up amid the islander boats. He'd tied himself to a lobsterman's buoy rope and hung from the bow. His limbs ached. He did not know how much time had passed. The Kelly Nova, twenty feet away, still scraped against the yacht. He dog-paddled toward the Nova but stopped. Heiden could be crouched in the gunwale. That's what Ryker would do: make sure the enemy didn't come up again, smash him with a ballast brick if he did.

He felt blood dripping down his face and traced the gash from temple to cheek. It was deep but not dangerous. He was almost crazy with rage. If Heiden was on that boat, Ryker would kill him. If he wasn't, Ryker needed to walkie-talkie to summon his men. He squinted toward the wharf. Heiden wasn't visible but the dinghy was still tied to the dock. The lone duck had been joined by a flock. Ryker made sure none of those forms was a human head.

The boats blocked his view of the headland. He couldn't tell if Heiden had gone that way.

He dog-paddled around another Nova and hefted his head above the bulwark. He still couldn't see Heiden. He stared toward the headland but the bright sun had turned the water into a dazzling sheet. Cursing, he climbed onto the deck for a better view. No Heiden. The Kelly engine room was open.

He took a gutting knife back into the water. When he reached Kelly's boat he put his ear to the rocking hull. All he heard was scraping. With a single swift motion, he pulled himself over the side. Fish heads lay all over the deck. He wiped trickling blood from his chin. In the engine room, the walkie-talkie was gone.

He smashed the door in frustration. But now another thought struck him. Suppose Heiden hadn't left the cove at all but had hidden on another boat? Suppose he was waiting for more sailboats? Or simply for Ryker to leave so he could try for the dinghy? Ryker spent twenty minutes searching the boats. By the time he swam ashore he was ready to take the wharf apart plank by plank. He took ten minutes to collect the four Austrians stationed in town. They were smart enough not to ask about his face.

Ryker left two men at the wharf and took two to the

jetty. Since Heiden had not taken the dinghy, Ryker figured he'd gone back the way he had come. They found no footprints but Axel spotted blood on the cove rocks. There was blood in the forest and blood near the sea.

They stood on the rocks, looking east, over the swells.

Private Neuman shielded his eyes with his palm. "A sailboat could have picked him up."

"He drowned," said Axel. "I saw the sailboats. No one swam out to them."

Ryker stared at the cobble beach a hundred yards away. "He didn't drown and a boat didn't pick him up. He went back to the island."

"Sure of that, are you?"

"He wouldn't have gotten into the water here if he was heading out to sea. He would have gone in from the end of the jetty. Less swimming that way."

"Unless he wanted to fool us." Axel suppressed a smile, looking over Ryker's face. "Seems like he did it before."

Ryker's lips whitened. With his finger he traced lines on the beach. "He would have come ashore . . . there."

"Blood on the rocks if he did," said Axel.

"Maybe," Ryker said. "He wasn't losing much here."

He called for more troops on Axel's walkie-talkie. The three raiders ran back along the jetty, toward the beach.

Heiden walked out of the forest and into Jeremiah's salvage yard, conscious of watching eyes. He glanced across the sea of junk toward the Cape Cod cottage, a hundred yards away. He guessed the raider was there.

I left a man at Jeremiah's, Ryker had said. *A man. One* man. It was funny, thinking of a German in that house, surrounded by Jeremiah's civil service helmets, his war maps, his what-to-do-if-attacked articles. Heiden pictured the raider at the attic window, munching tomatoes from Jeremiah's victory garden.

He had circled the junkyard before exposing himself, to make sure the guard wasn't in the woods. Then he'd seen the attic curtain move. The window commanded a good view of the yard and Jeremiah's dock below the the cliff.

Ryker would have waited by the window.

Heiden kept low. The yard was crisscrossed by meandering idiosyncratic paths that had evolved over the years. Two salvaged hulls, a sailboat and a Nova, comprised the most prominent points. The rest was a mass of hubcaps, portholes, tires, refrigerators. Heiden saw gigantic engine blocks and pulleys, chains, a wooden propeller, a backhoe, cars. Rust and oil smell surrounded him.

A junkyard rope looped from his belt. He held the shovel low so that the sentry would not see. He imagined the Sten gun tracking him, yet still felt relatively safe. Sten guns were accurate at eighty yards; at one hundred and twenty they gave problems. Also, it was harder to shoot down, at an angle. And the raider would realize his silencer was useless in a junkyard, where stray bullets would ricochet on steel, alerting the enemy. No, the man would wait. Heiden drifted closer, staying out of range.

A rustling drew his attention. Three feet away on its hind legs, a monstrous junkyard rat sniffed at him. The rat disappeared into an old backhoe. Heiden shuddered and glanced at the house.

He reached the sailboat. Graceless in salvage, it towered, a thirty-foot-high monument to peeling paint. Heiden glanced at the three-foot hole caving in the side. "Must have been some rock," he muttered.

He left the shovel out of sight and stepped into the open,

fully exposing himself to the house. He didn't move for half a minute, then he ducked behind the boat.

He glanced out. His vantage point provided a view of Jeremiah's front and rear yards. Ten minutes passed and the German didn't leave the house. Heiden wondered if Ryker had lied about posting a guard. Or maybe, incredibly, the guard had failed to see him hide. Or had been relieving himself. Or had been asleep.

Heiden debated whether or not to step into view again, but at that moment caught a movement at the back of the house. A khaki-clad figure scrambled across the yard and into the forest. *He's circling around.*

Moving quickly, he recovered the shovel and squeezed down a shoulder-wide path, back toward the second boat. The raider would need three to five minutes to reach the point where Heiden had entered the junkyard. He would be heading for the sailboat Heiden had ducked behind. Heiden planned to ambush him before he got there, at the second hull, the Nova.

Just past a rusting Pontiac ahead, the path branched right and left at the Nova. What Heiden knew, what he hoped the raider would not realize, was that the hull was completely encircled by a path. Heiden had chosen the T-shaped junction of the circle and the main path as his point of attack.

He fastened the clothesline to the Pontiac's door. The door didn't budge when he pulled the rope. Unraveling the line, he reached the junction and turned left. He circled the back of the boat, making sure the rope didn't catch on the wreck. He emerged on the top of the T again, only now he stood where he would have been had he turned right originally, not left. He peeked around the corner. The raider was not yet visible on the main path. The clothesline, fastened ten feet away and on the opposite side of the path, snaked toward Heiden but around the left corner. He tugged it off the ground and relaxed his grip. The rope sank back to earth.

The sun was bright. The raider's shadow would precede the man by four feet. The German would notice the rope disappearing around the corner. He'd look left when he reached the junction.

Heiden would be waiting with the shovel, on the right.

It wasn't the safest plan imaginable, but under the circumstances he was proud of his ingenuity. He fixed on the spot, forty feet away, where the raider should appear. He reached back and leaned the shovel across his knees.

Five minutes passed. The German could be lost, could be approaching from the rear. Heiden didn't dare stand to scan the yard. He glanced back. When he turned around again, the first khaki leg was coming around the corner.

His heart beat in his throat. The shovel suddenly seemed paltry compared to the gun. Suppose the raider *didn't* look left. Heiden wished for a more diagonal junction of paths instead of a T, so as to provide a better hiding place.

The soft brushing of shoes was audible now. He pictured the black swelled Sten barrel moving side to side, swishing almost. The German must have reached the Pontiac. Heiden yanked the clothesline, heard it snap against the car ahead and the hull behind. If the raider had heard the second sound he might look right.

Heiden dropped the rope and gripped the shovel. The air grew hot. The shadow head appeared by his feet, grew a neck. The gun's snout came into view and—*Not yet*—he saw khaki. The raider looked left. Rising, unhesitating, Heiden swung the shovel with all his might.

NINETEEN

FRANTIC ACTIVITY MARKED the Portland docks. Amid whistles and groaning derricks, soldiers finished loading the convoy. Mewing gulls soared between screeching winches. Shipyard clanging fed the constant commotion, along with shouts and arriving trains.

"Up anchor in an hour," said the commodore. "Then up to Halifax. Iceland. Belfast." Silver-haired and fiftyish, he looked down, with two other men, from the wheelroom of the freighter *John Kukulka*. Sailors on the forward deck guided a laden net into the hold. "Easy," they cried. Red brands marked the crates inside.

"One torpedo, that's all it would take," muttered the second man. A fleshy, shrewd-eyed civilian in a loose-fitting suit, Joseph Cardi ran the waterfront unions in Portland and helped with convoy security. "Some camouflage," he said. "Marking explosives in red."

On the narrow pier between ship and warehouse, troops with carbines stood every ten feet.

The third man said, "You're a worrier." Charles Evans, special liaison between navy security and the OSS, added, "No one's going to reach this ship."

"That's what they said in New York." Cardi referred to the mysterious fire that had sunk the troop carrier *Normandie* in Brooklyn a few weeks before. The daylight blaze had been the catalyst for the security effort between navy and union.

The empty net rose out of the hold, past grey crates tied on deck: bombing planes for the RAF. Sailors leapt to lock the hatches.

The commodore faced both men. "You'd think *you* were going to England, not me." He was interrupted by a yeoman who announced that a navy repair team had left the ship. Then he swung to look at the harbor. Over a dozen ships wove in and out, seemingly at random, but they were forming up for the convoy. Each vessel flew two colored flags, to mark row and position in the open sea.

The commodore picked a coffee mug off a chart table. "We'll have a heavier escort than most," he said. "If *I* wanted to attack this ship I'd do it before the convoy formed up."

Evans stepped close. "I assure you. There's no U-boat in the bay." He tapped the chart table. "I know the sonic buoys went off two days ago, but we've secured the whole area since then. Destroyers, planes. Schools of fish can set off the buoys, so can waves."

"So can subs," said Cardi dryly, "that lie on the bottom, waiting."

Evans exhaled noisily. Straight-backed, the commodore faced the harbor, looking as if he were trying to see under the surface.

Cardi said, "We never caught the Kraut who came ashore at Milbridge," and Evans flushed as he said, "You don't know *who* came ashore." He softened his voice for the commodore. "I assure you. The convoy will reach England unscathed."

Cardi snorted, "Unscathed," and the commodore turned back. "An hour and we pass Captains Island, those guns. I shudder every time I sail under them."

Evans said, "The harbor's locked up tight. You have my word on it."

"And no more gas through Portland," Cardi said. "That was the agreement. Poison Boston next time."

Evans bowed. It was a curiously German gesture. "One more hour and you can go home, Cardi. Relax, both of you. What can happen in an hour?"

The supply launch floated to Captains Island and bumped the dock. Manned by two privates, it was a grey twenty-footer that had been requisitioned from a Portland shoe manufacturer.

"Get yer fuckin' perishable Sunday eggs," growled private Stanley Bernstein at the wheel. He scowled at two soldiers looking down at him. The canvas-topped truck was parked on the wharf, just like every Sunday. "And yer milk, you pansies. Makin' me work on weekends when Florence is in town. New guys, huh? Where's Mitchell and Henry?"

"Shipped out," said the blonde private on the dock. "To Pearl."

Bernstein couldn't make out the accent. He was a Brownsville, Brooklyn, boy and he hadn't had a lot of exposure to other accents until a few months ago. Midwest? Was Montana in the Midwest?

Then he noticed the wary way the other soldier gripped his carbine and he laughed. "No sweat. Nobody tried to hijack the eggs yet."

The unloading took twenty minutes, twice the usual time because the men on the dock didn't lift a finger to help. They just watched. Back on the boat, Bernstein whipped out his little bookie pad. He licked his pencil. "In the pool?" he asked.

The privates looked at each other. "Pool?"

"The baseball pool. Mitchell always went with the Cubs. You coming in?"

"In?" said the blonde man.

"Win big dough in the Bernstein pool."

"No thank you," the private on the dock said. "I don't gamble."

Bernstein slammed the launch in gear and headed into the cove. He nudged Private Gable as they passed the islander boats. "No wonder guys get weird out here. How do they stand it with nothing to do?"

They reached the headland. Bernstein muttered, "Doesn't bet, huh? What is he, un-American?"

Lance Corporal Albert Neuman knelt in the forest and fingered a broken twig. The pulp was still moist. "He was here," he said.

Axel's wrists stuck out of his sleeves. "The last trail was Krieger's," he growled. "Ryker's crazy, making us chase each other in the trees."

Neuman lowered his voice conspiratorially. "It's him. I know it. Something is written on the twig."

"Written?"

"It says, 'This twig was snapped by Americans.'"

Neuman started laughing. Axel spun suddenly and fired into the bushes. A voice cried, "Stop shooting! It's me, Krieger!" A stocky alpiner stepped into view. "Shit. I've been following *you*?"

Axel spat. Neuman said, "The situation improves. This can't be your trail."

Axel said, "It's probably Weissman's trail." Neuman suggested they team up, and several seconds later they found snapped fronds and crushed toadstools by an oak.

"He's heading northwest," Neuman said. "Toward the salvage yard."

The laughter was gone from his voice. It was obvious from the blundering path that an amateur had left this trail.

The forest was still as always, that was the crazy thing about it. Heiden could almost believe the Germans had never landed at all. His stop-and-go pace was deliberate now. He headed toward the base.

Once he heard trackers. He halted and spotted them after a moment. They passed, apparently following another trail.

Crossing the cliff where he'd made a fool of himself over the kids with the flashlight, he saw that the dry earth had preserved dozens of footprints from the night before. *This is where they landed.*

He didn't feel like Lieutenant Flashlight anymore, that was for sure. It was amazing how much more energy you had when you stopped wasting it being afraid. Using the protruding watchtower as a reference point, he skirted a pond and small reed swamp. He'd stripped the dead German at Jeremiah's, discarded Michael Kelly's fishing clothes, and donned the private's khaki denims. The raiders were dressed like enlisted men; now he was too.

He'd also changed into bedroom slippers in the house. If he left footprints now, they would look different.

The Sten gun felt sturdy and menacing. He smelled its oil tang mixed with the vegetable humidity. Heiden had tested the gun, clipping the lower branches of a tree, watching the flying wooden bits before he was even aware of pulling the trigger.

He would have to remember that the barrel rose left to right when he fired.

We use the battery this afternoon, Ryker had said. Well, it was afternoon now. He had given himself an hour to try to reach the base radio. Even a superman couldn't help the convoy if it passed before then.

He was skirting the northwestern coast of the island. Vines and creepers hung from trees as thick as any South American rain forest. A lone raven flashed across a field, against the green. The insect buzz grew incessant. At a deeper droning, he looked up. A navy patrol plane flew low, its boat hull casting a missile-shaped shadow across the savanna. *Closer,* he prayed, ready to shoot to catch the pilot's attention, but it headed out to sea. Fort Williams seemed a million miles away.

Climbing a steep incline, he flashed on his killing of the commando in the salvage yard. The man had half turned when Heiden's spade caught him in the temple, crushing it like an egg.

With the blow something had changed inside him. He had been sick at first, but then he felt as if some well of capability had been tapped. He felt stronger. The heat soaked into him; so did the forest air. He had an inkling of the sort of power Ryker had exuded, the same kind of rawness he felt now. But Ryker had so much more of it. With the realization, the extent of Heiden's luck on the boat became clearer. He shuddered.

The fence appeared. He crouched, scanning from behind a log. He heard the rap-rap of a woodpecker on a tree. The chicken wire broke the view into pieces, patches of green and brown in fibrous frames. But something was wrong.

It was the off color, the subtle change in hue that alerted him to the sentry's presence. Through an opening in the foliage, he saw a bit of khaki, lighter than the oaks. The six-inch patch shifted, a stone's heave away and easy target in the open, but Heiden had no way of knowing what might block his shot in the woods.

He propped himself over the log. Movement might be dangerous. Heiden slipped off the safety as the color slid toward a five-foot gap in the trees. In another second the man would break into the open.

Heiden's conscience tugged at him. Would he shoot an unaware man?

The German stepped out of cover.

Heiden pulled the trigger.

The machine gun seemed to come alive in his hands, rising left to right. He had to hold on. Hissing bullets sprayed into the trees, shaving wood bits and chopping wire.

Sixty feet away, the sentry cried out and threw up his hands; the Sten gun went flying. He backed, legs buckling, and fell sideways out of sight.

The gun barrel smoked with a cordite odor. Heiden started to stand but changed his mind. He took off his shirt and waved it on a stick. With the shirt back on, he crept from behind the log and south, parallel to the fence for thirty-five feet. Climbing the fence was the worst part. Tree to tree on the other side, he doubled back toward the fallen sentry.

Nobody was there.

Heiden dived for the ground and rolled. He came up

firing in a circle. Clipped leaves fluttered to the earth. A bird screamed in the trees. The sentry's Sten gun lay a few yards away but the man was gone.

Then he saw the marks, two jagged lines disappearing into a bramble patch.

Heiden felt the barb in his belly. Less than an hour ago he had killed a man by tricking him with a false trail. Even if the Sten gun had been discarded by accident, the raider would still have a knife. The man was probably watching, hoping Heiden would concentrate on the tracks in the ground. The raider would jump out from another direction.

He fired a burst into the brambles, but could not afford to use up the clip. Carefully, he skirted the bramble patch. A fly buzzed in his ear, settled. He felt it crawling but couldn't take his hand from the gun. The heel of a boot extended out of the bushes. He fired and the shoe jerked, but that could have been from the impact.

His mind screamed, *It's a trick.*

Heiden swept the bush aside.

The body lay face up, leaves matting the black hair. The man's hands hooked like claws into the earth.

Holes stitched the chest, each one the center of a spreading stain, the last one marking almost the exact spot where Ryker had stabbed Heiden.

It was the raider who had killed Turner. Heiden waited for the sick feeling but this time it didn't come. The corpse was practically concealed already. He only had to adjust the bushes to hide it completely. He recovered the sentry's gun and slung it over his shoulder. He had his own arsenal now, *two* Sten guns, plus the sentry's extra ammunition.

Heiden hurried toward the parade ground. On an overhead branch, an apple twirled, slashed by a bullet, red and white.

Ryker rocketed the jeep through the gate and past the parade-ground guard. He was still steaming over Heiden's escape, but visibly he had himself under control. He had wasted too much time in town. The convoy could be coming now.

The battery stank of powder and oil. He found Teacher directing a practice crew at the first cannon. Half a dozen raiders tracked a battleship in the strait. The swiveling seventy-foot gun extended out under a concrete lip and into the sunlight. "Five degrees," Teacher called over the hum. "Up, move it up." The concrete floor vibrated. Half a mile off, the vessel filled the waterway, monstrous, bristling.

Ryker called, "Teacher," and the head turned halfway. "Do I hear a voice?" Teacher asked. "A voice from the past?" He held up a hand to the crew. "Nobody tell me. Let me guess. It can't be Uncle Julius."

Even from the side, his gaunt face was filthier than usual, lined with fatigue. The men had been working at top speed, Ryker could see that.

An Austrian on the rotating platform called cheerfully, pointing at the battleship, "Plenty of sixteen-inchers there, eh Ryker?" Ryker patted his crotch. "Here too." At the roar of laughter the gash in his face went hot. *I don't feel it.*

Teacher faced him all the way now, his eyes traveling up and down the wound. He whistled, low and flat. "I have warned you, Ryker. Do not pet the dog when he is eating."

Ryker said, "Where's the convoy?"

"We haven't heard yet."

The lazy drone of a plane filled the emplacement. A

boat-hulled navy patroller swept low, the pilot's face a grinning oval. Men stepped into the sunlight and waved, then
the plane headed over the swamp and toward the battleship. Teacher's shoulders slumped. "Back to work."

The gun started tracking. Teacher removed his glasses
and cleaned them with his fingers, although it was unclear
which was dirtier, the lenses or his hands.

Ryker said, "Problems?"

"Men. I have only six on each gun. Had to send two into
town for a dairy shipment. They're on their way back. But
I'm happy you've brought back the others. Where are they?"

Ryker, who had left the men on the other side of the
island, said, "Any messages from the fort? Other boats?"

Teacher pressed his palms together like a pious church-
goer. He rolled his eyes toward the heavens. "On Sunday?"

Three six-foot bombs hung from steel pincers on a monorail track. Ryker hoped the ceiling, which under normal
circumstances would hold up one shell at a time, would
support the six-ton weight. He heard running footsteps
and the creak of carts from the main corridor, which, when
they walked into it, seemed much too vast for the handful
of raiders struggling to push powder charges to the guns.
Each silk-bound bag weighed up to six hundred pounds.

At the far end of the tunnel, five hundred feet away, a
splash of sunlight marked the second gun emplacement.
The whole battery vibrated. Condensation poured down
battleship-grey walls.

Ryker and Teacher went over the escape plan. When
the convoy was first spotted, two raiders in town would row
out to the Hudson yacht and one of the Novas. They would
reattach the distributors to the engines and drive the boats
around the island. The raiders had to wait until the convoy
appeared to do this because civilian boats were not per-

mitted in base waters, and a patrol plane spotting them would immediately radio ashore that something was wrong on Captains Island. The raiders would use the guns for no more than ten minutes. The U-boat, monitoring radio signals, would know when to surface.

"Safe and sound," Teacher said dryly. "I don't suppose you've thought of an alternative plan if the Americans land before our attack."

"They won't," Ryker said. "But if they do, we get out anyway. We offer a trade. That battery is worth plenty, as much as ten B-17s. Plus we have the islanders." He reminded Teacher how, in Norway, Erhard had designed a method to detonate an explosion from two miles off, using a walkie-talkie signal. "Set it up," Ryker ordered. "The Americans land first and we offer a deal. They let us go and they get the battery and islanders untouched. We see a single warship and we blow the base up."

"And planes, Ryker?"

Ryker nodded. "Planes are different. Why should the Americans trust us? They'll figure we'll blow the battery even if they let us go, so they'll need a guarantee. We'll allow a single fighter, a fighter, not a bomber, not a plane that could sink a sub. If we explode the battery the fighter sinks our little boats. If the fighter attacks first we blow up the battery. No warships for two miles. Once we're underwater the radio signal won't work, we won't be able to do damage even if we want to. The Americans will understand. If they send an antidemolition crew before we reach the U-boat, they'll never find all the charges."

They had stopped in the doorway of the powder room, which was high-ceilinged and packed with ammunition. "Enough here to blow the island to Vienna," Teacher said. "And the islanders are close to that wall."

Ryker shrugged. "It's the Americans' fault if the islanders are killed, it's their choice."

"Very generous of you."

"I saved your life. Got you out of Russia. Learn to trust. I know it's a gamble, a fallback plan."

"Unlike your other foolproof plan?"

"I take the same risks you do, Teacher."

Teacher smiled and spread his hands. "But I want to live and you don't."

Ryker colored. Teacher said quickly, "I'll need the men you brought from town. There's too much work on the guns."

"I didn't bring any men from town."

Teacher frowned. "I don't understand. If you found the lieutenant, why . . ." He trailed off and exhaled audibly. "Heiden did that to you and he *got away?*"

"Set the explosives," Ryker snapped. Teacher left. He had, he guessed, forty minutes until the convoy was spotted, maybe an hour to assemble the shells, drill with the guns. An hour for his men to find Heiden.

Ryker had felt his knife penetrate Heiden's underarm, but the wound couldn't be serious or Heiden could never have reached shore. Heiden knew the raiders planned to leave after the attack. He could save himself if he hid.

But Heiden wouldn't hide. Ryker cursed himself for telling him about the convoy.

Could Heiden know about extra radios on the island, radios Ryker had missed? Ryker didn't think so. Heiden would have already used one if he did. Swim? Heiden would have left from the headland. Ryker strode toward the far cannon. Would Heiden attack? He stopped. Ryker would try but Heiden wasn't him.

He started walking but stopped again.

Never assume. If Heiden did attack, what would he attack? Corrice was on the base, so was a radio and phones. It was barely conceivable that Heiden would return to the base. He also knew about the dinghy by the wharf, which he could use to reach Fort Williams.

Ryker bolted toward Teacher's gun. He had left only one sentry on the wharf. It was unlikely that Heiden could overcome the man, but if he did he'd have a Sten gun. And now Ryker remembered telling Heiden about the sentry at Jeremiah's, too.

The raiders looked surprised when he burst around the corner. He calmed his breathing before using the walkie-talkie. On the air, the raiders assumed Americans could be listening at any time, even with the special high frequency. They used a code and American names.

Ryker called the wharf, casually made sure the supply boat had left, and suggested that the guard "untie" the dinghy. That meant sink it. He checked with the lookout on the south coast, who watched for the convoy. The sentries at the base gate and fence would hear the oblique warning to stay alert.

He tried Jeremiah's. "Steve?"

No answer. "Steve!"

Neuman's voice answered. "It's Barry."

"I wanted Steve." Ryker envisioned sailors in the harbor, listening.

"We're going there now." Neuman's accent was emerging. He had pronounced the "th" sound as a "z."

"Call me when you get there." Ryker broke the connection. He shouldn't be using the walkie-talkies at all. If Heiden had gone to the junkyard knowing a sentry was there, he was after a Sten gun. He was smart enough to know Jeremiah's radio and submarine would be disabled. And there was only one reason Heiden would risk his life for a gun.

Incredibly, the lieutenant was switching to the attack.

Heiden could never hope to win, or even live, but that wasn't the problem. As a superbly trained athlete, Ryker knew that in order to ruin a fine-tuned performance, you don't have to block it entirely, don't have to beat it, you only have to throw it off, even slightly. Simply by staying alive, Heiden had already sapped ten percent of the attack force. He had forced raiders to constantly risk using the walkie-talkies. He had slowed preparations in the battery.

Now he might have a Sten gun. Back in the corridor, Ryker stopped a trooper wheeling powder charges and ordered the man to take up guard duty by the radio shack. Then he took over the cart. It was heavier than it looked, but the physical labor cleared his mind.

Except three minutes later he saw that the man had not left the battery but was helping the gun crew. Ryker couldn't believe it. Quite plainly, he had told the man what to do. The anger began burning as Teacher materialized at his side, reaching to soothe him. "I'm sorry, Ryker, really sorry. I was looking for you to tell you."

But for Ryker, the air seemed to have drained out of the battery. Even the greyness had left Teacher's face. The fear in his voice was the only mollifying aspect of the situation. "Please," Teacher said. "I have six men on each gun. I need fifteen. I have twelve to prepare the powder room, check the base schedules, to move fourteen two-ton shells and three thousand pounds of powder. They can't do it if you cut the manpower! The guns won't be ready!"

Ryker felt the muscles bunching in his neck. His fury over Heiden's escape was still fresh. What had Teacher said a few minutes ago? *He did that to you and he got away?*

And now Teacher had countermanded an order, a direct order, an order Ryker had given only minutes ago. He had trouble understanding the torrent of words, so consuming was his rage. The raiders had stopped working. They watched now. It had ended like this in Norway, a near mutiny settled with a bullet. And Teacher had been there, had seen it, had even warned the men about it. *Obey Ryker instantly.*

And now he, of all of them, who knew the breaking point, had not obeyed at all.

"You've got to listen," Teacher said. Sweat poured down his face. With supreme effort, he kept his hands at his sides, not compounding his danger by trying to defend himself. "You can't plan for every contingency. The guns need forty-six-man crews. We're behind schedule!"

His words combined with his tone and posture. Ryker forced himself to think. He could see the throbbing vein in Teacher's neck. *He's right, yes, but he didn't follow my order.* "I'll kill you next time," Ryker whispered. Relief flooded Teacher's face. "I won't do it again. We'll get him in the woods." Teacher whirled on the men. "Work, all of you. Now!" Sullen, they turned. Ryker felt their hatred and it made him feel better.

But then he remembered how Heiden had tricked him, fooled him. *He did that to you and he got away?* The men had gone back to their jobs and he stood alone. He caught sight of his reflection in the bright polished nose cone of a shell overhead. It widened his face like an amusement-park mirror. It aged him.

He felt a wild urge to empty the installation, comb the woods, find Heiden personally and pay him back. At that moment he hoped the Americans would attack instead of agreeing to his escape plan. This morning's takeover had been too easy. He'd been planning for months, he was sick of planning. He needed to fight.

The urge died. He whipped off his shirt and leaned into the cart, the sweat smell thick in his nostrils. He would wait for Neuman's call from the salvage yard. If Heiden had attacked the sentry, Ryker would send a guard to the radio shack, whether he was short of men or not.

That guard would be Teacher or Teacher would be dead.

Heiden paused in the high grass at the edge of the parade ground. Last time he'd been here, Ryker's trackers had been coming for him. Now he had two silenced guns; the situation was reversed. He gripped the stock and looked over the square, checking his plan for flaws.

A single guard, very much in range, circled slowly by the manhole cover, thirty feet from the battery entrance, diagonally across from the radio shack. At least one raider would be inside. But where was everybody else?

Heiden brightened. *They don't have enough men.*

That didn't mean Germans weren't in the barracks or officers' quarters. Empty windows lined the square.

The manhole cover was a curving slit seconds away. Heiden had unlocked the bolt a hundred times while supervising fuel loadings. He envisioned Corrice, Jeremiah, all the islanders looking up at him, surprise turning to amazement. In another few seconds more raiders could come out of the battery. *Get them out of here.*

Hating himself, he turned away. Once he invaded the parade grounds, the odds of getting out alive were minuscule. He would try to help Corrice later but he had to reach the radio first. His plan was to circle in the grass, hide behind the barracks, and make his way to the rear of the shack.

When he had gone as far as possible in the grass, he waited until the guard faced the other direction. A thrill of fear hit him when his feet touched the cut lawn. He reached the barracks and hugged the sloping green wall.

An odd, sickly-sweet smell wafted from an open window a few feet away. He slid over and glanced inside.

Heiden gasped and stood up in the window.

In two neat rows, the dead lay in their cots, pale arms dangling, magenta streaks on pillows and sheets. Cot after cot. Dust danced in sun shafts. Two men had half tumbled out of bed. Flies crawled on their shoulders.

It was worse than anything he'd imagined. Thick glasses lay beside most beds. Feet stuck out of covers, obscenely blue. He'd drilled with these men, joked with them, soldiers healthy enough for the army in Maine but not the battlefield.

They looked so undignified.

He turned away. The parade ground was unchanged, with its green carpet under a warm blue sky. A jeep and canvas-topped truck were parked by the other battery entrance. A sea breeze brushed his cheek and the sweet smell enveloped him. He gagged but kept from getting sick. *Reveille. Wake up. Blow the bugle and get up.*

He had overheard Teacher on the parade ground. "We killed all the soldiers." Heiden looked inside again. Seventy corpses lay in their beds.

He inched to the edge of the barracks. The guard was looking in his direction but turned away. Heiden made the twenty-five-foot run to the radio shack, ready to fire if necessary. The open rear window was decorated with lace curtains and flowerpots. He heard an unaccented voice inside.

"Sergeant Pulski's on furlough. I'll tell him you called."

At the click of the phone Heiden shoved the barrel through the window and pulled the trigger. He heard the flowerpot crash to the floor. The face in front of him was splintering, exploding into spray and bone. The Sten rose, driving the raider into the radio. Heiden couldn't stop firing. The man seemed to be coming apart before his eyes.

His finger clenched on the trigger even after the gun ran out of bullets.

Drenched, the raider sprawled over the radio.

Little fountains spurted from his neck and chest. Pools merged on the floor.

Heiden removed the other flowerpot and climbed through the window. He discarded his Sten gun and picked the German's off the table. The third gun still lay over his shoulder.

When the raider started to slide, Heiden jerked, but it was clear all life had left that body. Heiden peered out of the front window. The sentry had cocked his head as if he'd heard something. He turned in a slow circle, listening.

He shrugged.

All Heiden could focus on below was an untied shoelace. The room smelled like the barracks.

Heiden noticed a bare shimmering spot beside the body, a tiny sparkle in the light. He touched his face. He was crying.

Move, he thought. He reached for the radio.

It was smashed. Slowly, he realized he had shot it to pieces.

While on the high south cliffs of the island, Austrian Private William Protzer lifted Zeiss Ikon binoculars to his face and aimed at an oncoming freighter, emerging, miles off, to head a line of ships. Estimated speed: eight knots.

Protzer adjusted the focus, trying to make out the name. It was the *John Kukulka*.

He grabbed his walkie-talkie and alerted the base. Scrambling from his rocky perch, he ran toward a baloon-tired bicycle leaning against a tree.

With a backward glance at the convoy's rising smoke, he pedaled furiously for the base.

The ships would pass in twenty minutes.

TWENTY

HEIDEN'S BACK WAS SOAKED, his ears burned. All the heat in the world seemed to concentrate in the radio shack. The convoy was coming and he'd destroyed the radio.

The corpse grinned up at him from the floor. When the guns went off they would rock the island, blowing out windows, cracking trees.

Heiden reached for the phone. But you had to go through channels with phones, you couldn't talk directly to ships. He dialed with trembling fingers. The ringing seemed interminable.

"Fort Williams," announced a brisk female voice. Heiden snapped, "This is an emergency. Give me Harbor Entrance Control."

It was the nerve center in the bay, a radio plotting room staffed by army and navy. An order from that room could stop a convoy and dispatch troops.

Heavy static came over the line.

"Harbor Control. Corporal Allen."

"This is Tom Heiden, Lieutenant Heiden on Captains Island. *We're under attack!* Get your commander, move!"

"Do you know the code of the day, sir?" Allen had the monotone whine of a bureaucrat.

"The code?" The password was changed each midnight and chalked above the radio. But Heiden had been with Corrice last night. And the dead raider had fallen against the blackboard.

"It's smeared, I can't read it!"

"You don't know the code?"

"For Christ's sake! Yesterday was Zulu, Aaron Joseph the day before!"

"I'm sorry, I'm under orders. No password, no . . . did you say attack, sir?"

"Put on your CO!"

Heiden heard a hand cover the receiver. His wound throbbed, his arm was cramped, leveling the gun at the closed door.

"Major Calabrese! Who the hell is this?"

"Heiden, sir, Lieutenant Heiden. On Captains Island and . . ."

"Why don't you know the code?"

The code, Heiden wanted to scream. *Who cares about the fucking code!*

He said, "Our radio operator, everyone is dead. Germans. They came ashore last night."

"What?"

"They have the battery. Waiting for a convoy. The islanders, the whole town, prisoners."

"Holy . . ." The major caught his breath. "Where are you calling from?"

"The radio shack."

"The *base* radio shack?" The major seemed to be saying, I thought you said Germans overran the base.

"I got back inside. Killed a guard."

The static grew loud. "Germans took the base. Germans . . . The base. Let me speak to Major Savage."

"Didn't you hear what I said? Major Savage is dead!"

The major sounded impatient. "A hundred and fifty soldiers bunk on Captains Island. Are you telling me Germans killed them all? We've seen no ships, no planes."

"You have to stop the convoy!" Heiden wanted to weep with rage but he forced himself to speak more slowly. "They came from a U-boat."

"And killed everyone but you. Lucky you. Where were you when all this happened?"

"With my girlfriend." His jaw hurt, it was clenched so tight. "AWOL."

"Heiden. Now I remember that name." Heiden recognized the tone and grew hot. "You're the guy they call Lieutenant Flashlight. Sure, Captains Island. The guy who called the false alert."

"I—"

"Aren't you that Heiden?"

"Yes, but—"

The voice grew angry. "And you want me to stop a convoy?"

"Damn you, you've got to stop the convoy. Stop the convoy; they're going to die!"

"This has gone far enough."

Heiden pleaded. "Call any phone. On the island. Nobody can answer. You stupid ass, it'll be your fault!"

"When this turns out to be another story, I'm coming personally. Savage was too easy on you last time."

But Heiden caught a note of frustrated surrender. "You'll do it? Stop them?"

"I'll check your story, all right. Call those phones."

"And then?"

He could almost hear gnashing teeth. "What the hell choice do I have?"

"Send men! Hurry!" Heiden cut the conversation with a downward jab of his finger. He left the receiver off the hook so the phone couldn't ring and alert the guard.

His shirt was drenched; he wiped his hands on his trousers.

That stupid major better get moving fast. From the window Heiden observed the lone sentry. He slung the dead radio operator's gun and ammo pouch over his shoulder, beside the gun that had come from the guard by the fence. That made a thirty-pound load. He snapped a fresh clip into the Sten in his hands. He couldn't believe he might see Corrice in minutes.

Were raiders occupying the other buildings, looking out from the officers' quarters or other prefabs?

He took a deep breath.

Threw open the door and fired.

The sentry had been looking directly at the shack. The Sten came up fast but the man was knocked backwards by multiple impacts. He opened his mouth and dropped to his knees.

A single tortured groan emanated from across the parade ground.

Heiden was already running as the man fell, face forward.

He zigzagged, expecting bullets, but when none came he made directly for the manhole cover. The battery entrance loomed. The ground vibrated. The guns were moving. Heiden saw smoke rising over the battery, from out in the strait.

The major hadn't stopped the convoy.

He fought off the sick feeling, kneeling frantically to draw the bolt. It wouldn't budge. He smashed it with the stock of his Sten gun. It clanged open. When he lifted the cover the islanders were looking up. "It's me! Hurry!" He didn't wait to see them respond but aimed at the battery. He felt like a target, utterly exposed. Footsteps sounded on the ladder and Jeremiah's head poked above ground.

"Pick up a Sten. Safety's on the left. Take an extra clip in case you need it."

Jack Rye came out of the hole, Bobby Lee behind him. "Watch the other entrance," Heiden ordered. Rye ran off with a Sten gun. To Jeremiah, Heiden said, "Run that way." He indicated the quickest route from the parade ground, past the barracks and radio shack. "Into the grass, toward the ridge. Gunners guard the rear."

"I'll tell the women."

"I'm not talking about the women. I'm talking about everybody! Mrs. Rye! That way! *Corrice!*" They tore their eyes from each other when she ran. Jeremiah said, "You're not going to fight? Where are the Heinies? In the battery?"

Four Sten guns, Heiden thought, against an arsenal. No way to guard the seaside battery entrances. The raiders could spill around the side. No way to cover the top of the battery, the road from the base gate, the ridge. Jeremiah's babble enraged him. "I'm not digging in with a dozen people," he snapped.

"Why not? We'll trap 'em! The rifle club is ready!"

The line of fleeing islanders stretched from the manhole cover past the barracks. Heiden hissed, "Go, will you!"

Jeremiah thrust out his jaw. "I ain't movin'.."

He used his town-meeting voice, his Maine fisherman voice. He used his you-can-go-to-hell-you-weren't-born-here voice. Their noses were an inch apart. At that distance, all

Heiden saw was one gigantic eye. He said, "I don't need your shit, mister." The eye blinked in shock. Heiden said, "Killing yourself is your business, you're not going to murder your kids."

"But I—"

Heiden grabbed Jeremiah's shirt. "Question my orders and I just might shoot you myself."

Jeremiah looked at Heiden as if he had turned into Roosevelt himself.

Dumbly, he nodded.

"Now get over to the barracks and cover me. And when I leave, you leave, *understand?*"

"Yes *sir,*" Jeremiah said. Then he said, "Germans."

Heiden whirled to the soft hiss of Jeremiah's gun. He recognized the German called Teacher, fleeing back through the extending concrete arms of the battery, but a hammer blow drove him into the wall, pinning him. Heiden fired too. With supreme effort, Teacher pushed himself back, staggered a step and crumpled, his cry a rolling echo, "GOTT."

Unbelievably, he started crawling, but his cry must have alerted the raiders. Heiden yelled into the manhole, "Anybody left?" No answer. "Let's go!" He backed with Jeremiah toward the barracks. At the far end of the installation, Jack Rye ran frantically toward them. Heiden screamed, "Hurry!" Germans would start pouring from the battery in seconds.

Ryker perched on the circular railing of the gun three minutes before Teacher's cry cut through the battery. His heart thundered, his blood roared. A quarter mile off, the line of approaching vessels closed rapidly, the lead battleship so monstrous it narrowed the strait.

The raiders clustered along the catwalk, eyes fixed in excitement, one man pounding the rail. "This is it!"

The loaded barrel was rotated to its extreme left. Low, it stretched parallel to the ground. Ryker patted its underside. Beside him, Teacher lowered binoculars, clicked his heels, and bowed theatrically, although his expression was, for once, respectful. "The battleship *Indiana* has just steamed into range. Ryker, you may turn me into an optimist yet."

Ryker's face was a bronze mask, his cheek muscles prominent as whipcords. He sounded hoarse, throaty. "Tell me about it in Vienna." He had to raise his voice because they all wore earplugs, black rubber strips that dangled like animal ears, imparting a vaguely comical air to the men. The Sten guns leaned against a side wall.

Ryker ordered, "Remember, no firing until the first six ships are through. Start from behind. The other gun will open up on the escort."

He had already ordered the raiders in town to drive the escape boats to the base's cobble beach, a few hundred yards from the battery. Now he raised his walkie-talkie. "Joe, come in Joe. Come in." It was the coded order for the other men to return to base.

His eyes remained riveted on the ships. The strait would be transformed in moments, filled with explosions and arcing shells, with fire sheets of flaming oil, with screams from dying men.

He pictured the pandemonium that would grip the harbor. But the raiders would be off the island, diving in the U-boat, before the Americans understood what had happened. All because of Ryker. All because he was superior, better. All because he was stronger. He was dizzy with success. After months of effort he had changed Bormann's plan into reality. Forty years old, what difference did it make? Overwhelmed with the rising rush of his own pleasure, he sensed rather than heard Teacher's hushed intake of breath.

"The battleship," Teacher said in alarm. "It's turning away."

"They're all turning," cried someone else.

The wall phone screamed. A trooper lunged for it. "Ryker, it's the other gun. Should they fire?"

"No, no. We don't know why they're stopping. They could be waiting for another ship. Call Erhard. Maybe he heard something on the radio." The trooper on the phone yelled back, "I can't get through. It's busy!"

Ryker snapped at Teacher, "Get over there! Everyone else! Battle stations!" The raiders dispersed over the gun as Teacher disappeared. A minute later an anguished scream tore through the emplacement.

"Sten guns," Ryker barked. "Cover!" He knew a death cry when he heard one. The gun lay directly in line with the entrance, so an attacker firing in, even blindly, could hit someone on the platform. *Forget the convoy. No time to think about it.* The parade ground would be filled with American soldiers. But why hadn't his sentries alerted him? Unless they were dead, surprised and dead. *Or unless there were no American soldiers and the attacker was Heiden.*

Yes, *yes.* And now that Ryker thought of it, he hadn't heard any firing before Teacher's scream. American troops would have been equipped with carbines but no silencers. *It's Heiden, probably alone. We can get out.*

Ryker crouched, with half a dozen raiders, against the side wall of the emplacement. He waved at the men. "You, you, outside." He pointed toward the ocean, then jerked his thumb at the ceiling. They nodded that they understood he wanted them to climb to the top of the battery, where they would have excellent cover to shoot down on the attackers.

His mind had never failed him; he had complete confidence it would keep him alive. Four raiders sprinted from cover, back past the gun and into the sunlight. No one fired at them and Ryker knew Heiden was alone. Troops would have attacked the tunnel.

Less than fifteen seconds had elapsed since Teacher's cry. The escape boats would arrive momentarily, but the U-boat wouldn't surface until Ryker radioed an order. So he needed to reach the shack. With the harbor alerted, American troops would be heading for the island.

Clutching his Sten to his chest, Ryker crawled into the tunnel. The floor sloped upwards. He was amazed to see Teacher ahead, wriggling toward him, hips up, arms under his chest. His eyes seemed tiny without glasses, blind.

Ryker cursed the man for keeping the extra sentry from the parade ground. He propelled himself sideways, Sten up, ready to fire. Raiders in the main corridor looked down at him as he passed. Fifteen feet to the entrance. He saw grass and sky but no soldiers. Beyond Teacher's now inert body, wire frames glinted, a snaking crack dividing one lens in half.

Five feet. In the suddenly opening vista he saw the open manhole and an islander ahead, running toward the barracks. The man spotted Ryker and stopped dead. He didn't even try to fire. He arched backwards, blown off his feet when Ryker pressed the trigger.

To the left, the parade ground looked clear. Ryker glanced right. In front of the fleeing islanders Heiden and Jeremiah faced him, by the barracks, Stens already flashing.

Ryker jacked his body away, coming down inside the entrance as the air filled with the slap and whine of bullets. He bellowed into the installation.

"There aren't any troops! Only islanders!"

And now the rest of the men flowed forward, expressions murderous when they passed Teacher. A submachine-gun rattle began above. Raiders had reached the top of the battery and were discarding their silencers to get more bullet velocity. Other men crawled from the far battery entrance, sliding, running, zigzagging toward Heiden, circling the top of the parade ground, shooting from behind the truck and jeep. No defender could survive such concentrated firepower for long.

But the barracks were only fifteen feet from the communications shack and Heiden was keeping the raiders from the radio. "On, on," Ryker urged, moving out of cover. The side of the barracks seemed to be disintegrating. Heiden looked out and fired off a burst. Ryker heard Jeremiah yelling, "There! Take it!" He was shooting out from the other side of the woden prefab. Then there was a roll of thunder, the high, deep roar of an explosion. Ryker whirled to see the hood of the truck in the air, flying glass and metal, the ball of fire rolling from the cab and along the ground toward the officers' quarters. Bullets must have hit the engine. One man ran from the wreck, blood streaming through hands on his face.

"Rapid fire!" Ryker roared. The raiders rose, the heat at their backs. The officers' quarters were burning. *He did that to you and he got away?* Teacher had said. He fired, charging the radio shack, the bitter taste in his mouth. His only regret was that he probably wouldn't get to kill Heiden himself.

◊   ◊   ◊

"We can't stop here!" cried Mrs. Hudson, but the islanders had frozen at the sound of the explosion. They had not even reached the forest yet, they were just a few yards away. Horrified, they stared back at the black smoke rising over the brush and the parade-ground roofs. They couldn't see the fighting but a machine gun opened up below.

Judge Hudson gripped a Sten gun; so did Doug Donnelly. They alternated looking soldierly and amateurish, depending upon whether they watched the trees ahead or smoke below. Mrs. Rye wept openly. Corrice held her tight; but from the expression on her face she seemed on the verge of going back to the parade ground.

"Mom, we're in the open," urged Bobby Lee Rye. Mrs. Hudson pulled at the judge's wrist but he wouldn't budge. "I wonder, I should help Tom," he said. His tone was sonorous as always but at this moment he seemed dignified.

"You're not going anywhere," Mrs. Hudson said. "Who'll protect us if you do?"

Judge Hudson opened his mouth but no sound came out. His heels rose, his neck erupted in red.

Mrs. Hudson screamed. Doug Donnelly fired the Sten from his shoulder and a raider fell out of the trees. "Got him!"

"Germannnnnnnnnns." The forest magnified Mrs. Hudson's cry. She was already running, her husband behind, her movement a trigger. The islanders turned and bolted back the way they had come, toward the parade ground, the barracks, toward Heiden.

Doug Donnelly shouted after them. "It was only one man! Don't go back!"

"NOT THAT WAY!" he yelled.

"Shit," he said. Then he went too.

◊   ◊   ◊

"I'm hit!" cried Jeremiah. He'd whirled against the far side of the barracks, clutching his arm, his Sten gun in the open where he'd dropped it. "Leave it alone!" Heiden screamed. Jeremiah reached for it anyway. He seemed to be flung back, onto the ground. He sat up like a child, legs out. "Hurts, it hurts," he said.

The truck burned across the parade ground. Heiden fired a vicious burst and ran to Jeremiah. He was thinking he might drag the man into the brush before the raiders closed in, then he heard crashing behind hin. He swung to shoot as the islanders burst into view.

Trapped! "Into the barracks!" he cried. Corrice helped Jeremiah, and Heiden joined them all inside.

The world was caving in. Ryker was alive! When the man had appeared, Heiden had been seized with almost supernatural terror. He'd seen Ryker die, seen the cove close over that wildly thrashing head. *Ryker couldn't be here.*

But Jack Rye's death on the parade ground had been real enough. And Jeremiah looked close to dying himself, the skin stretched tight over his skull. He attempted a grin but failed. "Looks like we get to fight anyway," he said.

The rain of bullets sounded like a hailstorm. But the islanders had become aware of the corpses in the beds. "Jesus, Jesus," Clara Chadborne kept saying. Mrs. Hudson shook Heiden; she looked crazy. "This is your fault." Then the windows started shattering.

"On the floor!" Bullets ricocheted everywhere. "My arm!" cried Pat Rye. Doug Donnelly sprayed his Sten gun out the window, but he was afraid to show himself and he was aiming up. Heiden crawled to a row of carbines against a wall and started passing them out, along with boxes of shells. "Load here. Watch the kick."

The sharp rifle cracks improved the mood, but Enfields

seemed pathetically inadequate against the worsening firestorm outside.

Heiden took his Sten gun to Corrice's window. They were shooting together. She was flushed, her eyes burned. Her hair tossed wildly when she fired. He felt a surge of joy and fear, looking at her. "We'll get out," he said. "But if I'm going to live here after the war, there's something important I have to know."

"What's that?"

He indicated the attacking Germans with a nod of his head. "Does this kind of thing happen on the island every summer?"

She grinned.

"I love you," she said.

The bulb blew out overhead. Razor-sharp glass rained down on them. A long, cylindrical object sailed through the window and rolled under Pulski's bed. Heiden dived after it. It was a grenade.

Ryker kicked open the door of the communications shack. Erhard sprawled facedown by the toppled chair. The radio was shattered, there was no way to contact the U-boat.

At the thump of an explosion he glanced out. A grenade had been thrown from the prefab, sending up a mushroom of dirt in the square. The shooting remained constant.

Forget the U-boat. A simple call could save his men and kill Heiden. If he could stall the American attack until he captured or killed the islanders, he could negotiate escape.

Now he picked up the phone but realized he had no idea whom to call. *Think.* Military lines should have military operators, at least they would in Germany. Sten-gun firing picked up outside. The raiders were discarding their silencers. Ryker dialed 0.

"Fort Williams," announced a brisk female voice. Ryker pretended panic. "My God! There are Germans on the island! A U-boat! Help! Connect me to the commander!"

"Oh, oh God!" A series of rapid clicks ensued, then a Southern drawl, "Harbor Control."

Ryker spoke the same lines and was immediately connected to a gravel-voiced major. "Who is this?"

"Oberst John Ryker," he said, dropping the fear from his voice, giving himself his special rank of major. "Field Army of the Third Reich, special assault branch. We will talk." He was confident, in command; the major had to know it. "You know there are Germans on Captains Island. I have a hundred men. We've captured the base and the islanders. But I'll give them back unharmed."

The static thundered at him. The major said, "You sound American."

"I may sound that way," Ryker answered in German, "but I'm not."

"Describe the radio shack." Ryker did so, adding some comments about Major Savage's quarters. When he finished, the major said, "Bastard. There were one hundred and fifty men on that base."

Ryker congratulated himself on finding the right man. This major already knew what had happened here. "We killed soldiers, not civilians. Now we want to trade."

"Trade!"

"Your battery and islanders for safe passage. We'll work out the details."

"If you think I'm going to let you go," the major said, "go on dreaming."

"You're not calm, not using your mind. The battery is wired to explode. The islanders are inside. Send troops and you will have to fight. Taking the battery is impossible without direct assault, heavy losses. We won't surrender. We'll blow it up, everything. You'll never take prisoners."

He could almost see the major struggling on the other end. Domestic troops were unprofessional, they couldn't take pressure.

"I'll kill you," the major said.

"I'll give you my address in Berlin."

"What's that noise?" The major had picked up increased firing outside. Ryker cursed inwardly but answered with calm. "One of your soldiers. He'll be dispatched momentarily."

Static. "You better not harm civilians."

"No, no. It's up to you."

There was always a way out, Ryker thought. You just had to figure hard enough. People gave up, that was their weakness. He'd missed the convoy, but the raid had been a success. A battalion slaughtered, a base captured. Panic would grip the American coast. Bormann had said, *Roosevelt will have to divert millions to coastal defense. Your raid could be decisive.*

"I will tell you my offer," Ryker said. But now he realized the firing was letting up, he didn't hear machine guns anymore, only the rifles. And then a new sound, a familiar, hated droning. Reconnaissance plane! Or worse, a fighter! Of course planes would come!

The major was waiting for a report.

The raiders were under strict instructions about planes; they were not to let pilots see fighting. But from the air the situation would be obvious, a truck and building in flames, soldiers converging on the barracks. The pilot would radio the truth!

"Remember, keep your troops off the island," Ryker

commanded. He watched the ceiling as if tracking the plane through the roof.

"Of course, you have us in a bind." But the major was a bad actor; his voice had changed. A more aggressive note tinged his anger, the helpless undertone was gone. "Give me time," he said.

Ryker envisioned an aide handing him notes. *"Fighting on Captains Island."* Or maybe the radio was in the same room. The major said, "I need to contact the general. A decision like this comes from the top. I'll call—"

Ryker slammed down the phone, breathing hard. A burning sensation began at the rear of his neck. Troops coming, planes coming. *I'm not afraid. It's an adrenaline problem.*

The droning faded and his amazing resilience returned. The solution to defeating them was still right here.

Hadn't the major been prepared to negotiate until he learned of Ryker's failure to secure the base?

Ryker strode from the radio shack. Stens were firing again, raking the barracks. Axel and Neuman waited outside; they must have just come down from the ridge. Their faces bore a peculiar look of hatred, which told him they'd learned Teacher was dead. But hatred wasn't a problem. When his men stopped looking at him like that, then he would have trouble.

"American boats coming," Axel said. Neuman added, "Troop launches. From the convoy."

"How far away?"

"Three, four kilometers."

Ryker waved a hand. "Then I'm not concerned."

"Ryker, they'll be coming from all directions!"

"Ten minutes is all we need."

Axel stood at eye level. "Teacher didn't even have a gun. You sent him out without a gun."

"He left his gun himself. Stop firing!" Ryker raised his voice. "*Cease fire! Heiden! I want to talk!*"

"But the boats," Neuman hissed behind him. "The boats!" Ryker looked down at him, a little frightened private crouching behind a shack. Had he really relied on these men? "We won't even have to fight them," he said, meaning the troops and islanders both. "The islanders will come out by themselves."

Silence spread across the base.

Sten held easy, Ryker stepped into the open.

He saw rifle muzzles at windows, aimed at his chest.

He thought he saw Heiden's silhouette. It gave him a little chill of satisfaction.

"I think we've had enough fighting here," he said. "Don't you?"

Heiden waved the islanders from the windows but they didn't listen. If the raiders opened up now, there would be a massacre.

Choking smoke churned beneath the sloping ceiling; the stench of cordite mixed with the smell from the beds.

Jeremiah lay unconscious on the floor. Mrs. Rye's arm was bleeding, Doug Donnelly's forehead grazed.

Heiden called, "What do you want?"

Ryker's voice was friendly, the voice Heiden had heard when they first met, the voice of the vacationer he had driven around the island. A warm voice, a concerned voice. "I don't hurt civilians," Ryker said. The man's audacity was inhuman. He stood in plain view, an easy shot, one hand hooked in his belt like an old uncle. He still wore his flannel shirt. Somehow, he made the Sten gun at his hip appear incongruous.

Corrice was trembling. Ryker said, "We'll beat you, you know that." There was no threat in his voice, only reason. Heiden reached to touch Corrice. Her arm felt cold.

"You have to know when to give up," Ryker continued. "It's an honorable surrender. We wouldn't have taken you prisoner before if we wanted to hurt you."

Heiden couldn't read the islander expressions.

"Do you think we're butchers?" Ryker asked. "To kill women and children? Look around. At the soldiers in their beds. Do you want that to happen to you?"

Heiden stared into the dead faces. He would be responsible if more islanders died. In an anguish of self blame he called out, "You won't hurt them?"

"He's lying." Corrice tugged at his elbow. "He killed my father."

Mrs. Hudson called, "Jeremiah needs a doctor!"

"He'll have one! Why shouldn't I tell the truth?" Ryker advanced half a step. "You think I'm afraid to fight?"

Doug Donnelly shook his head. "Our boys are coming. He wants us to come out first."

Ryker said, "We'll put you back in the fuel room! I promise!"

"Bobby Lee," Pat Rye said, "we'll go outside."

Heiden said, "I don't think he'd hurt the women and children, at least. And he's right. We can't fight them."

In one swift movement, Corrice shoved Heiden from the window, brought the Enfield up, and yanked the trigger. The shot went wide. Ryker dived behind the radio shack. Machine guns opened up and the battle was joined again.

Ryker's head pounded, his hands shook with rage. "No quarter," he said. Neither Axel nor Neuman moved. "What are you waiting for?"

"The boats, the Americans, they're coming," Neuman said. The fearful look had left his face. His voice was flat.

"Do what I say!"

"Everything's folding up," Axel muttered. Ryker realized several other men had deserted their posts to run for the battery. They were watching the boats. Neuman stood his ground. "We kill civilians and we kill ourselves. The Americans won't let us surrender even if we want to."

"Surrender?"

A tepid wind blew in their faces. Ryker backed a step. He didn't have time to discipline the men and take care of the islanders both, or he would have started shooting already. Raiders watched him, he felt the eyes. What had they decided while he was in the radio shack?

He said, easy but alert, "The Americans won't know the islanders are dead. Nothing's changed if you only have the courage."

Neuman and Axel took half a step apart.

"I'll get you back to Austria," Ryker said. "You'll end the war as civilians, not in a prison camp."

No answer.

"They'll kill you anyway after what we did."

No answer.

"Fire at them!" Ryker screamed.

"The whole purpose of war," Neuman said, undeterred and strangely Teacher-like, "is to save one's own skin."

The three guns came up but Ryker's was faster, he had always been faster, and he dropped to one knee and shot them both across the bellies. Neuman dropped the gun as if it were hot steel. He pressed his palms to his groin. Axel began coughing.

Ryker rolled, not even looking at the other men, leaping into the tall grass as the thin rain of steel came after him, clipping the rough turf but missing. Low, fast, he headed toward the ridge. He knew where he was going. He had provided for this, too.

The raiders gathered by Axel and Neuman, Neuman still alive, tears running down his cheeks. Blood gushed between splayed fingers over his belly. "For what?" he said. "For what?"

Gradually the islanders stopped firing. Corporal Protzer called for Heiden from behind the radio shack. He had no intention of stepping into the open like Ryker.

"We were dressed like soldiers!" Protzer called. "Not spies! Our sweaters had insignias. Clemency, we request clemency!"

They heard weeping from the barracks, the scrape of metal beds being moved. Smoke wound behind smashed windows.

The smoldering truck was a steel skeleton, but the fire still burned in the officers' quarters. Crackling filled the parade ground.

Heiden called, "What do you want now? We gave you our answer!"

"You don't understand," Protzer replied. The men grouped behind him, Stens facing the tall grass, watching for Ryker. Protzer said, "We wish to surrender!"

Wary, Heiden ordered the Germans into the parade ground. He told them to pile their Sten guns and step five paces back, to raise their hands, to turn around. With each compliance his amazement grew.

Mrs. Hudson hissed, "Shoot them! Kill them"

"Nobody fire," Heiden said.

"Why not? Look what they did!"

The Germans stood in a row, like the corpses in the beds, helpless, able to hear the conversation. Mrs. Hudson screamed into his face, "Tell me why!"

Heiden craved release.

The islanders would do what he wanted; he felt it with absolute certainty.

"We're not them," he said. "Leave them for the army."

Then he realized who was missing outside. "Ryker," he said to himself. He called out the name. "Ryker!"

A German answered. "He ran off. Into the woods."

Heiden ran as fast as he could, for the jeep.

TWENTY-ONE

RYKER CRASHED THROUGH THE FOREST, slashed by brambles, half-blinded by sweat. The shooting had stopped behind him. The whole island smelled of smoke. The fire must be worse on the base. He'd glimpsed approaching troop launches from a cliff and thrown away his Sten gun. Speed was what he needed now, not firepower. He was desperate to reach Jeremiah's before the boats arrived.

There's air in my sub for six hours, Jeremiah had said. Ryker needed four. He'd surface up north, find a radio, and summon the U-boat. He'd disabled Jeremiah's sub himself when the raiders took the island, so he knew how to fix it again.

Now, as he ran, he promised his men, *If the Americans don't kill you I will.*

He ripped honeysuckle from his path, plunged through heavy trees, and broke onto Jeremiah's bluff.

To his right, a sheer cliff, the sea, launches heading his way. Ahead, another cliff, this one overlooking the inlet. Then the junkyard, the sagging house, a hundred yards off. Ryker ran harder; there was a stabbing in his chest. Heaving, he stopped at the top of the zigzag path to the inlet. Calm green water lay below, the granite-walled cul de sac, the sub. It seemed so tiny. He would have to hunch in the turret the whole trip, looking out that little window. He envisioned the cramped white cabin, the bunched wires and salvaged valves. And Jeremiah's instructions, scrawled on the walls in black paint: OPEN. OPEN. CLOSE.

Fighter planes swept overhead, diving for the base.

Ryker shuddered, despising small spaces.

I made it, he thought.

Then the jeep shot out of the forest, eighty yards off, skidding sideways by the house, throwing up dirt.

Heiden had arrived.

He'd driven like a madman, knowing Ryker would be here. He'd shown the man this place himself, listened while Ryker learned about the sub.

Ryker faced him, presence powerful even at eighty yards. Heiden brought the Sten gun up in the jeep.

As he fired, Ryker fled out of sight, down the path.

The junkyard blocked the jeep. Heiden leapt after Ryker. His shoulder burned; he figured he had half a clip in the gun. He reached the cliff to see Ryker below, slipping the sub from its mooring. Heiden's shots kicked up the water. Ryker was already opening the hatch.

Bullets clanged uselessly on steel.

Ryker slammed the hatch behind him.

Heiden cursed and tore forward, stumbling on the steep path but staying up. Pines sprouted from the banded granite, exposed roots blocked his way. The sub just sat there, absolutely still, and he realized *Ryker had to fix the boat before he could start it.*

Halfway down now. Forty feet to the dock.

Thirty.

The sub belched blue smoke. White water churned under the stern.

Heiden shot down the ramp.

The sub started moving.

He leapt four feet and crashed on the deck, sneakers giving out on the slippery hull, knees crashing into steel plate. He almost lost the Sten but pulled it from the water. A hundred feet ahead, the headlands came together as if to crush the sub. The deck sloped dangerously, water foamed at his legs. He pulled himself up the turret but the hatch wouldn't open. He hammered on it in rage.

The sub accelerated. He heard thumping noises from inside. Ryker was only feet away but totally invulnerable, encased in steel.

No! Not invulnerable! There was a window!

But he would have to circle the turret to reach it, a near-impossible task because the turret took up the width of the hull; there was no room to pass.

He slung the Sten gun over his shoulder, wincing at the pain, grabbed handles on top of the turret, and, legs dangling, began inching around to the front. The sub reached the headlands. Sheer wall rose on both sides. The ocean grew rougher, lashing at him.

The sub drew into the open sea.

It slowed. Heiden heard a humming, grinding noise.

We're going down.

He reached the front deck and pushed himself off the turret. He was looking directly into Ryker's face. Ryker wasn't moving, just staring at him from the other side of the window, a foot away. Water cascaded across the pane, distorting the mouth, the hard, fixing eyes. The thick lips moved. Heiden couldn't hear words but knew, with absolute certainty, that if he didn't kill Ryker now the man would come back for him.

He straddled the narrow deck, riding backwards, the water rushing at his waist. The window, one inch thick, had been designed to withstand pressure eighty feet down. Heiden smashed the gun against the pane. It bounced off.

Ryker drew back.

Heiden reversed the gun and fired.

The air filled with hissing; razor glass shards cut him, slicing his cheeks, his wrists. He heard a buzzing like an electric drill. The bullets were eating through the thick glass, spalling it, not penetrating it, cutting it away.

He fired a second burst.

The water was halfway up the window.

The clip ran out of bullets.

And the ocean closed around his neck. Suddenly he was underwater. The pressure pushed him toward the turret, the sea clogged his nose and mouth. *The window wasn't broken.* He'd cracked it, cratered it, but it was still intact.

Ryker's face came close to the window, inspecting damage.

Heiden rammed the gun into the weakened pane.

A mass of glass and air bubbles exploded out at him, knocking him back. He couldn't breathe, couldn't see into the sub anymore. But he didn't want to surface, because Ryker had gotten away last time.

The sub shuddered, clanked. *He's trying to get back up.*

In the fraction of a second remaining, Heiden jammed the Sten gun between handles on the turret, barring the hatch.

He kicked, rising too slowly, his sopping sneakers like dead weights. His ears rang. He saw the sub, dimly, still descending, not as steeply but dropping, trailing two streams of bubbles, and as he watched *a hand came out of the bubbles, groping for the Sten gun.*

The hand touched the gun.

Heiden broke surface.

He was coughing badly, the cliffs seemed too far away, but he heard the sound of a motor slowing and the launch was there, hands pulled him from the sea, laying him down as faces went in and out of focus. "Was that a submarine?" "Are there Germans on the island?" He kept seeing the hand. "Don't leave," he gasped. "He's trying to get out. He did it before!"

"He's delirious," a voice said. "Get him to a medic."

"No, you don't understand. You have to stay here!" He couldn't fight them all. They were holding him down. The voice said, "Move it, let's get him back to the ship."

"The hand," Heiden gasped. The pain was burning up his shoulder. "Listen to me. The hand!"

He blacked out.

TWENTY-TWO

ON A CLOUDY AFTERNOON in mid-August, 1942, the Portland ferry made an unscheduled stop at Captains Island, Maine. A lone black Cadillac idled on deck, drawn curtains obscuring the back seat. Two serious-faced men stared straight ahead in front.

Strangely, the wharf, which always filled as the boat sounded its horn, remained deserted.

When the ferry docked, the car slid up a cobblestone hill into the tiny seacoast village. A tricycle lay in the middle of the road, unattended. No customers gossiped through the plate-glass window of Cora's Store. No postmaster peered from the olive-drab post office.

A lone Labrador retriever, tail tucked low, choked on dust thrown up by the wheels.

The dog cringed at the metallic intercom voice directing the driver. "Stop. This must be the Kelly house. The Turner house over there. Drive to the base."

The car slid past porches and pines, slick cobble beaches, New England coastal marsh. Around a bend it came to an empty guard booth. The parade ground was totally deserted. The burnt barracks had been torn down, the blackened truck removed.

In town again, the car halted before a small white church guarded by soldiers, who froze at attention. The plainclothes guards opened the back door of the car, leaned inside, and began struggling with something. Immediately a small dog began yapping inside the car. The voice that silenced it was nasal, commanding, "Fala!"

One bodyguard unfolded the wheelchair and both carried it up the church steps. The narrow pews were filled with about thirty islanders and summer people. Roosevelt rolled down the aisle, smiling, reaching. "You are ma-velous, ma-velous people. You've done so much." The islanders seemed somber, tired, and proud.

When he reached the front he turned, his voice hardened. "Now you must do more." From photographs, he recognized Heiden in the first row, beside Corrice Kelly and the salvage operator, Jeremiah Leeds. Leeds was swathed in bandages but alert.

The bodyguards remained at the rear of the church.

Roosevelt said, "I've come to explain my plan for this island. The war hangs in the balance. You few people can change the outcome of the conflict."

It was for this reason, the importance of his plea, that he had refused to entrust it to an emissary. The cover-up was massive and had only a slim chance of working. He prayed for its success. The soldiers who had removed the raiders from the island, buried the dead Americans, and torn down the burnt barracks were being shipped to North Africa. They'd been sworn to secrecy and threatened with court-martial if they talked. Other GIs, support troops, and navy personnel had been told the whole emergency was an "exercise." Now he had to convince the islanders. In Washington, the press and Congress thought he was bedridden with flu. He'd arrived in an army plane, had not once opened the limousine curtains on the trip here.

"I have viewed the devastation," Roosevelt said. "I was horrified. You are heroes. American citizens, untrained in combat, repel the Hun. I grieve for your losses. But now, from you, who have sacrificed so much, I must ask even more. We Americans are a friendly, a gregarious people. Suspicion does not come easily to us, but today, in these extraordinary times, in these perilous times, workers in factories do not discuss what rolls down assembly lines. Scientists designing great weapons, weapons to shorten the war, sailors bringing supplies to our troops, even myself, my cabinet, our generals, all safeguard our plans in the conflict from the public. The enemy listens, desperate for information.

"Yes, I'm here to grieve, but also to ask, as your commander in chief, for you to remain silent about the tragedy which has befallen you.

"After the war is won, our nation will learn of your sacrifice. For now, we will help rebuild the island. But you have become part of another kind of war, a war for information. A war which determines whether we feel constant fear or walk with heads high, whether we look over our shoulders even in the bright sunlight. A war of perception. An army which feels strong is strong. A people who feel strong are more productive. I promise you, our shores are safe. Patrols have been increased up and down the coast. But we must not allow doubt to hamper our effort, to damage our fight."

He was having trouble gauging the reaction, the islanders hadn't changed expression. "I'll be honest," he said veiling the threat. "Some in Washington wanted to place you in detention, to safeguard our secret until the end of the war. I did not believe that was necessary." The truth was that he'd rejected detention because there were too many islanders, there would be too many curious friends and relatives. Especially Heiden's father. A senator.

Besides, if the islanders had escaped from armed Germans, he didn't think they would stay detained if they wanted to get out.

"Will you keep our secret?" Roosevelt asked.

He had also not told them about the shock in Washington since the attack. The War Department had been monitoring Berlin radio, praying Hitler was unaware of how close his men had come to success, waiting for the crowing announcement that could shatter the European war effort, forcing Roosevelt to divert millions for coastal defense.

Now he was surprised when Major Heiden rose as spokesman. Roosevelt said, "I didn't know you were from the island, Major."

"I am now." The islanders seemed confortable with the statement. "We've discussed all this," Heiden said. "We're a private people and do not crave attention. We'll help, yes." He added, "We know how to keep secrets."

Roosevelt felt vast relief then, but had the sudden additional feeling that the islanders were manipulating him too. There was something about the way Heiden said "secrets," some subtlety accentuated by two or three glances directed at his fiancée by islanders. Roosevelt, the crowd expert, sensed a protective cloak, a mental energy flung over the girl.

He beamed at the audience in gratification, but he was shrewdly judging Corrice Kelly, wondering what she had done to merit the protective shield.

He felt as if the islanders had offered not compliance, but a bargain. They were saying, "You keep our secret, we'll keep yours." And the truth was that he was a politician, more comfortable with a deal than a favor.

He rolled back into the aisle to shake hands and talk to the islanders, one by one. Whatever you did, Corrice, he thought, you're lucky to have people who love you.

At the rear of the church, one of the bodyguards looked at his watch in a signal. Roosevelt had an important meeting with the British ambassador this evening. His remarkable recovery from the flu would be announced in Washington at six.

After Roosevelt left, Heiden and Corrice strolled the island. They dropped hands when they reached the base. Heiden's new troops, veterans specially chosen for reliability with classified information, had not arrived yet. Offshore patrols had been increased to protect the island, but the new men would only guard the battery, not operate it. Roosevelt wanted as few people as possible to have the opportunity of finding out what had happened here.

With the burnt barracks gone, the parade ground was peaceful, mowed. Undisturbed, a bluejay watched from the top of the radio shack.

Corrice wore Michael Kelly's gold necklace. And Thomas Heiden's engagement ring.

Heiden wore the dress uniform of a major.

They did not speak until they reached the top of the battery.

"Sometimes," she said, "I think he didn't die in the submarine. At night. If I get up. He's in the hallway or outside. I hear him on the porch. That's silly, isn't it?"

The sea was Mediterranean blue. Mewing gulls swept

over the strait, the impassive straining guns. A convoy passed the island, the soldiers hugging the rails too far off to be seen individually. They appeared as a brown solid mass.

Heiden slipped his arm around her shoulders. "Why would the divers have lied?" he asked. They'd found Jeremiah's submarine two days after Heiden's fight with Ryker, wedged fifty feet down in a sandbar. "The Sten was in place," a frogman had told Heiden. "But Ryker had forced one shoulder out the window. There was glass in his neck, big pieces. He was all cut up. The fish had been at him. I don't know if he drowned first or tore himself to shreds, trying to get out."

He'd made the diver tell the story three times before he believed it.

Now he said, "I have a telescope in my room. I used to look out to sea with it. I wanted to go to Europe. To fight." He shook his head. "It's so clean here it's almost as if nothing happened. Maybe that's the way it's always been. The people who do the fighting don't want to remember, they want to get back to how things were. Other people call them heroes but they don't feel like heroes. They don't even want to talk about it. Then the next ones to come along see the new paint job and the whole process starts again."

"You know what I think," Corrice said. They faced each other. "I think we were lucky."

"You know what I think?" Heiden asked. "I think we're still lucky."

She still blamed herself for what happened sometimes. They were quiet for a while. Then she shook herself and took his arm again. "*I'm* the lucky one," she said.

"Flip you for it."

When she laughed he said, "You know what they say

about soldiers." He pulled away, then extended his arms and lurched toward her, like Frankenstein. "I feel the rape and pillage instinct coming on."

She was really laughing now. "I'm just a country girl," she said. "Your prisoner, Major Heiden."

With time, he knew she'd be all right. He took her into his arms. "Call me Major Flashlight," he said. "All my friends do."